WRONG TIMING

MALLORY GRANT

WRONG TIMING

MALLORY GRANT

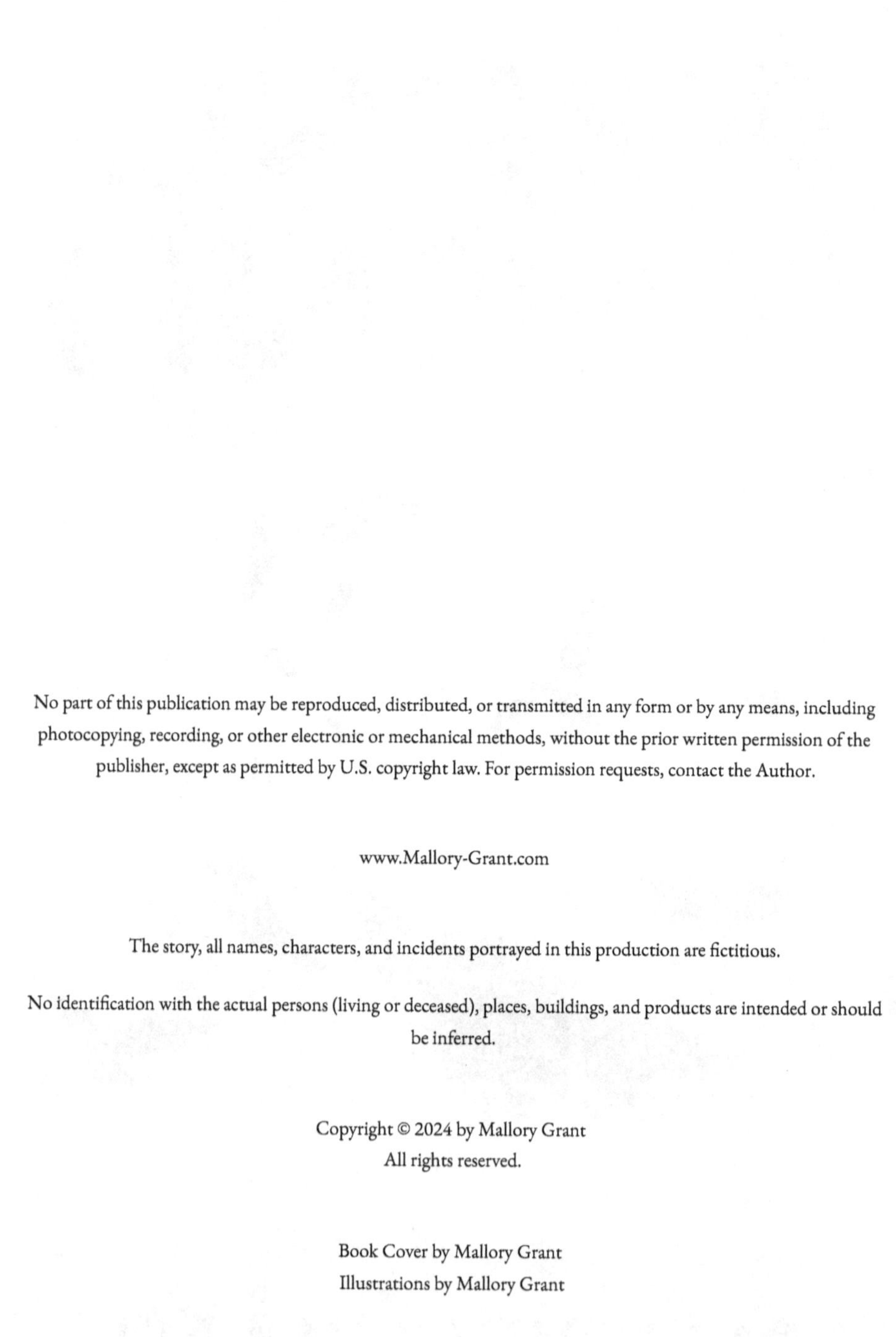

For those who have been silenced by their pain. Your voice matters, you matter. Speak your truth, no matter what stands in your way.

Content Warnings

This book contains scenes with child abuse, domestic violence, mild language, a parent with mental illness, mention of attempt of suicide scars, and homophobic slurs.

Playlist

Where's My Love- SYML
Wherever You Are- 5 S.O.S.
Invisible Battles- Carolina Rial
Broken Parts- Clide
Ocean Eyes- Billie Eilish
Lifeline- Reuben
Sometimes- Camylio
Nightlight - We Three
IDK You Yet- Alexander23

Chapter 1
Luke

I lay on my back as I stared up at the ceiling and counted the stars that glowed above me. They were faded in some places, the glow-in-the-dark stars scattered across the ceiling from old age. I liked it though, the way they faded in some places and shone brightly in others.

"What are you doing?" I flinched at the harsh sound of Isabella's voice over the speaker and pulled out of my thoughts as I gripped the leather in my hands, the straps of the football against the pads of my fingers.

The phone lay against my chest as I stared up at the ceiling. "I'm peeing in the damn cup," Kinsley replied crossly.

I grinned, a deep chuckle spilling from my lips as I rolled the football around my fingers back and forth over and over again. I loved the leather smell, the feel of it in my hands. I loved how constant football was. In a world filled with change, it was nice to have something steady. "Again? Didn't he just make you do that yesterday?" I whispered.

I didn't know why I had been trying to be quiet. My roommate had passed out with headphones on, and the loud sounds of Metallica had spilled from his bunk to the point where I was worried he was going to lose his hearing.

"He said I must be on drugs for spilling my drink all over Lacy," Kinsley replied with exasperation. It was quiet for a minute, and then the toilet flushed and the sound of knocking was heard. "Yeah, I know, Dad. Here's your liquid drug pee, nice and warm and fresh for you, you psycho!" Kinsley called out as Isabella and I cackled.

Kinsley's voice faded away as he moved to talk to his father. "How's camp, Curly?" Isabella asked to fill the silence.

We had gotten closer over the past few months. She still strangely competed with me over the main place as best friend for Kinsley, but we had started to become pretty close ourselves in a way. The three musketeers, she called us sometimes. Other times, Izzy liked to make paper airplanes and sail them down onto the football field. She liked to try to hit me in the head as we practiced down below the art room.

Coach hated it, but was strangely terrified of her for some reason Izzy refused to tell me, so she never really got in trouble for it. Coach found out she was one of my friends and insisted that I had to clean up her mess. I shrugged, even if she couldn't see me.

We all could have Facetimed, but the internet connection was awful here and while my strange roommate seemed to be able to sleep to the loud sound of the guitar and screams in his ears, he woke up instantly when I had the light on. "It's camp," I muttered stupidly.

She was rolling her eyes. I couldn't see her, but I knew her well enough to know by the sound of her clicking her tongue against the roof of her mouth that she had to have rolled her eyes. "Boys are so stupid," she muttered as a grin spread across my lips.

I did enjoy being at camp, it was always the best part of the year for me. However, over the past few months of being friends with Kinsley and even Isabella, this was the first time I wished I was home. The rest of the school year wasn't too bad after spring break. People had been curious as to why the three of us were constantly together after I had punched Roan, but no one wanted to mess with me after I punched him.

He still had his remarks, even a few about me. However, with Isabella there, almost everyone seemed to think that either we shared her or she was my girlfriend. Pretty sure the last rumor that had been circulating was she had been Kinsley's and I took her from him.

It didn't help that Isabella seemed to love making me give her piggyback rides or her strange habit of holding hands. It wasn't just me, she held Kinsley's hand all the time as well. A few times I had gotten so used to the feel of fingers laced with mine, that more than once I caught myself just as I slid my fingers against Kinsley's, and had to pull away with a muttered apology and a slightly redder complexion plastered on my cheeks than before.

"How are your parents doing?" Kinsley asked. I could hear the sound of his computer loading up and smiled, I knew that meant he'd start to draw something now. Over the past few months, I had found myself enamored by his art.

Football practice finished in time for me to make it up to the art room, where Isabella and Kinsley were by themselves at their little table surrounded by their art. The other side of the room was filled with freshmen smoking, and while I always ended up being late to work, that hour I spent with them babysitting the freshmen while I watched Kinsley draw was probably my favorite time of the day.

However, the past few months were a lot harder at home. As much as I wanted to, I didn't stay at Kinsley's again. My father refused to let me spend time with him, to have contact with him, and constantly watched me. He couldn't do anything while I was at school, and Kinsley dropped me off at work far enough away that my boss thought I ran there instead.

My father would interrogate my boss who didn't know anything. From what he could tell, I always ran to work every day. Father started to pick me up after work and drove me every morning, even if he was tipsy from the night before binge he often had. He suffocated me, made sure I didn't do anything he didn't want me to do, and I could barely sneak out to hang out with Kinsley and Isabella.

Not to mention the fights. I gripped the football tighter and threw it blindly into the air. The darkness hid it from view as the straps glittered in the dull light from the stars plastered on the ceiling before I caught it by the tips of my fingers. The fights were worse ever since my mom stuck up for me that day. My father was ten times worse than before. The bruises left my stomach and spilled over onto my face.

It made the rumors of me being in a gang float around the school more than ever before. Our town wasn't much for it, but the next town over was about an hour and a half away and there were a lot of rumors about drugs and guns, and gangs where stuff was sold and brought in illegally. I wasn't part of any of that, but the rumors made it sound like the kids in school thought I was.

I guess all I had to do was punch Roan one time to be considered in a gang, whilst he beat people up constantly and he was never looked down on. Then again, we were on a completely different level. Him with his rich and influential parents, and me with my storm.

My mother had to call out a few weekends to hide the bruises for wounds I wasn't there to receive for her, and Shawn was barely around now. He came in and out like a shadow, hanging out with his best friend Brett, most likely. I hadn't met him much, but he stuck up for Shawn at school, protected him, and watched him, so I figured he couldn't be too bad.

"I'm not sure. Shawn hasn't said anything to me recently," I replied dryly. It was never a conversation I wanted to have, especially with Isabella there. It's not like I didn't like her, but she wasn't Kinsley. It was funny, how a handful of letters back and forth was enough to make Kinsley my best friend. I've now spent more time with both Kinsley and Isabella in comparison to the amount of time I spent on letters, but Kinsley was still at the top for me.

It both worried me and made me smile to know he'd probably always be at the top. I was just afraid that he was going to leave and forget all about me. I was nothing, after all, so it was pretty much expected that once we were all apart, I'd be forgotten.

Kinsley made a sound of affirmation, the silence that came from his slow breathing and steady taps on the keys was like a lullaby to me. There was always something about his silence that calmed me. I found my eyes starting to close not because I was tired, but because he made me feel at peace. "I'm going to get off, Mami yelled at me to go to sleep. Peace out, princesses," she said as Kinsley and I both chuckled and said our goodbyes to her.

I heard the beep of her hang up as I transferred my phone from my chest to my shoulder and took it off of the speakerphone. "What are you doing?" I asked after a few minutes of his peaceful silence.

The soft tap of the keys paused. It was funny the number of times I was on a three-way call with the two of them, but when it was just Kinsley and me all I could do was smile. As I closed my eyes, I imagined him seated there with his knees pulled up to his chest, a long-sleeved shirt that covered his slightly muscular frame as he brushed his blond hair out of his cerulean eyes. I couldn't draw, not really, but more than once I wished I could, just so I could draw the images of him that were constantly in my head. "It's a secret," he breathed into the phone.

A shiver ran through me at how close his voice was to my ear; he must have moved his phone from the speakerphone to his shoulder as well. I licked my lips absentmindedly and tried to get rid of the dryness I felt as my chest started to feel lighter. "Tell me your secrets, Kins,"

"Will you tell me yours?" he countered. I opened my mouth, closed it, and sighed.

"How was your date?" I asked instead. I didn't know why, but I hated the way that word sounded in my mouth. *Date.* Like I had suddenly decided to grab a handful of chalk and stick it in my mouth in an attempt to chew on the tasteless dry sticks.

The typing stopped, and he closed his laptop; the conversation was too much of a distraction to continue whatever his strange secret was. I kind of wanted to tease him about it. Ask him if it was a secret dating site or something, but the joke just wouldn't sound the same with him as with someone else. I couldn't tease him the same way I teased Tony or Bobby. Even though they were all guys, it was different with Kinsley. I figured it was just because he was my best friend, and they weren't more than just regular friends.

It started about a week after the strange dinner with Kinsley's family, the dates. Being the son of a prestigious family, Kinsley was expected sometimes to dress up accordingly in a suit and tie and attend family dinners and meetings with others.

He was expected to go to galas, fancy events, and company meetings, and even appear on TV with his father as he talked about his ever-growing business and how he was opening a branch in Texas. All of this Kinsley took in stride, but I knew he hated it. Now that I had started to know him better, I could see a little bit under the smile that Kinsley wore all of the time. To the little boy who wished so desperately that his parents liked him for who he was, and not just paid attention to him when it was for an event.

I knew his inner boy because I had my own inside me. Curled in a ball as I wished my father would shower me with kind words, instead of his fists. Wished that my mom would stop abusing her medications and take them accordingly so she could be the mother Shawn and I needed, instead of just being absent.

His father started to make sure another family sat at the same table as theirs at all the events. A family that had a pretty and available girl he could be forced to sit next to. I wasn't sure why, but for some reason whenever it came time for Kinsley to go to a new event, I felt a tightness in my chest. My eyes instantly lowered as I grew quiet. I felt a sadness spread throughout me. I didn't know what it meant, but until he said those few words, the tightness remained.

"It was shit," Kinsley replied after a moment of silence. My body visibly relaxed against the pillow as I tried to think about why I always reacted this way. Why I was always worried so much, but then would feel relief so soon after he made some sort of annoyed remark about the encounter. I never felt this way before Kinsley. "She had this obnoxious laugh and tried to constantly do that stupid thing girls do. You know the thing, the boobs thing where they press their arms against their breasts to try and make us look at their cleavage." I laughed quietly.

I heard the soft swish of the blanket as he got into bed and clicked his lamp off. We always ended up on the phone longer than Isabella. For hours sometimes, and more than once, we woke each other up in the morning when we accidentally forgot to hang up before we drifted to sleep.

"She tried to touch me so many times I spilled my drink down her dress. Lacy was pissed. She screamed stuff about how expensive her dress was, and when I offered to hand her a few hundred dollars, she said I called her a prostitute and ran off. It was the strangest arranged date of all of them so far," he muttered with a dry laugh.

I grinned. "You know her name is Lana, right? I'd know that obnoxious laugh and that screeched scream over her clothes any day. That was my first ex-girlfriend." I remembered Lana. She always wanted to offer to buy me things because she was probably almost as rich as Kinsley and saw me as a project that needed to be fixed. I refused because I felt awkward and unhappy about it.

She pushed herself on me constantly, tried to stick her hand down my pants, and the one time she managed to brush her hand against my crotch she screamed about being ugly because I wasn't hard for her. We had the strangest split up, and I had no idea all of the weird rumors she managed to get out about me.

Kinsley was quiet, but I could hear his breathing. I knew by now the sound of his breathing. I could usually tell whether or not he was asleep or not by the way his breathing shifted to a deeper sound when he fell asleep. He never snored, but every once in a while he made a soft hum noise and for some reason, it never bothered me. Honestly, I kind of thought it was cute. "Did you, was she..." He stammered softly.

I waited, curious as he cursed under his breath and let the question fade away. For a moment, I just listened, my eyes closed as I curled into more of a ball on the uncomfortable bed. I moved side to side slightly to let the blanket curl against my back, around my front, almost like I was being cocooned in warmth. It reminded me sometimes of the way it felt when I woke up wrapped against Kinsley, so many months ago. For some reason, it helped me sleep better this way. "No. We didn't sleep together," I spoke after a few minutes.

He let out a deep breath, and I wasn't sure if he was getting sleepy or trying to figure out how to say what was on his mind. Kinsley and I seemed to have our own language of stares and silence, but when we were hours away from each other, it was difficult to read him sometimes. I never did like to read, but if Kinsley was a book, then he'd be my favorite one. "But you have before?" he asked after a few minutes. "God, that's none of my business, I'm sorry-"

"Once," I replied as I cut off his ramble. I didn't like questions from most people, but from him, I didn't mind. In a way, it was his business because we were best friends. I was his business, and he was mine. "Not with Lana, but I did do it once, with my second ex-girlfriend, Alison Miller." He was quiet, I could hear the soft sound of fabric being scrunched. I knew from the sound of it he most likely started to graze his fingers against the sheet. He did that a lot when we FaceTimed before I went away to camp. "How about you?" I couldn't help but wonder.

He didn't even hesitate to answer me. "Nope. I've never slept with anyone. Never had a girlfriend either."

"A boyfriend?" I wondered. I chewed on my lower lip as I tried to figure out why that was a weird thing to ask. Then again, all of this conversation was weird, but because it was Kinsley, it didn't feel weird.

He chuckled. "Nope. I was in a kind-of-but-not relationship with a person I thought was a girl, but was actually a boy for a little while, but that's it."

I had a smile on my face, it was bigger than it had been all day, and I had no idea why. It just seemed to be the fact that it was Kinsley's voice, Kinsley's words, and Kinsley's laugh in my ear was enough to make me smile. "It was the best kind-of-but-not relationship I've ever been in," I joked as he quietly laughed.

We were silent for a while, and I absently stared at the carvings on the wall beside me. The number of initials marking who lived in this bunk for six weeks, and even my own were on here at some point. From middle school until high school, our football team went to the same camp every year for summer. It didn't need money for us to go, but a lot of the rich families donated to it anyway to make sure their kids had the best mattresses and weatherproofed cabins, and equipment to play with.

There were some of the really rich kids like Bobby whose parents sent them to work with professionals over the summer because they wanted their kids to turn pro when they graduated, but mostly we all came here year after year. This was the first year I wished I was at home because at least with the storm, I knew I could just call up Kinsley for the calm I craved.

"Me too," Kinsley replied after a few minutes. His voice was softer for some reason. He didn't sound tired, he sounded slightly pained, a hitch to his voice that he cleared away with a small cough.

I could hear him sit up and grab a glass from his nightstand, the ice in his water jostled around as he gulped it. I teased him about it sometimes, called him fancy for his need to have ice in his water when it was all just water anyway. It was stupid teasing and he knew it, he was probably the only kid around who floated in the land of money but didn't care in the least about it.

He liked to drive to malls to buy things for Isabella, who gladly took him up on the idea. His parents wanted him to spend his card at fancy stores and check his bills, so he had to pick things out so he could escape their wrath of strange multicolored designer clothes being flung at him. I never grabbed anything, and he never made me. We mostly just had fun and tried on weird clothes while Isabella constantly kept re-dying her hair. I never knew I could have fun like that until I met Kinsley.

I never expected any of this, but it was okay because it was him. I couldn't help but notice over the past few months that Kinsley was a maze, and I slowly started to realize I was lost in him. It was a thought that both surprised me and terrified me all at the same time. "Hey, Luke?" Kinsley whispered.

I blinked, surprised for a moment because I had thought he had fallen asleep. "Hmm?"

"It's midnight," His voice was deeper, a slight rasp to it that never really mattered to me before that one week I stayed at his house to help with his wounds, but I couldn't help but notice it now. It made my chest feel tighter all over again.

"Is that your way of telling me it's bedtime?"

He laughed, a soft chuckle that made me close my eyes and bite my lower lip to try and stop my smile as it threatened to spill onto my cheeks. "No, silly. Happy seventeenth birthday, Luke Wilson," he muttered with a yawn.

I was quiet, my eyes wide as I stared at the wall, and I clutched tightly to the blanket on top of me. I took a deep breath, and then another, as my eyes started to burn. "Thank you," I whispered. *Thank you for caring. Thank you for remembering. Thank you for slipping your letter into the wrong locker.*

"Thank you for being born," Kinsley muttered, his voice soft as he slipped into his dreams. I gently placed the phone beside the pillow, curled my knees up to my chest, and silently cried.

Thank you for being my Kinsley.

If Kinsley was a book,
then he'd be my favorite
one.

Chapter 2
Kinsley

I lay there with my eyes closed and listened to the soft deep sounds that came from over the phone. His roommate woke me up, the strange boy who shared a room with Luke but constantly woke at four in the morning to go run and exercise. He was loud, and normally it would wake up Luke as well. Usually, we'd lay here and laugh about the fact that it was four in the morning because, for us, four in the morning was something special.

I didn't know what it was about that time, but it seemed like secrets didn't feel all that secret, whispers were ceaseless, and the sound of soft quiet sobs was okay, as long as we knew the other was on the other side of the phone listening.

That first time Luke called me in tears didn't end up being the last, and more than once I'd lay here in my silent anguish as I listened to him break apart into a million pieces. I wanted nothing more than to wrap my arms around him and tell him that everything was going to be okay, but at the same time, how could I promise that? I didn't know the future, I didn't know the extent of his life, only small guesses and assumptions that remained silenced as I waited for him to explain.

This world was big, it was vast and startling, and in the end, I couldn't promise him something I wasn't sure I could do. I wanted to protect him from everything, but we were only seventeen. While we seemed to believe we were so grown, we knew we weren't.

On the inside, hidden behind every tough guy and every conceited smile, was just a small boy curled up in a ball who watched the world move on and on around them. A small boy that wished desperately it would slow down just a little bit, just for a moment, so they could figure out how to catch up with the rest.

The second time he called me in tears was the night before he came to school, the first Monday back after spring break with a black eye. It was right after my seventeenth birthday since my birthday had been the Saturday before spring break ended. Everyone gossiped, and the rumors of him being in a gang surfaced, but he took it all in stride.

I tried as hard as I could to hold back my questions, to force Isabella to hold back hers, because I had to have hope that he'd tell me when he was ready. Honestly, I wasn't sure if I'd ever be ready to hear everything he hid from me. He called me brave, and he called me to cry because he didn't want to be alone, but at the same time, he never explained why. I never asked, I just tried to be there for him.

When your world shattered into a million pieces over and over again, all you could do was cry and lean on those who were there for you. For me, I was always going to be there for Luke, as long as he wanted me to be. I was fairly certain I'd always be there for him, even if he tried to push me away. I'd wait forever for him to remember me.

When it came to Luke I felt terrified. I wanted to know his secrets, but at the same time, I was scared if he gave me everything all at once he'd walk away. He might feel like he had nothing else to give. He was like a book, filled with mysteries, twists, and turns. As exciting as he was to read, I wanted to take my time, to turn the pages slowly. To breathe in the book smell and take time to soak in every line and every curl. To brush my fingers lovingly down the pages and saturate myself with every detail. So that when the book was finally done I'd feel okay, watching him leave.

I wasn't sure if I'd ever feel okay without him, but I had to try if it was what he chose. I didn't think we'd stay friends forever, I wasn't naive. Isabella and I had already planned our move to New York, and Luke hadn't talked about his future. Whatever college would take him pro, most likely, unless he had some other secret talent I wasn't sure of. I knew nothing about sports, but I didn't think New York was a football-type city. Logically we'd split up, and then he'd realize he didn't need me anymore. He'd realize he never needed me, from the start.

What scared me the most was the four in the morning calls. What if he found someone else to call at four in the morning? I didn't think I'd ever be okay with that. Those calls were reserved for me, as childish as it was to claim them, and I thought it would shatter something inside me if he chose to call someone else.

The roommate hummed off-key to some song I didn't recognize and for some reason, Luke stayed asleep. He did tend to sleep deeper after he cried, and when he worked out all day. The last thing I remembered before I fell asleep was his laugh as I told him happy birthday. I had planned to do more than just say it. I tried to work myself up to being cheesy and sing it to him, but maybe my pride overwhelmed the nerd side of me and forced me to go to sleep before I embarrassed myself.

I closed my eyes and thought about our words, our conversation before I fell asleep. A blush spread slowly over my cheeks, and I stared at the back of my eyelids. Sparkles erupted in my mind as I watched them move back and forth, almost like stars. It wasn't a strange conversation, not for us, despite how deep it was. To ask about past relationships, joke about the letters, it was simply us.

No matter how much he liked to reach out and touch me, or how accepted he was of me when I randomly did the same. No matter how much our conversations sent a flutter through my chest like the wings of a hummingbird. In the end, Luke was straight, and that was okay. It had to be okay. We didn't get to choose our sexuality. Some might experiment when they got older, and some might experiment when they were in high school, but those of us who figured it out young just lay there and stared at the backs of our eyelids and tried to hold in our sighs.

I had thought about ending the call. Instead, I lay there and listened to him breathe. I opened my eyes and turned on my side, glad I wasn't bruised anymore. Ever since Luke beat up Roan, he left me alone, especially since Luke walked me to and from class now with Isabella in the middle of us. She'd hold our hands and give them all the stink eye.

As I listened to Luke's slightly deep breaths, my fingers glided over the spot he had used to lay so many months ago almost on impulse. To search for the warmth of his body or the indent he left behind. Neither were there any longer, but my fingers still searched for it anyway. A habit, one he teased me about whenever we Facetimed, but he never knew quite why I did it.

I doubted I'd ever tell him the real reason why. To tell him I tried to feel his shape on my bed, to smell his warm, safe smell, to feel his body tangled against mine once more. No, I doubted I'd ever be able to tell him that. As I listened to his breaths, I closed my eyes tightly and my fingers rhythmically slid back and forth over the soft blanket. I remembered back to spring break. The week after he had started to sleep back at his house again, the Saturday of my seventeenth birthday.

I felt a smile brush over my lips as I moved my head silently against the blanket and rubbed my skin on the soft material. I was glad it was on a Saturday instead of a Sunday.

When my birthday fell on Sundays, I had to be forced to go to church and listen to how people like me who liked those of the same gender as me would go to Hell. It was not a fun birthday gift, especially so early in the morning.

Not to mention the family dinner, I would be forced to sit there while my parents talked to Kennedy and forgot that it was my birthday. Or Kennedy would hand me a gag present of something ridiculous and my parents would look at each other uncomfortably and promise me that their present was them upping my credit card limit. As if I'd ever really used the limit they gave me, to begin with. But this year it had been on a Saturday, and this year I had two best friends I spent it with.

Isabella and I had a routine if I wasn't forced to be with my family. I'd pick her up at seven in the morning, and we'd run around the city. We did silly, nonsense, like trying to tag during the day without getting caught, or we'd draw all over each other's bodies and walk into local grocery stores covered in paint. Random things that made no sense but were funny to us nonetheless.

This year when I picked Isabella up, I drove past Luke as he had started to work and practically dragged him into the car. He protested at first, but after he called his boss and told him he was too sick to work, he seemed to get past it pretty easily. We did some of the same traditions and ate the most sugary treat we could find as early as we could until the point our stomachs were churning.

It didn't matter what we did, because Luke had been there and he had smiled, he had laughed, and I loved his laugh. To see him relax like that made me feel like he was starting to trust me. All I wanted was for him to trust me.

I smiled as I remembered how Luke had been so adamant that we buy a cake. Isabella and I didn't care about cake for birthdays, she said it was too obvious and would rather eat pie or steak, something the complete opposite. She was a hypocrite, however, because every year on her birthday her mom gave her a large Tres Leches cake, but it didn't matter.

I was humbled by it because Luke -who was never demanding- put his foot down and demanded I drive him to the bakery so he could buy me a cake. He refused my money, said it was his present, and I didn't have the heart to tell him how important that cake was to me. I don't remember the last time I had gotten one for a birthday.

Isabella had to go home by then, and it was just Luke and me who climbed up the side of the abandoned apartment building. Our legs dangled over the edge of the building as we watched the sunset and ate cake together.

It wasn't the biggest cake, a small round one, but we devoured the whole thing together. I could still remember the way his cheeks were flushed from the ever-changing spring weather, one moment it was hot and one moment it was cold, or the next you'd find it to be raining as people would come out onto their porches and stare up at the skies in search for the tell-tale dip of a forming tornado.

As the moon came out I lay down, one leg resting over the side of the building as Luke gently lifted my head and laid it in his lap. We quietly stared at the setting sun, our breaths visible in the lowered temperature as he absentmindedly brushed his fingers through my hair.

He stopped to pull a cigarette pack out of his pocket, banged the bottom of the pack as I squirmed on his lap, and fished the lighter out of his coat pocket for him. Luke smirked down at me as I flicked my thumb over the little roll, the soft click sounded once, twice, before a flame was lit. I lifted it high as he dipped his head, his eyes lowered as he peered through his long lashes. I admired his chiseled cheekbones, his sharp jaw, and the beautiful curls that framed his eyes. Luke curled his hands around mine, and my other hand tangled with his as we covered the flame together.

He sucked in a deep breath, his eyes automatically closed as I studied his features in the darkened sky. Then he opened his eyes and smiled softly at me. I loved it when he was this close to me, close enough for me to see the golden specks that dotted across the light green of his eyes. It looked like an artist drew them green and decided at the last second to dip their fingers into the gold paint and splash it against his irises.

I lowered the lighter and he lowered my other hand, his fingers still tangled together with mine as he held my hand above my head. I slipped his lighter into my pocket as he held the cigarette with his free hand, no indication that he cared about us holding hands. I knew it was nothing, not for him.

Luke was used to Isabella by then, and more than once Luke would accidentally slip his fingers against mine before pulling them away with a muttered apology. It was a familiar act that told me that even though he held my hand then, his thumb gently brushed up and down against my finger, and that he didn't notice he did it. Otherwise, he'd pull away, and I desperately didn't want him to pull away.

He never did let go of my hand that night. He allowed me to hold his left hand above my head as his fingers brushed against my thumb, and occasionally against my hair. "I love the stars," Luke said quietly. His voice had a soft rasp to it, his head tilted back as I watched his Adam's apple bob slightly up and down. I had come to love the rasp that came when he smoked, despite how bad it was for him.

I lov- "I love them too," I replied quietly as he looked back down at me. Even though we talked about the stars, we looked at each other. We were ever silent, our souls talked back and forth as we stared. He lifted his eyes to the stars once more and I watched him watch the soft scatter of falling stars. I couldn't help but wonder if there was a chance I made a wish, if mine would come true.

Luke's smoke slowly lifted to the stars, and I found it hard that night to tell myself I needed to get over him when he slid the rough pad of his thumb against the side of my forefinger. His hand moved even closer as he pressed the back of my hand against my hair, so he could trap the strands of my hair in between my finger and his thumb to twirl and play with absently while he stared up at the stars.

How to tell myself I needed to get over him when he touched me on the inside and the outside? How could I tell my soul to turn away from what made it whole? I knew I needed to get up, to move, to smile that smile that made him know everything was okay even when I slowly shattered on the inside, but that night I didn't. That night, I let myself be spoiled by his touch, his smell, in him. Maybe in a way, it was my own birthday present.

I lay there in my bed, now on my back again, and listened to the sounds of his breaths as I pressed my hands against my eyes. I could still see the sparkle in his eyes as the sun rose, the way the golden hues lit up the natural blond streaks in his hair that only stood out when it started to get warmer and made him look like he was glowing. "Happy birthday, Kinsley. I know we didn't do much, but I hope you had fun," he had said.

I could still hear his voice, the deep rasp to it as he flicked the bud of his cigarette down off the side of the building to fall to the ground below. I wanted to tell him it was the best birthday I had ever had, simply because he was by my side the whole time. It was the first time I had stayed out all night, the first time I had watched the sun set and rise. He seemed to take all of my firsts, and I was glad it was him, even if he couldn't reciprocate my feelings. It was enough, just being by his side. It had to be enough.

I wondered when it was the last time someone had told him happy birthday, someone who mattered. Shawn probably did. I didn't know Shawn much, I'd seen glances of him here or there when Luke thought it was safe for me to drive up to his house. He didn't look much like Luke, but I did remember how his mother looked and was fairly certain Shawn looked more like her. He was quiet, but from the rare stories Luke told, I knew he had a temper inside him, an anger that bubbled, just waiting to explode. Other than Shawn, I wondered if he'd ever been told happy birthday.

Was my happy birthday his first outside of the family? I let out a soft frustrated groan. I wasn't quite sure if what I had said was good enough. Although Luke had said less to me, it still meant more to me because he was there. Luke wasn't the same as me. He didn't feel the same as me, so it probably didn't matter if it wasn't enough.

I picked up my phone and opened the messages section. Luke's was at the top because I had it set where the most recent texts would be on top. Despite him being in camp he was lonely and bored, and we tended to text a lot more this summer than we ever had during the school year.

Isabella's text messages were underneath Luke's, my parents under that, and then one of Kennedy's at the end. My family's texts were old and hadn't been used in a good month or two as they sat there. I clicked on Isabella's name and opened up the bright screen to show off a gif of a cat that shook its butt with sunglasses on that she had sent me earlier today. I grinned, shook my head at the GIF as I chewed on my bottom lip, and started to type. *'When Luke gets back it'll still be two weeks until school starts. Find a way to sleep over, we're going to have a birthday party for Luke.'*

I was surprised that she had texted back. *'Dios mios, Pretty Boy! It's four in the morning!'*

I grinned. *'My favorite time of the day,'* I replied to her, even though she wouldn't understand why.

I just knew she had to be over there with a grumble as she cursed me out. *'Fine, remind me of the party again when it's not the crack of way too freaking early, and I'll prepare for it.'*

I sent a few kiss emojis to her as a reply, to which she promptly sent me a picture of her bedroom wall near her dim lamp, and her finger lifted as she flipped me off. I barked out a soft laugh and shook my head back and forth.

I went back to the call screen to make sure I hadn't accidentally hung up on Luke and put my phone on my nightstand. Luke shuffled around quietly, most likely he had turned over in his sleep. "Good night, Luke," I whispered to the bright light that radiated from my screen in the dark of the room. He didn't reply and I didn't expect him to. It was just enough to hear his breath on the other side of the phone as I sunk my fingers into the bed and imagined he was there once more, beside me.

Luke was like a book, filled with mysteries, twists, and turns. As exciting as he was to read, I wanted to take my time, to turn the pages slowly.

Chapter 3
Luke

I knew today was going to be a bad day the moment I stepped out of the bus. I searched the parking lot looking for him even though I knew he wasn't going to be there. I wanted to see him. The two weeks at the camp were fun but long, and I couldn't help but sigh as my lips lowered into a frown. I pulled out my phone, my finger hovered over the call button but pulled my finger away. *It's fine,* I told myself. I'll see him another day. I'll get to see both of them another day.

I knew Kinsley was busy with a party he was being dragged to anyway. The pictures of him in a tux were scattered through the group text message between Kinsley, Isabella, and me that Isabella had started a while ago. I opened my texts, my fingers slid through the messages. The texts were full of Kinsley complaining as he snapped and shared pictures of himself through his dressing process.

He complained about the shirt being too big and showed off quite a bit of his chest since he hadn't buttoned it yet in the picture. Another picture of him holding up three different ties as he begged us to help him color coordinate for him, a confused and disheveled look on his face.

I hummed under my breath, a smile slipped to my lips as I scrolled to a picture of Kinsley with his hair stuck straight up, gelled into a strange mohawk of sorts. He asked if we thought he should risk it and see if his parents would notice.

The chat was flooded with Isabella's laugh emojis, she dared him to do it and begged him to let her dye his hair. I grinned, my comment was next, and in it, I told him they'd probably try to shave his head. He was horrified and promised he was going to fix his hair properly. In the last picture, Isabella had asked to see the final result and he was slightly shy. A coral-colored blush lit up his cheeks as he stood in the bathroom. He wore a tux, a light blue tie that made his eyes pop. His hair was slicked back, and a few strands hung onto his forehead.

I had been silent while Isabella praised him. I had been silent as I stared at the picture with wide eyes and tried to understand the way my chest ached. When they finally asked me what I thought, I simply replied with a: *'looks good, Kins,'* and hoped that would be enough. I wished I could figure out how to make the pain in my chest go away.

I shut my phone and slipped it into my pocket in frustration. I knew he was going to a party, knew he was going to be next to some rich girl that his father was going to shove him on, and my chest ached. "Do you need a ride home?" Bobby asked hesitantly.

I clutched the strap of my bag tighter on my shoulder and frowned. Bobby didn't go with us to our camp, his parents had him go off to other places, but when he got back from the airport he came straight here so he could talk to the guys on the team and ask us how camp was. I kind of felt sorry for Bobby in a way, the fact that he just wanted to be with everyone else, but his parents kept pushing their ideals on him.

The sound of my helmet and my pads clicking together from the jostled bag was soft in the air, the parking lot was like a zoo right now as everyone scattered out of the bus and headed towards the few cars that were parked there. Half of the team whooped and ran down the road, some of the guys messed around and tore off their clothes because of a dare they had the other day at camp.

Two losers had to run butt-naked down the road in front of the school. Parents who were there to pick up their kids were a mixture of horrified and humored at the obscure scene as the few teens with cars beeped their horns and whooped loudly at the sight.

Bobby grinned. He shook his head at them for a second then turned to look at me once more. "My dad," I mumbled with a flush on my cheeks as embarrassment settled in. I knew what my dad did. He had called up Bobby's mom, pissed her off, and made me unable to get rides from Bobby anymore.

Bobby shuffled his feet from side to side, and I wondered in another life if I would have been able to befriend him. He certainly tried hard enough. He offered me rides and wanted to buy me food constantly. But when he started to want to come over to my house, I had to shut it down, and all it did was make him feel offended. It was lonely, living in the middle of a storm. "How about I drop you off at Kyle's house? It's a block from yours. Your dad wouldn't even see you," he said with a grin. "Less walking, bro."

Bobby pulled a cigarette out from the lining of his hat and offered me one as I shook my head no. I had been trying to quit and only started to have one every once in a while. It seemed like when I was with Kinsley and Isabella, I didn't need to smoke as much anymore, and I realized I wanted to stop just for the fact that they didn't smoke. "If that's cool with you, we can try it. I just don't want you getting into trouble,"

He grinned, his cigarette still unlit as it dangled in between his lips. "It's all good, bro," he said with a punch to my shoulder.

I stared at him as he walked away and followed slowly behind him. For the first time, I really looked at him. I could still hear it, the sound of my father's voice as he called me a slur in my head for my eyes lingering, but I was curious. I traced the way his neck curved into his shoulder, his thick muscular arms, and his overly built back. I risked a glance at his butt, his hands, and his calf muscles, and looked away before anyone could see.

I didn't know what I was looking for, but I didn't feel anything. Looking at him didn't do anything to me. It didn't make my chest ache, it didn't make me uncomfortably hard, and it didn't turn me on. I had allowed myself a little to wonder over the summer as I laid there in my bed just what this feeling was when I thought of Kinsley, but it seemed like my curiosity was wrong.

I had dangerously ventured closer and closer to the feelings inside me that I kept bottled up, and I was curious. However, I felt a sigh of relief escape me as I realized all of my curiosity was for nothing. I wasn't attracted to Bobby, to any of these guys, and I felt like a weight had been lifted off of my shoulders. I remembered the time I had sex, the one time, and how weird it was. How hard it was for me to get excited for her, and while she was understanding and accepted it was nerves, she still mocked me for it later on with her friends.

I glanced over at the cheerleaders as they got off another bus, they had come home from their cheer camp the same day as we did. I looked at their legs, the short skirts, and the midriff of their stomachs since most of them were still in their uniforms. No jewelry in their belly buttons, it wasn't allowed, but I knew at least a few of them had it and took it out when they were at games. The high ponytails, their chests of various sizes, and their soft curves. I looked at them and felt confused once more because just like with Bobby, I felt nothing. They were pretty, but I wasn't excited.

Maybe I was useless after all. I wondered about it sometimes, what could be wrong with me. Maybe my parents had ruined me. The more I wondered about the strange throb that came and went in my chest, the more I pushed it aside. I wondered if I'd always just be alone. Maybe it was better that way. After all, how could I introduce someone I loved to my parents? To my home? To see the beautifully painted house with the pretty flower beds and the walls that were drenched in dried blood and broken holes. No, It was better if I was alone.

The ride home was loud. The country music boomed, and older couples in cars that drove near the truck gave us dirty glares. I sang along with some of it while Bobby punched me in the arm as he grinned, and for a moment, I let myself smile. These people weren't like Isabella and Kinsley, but I wondered if it would be okay to let them in just a little bit. Not best friends, not people I could trust, but friends all the same. Maybe there wasn't anything bad with having friends, even if I had to keep them at a distance. I realized I had started to crave more, now that I had befriended Kinsley and Isabella. More fun, more smiles, more happiness. Maybe I was worth it after all.

We stopped and I got out with Kyle. A few guys fought over the front seat as we waved at them and walked in separate directions. I felt a little lighter as I walked down the road towards my house. A smile tugged on my lips, lifted and lowered, almost like it wasn't sure if it was okay or not to be there. Maybe it was fine, being happy. Maybe I was allowed after all, if even a little bit.

I looked at my phone as I stood in my front yard and noticed the text from Isabella who, as usual, whined about being lonely on the nights when Kinsley was too busy for her. *'Are we going out tonight?'* I asked her.

Her reply wasn't that fast, but didn't take forever either. I knew it wasn't that easy for her to sneak out. *'Possibly, but it would just have to be you and me, Curly. Our Pretty Boy won't be back until late. They paired him up with Lana again. She was making him take her out to dinner afterward.'*

I frowned, annoyed by the fact that he wasn't going to be there because he was being forced to be with Lana again. Despite that, my heart lifted at the words. Our Pretty Boy. Ours, mine. My Pretty Boy. *'I'll see if I can get away. Maybe we can just play at the park?'*

She replied with a thumbs up as I put my phone in my pocket, and I looked at the door with a sigh. I wondered not for the first time just what part of the storm I would walk into.

Would it be the silence of lightning, the deadly silence? Or would it be the loud crack of thunder, to boom through every part of me?

I opened the door to thunder today.

"I want you out of here! I'm done with this!" My mother screamed as I stepped inside.

I shut the door fast, my eyes wide as my back pressed against it. I watched in surprise as my mother flung a lamp at my father. He was angry, his eyes red, and he staggered as he tried to knock the lamp away. "Come on, it's not even what you think," he slurred.

I looked around, unsure if I should even be there. I couldn't dart past them, father would see me and grab me where he stood. Shawn was seated on the stairs, his back pressed against the wall as he stared off into the space in front of him. His brown eyes were dull and lifeless, his glasses slid down his nose ever so slowly as his black curls hung in his eyes.

He listened, always quietly listened, as I always told him to. To check to see if he needed to run down the stairs and try to run out the backdoor before he got hurt or if it would just blow over so he could go back upstairs and finish his homework. He was smart, smarter than I'd ever be. I needed to protect him, to protect his future.

I wanted to open the door and run out of it, but at the same time, I couldn't, not like this. Not when my father took a drunken step toward my mom or the way she flinched despite her angry words, and fear on her face. I couldn't leave as Shawn sat there so helplessly staring. I needed to protect all of them. To catch the blows for her, to make sure he got away because I was there to receive his anger.

"I saw you with her! I saw the picture! Do you know how embarrassing it is to have a text message from a coworker showing me they recognized my husband with another woman?" She asked with wide eyes slightly wild, the result of so many missed doses of her medication. It wasn't the first time I had seen it.

I took a deep breath, then another one as I slowly slid my phone from my pocket to my bag and slid it inside the clothes. I didn't care that most of them were dirty because I'd rather have a phone that needed to be cleaned afterward than a broken phone. Slowly, I slid my bag to the ground and hid it beside the door where all of the winter coats hung waiting for us to need them. I didn't want to, but I took a few steps toward her, my body tense and focused.

Shawn's eyes fluttered over to me and a mixed look of relief and sadness washed over his face as tears started to pour down his cheeks. He pressed his hands to his face as if he was glad I was there but guilty that he was glad he didn't have to help now. I didn't judge him for being glad, for being relieved that I was there. He was just a scared kid, just turned fifteen years old. I guess I was a kid too, right? I couldn't quite remember the last time I'd been a kid.

"So what, you're getting it on with your coworker now? Why do they have your number? What did I tell you about that?" Dad sputtered. He took a step toward her, tension radiated from every drunken pore. "What did I tell you about friends, hmm? You can't have those, they aren't real friends. You just want to get with everyone, you dirty whore!"

I took a step forward and caught his fist with my face. Mom screamed and clutched onto the back of my shirt as she pressed her forehead into my spine. I sucked in a deep breath at the sting from his ring against my cheek, the slow trickle of blood that slowly slid down the curves of my cheek and to my jaw. "You're no better than her! A fucking coward, weakling! A faggot!" He spat at me.

"Get out of my house!" Mom screamed. Her hands shook as she clutched onto my shirt.

Dad took a step back and I tried to hold my hands tight, to hide the way they trembled. To hide the fear I felt at how tall he was, how strong he was. No matter how strong I got, he was always stronger.

He looked at me, his eyes softened for a moment and I paused, searching. I thought back to the past brief moments of happiness that I could remember. A fishing trip, here or there. The sound of my father's laughter was something I hadn't heard in a long time. Before my mother started to get worse, before everything started to fade away into the forever churning storm. I wanted to reach out my hands and hug him, to feel his embrace once more, like I had so long ago. What it would feel like to have him smile at me, to tell me he was proud of me, the child in me wished to know.

"Fine, you know what? You'll have your wish. I'll leave, and I'll take everything too. The kids, the house, the money. You'll have nothing!" He screamed.

"They won't let you have the kids!"

He stared at her through me, as if I wasn't even there. "You're mentally unstable. They'll give me the kids," he promised. His eyes finally lifted to me, appraised me as I stood still, and I heard Shawn on the stairs quietly crying. I was so mad at myself for expecting anything from him.

"Well, you can keep this one," he spat, his eyes flickered down to my wrist with disgust. "Luke is broken, I don't want him. He's broken like you, disgusting. I won't let your sickness corrupt Shawn too."

I felt my world growing smaller, even smaller as my body quietly shook. I chewed on the inside of my cheek, ignored the taste of blood from when he had smacked me and I bit down hard. *Worthless,* I couldn't help but think. I was always going to be worthless to him. To everyone.

"He's broken because of you! You broke him!" My mother screamed, coming out from behind me to glare at my father.

I took a step back because I knew from experience that the fight was mostly done. Dad walked to the bedroom and he started to slam the drawers and the closet as he screamed for Shawn to get packed, to get ready to leave. Shawn slipped down the stairs and ran out the backdoor, and I couldn't blame him. I wasn't stupid, I knew the law at least that much.

Mom had been in and out of psych wards for the past few years, and she hadn't been taking her medication properly again. Dad was an asshole, but he was right. By law, he'd get custody of us. Mom had no bruises on her, no scratches, and Dad could say mine was from football. There was no way to prove the abuse. I felt small as I grabbed my bag, my mother fell to the ground in the middle of the living room and sat there staring at the wall, already checked out.

I felt small as I walked quietly past my father's room, the screams and slurs he yelled echoed through the house. With a quick change of my clothes, I grabbed the textbook filled with Kinsley's letters and slipped it into a small bag, determined not to leave it behind. As I ran down the stairs, Father screamed at me to find Shawn, but I ignored him and ran past my mother as the tears started to slip down my cheeks.

I didn't know I was broken until my parents told me. I suspected it, the sadness I felt, the emptiness, and the way I was with my exes. Maybe they were right, maybe I was broken.

My phone vibrated and I looked at it, already heading towards the park and as far away from my parents and that beautifully painted house as I could. Distantly, I noticed a few of the houses at the end of the street were halfway down as construction workers stood beside the machines and took a break. I had heard some rumor about someone wanting a mall here, but so far most of the neighbors just argued about it. *'Hey, Curly. I got out, I'm at the park,'* Isabella said.

I breathed out a sigh of relief, happiness spreading throughout me as I told her I'd be there soon. I wiped at my cheeks, the stupid tears frustrating me as I ran to her. I had wanted Kinsley, I realized as I ran to her, but she was close enough. She was my friend too, after all. Isabella was seated on the swing as I stopped in front of her. I took a second to catch my breath as my bag fell to the ground behind me.

"Why are you crying, Curly?" She asked softly. I shook my head no, upset that I hadn't stopped the tears. She stood up, her hair a mix of dark brown and dark green as it fell in a wave around her shoulders. Her brown eyes were wide as she stared at me and clutched my shoulders. "Is it your family? Did something happen?"

I nodded, unable to explain, the words stuck in my throat. I trusted her, but she wasn't Kinsley and I hadn't even told him. If I couldn't tell him, I wasn't going to be able to tell anyone. She started to curse in Spanish and I caught only half of it. "I'll go home and get some crutches, and I'll be right back," she snapped at me.

I let out a pained chuckle as I shook my head at her. "Why do you have crutches? And why were you grabbing them?" I breathed out as I attempted to stop my tears.

She clicked her tongue against the roof of her mouth, trying to keep her anger in check. "I had sprained my ankle freshman year when I tried to climb out of my window to meet with Kinsley, but that's not important. The most important thing is I'm getting them because when I'm done with your family, they're going to need them."

I couldn't help it. I leaned forward, wrapped my arms around her, and hugged her tightly. She fell to her knees with the weight of me on her and I followed her, my nose pressed against her throat as I sucked in a deep breath because she smelled like Kinsley. "You smelled like Kinsley," I muttered softly.

She patted my back awkwardly, her head bobbing up and down in a nod. "I saw him, right before he left. He stopped by to steal one of Mami's tamales. I probably still have his cologne on me." I took another deep breath, and another one as I silently breathed him in.

Finally, I pulled away from her, my eyes dry, and a soft smile on my face as I shrugged apologetically to her. "I'm sorry. I feel better now, stronger I guess,"

I needed to be brave, after all. Brave like Kinsley. If it had been him, I doubted he would have acted like this if his parents had threatened divorce. If his father had threatened to separate him and Kennedy from each other. He would have been fine because Kinsley was strong, he was brave.

I stood up, helped her stand, and I apologized to her once more. I was kind of embarrassed she had seen me like this, but in a way, it made me happy. Happy to see how angry she got at my expense. Happy to have a friend like her and Kinsley who care about me. Maybe I wasn't as worthless as I thought I was, at least not in their eyes.

Isabella looked at me with a glance as she lifted her shirt collar so she could breathe it in. Her chocolate eyes peered into mine. When she looked at me like that, it felt like she saw right through me, every part of me. "It's okay if he makes you strong," she said with a soft knowing smile.

I stared at her, my eyes wide as the wind blew around me, my curls wrapped around my forehead, and all I could do was stare.

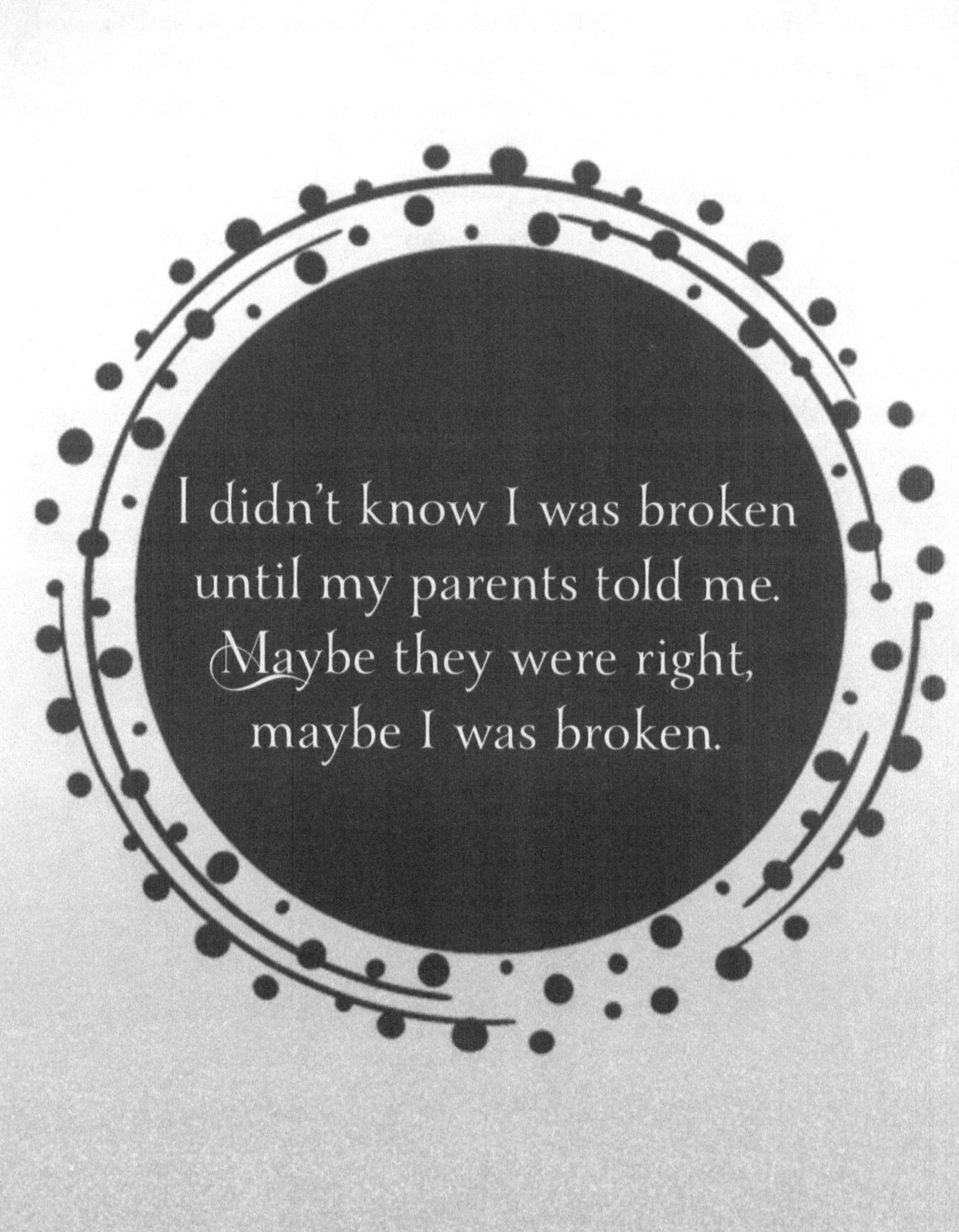
I didn't know I was broken
until my parents told me.
Maybe they were right,
maybe I was broken.

Chapter 4
Kinsley

"Where are you going? The night isn't over yet!" Lana screeched. I was halfway out of my chair, my eyes on my phone as I stopped and looked at my so-called date with an annoyed frown.

Honestly, though. I had just spilled water on her the other day, why was she still trying to get with me? Then again, amidst all of the talk tonight, her father mentioned something to his wife that I probably wasn't supposed to overhear. Something about a stock dropping, and their money not being what they expected it to be anymore. They probably told this Lana girl to keep trying to get with me for the money my parents had. I freaking hated how the rich world worked.

"I'm tired," I tried to say as she glared at me. I could see from the restaurant window that it was dark out now, and as I closed my phone I frowned, putting it back into my pocket. I had gotten a text from Izzy, telling me I needed to get to the park because she had a feeling there was something there I needed to see. She had told me to hurry, which meant it could be nothing, or something really big, depending on her. Izzy didn't have an in-between, she was either one extreme or the other.

My parents had left for the evening a while ago, having to rush back to their office for their work, and Lana's parents gradually left as well, probably trying to be inconspicuous with their fists pumping in the air as they tried to tell their daughter to get me to like her. I wanted to ask them if they realized they were pretty much pimping their daughter out for money but figured that wouldn't go over well with my parents if they heard what I said. "I have a case of raging diarrhea," I added, without any ounce of care in the least as the table next to us grimaced and scooted their chairs farther away.

Lana's eyes were wide with disgust and horror as a waiter came over to me. "Sir? Is there anything I can get for you?" he asked. I could tell he was trying to be nice, but the idea of calling a seventeen-year-old boy sir was grating on him.

He was probably thinking I was one of those rich kids who flaunted their parents' money, trying to get girls out of their league. Honestly, Lana might have looked out of my league, but her personality sure wasn't. "Yeah, let her get whatever she wants and order her a cab afterward, okay? It's on my father's tab. Hell, sit down, order something with her, I don't care," I said, nudging his shoulder. I leaned over, whispering in his ear. "Maybe she'll date you, she's single, ask her out," I motioned for him to sit down.

He was shocked, and she was fuming as I turned around and walked away, ignoring the stares of those in the restaurant. *'I'm coming,'* I texted.

Isabella sent me a thumbs-up as I grabbed the knot of my tie, pulling it just enough to loosen it a little as I unlocked my car and sat down in it. It was a good thing I had forced my parents to let me drive myself. Normally, we all went together, but after I embarrassed them enough to need to take a drug test the other day, they agreed that it would be best if we drove in separate cars, if only so they could pretend not to know me when I did something embarrassing for them again.

This stupid restaurant was a town over, and it took forever to get to the park. I was worried because I hadn't seen a text from Luke in a while, but I figured he was probably catching up with his family from being at camp for so long. I was worried because of the same reason. I didn't know what was going on with his family, but the small bit I could figure out for myself was enough to worry me. *'Are you doing okay?'* I texted Luke separately.

I could tell that sometimes he got overwhelmed with the group texts. Isabella was loud and wild sometimes, and Luke would get so quiet while she would message one after the other. She was excited to have someone else in our tiny little group, but at the same time, Luke was still gradually getting used to having friends that he could call real friends. *'I miss you,'* Luke replied.

I sucked in a deep breath as I parked, looking at my phone with shaky hands and a blush spreading on my cheeks. I felt kind of exposed right now without my hoodie, having driven here still wearing the tux and such, and smacked my face a few times to try and shake myself out of it before seeing Isabella. I was glad it was dark out because maybe she wouldn't be able to notice my flushed cheeks with the dim lights that lit up the park. I stepped out of the car and shook my head, looking at the text once more. *He misses me, but as a friend,* I told myself. Always, only as a friend. *'I miss you too,'* I replied.

I was getting better at pushing these feelings down, and I wondered if one day I'd be able to look at him without feeling my heart racing and without trying to catch my breath. As I walked onto the sand and around the large slide to the swings, I was surprised to see it was Luke sitting there with his phone in his hands as he bent down and stared at it, a bag at his feet.

Luke looked up at me with tired eyes, his light green eyes shining in the dim light that flickered on and off behind him. His mouth curled into a warm smile as he looked at me, to which my heart responded by fluttering like a hovering hummingbird. I realized today wasn't going to be the day I was able to look at him without struggling to breathe. Maybe tomorrow, but certainly not today.

"Miss you more," Luke said softly, closing his phone as I crouched down in front of him. I lifted my hands to cup his cheeks, my thumb lightly sliding over the dry blood from a wound, a bruise forming against his tanned skin.

"Who did this to you?" I wondered, feeling the tightness of his skin, knowing that it meant at some point he had been crying and hadn't washed it off yet. He shook his head, leaning against my hands and I sighed, watching him wince as I accidentally put too much pressure on his cheek.

He lowered his eyelashes as he shrugged, and I wanted nothing more than to hold him and never let go. It was funny how much stronger he was than me, but how much more I felt like I needed to protect him. Maybe just because he was strong on the outside, didn't mean he was strong on the inside. "Come home with me,"

I took a step back, letting go of his face as I held my hand out to him. *I'll take care of you,* I wanted to say to him. *I'll protect you. I'll never let you get hurt again.*

He took my hand hesitantly, leaning down to get his bag as he stood. When he went to pull his hand away, I laced my fingers with his, holding him steady, anchoring him to me as he leaned his head on my shoulder. "Your parents-" He started to say as I shook my head no.

"They're not home, they're never home. It will be fine, Luke," I reassured him. My phone went off and I grabbed it, rolling my eyes at the text from Isabella saying she had to leave but there was a package for me to take care of at the park. I could only assume Luke was the package.

Luke nodded, his cheek scraping against my suit as he took a deep breath, and then another one. It was like he was breathing me into him, breathing my soul into his, and holding it there where no one would ever be able to touch it. I was scared I'd never be able to exist without him, since two halves were meant to be whole, and surely he was mine in any sense of the word.

We were silent as I drove to my house. He was lost in his thoughts and I wanted more than anything to split his head open and dive down deep inside it, to learn all of his secrets, to learn every part of him. As we walked up to my room and shut the door behind us, I sighed, watching him place his bag on the ground and plop down on my bed.

He had his shoes off already, left at the door downstairs with mine. I leaned against my door, watching him press his hands against his eyes and lay his head on my pillow. I felt like an asshole for being happy he was laying there once more, knowing that at least for the next few days I'd have his scent on my pillow again.

I walked to the bathroom as I yanked off my tie, draped it over a chair, and added my suit as well. I unbuttoned the top two buttons and ran my fingers through my hair, messing up the gel and making it fall into my eyes again. I grabbed the first aid kit, a clean wet rag, and moved back to him, casually spreading his legs and sitting in between them as I grabbed his shirt and yanked him up to me. "I, what-" Luke started to say as he grabbed my shoulders to steady himself.

I grinned, opening the kit as he grumbled, sitting up straight as he curled his legs around me. He closed his eyes, his hands resting casually against my knees as I started to press a wet rag to his face and clean off the tears and the dry blood. "Tell me what happened, Luke," I said softly as I ran my finger against his soft long eyelashes.

He shuddered under my touch, his hands clutching the material on my legs tightly as he kept his eyes closed. I grabbed some peroxide and warned him ahead of time before spraying it on the cut, watching the little white foam bubbles dot against the cut. "It isn't four in the morning, Kins," he said, his lips fluttering into a smile as I grinned.

I stared at his lips, so close to mine, and imagined what they'd feel like pressed against me. "We didn't have to wait until four in the morning to tell each other our secrets, Luke," I whispered.

He shivered and I realized I had moved closer to him, my lips close enough to his that he could feel my breath against him. I had pressed a bandaid to his cheek, my fingers sliding gently over it as I moved down his face, to slide my finger against his lips. His breathing thickened, his chest moving faster as he parted his lips, before he closed his mouth and backed up a bit, his cheeks red as he opened his eyes.

"I was looking to see if there was a cut," I lied. I felt immediately guilty for it, knowing this was the first time I had lied to him. I didn't want to ever lie to Luke, but I stepped out of line and I was scared he'd be disgusted, that he'd leave. *Just this once,* I told myself. *Then never again. I'll never lie again, not to him.*

He nodded, taking a deep breath as he moved backward, his legs crossed in front of him as I closed the first aid kit. "I didn't bring any clothes,"

I stood up by putting the first aid kit in front of my lower half, trying to hide the way just touching his lips, just thinking about how it would feel if I pressed mine against his, had made me feel. "I have a bunch of clothes that don't fit me. Mom wants me to be bigger like my dad, so she bought me clothes that would fit him at my age. They'll probably fit you, to be honest. They are in the second dresser if you want to look at them, all new, never worn." I was embarrassed over my predicament but glad he had stood up and gone to the dresser, not looking or noticing what I was hiding.

We took turns showering, the clothes fitting him nicely as we both went to bed together wearing long-sleeved shirts and different kinds of sweatpants to bed. It was dark, and we lay on our backs facing the ceiling but were silent. The only sounds I could hear were my breath and my heartbeat, and I wondered if he could hear how fast it was pounding in my chest. "Everyone expects me to be perfect, to be how they want me to be," Luke said softly.

Honestly, I wasn't sure if he was asleep or not until he spoke. He had a way of breathing when he slept, the softness of it, the small little sighs, and it was hard to tell when he was simply just laying there or if he was sleeping. He said it was easier for him to tell with me, that my breathing got deeper. He probably knew I was still awake, my head turned to the side, staring at his black silhouette as I waited for him to keep speaking.

I reached out my hand, gently finding him, brushing my pinky finger against his for a moment. A brief touch, nothing big, just enough to tell him to go on, that I was here, that I was listening. I was surprised when he looped his pinky finger with mine, holding it there tightly against his. The first time he had touched my hand, noticed he was touching my hand, and held it there without pulling away with a muttered apology.

"But look at me. This is far from perfect," he said, letting out a choked laugh. I wanted nothing more than to stop him because, even though he was opening up to me just a little bit, he was in pain, and I never wanted him to be in pain again. "No one understands that I could be so much more than what they're expecting."

In a house full of silence, full of non-important trinkets and quiet rooms of beds barely slept in, he whispered as if he was scared to voice his secrets out loud. Scared of being heard. It humbled me that he trusted me, even a little bit. "No one would understand the things that go on in my head, Kins," he said. He turned on his side, his left hand still looping his pinky around mine as the fingers on his right hand slowly slid up and down my arm.

Even on top of the cloth, I could feel his touch burning me. I wondered what that touch would have felt like against my skin. "But jocks have scarred wrists too, whether we bleed on the outside of our skin, or are hidden under the surface." I felt like I was shattering with him.

I wondered if he realized he was crying again. I rolled onto my side as well, my right hand trapped by him but my left hand free, and I pressed it against his cheek, gently running my thumb over the soft wetness gathered there as he let out a soft sob. I had heard him cry before, more than once, but this was the first time in front of me. I couldn't help but cry too, even if my tears were silent.

"I can't be perfect, I don't know how," he choked out, his body trembling.

I wasn't sure how to help him, but I knew more than anything I wanted him to know I was there, that I would always be there, and that he was so much more than he thought he was. "Those people don't matter, Luke. Because what you just said, just told me what I've already known."

He lifted his head slightly, brushing his cheek against my hand. "What's that?" he wondered.

I was quiet for a moment, wondering if I should even say it. Would it scare him away? Would he hate me? I had been so proud of myself the past few months, accepting the fact that he was straight, that he was never going to be mine. Accepting the fact that I needed to move on and find someone else to love eventually and that he would find someone as well.

That I'd have to be okay with that, or else I'd lose him. But as I felt his fingers sliding up my arm to my armpit and gently slide back down my arm, stroking my arm through my shirt, all I could do was sigh. It looked like I was really bad at holding myself back when it came to him after all.

"That you're perfect, just the way you are," I whispered.

His fingers stilled, and as I pulled my hand from his cheek I wondered if I had gone too far. "Kinsley? Can I... cuddle with you? I know that's weird, I'm straight, you're not, but as friends I just... can I cuddle with you?"

He was breathless, fear in his voice as I blinked, surprised by his question. I was glad it was dark so he wasn't able to see the way my cheeks were painted with the brightest shade of red I'd ever be able to find. "It's okay, you can say no. That's a weird question-" he started to say as I grabbed his arm and yanked him against me.

He gasped in surprise as his nose pressed against my collarbone, my arm slipping casually under his head as I wrapped my arm around his back, pulling him closer. Almost instantly, he slid an arm under my waist and another above it, pressing his body against mine. My knees were curved against his stomach as his legs curled under mine, his face buried in my chest as I breathed in his tickly curls.

I was trying not to cry, but the tears endlessly spilled from my cheeks, soaking against my pillow as his head warmed the spot on my chest, right above my heart. I wanted to ask him if he could hear it breaking, the way I was able to be so close, to touch so much, but not enough. *Straight,* he had said, *friends.* Always, always friends.

I knew it was my fault, I could have said no. I could have said it would make me uncomfortable, but in a way, I craved his touch too much to say no. I knew everything I felt was my fault, not his. I wondered if he knew just how perfect it felt wrapped around him, how right this felt; for me.

I wondered if it was the same for him, even if it didn't mean the same thing. I wanted to tell myself this was okay, that this would have to be okay. At least I was important to him, even if I'd never be the one who was the most important to him.

"If it wasn't for you," Luke whispered against my chest, his breath warming the cloth and setting every part of me on fire. "I wouldn't have been as strong as I am right now. I'll keep getting stronger, and hopefully one day, I'll be as strong as you." Despite his words, I'd never felt weaker in my whole life than I did right then wrapped in his arms, wishing my lips were pressed against his.

'It's okay though,' I told myself. It was going to be okay. *'This is enough, just like this,'*

I wondered distantly as the darkness started to spread around me, if now I was going to start lying to myself.

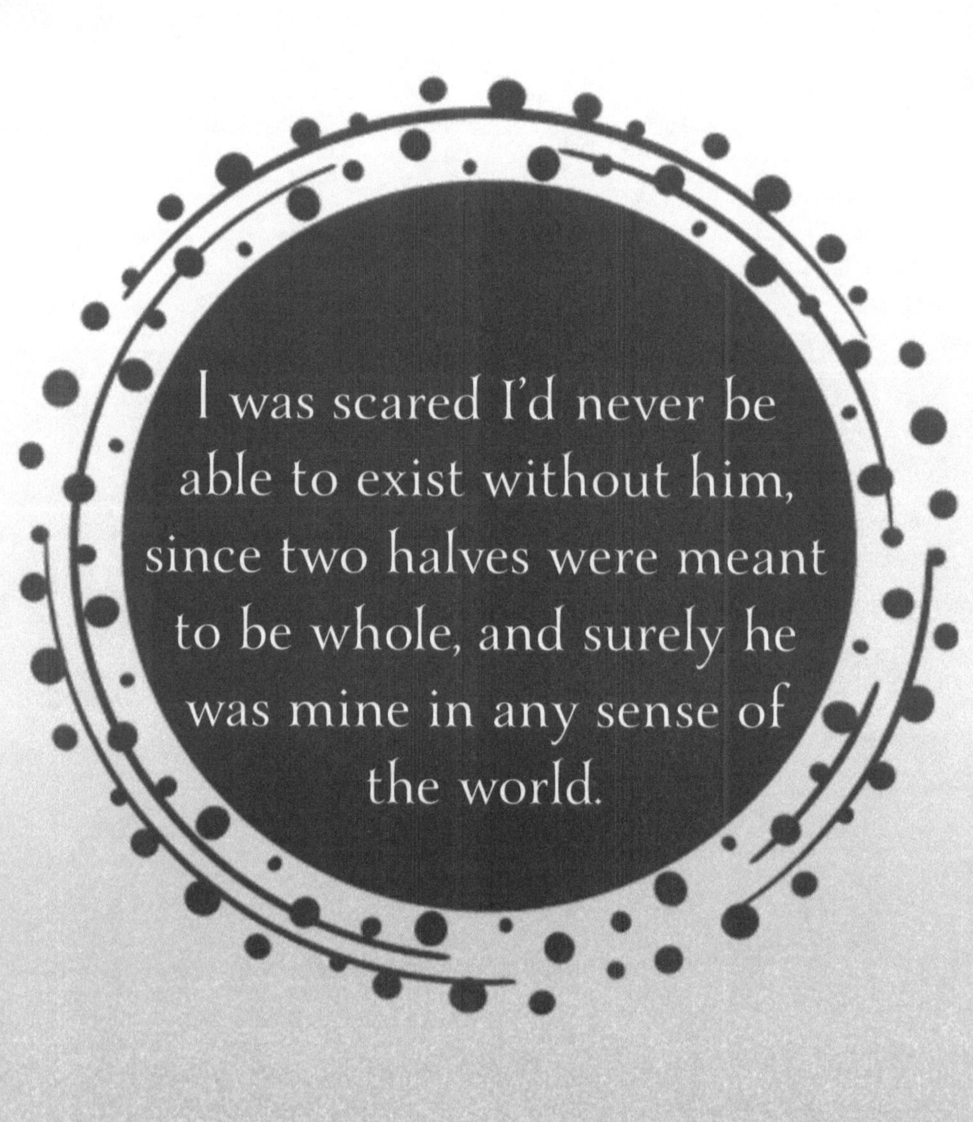
I was scared I'd never be able to exist without him, since two halves were meant to be whole, and surely he was mine in any sense of the world.

Chapter 5
Kinsley

I woke to the sound of my phone ringing. The alarm was soft, the melody of a piano, but I knew if I let it keep going it would wake Luke. I could feel him stirring in my arms, still wrapped around me the same as he was when we had fallen asleep and I wanted nothing more than to curl back up against him and never let go. But the phone was getting louder, and I knew this song, I knew this ringtone, and I knew it was going to get louder the longer it went on. I also knew it was Isabella.

It wasn't the first time she called me in the middle of the night. We both were kind of night owls and tended to wake each other when we couldn't sleep. I was more awake than I used to be, more alert, but I figured that was because my body had gotten used to Luke's roommate waking us both up so we could stay up and talk for another hour. It was weird, waking up to the phone ringing and it not being him, because he was already tangled around me.

I untangled from him slowly, watching his nose scrunch up in annoyance, his fingers grasping at the blanket where I had been just moments before. I silenced the phone, walked to my bathroom, and shut the door behind me. It was cold, sitting on the linoleum floor, and I found myself shivering as I called her back. "Are you okay?" I whispered as she answered the phone.

"Why are we whispering?" Isabella asked, letting out a soft giggle. I smirked, pulling my knees up as I rested one elbow on them, the other tucked in between my knees and my chest as I pressed my phone to my ear. "I wanted to see if everything was alright. Mami caught me sneaking back in and I just now got done with deep cleaning the house. I don't think I'll be able to sit down for a week, I can still feel the crack of her shoe against my behind."

I grinned, shaking my head at her. "Naughty girl, little Izzy," I said quietly as she made a sound I knew very well to be her sticking her tongue out at me. "Everything is fine. I received your package."

"Good, because I tried to make him go home and he said he wanted to stay there. He was so upset, I don't think I've ever seen him cry before. He hugged me, I just wanted to find whoever hurt him and tear them a new one. He's like a giant muscular baby and we have to protect our giant muscular baby," she cooed.

I shoved my jealousy down, knowing it wasn't allowed. Isabella wouldn't date him, she knew about how connected Luke was with me, but at the same time, he was straight. If something did happen between them, I couldn't do anything to stop it. Maybe if I let it happen, no matter how hard it would be for me, at least I'd still get to keep him. Even as a friend, at least he'd always be my friend. "Did you take him home?" She asked, snapping me out of my self-pity.

"Um," I stammered, pressing my ear against the door. I couldn't hear much, but that was okay. He wasn't calling for me, so he was probably still asleep. I figured he'd probably sleep for a week after having all of that training. Not that we made it easy for him, being on the phone with him every night. "He's sleeping in my bed."

She was quiet for a few minutes before she chuckled. "Kinsley, did you get poked by Curly? Or did you do the poking?"

I was quiet, trying to think of what the heck she was talking about before it finally registered in my head. "Isabella!" I shouted in a whisper voice, making her giggle. "He was hurt, he was upset, and he didn't want to go home. I don't know what happened, but I brought him here. I cleaned his wound, we took separate showers, and-" *we connected. We cuddled. I had to physically stop myself from kissing him.* "And fell asleep," I added lamely.

She sighed, and I knew she was done teasing me for now. "He wasn't in a good place, Kinsley. And the more I get to know him, the more I worry. Something is going on he isn't telling us about."

I nodded, even though she couldn't see me. But that didn't matter, because as much as I loved Isabella, I wasn't going to talk about my assumptions with her. If Luke told me, but not her, I'd keep it quiet, just like I hadn't talked to Luke about Isabella's past either. They were their truths to tell, not mine. "I think he's a little broken right now, but who isn't a little broken, right? It'll be fine, Izzy. I'm looking out for him." *I'm going to protect him.*

I could hear her drumming her fingers on a desk and remembered she hadn't even gone to sleep yet. I opened my mouth, ready to remind her when she spoke first. "You have to stop trying to fix things that you didn't break," she said softly. I knew almost immediately what she was talking about. I had tried to fix my relationship with my parents countless times, I tried fixing my relationship with Kennedy, and when Isabella had been shattered by her ex, I tried to fix her, too. "It's not your responsibility. Some things are just broken."

I closed my eyes, making myself smaller, because as much as I didn't want to hear it, she was right. What if no matter how hard I tried, I wasn't ever going to be able to protect him? I wanted to ask him about the song, the mention of scarred wrists earlier tonight made me realize he was always wearing long sleeves. I wanted to ask about that, but I was scared.

"Some people are broken. You didn't break them, Kinsley. You didn't break the thing or the person. You know that, right? Yet you're almost about to break yourself trying to fix him. Don't do it, okay? Everything is not your responsibility."

I wanted to scream at her. To yell, to tell her to mind her own business but I didn't. I knew she was scared for me, scared I would get in too deep and become unable to dig myself out. I was already too deep, it was already too late. "Some people are worth breaking for. If it happens, if I break, maybe then I can put the pieces back together, and show him how to do it at the same time."

She was silent for a moment until she breathed out a sigh. "You are the strongest person I know, Kinsley. The best person I know." It wasn't long after that we hung up. I used the bathroom, since I was already in there, washing my hands and running the water over my face. My eyes were red, I was tired, and I noticed it was only one in the morning. I was used to staying up until midnight or later with Luke on the phone, but it seemed like all of the crying we did earlier was enough to wear us out. That, and the comfort of being wrapped in each other's arms.

I wondered if he would think it was weird, to ask him to stay here. To tell him I never wanted to sleep without him again. It probably wasn't something you said to your straight best friend.

I was relieved to see he was still asleep, his fingers gently searching the blanket, curled in a tight grip that I had to untangle to slide myself into. I silenced my phone before putting it away, wanting nothing more than to be at peace with him. He wrapped around me again with a relaxed sigh, and I remembered Isabella's words as he cuddled against my chest. *'He's going to break you,'* she had said. I didn't doubt that for a single second.

I felt like I was barely asleep, before being woken up once more. At first, I wasn't sure what had woken me. I opened my eyes and stared straight into Luke's closed eyes. His left hand was under my neck, his fingers tangled in my hair, and his right hand was tangled against my shirt, anchoring me to him even in his sleep. He didn't need to anchor me, no matter how much I tried to get over him, I was already his.

I leaned forward, my forehead resting near his lips, enjoying the feel of his breath warming my skin as I closed my eyes. "No," he whimpered, his lips sliding softly against my skin. I shuddered from the feel of it, trying to push all the ways I wanted his lips to touch my skin from my mind as he let out a soft whine, the sound that had woken me before. "Don't do it."

I realized he was having a nightmare. Lifting my face to his once more, I moved my fingers to his cheeks, ignoring the soft sting of him pulling my hair. "Luke, wake up," I whispered, gently sliding my fingers up and down his cheek.

"Don't hurt me," he whimpered.

Never once in my life had I ever felt as much hatred for a dream, or for whoever it was that he was dreaming about as I did at that moment. "Luke, please, you're safe," I said, slightly louder. His eyes shot open and he jerked backward, but because he was still holding my hair I fell with him.

We tumbled off of the side of the bed, wrapped around each other with blankets tangling us together. He was on top of me as he lifted his face, his eyes red and shining. "You're safe, Luke, I promise. You're safe with me," I said, laying there calmly while he regained himself.

He wrapped his arms around my neck and buried himself against me, his body shaking as my shoulder grew wetter and wetter. I was quiet, he was quiet, and I wondered which type of tears were sadder. The kind you cried loudly when you couldn't control yourself, or the ones you cried silently because you were scared of what would happen if you were heard.

I ran my fingers through his curls with my left hand, my right hand sliding up his shirt and rubbing soft circles on his skin. "My dad," he whispered against my neck. I didn't need him to say any more than that. In an instant, it all snapped into place.

The night he stayed out with me all night long on my birthday, then came to school the next Monday covered in bruises. He wouldn't get rides unless I dropped him off away from his job. He couldn't sneak out as much, and couldn't sleep over again. The four in the morning calls of nothing but silence and tears, the bruises that he claimed were from football. It all made sense, and I wished more than anything that it didn't.

"I don't want you to go home again," I said sternly.

He chuckled, sniffling, before cursing under his breath. I couldn't help but smile, knowing he had gotten snot on my shirt. "I'm seventeen, Kins. Reality check. We can't just blow off our parents and do whatever. Not my dad. He would come to the school to find me. He'd drag me home and-" He stopped, and I found myself not wanting to know what it was he thought his father would do. I was scared he was right.

He got off of me then, both of us stumbling to untangle the blankets as I lifted my shirt over my head and ran the sleeve of it against his face. It was already ruined, might as well use the rest of it too. As I lowered the sleeve and flung the dirty shirt towards the bathroom door we stood there. The moonlight was shining into my room, lighting up his eyes as he stared at me.

His eyes slid over my chest, down my stomach slowly, before lifting to my face once more. I never knew I could feel touch through a gaze, but I found myself wanting him to do it again. He took a step towards me, and I held back a whimper, his fingers sliding down my chest slowly.

I closed my eyes and took a deep breath as I felt every touch, every slide of his fingers as they lowered down my sternum to my stomach. He moved his fingers to my hip bone, and I chewed on my bottom lip, my head lowered because I was scared he'd see my expression. He grabbed my wrist and pulled it towards him, and my heart sank as low as the fish in the deep blue sea.

All he wanted was to look at my tattoo. Of course, that's all it was. I was stupid for thinking it was something else. He lifted my arm towards the light and held it with one hand as he ran his fingers down the tatted skin with the other, studying it. Before he could ask, he yawned, his eyes closing for a moment like a cat, his tongue sticking out of his mouth as he rolled his shoulders, stretching them. "Back to bed?" I wondered. I hoped he couldn't hear how breathless I was, my mind filled with images and touches and things that I wanted but could never have.

We lay back down fairly close to the same as before, and I regretted not grabbing another shirt. I could see his hesitation to bury his face against me like before. Instead, we tangled our legs together and rested our hands beside each other, lying where we could stare. We were touching, but it wasn't enough. I wanted to touch more of him. He had one palm face up, and the other curled into a fist against his chest. The face-up palm was next to mine, and I moved my hand to his, my pointer finger out like a pencil, and drew a letter. *'L.'*

"What?" Luke asked, a confused smile fluttering over his face.

I grinned, simply for the fact that he was smiling. "Didn't you ever do this?" I asked, drawing the same letter once more. He shook his head no, the smile growing brighter as he watched me in the dim light from the moon.

"Back when my parents actually," I took a deep breath, trying to keep my voice light, despite how sad I was to mention this. "Back when I tried to play sports to appease them, whenever I had a nightmare my mom would put me back to sleep by tracing letters or numbers on my hand and have me try to figure them out."

I felt stupid for even mentioning the past, for mentioning the things that I once had, so long ago, before my parents stopped trying to understand me. But Luke was waiting, and he was watching, and I was supposed to show him how to be brave. I took a deep breath and forced a smile, shrugging. "It distracted my mind, I guess. It helped me not be scared anymore."

He was staring at me, and I wanted to ask him just what he thought when he stared at me like that. Did he see me, or my past? Did he see the sadness hidden behind the smile? "Okay, go for it. Do it again."

I smiled, letting out a breath I couldn't help but try to hold in. It was like time with Luke was measured in breaths, and when I was with him, I had fewer breaths than normal, as if my body was holding in each one, wanting it to last longer. Wanting it to last forever. I wondered if this time next year when we would be parted to go live in the dorms of whichever college we went off to, he'd be laying side by side with whoever his new roommate was going to be, cuddling them when he was sad.

Maybe he'd find some girl by then, someone sweet and kind and understanding, someone perfect for him. Someone who wasn't me, someone who was the right gender for him.

"You wrote hello, right?" he asked. He was smiling, a soft giddy laugh spilling from his lips like a small child, and I pushed away all of my sadness, all of my frustration, and smiled.

"You're right, your turn," I said softly. I was always amazed by this Luke whom I rarely saw. The carefree Luke, the smiling laughing Luke. My favorite kind of Luke. He drew a circle, and I laughed. "It's supposed to be words, Luke, not shapes."

"What? It was an O! That's a letter," he said with a scoff, looking offended.

I laughed, and he ran his fingers gently over the palm of my hand as he laughed with me, and all I could do was smile. I moved my finger slowly, letting him take time to guess the letters. "Fun? That's easy. My turn, okay?" He asked.

I wondered if he realized how excited he was, and how adorable this was to me. I was glad he forgot he was sad from his nightmare. I still wanted to ask him about it, to make him elaborate on exactly what he meant when he said his dad. I knew what he meant, but I wanted him to tell me all the same. To trust me with all of his secrets, even if I couldn't tell him mine.

I realized he was finished drawing on my hand and frowned, trying to remember what he had done, and shook my head, sighing. "I don't know what it was. Was it pizza?" I asked.

Luke barked out a laugh, his cheeks reddening as he smiled embarrassedly, looking around the dark room as if he expected someone to pop out and yell at us for being loud. We were both getting sleepy, the adrenaline slipping away as we moved closer to each other. I could feel his breath against my cheek, my forehead pressed against his nose as we held each other's arms together to draw on the palms of our hands. "How did you get pizza from that?" He breathed. "I wrote: How are you? There was even a question mark at the end."

I shook my head, my forehead brushing against his lips but he didn't move away, and neither did I. We went a few more rounds, but suddenly mid-word his finger fell on top of my hand and his breath softened. I didn't need to look at him to know he had fallen asleep. I lay there for a few minutes listening to the sound of his breathing, feeling his lips part and press against my forehead. I turned his hand over and pressed my finger against the soft pad of his palm. *'I love you,'* I wrote.

"Do you feel that?" I whispered, my voice breathless with the pain that was building in my chest. But he was asleep, and I curled his hand up and pulled it against my chest, to lay against the skin over my heart. "It feels like this."

He remained quiet, lost in his dreams, where I wished I could one day reside. I closed my eyes, feeling his hand slide down my chest, his fingers cupping against my hipbone, pulling me closer to him. I thought back to the letters, to once upon a time when I thought Green was a girl, when I thought I'd meet her one day, and everything would be simple. When I thought that she'd be mine.

But Luke wasn't a girl, and nothing was simple. Nothing was ever going to be simple. He had only been mine long enough to fall in love with. Now I was going to be forced to watch him go off and be someone else's.

"I give up," I whispered into the quiet night. I closed my eyes once more, imagining a box, and trying to shove all of my feelings into it, to slam the lid, to shut it, to lock it away. I just had to hope the box was big enough to contain it all.

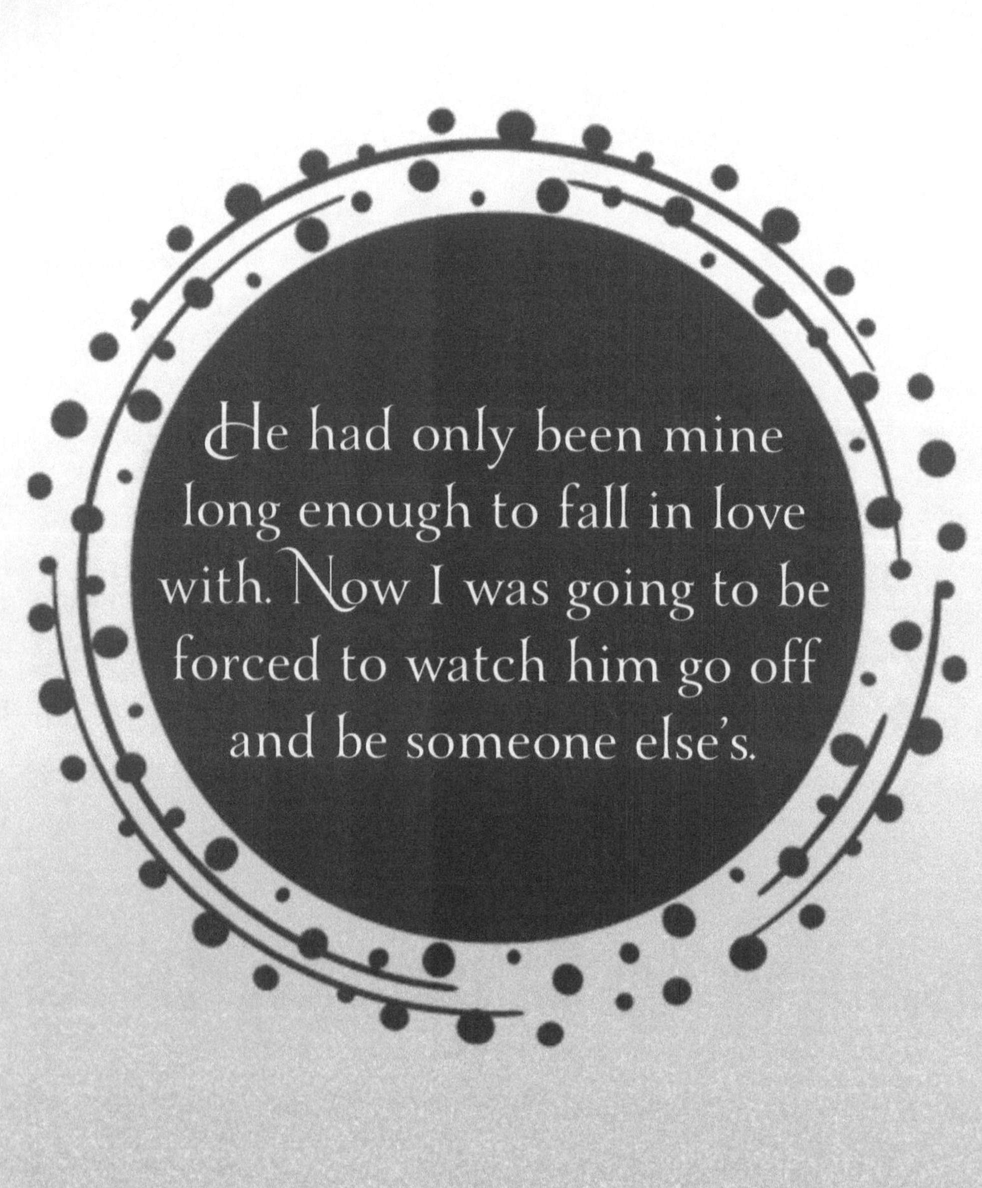

He had only been mine long enough to fall in love with. Now I was going to be forced to watch him go off and be someone else's.

Chapter 6
Luke

"Alright, guys! It's time to party!" Isabella screamed.

I felt awkward standing there in the doorway, watching them. This morning, I had woken up in Kinsley's arms again, and I was still reeling from everything I was feeling. It was like a roller coaster in my mind. I had lain there telling myself I needed to move, that I needed to get up and get out of his arms, but I had stayed there. I enjoyed the way his arms felt wrapped around me, how his chest felt against my cheek, and his heart beating slowly and calmly against my ear.

Boys shouldn't hug like this, I tried to tell myself, but no matter how hard I tried, I wasn't able to convince myself to move. The only thing that made me move was when my father's voice started to echo in my mind, calling me that word I hated more than anything and reminding me just how broken I was.

"Luke, come get a piece of cake!" Kinsley said, grinning at me. "Before Isabella eats it all."

Isabella smacked him and he giggled, and for a moment I was entranced by it. The soft sound of his laugh, the way the smile slipped so beautifully over his lips, his dimples deep in his cheeks as his cerulean eyes shone. I wondered how it was possible that when one boy smiled, the world seemed to stop moving, if at least for a moment.

I smiled softly at them both, walking towards them hesitantly. It felt weird now, after last night. A night of loose lips and spilled secrets. I kept thinking about how I had told Kinsley about my father. I didn't elaborate, but Kinsley was smart, he knew what wasn't said. He told me to stay here, and I wanted more than anything to never leave.

I knew I was probably in a lot of trouble, the way my phone had been going off with multiple texts from both of my parents. I ignored them all, putting my phone on silent, so I could enjoy one more night of freedom.

Kinsley handed me a plate with a large piece of cake on it. It was a vanilla cake, with a slab of what looked like cookies and cream ice cream in the middle of it. The icing was a light green, and from the way it was cut, I could see a few letters. An A, an R, and a L. "Um, what is this?" I asked, confused.

I had told Kinsley that morning I had to go back home, but he had begged me to stay just one more night. He had told me he had plans in place and it was a good thing I was there now because he had been planning on kidnapping me tonight anyway. As strange as it was to admit, I felt happy inside knowing he had made plans with me without even feeling like he needed to ask me. He wanted to spend time with me, he missed me just as much as I missed him.

However, I was surprised when Isabella showed up with a large white box and a dark red bag. Kinsley looked down at the cake in my hand, then at me, his eyes wide in a way that showed off how horrified he was. "Oh my god, Izzy! We did this all wrong! You're not supposed to cut it first!" He turned his back on me and took the cake with him.

Isabella threw her hands up in the air and pinched her thumb and her finger against the bridge of her nose. "Well, you never said you wanted to be traditional, Pretty Boy. You should have specified,"

"Um, what?" I wondered, watching Kinsley move around the island to search drawers. I had no idea what was going on at that point, let alone why there was cake there.

He pulled his phone out of his pocket and called someone, putting the phone against his ear and his shoulder. "Hey, I have a question. No, you don't have to come, it's okay, I just needed to find something. Do we have candles somewhere?" He asked quietly.

He paused, stood up straight as he listened, before shaking his head. "I'm not going to cook anything, Gloria!" he exclaimed with a huff. "I know, I know, you'd beat my ass if I tried." I grinned, unsure what the hell was going on but remembered his story about her getting mad at him for burning water and setting a dish rag on fire.

It seemed like she had directed him to the right drawer and he hung up with her, grabbed a box of candles, and came over to me. He reached his hand into my front pocket, so used to touching me that he didn't even bother to think to ask first. I felt my cheeks flush as his fingers skimmed the material against the inside of my leg, my breath caught in my throat as he grabbed something in my pocket and pulled it out.

I was disappointed that he was just searching for the lighter and confused that I wanted him to touch me again. "Give me a second," I muttered as I turned around and walked out of the kitchen.

I gasped as I pressed my forehead against the living room wall, looking down at my tented pants with a soft whimper. Of all the times my exes touched me, even purposely trying to excite me, it had never caused a reaction like this. "I thought I was broken," I muttered quietly, unsure of what was going on. Maybe this was just more proof I was broken, in a way. I had no idea what to think about this.

"Luke! Stop peeing and hurry up! Before Kinsley lights the kitchen on fire!" Izzy yelled. I looked around the living room desperately, my eyes wide as I made sure no one was around. The housekeeper was quiet, I've come to find out. She could pop out of nowhere at any time. Quickly, I reached my hand into my pants and fixed myself to hide the problem, smoothing my shirt down to try and hide it.

I wished I had one of Kinsley's hoodies to wear, but this particular shirt he gave me was a little bit big on me so that helped. He did have a drawer full of clothes that were too big for him and it made me sad that his parents were trying so hard to turn him into someone he wasn't. I thought he was perfect just the way he was.

As I walked back into the kitchen, I was met with a square that was brightly lit, the lights dimmed, and the whole square looked to be on fire. But as I took an alarmed step towards it, I sighed in relief because it wasn't that it was on fire, but there were so many candles jammed all over it that it looked practically covered. "What is this?" I asked, letting out a breathless laugh.

I could barely make out black words written on the green icing. The cake was cut and falling slightly apart as it started to melt, and all I could do was laugh. They had cut it first, then tried to put the pieces back together to put the candles on it. They were the strangest, most amazing people I'd ever known. "Happy birthday!" Kinsley said, his eyes shining as Isabella clapped and hugged me.

"A birthday cake? For me?" I wondered, my eyes strangely filling as I stared at the candles. Isabella pulled away from me and I felt Kinsley brushing his fingers down my arm, gently holding onto a corner of my sleeve. "Thank you," I said quietly, unsure how to express how I was feeling.

"Hurry up and make a wish. It's all starting to melt. Maybe it's all the damn candles. Kins, he's not over a hundred years old, you only needed seventeen!" She said with a sigh.

Kinsley shrugged, an embarrassed blush spreading over his face as he laughed. "I just wanted to be safe, you know? Who knows how these cakes are supposed to work?" he wondered.

"We were by far the strangest group of friends ever made," Isabella mumbled.

I leaned down, my hands on the edge of the island. A piece of cake fell to the side slowly, one of the candles dangerously tipping as a stream of white speckled liquid started to come out of the cake, the ice cream slowly melting. I closed my eyes and smiled, listening to Isabella and Kinsley bickering as I made my wish. *'I hope I can be with them forever,'* I wished, before blowing the candles out.

It was harder to blow out all of the candles than I thought it would be, but having a bunch of candles didn't help. In the end, Kinsley blew out the few near him while Isabella blew out a few others, all of us trying to stop the melting of the cake. We were left with a strange lopsided thing and despite the way Kinsley was apologizing to me, I thought it was beautiful because it was made for me.

My first cake ever since I was a small boy, just for me. I remembered back before my mom got worse. Small cakes, the singing of birthday songs. My dad would dance with her around the kitchen as Shawn giggled from his highchair and I felt like the happiest boy in the world. But soon the birthdays faded, the dancing stopped, and the storm appeared, getting fiercer and fiercer as the years passed.

Quietly I wiped a tear from my eye as Kinsley and Isabella battled the candles. Kinsley grabbed three large bowls and spoons, and we ended up each getting a really big bowl of melted ice cream cake. I wiped down the counter as Isabella grabbed all of the bowls and practically ran up the stairs. "Come on, there's more," Kinsley said. I didn't know I even deserved this, let alone more.

He grabbed my wrist and I pulled away, instead sliding my fingers with his, lacing them together. Kinsley looked surprised for a second before smiling, pulling me with him from the kitchen and to his room. Earlier they had kicked me out of the room so they could do something secret, and I laughed out loud as I walked inside and was immediately hit with a spray of confetti.

The room was covered in balloons and confetti, streamers thrown over different surfaces. I was humbled that they'd done all of this for me. I leaned down and grabbed a balloon, holding it gently in my hand as Kinsley pulled me to the middle of the room and made me sit down on the carpet. "Here's my gift," Isabella said with a grin.

I dig into the red bag, feeling like a small child as I pulled out a picture frame. I wiped the small pieces of confetti she had thrown into the bag away and blinked, staring down at it in surprise. Before this moment, I had believed Kinsley was better at detail drawing than Isabella was because all I'd ever really seen her draw was graffiti or those stencils she spray-painted.

However, I was surprised by the immense detail she had put into this picture. I remembered that day. It was after spring break, and I had visited them in the art room. I had fallen asleep next to Kinsley, and he was sitting there quietly drawing. We both were sharing a headphone since we both realized that over time with letters, we liked the same music. He was looking down at me, his eyes lowered and a soft smile on his face as his pencil hovered over his paper, and I was lying on my arms.

I guess at some point, Isabella had captured the moment, and I was speechless. Before I could say anything, however, Kinsley handed me a small box with a sheepish grin on his face. Gently I placed the picture back into the bag, the masterpiece that I knew I'd hold just as dear as Kinsley's letters and his angel drawing, and grabbed the box.

I shook it, confused as I heard a clinking sound, before opening it. There were two folded pieces of paper, one shiny and one that looked to be a regular piece of paper, and two keys on a chain inside. "This paper is what you show the guy at the gate, giving you access to come in here whenever you want. You put it on the windshield, it makes it easier to see during the rain and such," he said, pointing at the shiny paper.

"I don't have a car, Kinsley," I muttered. I still felt touched though, that he had thought to give me access to get inside whenever I wanted.

He grinned, pointing at the other paper as I started to open it. With wide eyes, I read over it, my mouth falling open. "This is a list of all of the parts your boss said you needed to get your car fixed. I knew you'd give me shit for buying you a new car, so I just got the parts instead. They are already ordered, and my favorite mechanic is going to have to put it together. So you'll have a place to put the paper to get in." He said with a grin.

"Though you can walk up and show it to the gate too, you know. You don't have to wait until your car is finished to get in here."

My voice was breaking, my eyes filling with tears as I pointed at the two keys. "And these?"

He ran the palms of his hands over his jeans, chewing on his lower lip. "This one is the key to my house, and this one is the key to my bedroom door. If you ever need to come over, just come over, Luke. Even if I'm not here, you're always welcome here. I want you to know you'll always have a safe place to go if you need one."

I broke then. The box and the papers fell to the carpet as I pressed my hands against my face. Isabella moved to the side of me as I buried my face against Kinsley's neck, his fingers slid through my curls while Isabella rubbed my back.

A house was nothing. A house was always going to be nothing to me. The key to his house wasn't what broke me, but the fact that it was a key to him. Kinsley was my safe place, my home. I just wished I knew what that meant. It terrified me how little I understood.

We quieted down after a while. Kinsley ordered pizza, and we all got our own box of different toppings as we ate our bowls of melted ice cream cake. It was funny, there was a large empty house but we still stuck to his room as we watched movie after movie on the TV, uninterested with the rest of his large empty house.

Maybe most kids wanted their seventeenth birthday celebrated big and wild, a party that shook the house and endless sweaty groping bodies sliding against each other as they danced through a haze of alcohol. But this was perfect to me, more than I'd ever had before, and more than I'd ever expected to have.

Isabella disappeared somewhere in the house as the last movie ended, and Kinsley started to chuckle, moving some of the confetti aside so we could sit more comfortably on the couch. I felt quieter than usual, humbled by everything they'd done for me. I didn't know if I was allowed to feel this happy, this safe and warm.

The last thing I remembered from my house was being told I was broken, but as I laid my head against Kinsley's shoulder and watched the movie credits flash on the screen, I was starting to wonder if it was true. Maybe I wasn't the one who was broken, after all, maybe it was just my parents.

"Okay, ladies! Let's get the after-party started!" Isabella called out as she turned the lights on. Kinsley and I grumbled, pulling away from each other as the light blinded us. I pulled my phone out of my pocket to check the time and was surprised to see Shawn was calling me. As Kinsley got up to see what Isabella was doing, I hesitantly stared at my screen, unsure if I should answer it or not. I could hear them talking quietly near the bathroom door and I saw Shawn's name fade as the call ended, and then flash on the screen once more as he tried to call me again.

I muted the TV and answered it. "Shawnie?" I asked quietly. "Are you okay?"

"Where the hell are you, you faggot? I can't find your brother and your mother is fucking useless. If you're hiding him somewhere I'm going to kill you, do you understand? I'll kill your mom, and then I'll kill you. Get your nasty faggy ass back here and bring me back your brother," My father screamed into Shawn's phone. "If you're not here by tomorrow, Your mother is going to find herself in a lot of pain."

I was silent, as I hung up on him. My hands were shaking as I pressed down on the end button hard, watching the screen turn black as it turned off. My heart was racing, and I was trying so hard to breathe as I dropped my phone on the couch like it had burned me. "Luke! Come here! After-party!" Isabella said.

"Izzy, I didn't think Luke wants that-" Kinsley said as I quietly walked over to them and grabbed the bottle out of her hand. I looked at it, then at Kinsley, the worried look on his face as Isabella held up another bottle and wagged her eyebrows. "You don't have to, Luke." He said softly as I read the label.

Maybe it was because of my father's words in my head, his voice fresh in my ears. Or because the brand was different from what he'd drink. Maybe it was because my fingers twitched to my pocket, to the pack of cigarettes I had been trying so hard to quit smoking, only to find myself suddenly craving again. I gave Kinsley a soft smile, hoping he couldn't read through it, wondering what it would be like to just be normal for once. To live a normal life, with normal parents.

To be a teenager that went out on the weekends to parties and got drunk and fucked girls without care, and woke up Sunday morning with a hangover. To move through the school hallway and instead of seeing a bunch of fake people, to blend in with them.

Maybe if I was normal, my father wouldn't call me that word anymore. Maybe if I was normal, he'd want me, too. "Sweet," I said thickly, grabbing the bottle opener and popping it open.

"The last time either of us drank we were fifteen, Luke. We don't do this very often at all. I don't know why she even thought to grab it," Kinsley said, frowning at Isabella as she tipped her bottle back with a giggle.

"It's fine, Dad," Izzy said with a laugh. "It's a party, our Curly's first party with us, we have to celebrate our baby turning seventeen!" She said loudly.

I shrugged, handing him the bottle opener. "It's fine, Kins. It's not like we're going to get wasted or something." I wondered if this was how the kids did it. Was this the way they spoke, when they tried to be cool? I pressed the bottle to my lips and tried not to cringe over the harsh smell, taking a deep breath, and swallowing the burning liquid.

Kinsley was watching me like a hawk. While I normally liked having his eyes watching me, right then, I wished everyone would leave me alone while I tried to sort through these feelings that were swirling around me. Breaking through me, mixing with the fear of what my father had threatened.

It seemed that the feelings I couldn't understand were sliding out of the place I'd been trying so hard to shove them, and I wasn't sure what to do about any of them. It was easier, the second sip. The third didn't burn as much, and the fourth tasted better. All the while I felt his eyes burning on me and I smiled, feeling everything get hazy and light. "I like your eyes," I slurred.

He laughed, seeming to think everything was okay as he patted me on the back and took a sip of his bottle. "I like your eyes too, Luke," he replied.

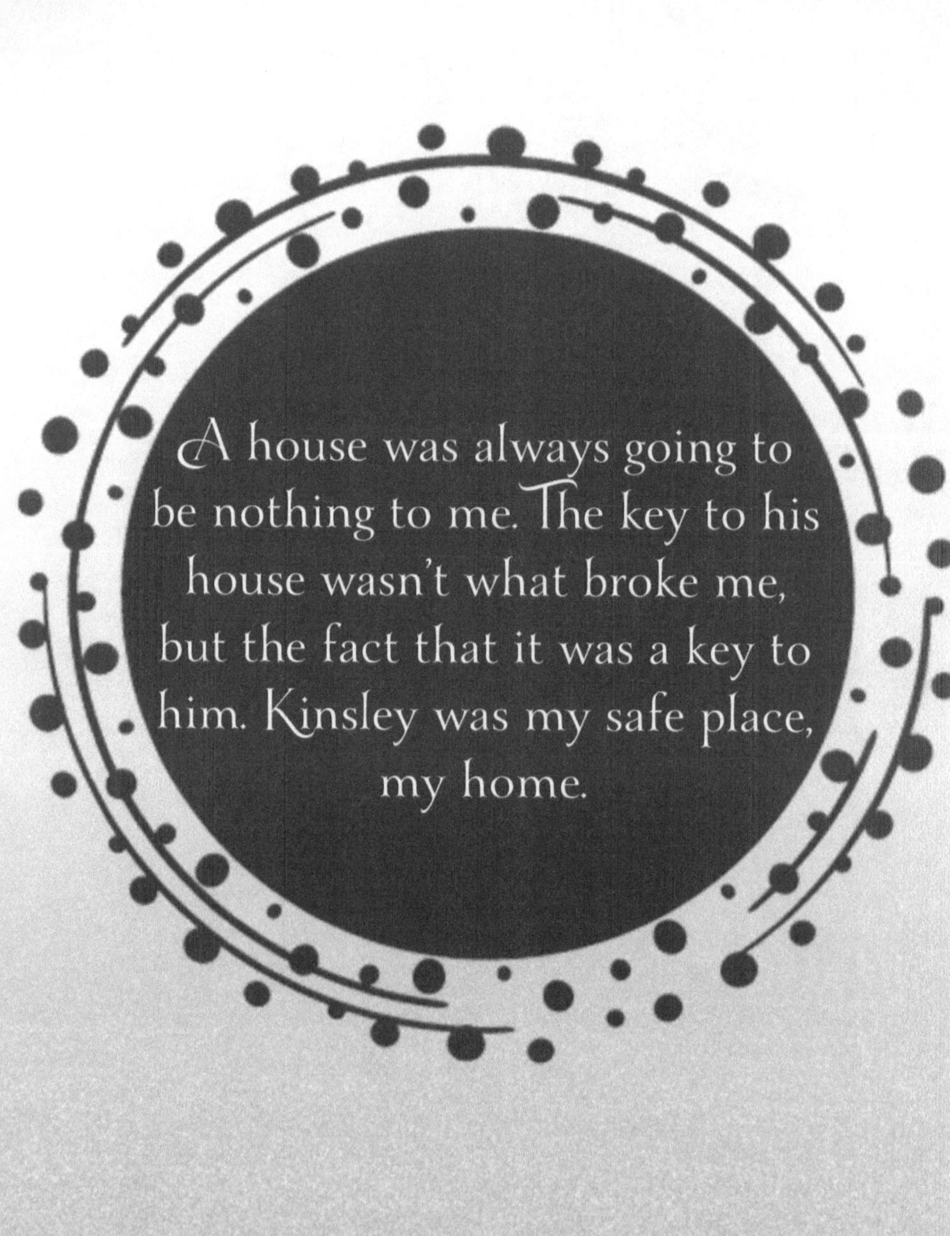
A house was always going to
be nothing to me. The key to his
house wasn't what broke me,
but the fact that it was a key to
him. Kinsley was my safe place,
my home.

Chapter 7
Luke

The feeling of the ice-cold water against my skin was like a jolt. I held my breath, my eyes closed as I curled into a ball. I sunk lower and lower as my lungs started to scream at me. My eyes opened automatically and swam towards the surface. It looked strange, the deep end of Kinsley's pool in the darkness. There were small lights lit up around the pool to lead me to the top, and I followed them.

As I broke through, I took a deep breath. The pounding of the music coming from the house was louder as I looked up at the others. "Oh my God! I didn't even think about that! What if he couldn't swim, Kinsley?" Isabella slurred, staggering sideways and falling into a lawn chair. The bottle in her hand fell to the ground, shattering against the cement and spilling the rest of her alcohol everywhere.

Kinsley was giggling. He couldn't stop giggling, his face bright red and his dimples bigger than ever as he fell to his knees, pointing at her like she was a little girl. "You tripped," he teased. She stuck out her middle finger at him, her tongue sliding out only a second later.

"I can swim," I said stupidly, my head pounding to the beat of the song that was blaring through the open windows. I didn't recognize the tune, something girly, and Isabella was bobbing her head along to it as she lay there sideways on the lawn chair.

The back of her neck pressed against one armrest as her legs were draped over the other one. Kinsley dove unexpectedly into the water and I gasped in surprise as one of his arms went around me and dragged me down with him. I was struggling, flailing in the water as it went into my mouth, sliding down my throat and suffocating me.

Then I felt an arm grabbing me around the waist and pulling me up towards the surface once more. Kinsley pressed me against his shoulder as he smacked my back hard over and over again, water spilling from my lungs as I coughed it all up onto his shoulder. "I thought you could swim," Kinsley said with a frown as I pulled away from him. His words were reprimanding but the bright smile was still on his face, his nose red as he giggled.

Maybe if I was more sober, I'd remind him that I was swimming just fine before he crashed into the pool with all of his clothes on, falling on top of me. "You saved me!" I said instead, throwing my hands in the air as Isabella started to sing loudly to the song that was playing. She had her head thrown back, her hair inches above the spilled alcohol as her arms were lifted into the air, waving around like a conductor conducting an orchestra.

I looked up at the house in wonder. The largeness of it all was intimidating from there, as every single light blared through the open curtains. It was one of Isabella's dares for Kinsley to go through each room and open all of the curtains, turn on the lights, and leave it like that. My dare was to balance across the side of the pool without falling over, but it seemed I lost.

We had been playing truth or dare for a while now, but it might as well have been called dare since we had all kept picking dare. There was just something more fun about dares than truth. Plus, I was scared of what they'd ask me, and even if this wasn't my actual birthday, it was my party, and I didn't want to think about heavy questions and answers. I was just glad I had long ago forgotten about the thing that upset me enough to make me want to drink, to begin with.

"I guess this makes me your hero!" Kinsley said, grinning at me.

His hair was usually always in his eyes, slanted in that emo way that helped hide him. I found myself wanting nothing more than to touch that hair, to run my fingers through it. I wrapped my arms around his shoulders, his hands automatically wrapping around my waist as I ran my fingers through his hair, brushing the wet blond strands out of his face.

Kinsley looked up at me, his lips opened in the shape of an 'O,' and I wanted to touch them, too. "My hero," I whispered to him, my voice slightly deeper than usual.

A shudder ran through his body, his fingers digging into my skin as the drops of water on my face fell onto his. "You lost your dare, Curly!" Izzy screamed, a strange cackling sound coming from her as we broke apart reluctantly.

"You also lost your shoe," Kinsley said as he hoisted himself out of the pool slowly. He slipped once, falling back down the side of the pool. His face settled in a determined scowl as he tried once more, his knee banging painfully against the side as he sat down, trying to fan the air above his knee as if that would do anything to stop the pain.

I followed behind him, both of us fully clothed and soaked as we sat side by side, our clothes clinging to our bodies. I stared down at my feet, one with a shoe on it and one with only a sock, and threw my head back, laughing. I wasn't entirely sure why I found it so funny, but for a good few minutes or so, I struggled to breathe, to stop the laughter from spilling out of me. "I don't even remember putting shoes on," I said after a few minutes, my voice slightly breathless.

Kinsley, however, frowned. He stared down at the pool with a sad look on his face, lifting his cerulean eyes to peer into mine as he chewed on his bottom lip. "Now it's lonely," he said softly. He held the bottom of his shirt between his fingers, moving them back and forth like a child would.

I couldn't help but feel sad, looking at Kinsley as he looked like that. *A pretty boy shouldn't be so sad*, I couldn't help but think as I kicked the other shoe off and watched it fall into the deep end of the pool. I couldn't see down to the bottom of the pool to tell if the shoes were next to each other.

I watched as the water rippled, the large house reflecting on the surface moving with the ripples, looking like something out of a movie. I looked up at Kinsley with a smile on my face, hoping he'd do the same. I liked Kinsley the best when he was smiling. "They're together now."

"I'm jealous," he slurred, holding out the s for so long I wasn't sure if he was even noticing what he was saying. I frowned, my head tilted to the side as a wave of dizziness spilled through me, and although I wanted to ask him why he was jealous, I was unable to form words. I whined, hoping the dizziness would fade.

Izzy grabbed the back of Kinsley's shirt, yanking on it. "Quit trying to reboot and come on! We have to play spin the bottle!" she shouted, yanking Kinsley to his feet.

"But there's only three of us, that's boring," Kinsley whined.

I followed behind Izzy, pulling Kinsley, and felt like pouting. My head was fuzzy, and the music was everywhere. "You guys can't lose your first kisses playing a party game!" I shouted at them over the music as we all practically crawled up the stairs to Kinsley's room.

Two of us were soaking wet, all three of us groaned as we slipped and slid, and I wondered if these stairs had been this dangerous before or if they had suddenly decided to take vengeance out on us. Kinsley slid down the steps a few times and burst out laughing, rolling around as I grabbed his wrist or his ankle, hoisting him back up the stairs only for him to slip once more barely a second later.

We finally made it up to Kinsley's room and Kinsley yanked off his wet shirt, a disgusted look on his face as he went to throw it towards the hamper. He spun in a circle, falling over in the process. Isabella turned down the stereo since we didn't need it set to the highest setting now that we were inside again. "You're just going to assume that I hadn't had a first kiss yet?" Isabella asked as she grabbed a pair of sweatpants and a short-sleeved shirt out of Kinsley's dresser, flinging them at him.

Kinsley had just managed to stand up again before falling over, giggling as the clothes-ball knocked him back down. I grabbed some clothes out of the dresser that I had pretty much claimed as mine and moved to the bathroom. I was trying not to notice Kinsley yanking his pants off without a care in the middle of the bedroom, singing along quietly to the music.

"Okay, who was your first kiss?" I asked Izzy.

I had left the bathroom door open, standing behind it so I could hear while I got dressed, but I couldn't be seen. Despite that, she still waited until I got out to reply to me. Kinsley had managed to get the sweatpants and the shirt on and was attempting to pull a hoodie over his head.

"Her name was Samantha Peterson," Isabella said with a soft sigh. I blinked in surprise because honestly, I had thought this whole time that Isabella was straight. "She smelled like cotton candy, and I thought she was a boy. We were seven, she wore boy clothes and a baseball cap and went by Sam,"

"And that's how I met your father," Kinsley said in a monotone voice as we all started to cackle over the lame joke. "What about you, Lukey?"

I felt my cheeks heat up over the nickname and wondered if it was considered a nickname if it was longer than my actual name. "Lana," I said lamely with a shrug. I guess maybe I should have gotten all dreamy-eyed like Isabella did and told them about this big ordeal that I had gone through, but it wasn't to me. We were chilling on the couch at her parents' house, the same day she had asked me out.

I was nervous, unsure how to even be a boyfriend, let alone what she wanted from me. She grabbed my chin and kissed me out of the blue, and I remembered how I thought it was disgusting because she had been chewing gum and still had the sticky residue on her lips from blowing bubbles every five minutes and popping them.

Kinsley nodded, understanding, since his father was still trying to set him up with Lana. I still kind of thought that was funny, to be honest, even if it did worry me constantly. "What about you?" I asked him.

Kinsley shrugged, grinning sheepishly at me. "Izzy was my first kiss."

He looked at Isabella, and they both started giggling together. For the first time since I had met her, I found myself being jealous of her. They were staring at each other in a way that I didn't like, not because it was a together way, but because they were talking without talking, and I didn't like it. I knew it was stupid, but I wanted to be the only person who could understand Kinsley without needing words to do so.

I frowned, looking down at my hands as I chewed on my bottom lip, trying to understand why I was upset. Before I knew it, I felt small and narrow fingers pressing against my chin as soft lips pressed against mine, a chaste kiss. It was only for a second before Isabella pulled away from me, and I blinked in surprise as I touched my lips, confused. "What?"

It felt like nothing, strangeness. Kind of like kissing a sibling, in a way, not that I had ever really kissed Shawn to know. I had never really liked kissing much, even with my exes. I didn't understand the point of it. Two lips touching, it had never really done much for me. Isabella grabbed my cheeks, squishing them together. "It's okay, Curly! You don't have to feel left out. I know! We can fix this. You can kiss Kinsley too, then we're all good!" Isabella said with her strange drunken logic as she grabbed the back of my head and pressed my face against Kinsley's.

We didn't kiss, not really. We were both wide-eyed and surprised as we were shoved against each other, my lips pressing against the corner of his lips as his tooth grazed lightly against my cheek. As we pulled away from each other, Kinsley was the deepest shade of red I'd ever seen. I pressed my fingers against my cheek in quiet surprise, wondering why it felt like it was burning when he hadn't even broken the skin.

I felt slightly disappointed for some reason as Isabella moved past us giggling and turned the stereo up once more. "Have some more liquid courage!" Isabella screamed at us, handing us both some bottles as she opened a third. I wasn't even caring anymore as I tilted my head back and chugged it. I think I was on my fourth bottle, and maybe in the morning, I was going to hate myself for drinking after saying I never would, but tonight I didn't care.

The three of us were dancing in a way that probably looked ridiculous, three drunk teenagers holding bottles of alcohol sloshing around all over the room as we kicked at the balloons floating around our feet, the confetti scattered throughout the carpet. Kinsley leaned down and grabbed a handful of glitter and confetti and scattered it all through Isabella's hair, causing her to squeal in horror and run out of the room and down the stairs.

"There's a bathroom in here!" Kinsley called out as I put my hands on my knees and laughed. All of a sudden, Kinsley was grabbing my wrist, yanking me over to him with wide eyes as he grinned at me. "I love this song!" He shouted, jumping up and down as the new song started.

Kinsley explained to me before that he and Isabella had fairly different tastes in music, so to compromise, they had created a playlist of both of their favorite songs. Whenever Isabella could convince her mother, she would claim to be sleeping over at some girl's house, and they would blast their mixed playlist. Kinsley had his right hand up in the air as he jumped up and down, his beer bottle splashing around and around in his left hand as he sang along to the song: *Kissin' When We're Mad,* by We Three.

For the first verse, I just watched, mesmerized as Kinsley sang along to the song without a care. I wondered if he knew just how amazing his voice was, how amazing he was. He was practically shining, his eyes sparkling, and as he jumped up and down, his hood fell back. Kinsley's blond hair was mostly dry by now, longer than mine, so it took longer to dry. The bangs hung in his eyes as I grabbed his now empty bottle and placed it down on the nightstand next to mine.

Perfect, I couldn't help but think as the chorus of the song came on. As the music got louder, so did Kinsley, and I found myself wishing the stereo was turned off so all I could hear was Kinsley singing. I grabbed his hand, and he blinked in surprise, a soft giggle spilling from his lips as I twirled him around in a circle before pulling him closer to me. We were touching by our fingertips as we both started to dance together, the brightest smile on my face as I burst out laughing.

Why is it so easy to touch him? I wondered, sliding my fingers down the length of his, pressing the palm of our hands together. With my free hand, I grabbed the collar of Kinsley's hoodie, yanking his face right next to mine as he stared up at me with a surprised look on his face. His eyes were red this close to him, slightly droopy as he staggered against me. I let go of his hand as he clutched onto my shirt tightly, my hands finding his cheeks as I helped hold him steady.

He let out a soft laugh, his body shaking against mine. "You're like a beanstalk, so freaking tall," he slurred as he blinked at me. I thought that was funny because I was taller than Kinsley, it wasn't by much. He was probably only a couple of inches under me.

I grinned, trying to figure out why everything was so much easier with him. So much better, so right. My left hand slid down the length of his jawline, tilting his head higher as my other hand moved to his bangs, running my fingers through his hair as I pushed it back off of his face.

His eyes were wide as he stared up at me, and I found myself hovering above him, my lips resting right above his, barely a hair's breadth away. I could feel his breath against mine as he let out a soft whimper, his fingers pulling my shirt closer, closer, but not close enough.

Nothing felt as right as the feel of Kinsley's lips against mine. They were soft and hesitant at first, but as I pulled him closer to me, he parted his lips and melted against me. The cold night air from the open windows flooded the room, but the heat from Kinsley's body enclosed me as he pulled me even closer. I felt a mixture of dizziness and wonder as I breathed him in.

Everything around us dropped away, the music faded, and the cold air became a distant memory as Kinsley's fingers slid down my shirt and to my stomach, sliding up my shirt and gripping tightly onto my waist. I slid my tongue against his, like a dance all on its own as wave after wave of heat and cold collided inside me, around me.

Breathlessly, I broke the kiss for a second to take a breath of air. Kinsley's eyes were closed, his eyelashes fluttered against his skin and I felt like I was boiling. I closed in on his mouth once more, kissing him fiercely in a way I'd never done before with anyone else, especially with this much enthusiasm. I never knew kissing could feel like this. A shudder ran through my body as his fingers slid over my abs, touching me, and I never wanted him to stop.

As I kissed him deeply, it was like I was asking a question, a question I wasn't sure I knew how to form into words. He kissed me back with as much passion as I was giving, and despite the words, the answer was there, waiting for me to touch it, to understand it.

We pulled away, both of us panting, falling to our knees unsteadily as we fell in front of each other. Our foreheads pressed together, our eyes burning a dark red, alcohol thick on our breath, and churning in our stomachs. Everything was hazy, and I wasn't even sure how any of this started.

A dare, maybe? A dance? Was it a song? But as I stared Kinsley in the eyes, none of that mattered right now. His eyes were asking me questions, and I wasn't sure if I was even able to answer my own questions, let alone his. I felt my stomach churning once more and pulled away, pressing my fingers against my lips as sudden waves of sickness spilled through me.

My body jerked, a blush rose to my cheeks, and I took a deep breath, trying to settle my stomach. Kinsley looked at me with an unreadable expression, a wave of hurt sliding over his features before he turned away, pressing his fingers against his swollen lips.

I wanted to hug him, I wanted to push him down and kiss him again, but I wasn't sure if he was mad at me now. I kissed him, I fucking kissed him, and he hated it. I wondered if he hated me now, too. If he was disappointed in me, like everyone else. Maybe my parents were right, all along. I was broken.

Isabella burst into the room holding a bowl of liquid nacho cheese and singing along to the new song that was playing on the stereo. The smell of the cheese and jalapenos filled the air with the crinkle of the bags of tortilla chips and it was enough to make me press my hand firmer against my mouth, stand and run to the bathroom, slamming the door behind me.

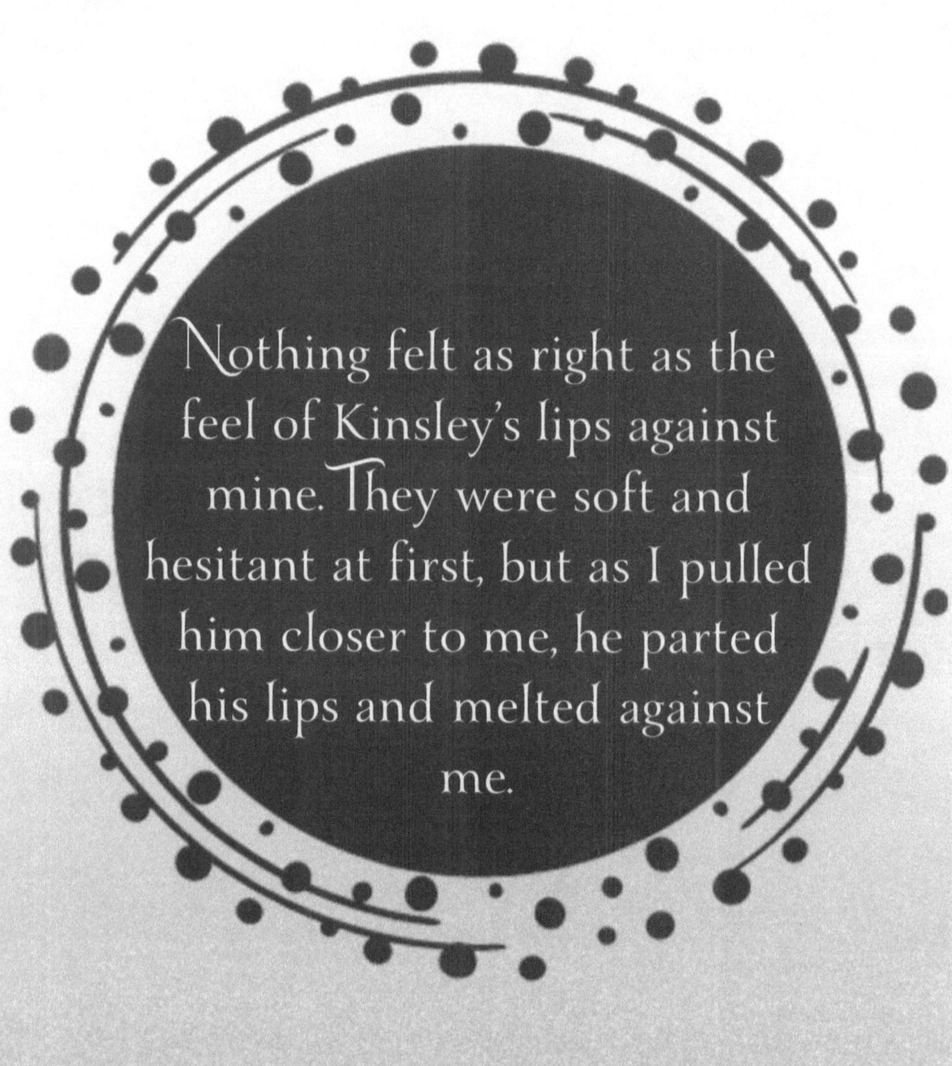

Nothing felt as right as the feel of Kinsley's lips against mine. They were soft and hesitant at first, but as I pulled him closer to me, he parted his lips and melted against me.

Chapter 8
Kinsley

I woke up with a groan. My body felt heavy, my stomach felt like death, and my head was aching. There was a weight against my stomach, and something on my ankle as well. Slowly, I lifted my head, feeling like a thousand bees were buzzing inside me as I licked my lips, disgusted by the taste in my mouth. My stomach churned as I took a deep breath and lifted myself so I was propped onto my elbows.

I was wearing all my clothes at least, that was something. Luke was lying on my stomach. My hoodie and my shirt were pushed up to my ribs as he lay on his side, curled in a ball facing me. He had on all of his clothes too, so that was also a plus and made my anxiety lessen more with every breath I took.

Isabella was lying with her head in the dip of Luke's side, her nose smushed against Luke's lower rib as her legs draped over my ankles, linking us together in some strange alcohol-induced triangle. She had on a sports bra and her shirt was draped over the side of the bed, but she had her pants on still, so I wasn't all that worried. I remembered from last time that Isabella was a notorious kisser when she was drunk and tended to strip off her clothes and run around screaming like a crazy person. Hopefully, nothing too bad happened last night. Well, I couldn't help but think as my eyes raked over the confetti and glitter mess all over my room. At least nothing that would ruin friendships happened last night.

I held myself up on one elbow as I lowered my hand to Luke's face, lightly running my fingers through his curls and pulling them away from his face. I studied his strong cheekbone, the small gathering of freckles that dotted under his right eye like a small handful of stars hovering against his cheek, waiting to fall and wash over his face.

I wanted to touch each freckle, to press my lips against each spot, to memorize the feel of him against me, but I knew I couldn't. I had already decided to give up on him. Luke turned his head and pressed his lips against my stomach and my cheeks flushed in surprise. He groaned and I lowered my hand, laying back down as I pressed my hands against my forehead and ran my fingers through my hair, trying to ignore the way my stomach churned.

"Kins," Luke whispered. I held back a shudder at the deep timbre of his voice, trying to tell myself that I was used to it. All the times I'd heard his voice in the morning, it shouldn't still affect me. I shouldn't have been affected by someone I was giving up on, but it seemed my mind and my heart wasn't on the same wavelength. I propped myself up on my elbows once more and found myself staring into Luke's resplendent light green eyes.

If I had to find the exact hue to color his eyes with, I'd probably pick seafoam green, maybe a parakeet green depending on how dark the background was. His eyes were soft as they peered into mine, and for a moment we stared without words.

Two souls resonated back and forth, talking in our own language that I wasn't sure Luke or I were ever going to be able to understand. Maybe one day we would learn the language of our souls, but for now, all we could do was stare. "Do you remember last night?" He asked quietly, hesitation in his voice.

I closed my eyes, knowing full well he was still watching me, waiting. I thought about the cake, remembering nearly lighting the kitchen on fire. I remembered watching movies and Isabella bringing in alcohol from my parents' cabinet. I remembered the water, how cold it was, and being sad about a shoe. I remembered the feeling of dancing, but that was all. It was like last night was a puzzle that was broken into hundreds of little pieces, and only half of the puzzle was completed, the rest forgotten and scattered around the house, to never be found, swept away, a puzzle that would never get completed.

"I remember getting drunk, but everything kind of fades after that. I remember water, but not sure why. I was also sad about a shoe for some reason, and the feeling of dancing," I whispered back to him. The feel of his fingers clasped around mine as he twirled me, but that was all. Was he looking like that because we danced together? I wanted to tell him it was okay, that nothing had to change just because of that. But maybe to him, it wasn't okay. I was scared I had ruined everything.

He closed his eyes for a moment, taking a deep breath as his calloused fingers lightly danced over my belly button. I couldn't quite stop myself from shivering and hoped he thought it was from the cold, instead of the touch. I liked the way he pulled my shirt up to sleep on my skin, wanting to touch me, instead of the cloth that was covering me. I was sure it didn't mean much to him, but to me, it meant everything.

When he opened his eyes, the pain in them nearly broke me. The shine lathered over his pupils as he chewed on his lower lip, his eyes moved to my belly button, then back at my face once more. "I see," he whispered. There was something about his voice, his expression, and I wasn't sure what to make of it. I was terrified. Scared he'd walk out the door and never come back.

"What's wrong?" Maybe it was the sound of my voice, the emotion I was trying to hold back that snapped him back into place again.

Luke let out a deep breath, and the arm he wasn't lying on lifted so he could brush his fingers through his curls. He looked embarrassed, shy, and unhappy. I didn't want him to be unhappy. "I'm mad at myself. I don't want to be like him." I was quiet, not fully understanding what he was talking about as I tilted my head to the side. "Drinking," he muttered softly.

Isabella let out a loud snore but continued to sleep as we stared at each other. I nodded because that was another puzzle piece to the question I had before. I wanted him to elaborate on what he meant when he said his father, about the pain, about being scared, but there was another clue right there. Drinking.

He must have done that a lot, I was sure. Enough to be a problem, at least. I wondered if he only hit Luke when he was drunk, or if he didn't need to be drunk to be abusive. "You're not like him," I promised. I didn't even need to meet his father, to see the differences.

"You're nothing like him, Luke. You'll never be like him," I talked sternly and calmly, trying to make him see just how serious I was. A boy like Luke didn't know what trust was. I hoped more than anything I could show him.

"You don't know him, Kins," Luke said hesitantly. I could hear just as loudly what he wasn't saying, as what he was. *You don't know him. You don't know how his fist feels, you don't know how my heart breaks with every swing, with every yell, with every curse.*

"I don't need to know him, to know you," I said firmly.

Luke let out a soft breath, his eyes moving to the side once more, and I considered telling him it was okay to cry. It was always going to be okay. Emotions didn't care what gender you were, only stereotypical adults who were scared of what they couldn't understand did.

"It's hard to think otherwise when I look in a mirror and all I see is him." He breathed out against my skin. I closed my eyes, trying to calm myself down. To tell myself there was no point thinking about wanting to beat up his father. I could barely even defend myself, let alone hurt someone else, but for Luke, I'd do anything. I was scared of the things I'd do for him. "I just don't want you to think about me, the way I think about myself."

I think I shattered, hearing that sentence. I rolled his words around and around in my mind because they were laced with the desperation of a young boy who wished desperately to have someone, anyone, see him. To see every part of him and still love him, just the way he was. I opened my eyes, studying him.

"I see you, Luke." My voice cracked as I took a deep breath, letting it out slowly. "I will always see you."

We were silent, both of us open in ways we'd never been before with anyone else. I could feel words on the tip of my tongue, words I was sure he'd never say, words I was sure he'd never feel for me. Those three words were dangerous, the most dangerous words I've ever known when it came to Luke Wilson.

Isabella groaned, rolling over onto her back in the dip of Luke's side, and threw her arms up above her head, accidentally punching Luke in the back of the head in the process. My eyes were wide as Luke groaned, his forehead pressing against my stomach as he winced in pain, and I chuckled as Isabella smacked her lips and yawned. "I feel nastyyy," Isabella sang.

Luke lifted his eyes to mine, and within seconds we were laughing. Isabella sat up and looked at us like we were crazy. Suddenly I shoved Luke against Isabella and stood on top of my bed, grinning down at them. "Bathroom's mine first!" I shouted, jumping off the bed. Isabella tackled me, and Luke ran past both of us, stopping only for a second to stick his tongue out at us while we both groaned before shutting the door behind him.

The morning was spent with me driving Luke home, making sure to drop him off a street over so his father didn't notice. He was quiet as I drove, his small bag filled with the presents we got him settled at his feet, his hands clasped tightly on his knees. I wanted to hold his hand, to lace my fingers with his, but it felt like something happened between us, and I wasn't sure what.

Luke sat farther away from me than usual, and when I accidentally touched him, he jumped backward away from me earlier. I wasn't sure what to make of it. Was it just us dancing that made him react so strangely? Or was it something more?

When I returned home, I was surprised to see Isabella and the housekeeper in my room talking animatedly in Spanish, cleaning the mess together. I didn't want to disturb their conversation, so I grabbed a bag and started to help, a smile fluttering over my lips as I heard the housekeeper laugh. She hugged Isabella for a moment before resuming to clean.

The housekeeper was a younger lady, in her twenties, I believe, and she had been very excited the first time I brought Isabella home and they started to talk to each other. Izzy told me she was lonely, that she had moved here with her sick grandfather and after he had died she was all alone. She needed the job to get the money to move to a new place with more people she could understand, but ever since she met Isabella, she had been introduced to Izzy's mom, and I wasn't sure if she was ever going to move away now that she had a friend.

The afternoon was filled with cleaning, Isabella leaving, and me just sitting on my window seat, looking down at the pool, trying to remember everything that happened last night. Little glimpses of laughter spilled into my head, the song we had danced to, and the way Luke's face lit up as he laughed. I can remember a game now, but not sure what it was. A game that resulted in me getting wet in the pool. From up here, I could see two black dots sitting side by side in the deep end of the pool.

As the sun lowered and my stomach started to growl, I stayed still as I heard the front door open and close. I had left my bedroom door open, and I could hear my father talking to someone on the phone while he went into his room to get something. Probably a change of clothes, since he and mom barely slept at home.

"Are you going to come check on me?" I whispered into the emptiness of my room, staring at my open bedroom door. I had my lamp on, so it was obvious I was there, my car was parked in the garage and my door opened to spill the soft dim yellow light out onto the soft carpeted hallway. "Are you going to remember I exist today?"

However, I wasn't surprised when his voice faded, Nor when the door slammed once more, or even the roar of his engine as he drove away. I sighed, looking down at the pool that was now as dark as the night around it, trying to ignore how it felt like the weight of the world rested on my shoulders.

I pulled my phone out of my pocket and stared at the group chat, noticing it was just me and Izzy talking in it for the rest of the day. Luke hadn't read any of it, it seemed, and I was worried. I looked at the time and shrugged, unsure if ten at night would be a bad time to call, and sent a text instead. *'Are you okay?'*

I miss you, I wanted to say. *I wish you were here. I wish you were safe. You'd be safe if you were here with me.*

He didn't reply to me, and all it did was make me worry even more. I dragged myself down to the kitchen, nearly decapitating myself as I tried to open a can of vegetable beef soup. I had gotten pretty good at making canned soup taste amazing, and I tried to distract myself from my silent phone as I poured in seasonings of garlic, minced onions, parsley, and a few other things to fix the originally dull taste.

I looked around the elaborately designed kitchen and chuckled, wondering if anyone realized just how useless those thousand dollars of expensive plates and accessories were when they were never even touched, unless it was once a week for the family dinners.

I walked through the silent prison back to my room, not bothering to close the door behind me. I was scared if I closed a door then Luke wouldn't enter it even if he had keys, and I wanted him to know he was always welcome. Was it the same for him, at his house? Or were closed doors a necessity there, locks a priority, to hide away from the storm raging inside quiet pristine painted walls and beautiful flowers to disguise the horror that was hidden inside?

'Have you heard from Luke?' I texted Izzy.

I didn't think I could be any more scared than I was when her reply came. *'No. I haven't heard from him since you dropped him off this morning. He's probably working late. Chill, Pretty Boy,'* she said with a tongue emoji.

I didn't want to tell her exactly why I wasn't able to chill. Secrets spilled at four in the morning were secrets I had to keep, no matter what. They weren't my secrets to tell, after all, they were just there for me to worry. I ate my soup, trying to calm myself down as the minutes passed. I took a shower, trying to clear my mind as the hour passed. I sat at my computer and typed away, my own secret that I'd never tell, as the hours passed.

When I decided I couldn't take it anymore, I looked at my phone and realized I had kept going long enough for it to be four in the morning, and I had been too worried to even sleep. I called him, lying down in my bed staring at the pillow he'd laid on just the other night, the groove of his head still perfectly shaped inside the pillow. I ran my fingers down the side of the bed where he had laid. It didn't even ring, it went straight to voicemail. I stared at it in horror, realizing this was the first time he hadn't answered a four in the morning call.

The next day was silence. I drove past his house to get to Izzy, but the beautifully painted house was filled with an eerie silence, showing off how much you never realize what's truly broken underneath the beauty that was covering the outside.

Windows with blinds covering them, a sprinkler turning on to freshen up the grass, and if one hadn't known of the pain inside, one wouldn't ever have been able to tell this home belonged to a storm. It made me wonder if there were others out there, other kids with fake smiles and broken hearts, with cracks etched in their souls as they forced themselves to smile.

Izzy and I drove past his job, but it was closed with an inventory sign stuck on the window. We went to the park and parked, and when it was dark, we tagged the side of the post office, but all the while my heart was quivering as I stared at my phone, worrying.

That night at four am, I called the hospital, instead of his phone. I was worried, as I asked if my brother was admitted there. I told them Luke's name, pretending to be Shawn since I knew they'd only release that information to a family member. The tired secretary told me he was never admitted there and told me the address to the next closest hospital. I spent that restless night calling hospital after hospital, searching for the other half of my soul, but to no avail. Another day of no reply, another day of no answer, another day that I slowly slid into darkness.

'What did I do wrong?' I texted him. He wasn't reading my texts, wasn't answering my calls, but he wasn't talking to Izzy either. We were both worried at this point, and I had to beg Isabella not to go to his house for fear of what that would do to him.

The next day, I lay on my bed, stared at the ceiling, and I cried. I never knew a heart could break for a loss it was never given, but even if we were never dating, even if we were never anything, I felt this loss like someone had ripped my heart out and thrown it into the pool next to Luke's shoes that rested side by side at the bottom of the deep end.

I kept my bedroom door open, hoping he'd walk through, but he never did. I thought he knew that a key was given to prove to someone they had a place they belonged, but it seemed he didn't feel like he belonged with me.

"Did I do something wrong?" I asked Isabella over the phone at the end of the week. Sunday dinner had been horrible, and we only had one more week left before school started. A night of parents trying to name pretty girls, my sister talking about her future marriage, and my mind on my silent phone resting in my pocket.

Isabella sighed, and I knew she was just as frustrated as I was. "Maybe he got mad about the alcohol. It's probably my fault, Kins, not yours. You didn't do anything that I could see. I barely remember that night though. We drank way too much. Maybe it's not even us, maybe it's something else. He'll explain, Pretty Boy. Just give him a chance to come back."

I curled into a ball, the pillow he had slept on pressed against my chest, my nose buried in the end of it as I breathed in his scent and cried. I wanted to tell myself this wasn't how you get over people, but who was I kidding? How could I expect my soul to try to get over that which made it whole? It was like cutting off my hand and trying to tell my body it didn't need the hand to draw.

It was four in the morning when I got the phone call from a number I didn't recognize. I had been sleeping on and off, rough nights filled with blank memories and fear of what could have happened, of what I must have caused to deserve his silence. I rolled over towards my phone and saw the time, my eyes lighting up in excitement, only to dim when I saw it was a number I didn't recognize. I let the number fade away, a frown on my face as I stared at it, confused. Telemarketers didn't call at four in the morning; they should know that this time was reserved for Luke and Luke alone.

The number rang again, and I considered answering it, to yell out my exhaustion and my fear to them. To have someone to scream to, all of these emotions bottled up inside me waiting to burst on the ground. The number faded, and I felt my heart race as it called once more. There was an urgency to the ring, something that pulled at me, like a little voice telling me even though it was a number I didn't recognize, I needed desperately to answer it all the same. "Hello?" I asked quietly, sitting up in my bed.

I stared at the darkness that was in the hallway, the door still open, waiting. "Kinsley," Luke breathed into the phone. I felt my heart racing at his voice, tears already pooling in my eyes as I opened my mouth and closed it, unsure what to even say. All of my anger and frustration faded away as I heard the pain and fear in his voice. "Please," he whispered.

"I'm on my way."

"I see you, Luke. I will
always see you."

Chapter 9
Luke

I remembered it.

I kept chanting those three words repeatedly as I walked from the street Kinsley dropped me off at to my house. I had my bag on my shoulder, and the fingers of my other hand brushed softly against my lips. I remembered, and he didn't. I wasn't sure what to think about all of this.

In a way, I was glad he didn't remember. I barely remembered last night myself, and I was wondering if it had happened after all. The dance he talked about, and twirling him. The song he sang along to, the way his face lit up as he grinned at me. I grabbed his hoodie, pulled him against me, and kissed him. The feel of his mouth against mine. It was hazy after that until the look of pain and disappointment on his face slipped into my mind.

Yeah, maybe it was a good thing he didn't remember. Just because he wasn't straight, didn't mean he was interested in me. "I'm straight," I told myself firmly, almost a tinge of desperation in my voice, the whisper slipping through the mostly quiet morning air around me. Though a part of me wondered if that was true, if that had ever been true, and just that thought in itself was enough to scare me more than anything.

I passed another house, the same wooden signs plastered in every yard now. These wooden signs were multiplying, filled with protests about something I never really cared to read. The sound of construction machines distracted me, and I shook my head, pushing all the thoughts away from me. I needed to shove it down, all of it down, and forget all about it. He didn't remember, and if he did, all I'd see is that look of disappointment, of sadness once more.

'It meant nothing to me,' I told myself fiercely, *'and it meant nothing to him.'* It was better he didn't remember, and that we could stay the same. I didn't think I'd be able to survive it if I lost him again.

I had borrowed a pair of shoes from Kinsley's closet, the side of the closet filled with clothes that he'd never wear, shoes he'd never try, everything given to a boy in hopes he'd wake up and decide to be everything they expected him to be. Everything I didn't want him to be, because he was perfect, just the way he was.

I was wearing the same clothes I wore when I went to Kinsley's, having dried since the incident of the pool, and wanted nothing more than to slip inside hopefully unnoticed, and take a shower to get the alcohol and the chlorine off of my skin. I felt like I was forgetting something, something important, as I walked onto my front porch, and frowned. A conversation, maybe?

As always, I pressed my ear against the door and listened. I could see my father's car in the driveway, with the little wooden sign next to it that hadn't been there before. I thought about going over there and seeing what was written on the little wooden sign, but thought against it, not hearing anything. I wasn't sure which side of the coin I'd be walking into, whether it was the side of thunder or the side of lightning, but as I opened the door I couldn't help but hope it was the silence.

At least with silence, there were no bruises, no cuts, and no screaming. My head was still slowly throbbing over everything that happened last night, small little pieces of the night coming back to me as I gently laid my bag down next to the shoe rack, kicked my shoes off at the door, and put them on the shoe rack. As I turned around and came face to face with my father, I realized a few things, the moment his fist went crashing into me.

The first thing I noticed was he was covered in oil and grease, a smell I had never really smelled on him before. The next thing I realized, as he slammed me into the wall, the sharp crack of my phone shattering in my pocket, was I had forgotten to put it in my bag. The last thing, as I tasted the sharp coppery taste of blood in my mouth, was I had forgotten about his threat to kill me. "Stop it!" Mother screamed. "Leave him alone!"

I was on my hands and knees now, my vision spotty as I looked at them, trying to see through the blurry vision. My head felt woozy and I could feel a trickle of blood down the side of my cheek, wondering absently where the wound was. As I pressed my finger against my pocket, I winced, feeling the sharp stab of my screen shattered and fragments jutting out of the fabric of my pants, cutting my fingertips. My father flung Mother off of him, her body fell with a soft thud against the couch.

I thought he would charge at her, but he whipped around once more and glared at me, charging at me instead. "Where is he?" He screamed, his eyes red and filled with the same dark veins I had last night. The same eyes, the same smell of alcohol on his breath. I tried to remind myself of Kinsley's words that morning, but everything was so hard to grasp right then through the haze of pain. "Where is Shawn?"

It was then that I noticed everything. The bags near the couch, and how there were quite a lot more than I would expect just for dad. With a jolt, I remembered the fight, the talk of divorce, and the talk of him taking us with him. I wanted to tell him he wasn't going to take me anywhere, but he didn't want me, he never did. I was just a broken boy, and that was all I was ever going to be. "You can't take him," I said, my voice quiet, my words slightly slurred from the pain in my mouth.

"What was that?" He asked, his eyes wide as he lifted me off of the ground by the collar of my shirt and slammed my back hard against the wall. I let out a breathy scream as my shoulder cracked into the frame. I was six foot one, with barely any body fat, my arms bigger than most of the other guys at school, and my abs strong as steel. But when my father lifted me with ease and flung me against the wall, I felt like I was five all over again.

I wanted to be five and let the tears fall down my cheeks as my father laughed and hugged me. I wanted to be five and feel my mom's kisses against my cheek as my father patted my head and told me good job. I wanted to be five again. When everything was right, when my father loved me, and I wasn't broken.

I realized, as he stared up at me with flaring nostrils, the vein pulsing in and out on his forehead, that I had stood up to him in a way. I had talked back, I had said it calmly, without fear in my voice. I had done that because of Kinsley. He wasn't even here, and he was my strength. Before I could reply or get beaten once more, the squeak of the backdoor was heard and I closed my eyes, breathing through my nose as I hoped beyond all hope Father hadn't heard it.

I wanted to shake Shawn like crazy for coming back. My father dropped me like a pile of trash on the ground and left me there. I opened my eyes, staring without really seeing at the wall across from me as the dizzy stars splattered across my vision. Everything throbbed with the pain that moved in and out around me. Shawn's screams, my mother as she begged Dad to leave Shawn alone. "Please," Shawn choked out. He sounded desperate, not that I could blame him. "I just came back for my phone, I didn't know you were here. I'll stay in a shed, at the garage, anywhere. Please don't make me go."

Dad replied by punching him. I couldn't see it, but I heard the crack of his fist against Shawn's face, the drop, and knew without needing to move he had knocked Shawn unconscious. My mother was pleading with him to stop as I sat there, feeling numb. My fingers tingled, I knew my left shoulder was dislocated by the horrible throb. I closed my eyes as my father walked past me, Shawn slung over his shoulder.

I kept my eyes shut tightly as he walked back and forth, my mother begging and pleading as she pulled on him, only to get ignored as he loaded bag after bag into the car. He didn't talk to her, and he didn't talk to me, he didn't want me.

As much as he was a monster, I wondered what that made me. For feeling physical pain that he had started his car and backed away, without even caring to say goodbye. *'Why wasn't I good enough?'*

'I see you,' Kinsley's voice filled my head, chasing away the little voice that constantly haunted me before it could even have a chance to speak.

'Would you still feel that way if you knew I had kissed you against your will? Or that you hated it?' But I couldn't think about the kiss, about what it meant, and I wasn't ready for that. I wasn't sure if I'd ever be ready for that.

My mother was breathing hard as she fell to her knees in front of me. Her eyes were wide, pupils dilated, and I wasn't sure what she'd do. Was she going to fix the cut on my head? Or my shoulder? She's a nurse after all, and has spent the last five or so years of this fixing the bruises and the cuts left behind by Father.

"Why did you let them leave? Why did you let him take my baby away?" she shouted at me.

My mind went blank as I stared up at the ceiling, feeling the blows of her fists against my chest. They weren't that painful, not really. She barely ate, she was weak and frail, but every blow hurt on the inside, more than the outside. The look of hatred in her wild eyes, the realization that I was never good enough for her, for him, for anyone.

'I'll always see you,' Kinsley's voice floated into my mind. It was like a light, shining in the darkness I was burying myself in. My light pulled me out of the darkness and reminded

me that I wasn't alone. I had Kinsley and Isabella. But would they still want me, if they knew? If they knew every part of me?

I didn't notice the sound of pounding, as lost as I was in my mind. Nor the air that streamed through the living room as the police pushed open the front door, where Father hadn't even bothered to close it all the way. I didn't even notice my mom wasn't hitting me anymore, with how numb I was.

My mother screaming as she was torn off of me snapped me into place as I stared with wide eyes at the strangers in front of me. She was screaming out insanity, her hair wild as she spit at the officers, telling them everything was ruined, and they needed to let her go so she could kill us both together.

When was the last time she took her medication? I should have been trying harder to make sure she was taking it. They cuffed her and dragged her out of the house, and I felt defeated as I stared up at the older officer in front of me. "She's not a bad person, she didn't mean it,"

"I can see you're hurt, so I don't want to make it worse. Will you voluntarily come to the car? Otherwise, I'll have to cuff you and drag you, and it might fuck up your arm even worse, son,"

I sighed, lifted my good hand, and ran it through my hair, wincing at the cut on my head. "Why do I have to go?" I held my hand out for him to pull.

He stared at the blood on my hand with disgust as he grabbed my wrist and helped lift me to my feet. I staggered backward, falling into the wall, before regaining myself. "You're under arrest, son. For the destruction of the garage you work at."

Two men in black suits, crisp ties, and slicked-back hair sat across from me. I had my good wrist chained, and the other one still dangled at my side, my good hand was cuffed to the table. They had taken me there, left me there. I stared at the cup in front of me, the water they pushed towards me, and contemplated drinking it. "Your mother threatened to kill you, son. Assault on a minor. The wounds on your body, it's not looking good, son," the older of the two said.

I frowned, looking down at the water. "She didn't hurt me." Not physically, anyway. Her little blows did nothing to me, on the outside of my skin. Her words, her eyes, had been crippling me for as long as I could remember, but her fists did nothing. "My mother has manic depression and she must have forgotten to take her pills this morning, but she didn't do this to me."

The younger man leaned back as he gripped his walkie-talkie. "Check the mom's room for pills. Son claimed she missed a dose this morning."

"Sir, from the damage in this house, it looks like she forgot a year of doses," someone said over the line with a laugh before it cut off.

I sat up straight, anger in my eyes as I glared at him. "She didn't do that to the house! She didn't hurt me, she didn't do any of it!" I yelled.

Both of them sat up straight, their hands automatically falling to rest protectively on their hips, where I knew guns were resting. I swallowed deeply, my throat bobbing in fear as I scooted backward in my chair as far as I could, ignoring the sharp pain in my arm. "Are you going to tell me it was you then, boy?" The man asked quietly.

I shook my head no, my good hand opening and closing over and over again as I saw it all in my mind. The anger in my father's eyes, the alcohol on his breath, the fear of his curses, his screams. I had never spoken of any of it before to anyone, just a few words here and there to Kinsley, but as I squeezed my eyes shut I tried to tell myself it would be okay. He wouldn't hurt me if he was behind bars. They would let my mother go, they would give back Shawn, it would be okay. I needed to be brave, brave like Kinsley.

I sat up straight, my head high as I looked at them, my heart racing in my chest. "My father did it, all of it," I spoke of the way my mother had started to slip into her depression, how my father had started to hate it, hate us, hate everything. I explained how he had gone from smiling one day to shoving the next week, to punching the next month.

Each time he hurt her and she didn't leave, it made him that much stronger. Each time I stood in front of him and protected her, it made him hate me all the more. I told them about the holes in the wall, how many times my shoulder had popped out of its socket, and how many times I had my ribs bruised and broken. All of the broken fingers over the years, the black eyes. I told them everything he had done to me, to her.

"He took Shawn, knocked him out, and carried him out of the house. He beat me up trying to find Shawn, thinking I had him hidden somewhere. He did it, not her," I explained.

They left me alone for a while, as I slowly drank the water. A tray of stale and tasteless food was brought in, and I ate it. The tray was taken away as the men came back with a few pills and a new cup of water. They were silent as I took the ibuprofen, swallowing the pills with the water. Then they spoke, and I wished more than anything they never had.

"Son, we have proof that your father has been living in another town for over a month now. The woman he's staying with, his fiance, her name is Tina. They signed the rental agreement together, over a month ago. We had an officer go over and talk to him, the rooms were nice and straightened, no boxes or bags to indicate someone had just moved in. Your little brother was asleep but no wounds on his body that we could see with a glance. Tina told us your father and your brother moved there over a month ago."

I stared at him with my mouth hanging open, confused, as they continued. "You asked to stay with your mother to finish your senior year, they said. Your father showed how many times he had called you the past day, how worried he was about you being here with your mother."

"He told us how she was crazy, always off the meds, and abusive. We have talked to her therapist and a pharmacist about the pill bottles we found, to show how little she's been taking the past few months. As for your claims of abuse, Luke. We have a report of you beating up another student at school, and rumors about you being in a gang. Your father said if you had ever been injured, it was during football practice, and your injuries were never as bad as you said. There were no hospital records to prove most of what you told us."

I wanted to cry as I lowered my head to the table, listening to the lies my father told and how the police believed them. To think he'd gotten a house with another woman while he was still with my mother was horrible. Not to mention he said they were engaged. What the hell was going on? The rooms were already set up, just waiting for him to leave Mom. He had been planning it for a while, it seemed, for it to be such a fast and smooth transaction.

I nodded because what else could I do? The hospital wouldn't have records of me because my mother was a nurse and took care of me at home. We had to hide it all, Mother would say. Otherwise, Father would be mad. "We do have a record of you slicing open your wrist though, Luke. And the fact that you refused therapy for it."

'There it is. This is where I get called crazy.' I closed my eyes, took a deep breath, and counted to ten. *'Maybe I should try again,'* the voice in my mind started up again.

I looked at my left wrist, knowing exactly what the scar looked like, underneath the long sleeves that hid it from view. The length of it, the way it cut vertically along the vein. "Your father said you're a compulsory liar, Luke, and we're starting to see why. Nothing you said measured up with the evidence."

"My mother, she'll agree with me," I muttered, hoping I was right.

"Your mother said it was all your fault. It was all she had been repeating, non-stop. So, are you going to tell me the truth, son?" I was quiet, as I stared at the cup. "are you going to admit to destroying the garage?"

I took a deep breath, feeling the tears prickle in my eyes. I chewed on my lower lip, realizing how hopeless it all was. "My father did it," I whispered, remembering the smell of the grease and the oil on my father's clothes. It wouldn't have surprised me, the way he was searching for Shawn. It wouldn't have been the first time Shawn and I crashed at the shop for a good night's rest without worrying about the storm.

As I looked up at them, I could see it. They didn't believe me, not from the start. The look of disappointment, of sadness, of pain, was so much like the look I had seen on Kinsley's face when I kissed him that I was struggling to breathe, trying not to let the tears fall. I wouldn't cry for them, for any of them. No one ever believed me.

Her charges were dismissed because of her mental health. She was placed in a psych ward, and I never got to say anything to her before she left. I was placed behind bars and labeled a liar. Destruction of private property was my charge. They never were going to believe me from the start.

The jailhouse had a doctor, a crude man who popped my shoulder back in place and stitched the small gash on the side of my head without numbing much of anything. Maybe they thought hardened criminals didn't deserve pain meds, but I kept my mouth shut through the pain, as I was trained to all of the years I had to stand there with fists raining down on me. They questioned me, but I remained silent, struggling to catch up to everything that happened.

My boss came and told me he believed it wasn't me, but just needed me to cooperate. I wasn't sure how much more he wanted me to cooperate when I was trying to tell everyone the truth and no one was listening to me. I was silent when they asked me where I had been that morning because I didn't want them to involve Kinsley and Isabella.

I lay there for days in the jail cell, curled in a ball on the uncomfortable mattress, staring at the stone around me, thinking about Kinsley. They took my phone, my clothes, everything I had on me. I was seventeen, but they needed to take me to trial first for a sentence, so they had me in a separate cell away from the adult males for the time being.

I was given one free call. I wanted to call Kinsley, but I didn't know his phone number by heart. I didn't know what time it was or what day it was until an officer finally opened the doors. "The owner of the garage isn't pressing charges, so you're free to go since it's his property. You better thank him. Your mother is going to be staying in the psych ward for a while; she needs a lot of mental help, son. Because you're underage, we contacted your father, and he'll be picking you up."

I ran out of the police station before they even finished their sentence, refusing to be there for him to finish the damage he caused. My phone was broken and thrown away, the glass was pulled out of the fabric of my jeans. My arm was in a sling, and I felt more broken than I had ever felt before.

They gave me my mom's phone and her wallet since she couldn't have it in the psych ward. The phone was dead, but I stopped at a gas station. The sun had already set, and the man behind the register didn't even look awake. I got a new charger cord and a portable battery for the phone, along with a pack of cigarettes and a new lighter. I knew I shouldn't, but he didn't even ask for my license, just accepted my mom's card without care, and sent me on my way.

It was difficult getting the cigarette to light while my arm was in a sling, but I managed. My mom's phone was plugged into the battery as I made my way to the closest place I felt safe. I was too scared to go home, knowing my father would search for me there, and I was too far away from Kinsley. I climbed the stairs of the abandoned building, up to the roof, and remembered the night of Kinsley's seventeenth birthday.

I remembered how it felt watching the sunset, the stars as they moved across the night sky, and the sunrise once more. I felt safe there, with Kinsley lying on my lap, my fingers in his hair, tangled around his. I had felt brave that night, holding his hand. I wanted to be brave like that again, but the look of disappointment, of pain on Kinsley's face, was too much for me to consider it.

As I sat down on the top of the roof, I opened my mom's phone, searching the phone directory for Kinsley's phone number. It wasn't registered, not that I was surprised since it was a cell phone, but I kept searching, desperately searching. I could call a cab and drive to his house, but I was too scared to go home and get my bag. I needed to get it; it had all of the things that were most important to me in it, but I didn't want to get it alone. Maybe if I waited a few days, Dad would give up and leave, and I'd be able to get it without worry.

I was growing desperate as I searched everything I could think of. Finally, I looked up Kinsley's Facebook and laughed out loud over how innocent he was. He had his address and phone number just right there, for anyone to see it. I made a mental note to tell him at a later time how he probably should have that hidden, as I called the number.

It wasn't until after I started to dial that I realized the irony of the fact that it was after four in the morning. It seemed that destiny was always going to link us together for our four in the morning calls. I frowned, looking at the phone as the dialing stopped, wondering why he wasn't answering. Kinsley was a light sleeper, a phone call would wake him without a problem, no matter what time it was.

I called once more, the cigarette burning my fingertips where I had held it for too long, and I yelped, letting it fall to the road below. My legs were draped over the side of the building as I listened to it ring, my fingers nervously dancing on my knee as I waited as patiently as I could, wondering what was going on.

The phone stopped dialing once more and I nearly threw it over the side of the building before taking a deep breath and trying again. I felt tears prickling in my eyes, desperate for him to answer, to hear his voice after everything that had happened. It was all I needed, just to hear his voice. I wondered distantly when he became so important to me. Maybe he'd always been this important, all along.

"Hello?" Kinsley's voice flooded through the phone. My hand was shaking so badly I nearly dropped the phone.

"Kinsley," I breathed, trying to take deep breaths, my hand pressed firmly against my chest, trying to calm the flutter of wings brushing back and forth inside me. How one word, coming from the right voice, could do so much to me was beyond me. "Please,"

"I'm on my way."

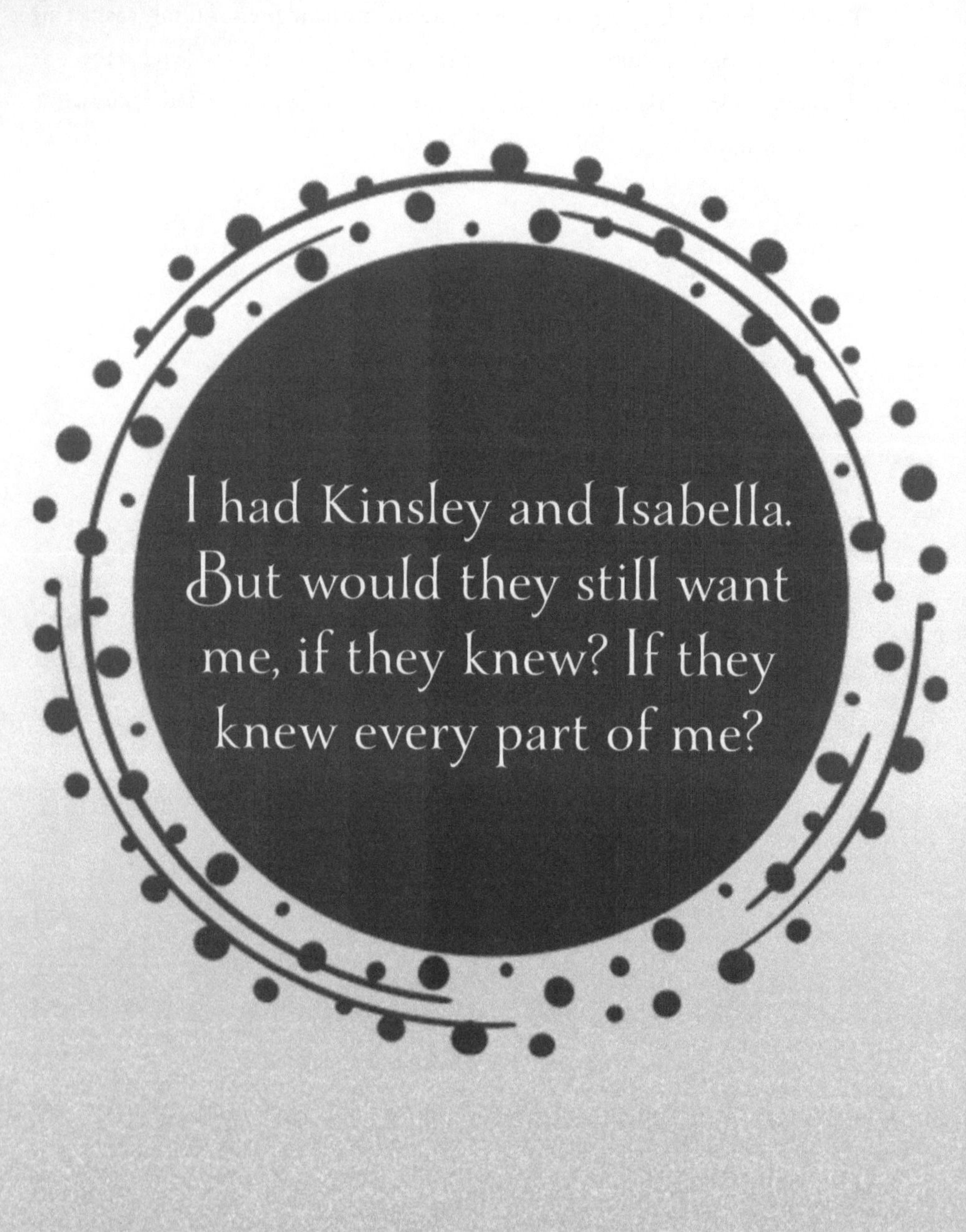
I had Kinsley and Isabella. But would they still want me, if they knew? If they knew every part of me?

Chapter 10
Luke

I wasn't entirely sure how he found me, to be honest. My mom's phone was barely charging with this cheap gas station charger, the battery was already dead after a few minutes, and for the next half hour, I lay there panicking. My legs draped over the side of the building, my good hand across my eyes as I lay on my back. I didn't let myself see the stars because wishes didn't come true, not for me. Maybe I didn't deserve the stars. Just a cemetery of dead stars, floating above us, waiting to fall and catch the wishes, hopes, and dreams of those who believed, only to crash to the ground, mocking us for our immature antics.

"Luke," I felt my cheeks heat up under my arm, the rasp in his voice was thick and I shuddered, either from the cold of the night air or from him. I wondered if it was a little of both as I lowered my arm and looked at him. He was falling to his hands and knees, his head bent at a lowered angle, staring down at me in a way that reminded me of the Spiderman movie and upside-down kisses.

I was glad it was dark, that there weren't many stars, and that the clouds were covering the moon because I was sure Kinsley would be able to see the way my cheeks were painted with my confusion. His eyes were so bright in the dark, so calming as he lowered his hand to my head, his fingers cool as they gently touched my stitches. I hissed at how good it felt, the cold of his fingers against the throbbing painful heat of my head as he went to jerk his hand away.

I grabbed his hand before he could move, pressed the palm of his hand against my head, and held it there as I held his gaze steadfast. "Luke," he said again, his voice more of a broken whisper as he cupped the back of my head, lifting me to place my head on his lap. I hummed, my eyes closing once more as I enjoyed everything that was Kinsley. The feel of him touching me, the smell of his cologne, how soft his fingers were as he stroked them against my cheek without pause.

It had been a week since the last time I had seen him. A whole week. He could have yelled at me and hung up the phone, but instead he came for me, he searched for me, he found me. Maybe it didn't matter if I was broken to everyone else because Kinsley thought I was worth searching for.

"What happened to you?" He whispered. I found myself staring at his lips, how full they were, knowing exactly how soft they were. I had been trying to tell myself all week it was a drunken fluke, surely my drunken self kissed him because Kinsley was so pretty, but here I was, completely sober, and all I could do was stare.

I swallowed, choosing to close my eyes instead of staring at him as he pressed his hand against my chest, right above my heart. I moved my hand that was holding onto his to press against the pulse on his wrist, and my heart slowed and mixed with his, beat for beat, perfect rhythm. For a moment, I felt whole, as if my soul was happy, touching his.

A soulmate, Kinsley had said in the letters. I wondered if either of us were even old enough to say that word, but at the same time, age didn't matter when it was right.

"I'm scared to just unload on you, Kinsley. I don't want you to look at me like he does, and I don't want you to think about me the way I do," I opened my eyes to stare at him once more.

He was silent for a moment, two souls staring back and forth, communicating in that way I wasn't sure if we'd ever understand. He leaned down, and for a moment my heart stopped. He pressed his forehead against the bridge of my nose, his eyes parallel to mine as I let out a soft shaky breath. I could feel his nose against my forehead, his breath against my hair, as he stared deep into my eyes.

"You don't have to hide anything, not from me. I promise, Green. I'm not going anywhere," I felt the tears spilling without warning or care from my eyes, silently flowing down my cheeks at his words. The words he'd written in the letters, the words I had embedded in my soul.

Kinsley squeezed my shirt tightly over my heart as I slowly but surely told him everything. I started from the beginning, my voice breaking only a few times as I spoke of when my mom's depression started to get obvious. I spoke of the first shoves, the first smacks, the first fist that flew through the air.

He was quiet, his eyes never wavering from mine as I talked, and I found peace in his silence. It calmed me, urged me to keep going, and made me feel safe. I told him about all of the fights, all of the words, the curses, the screaming. I opened my pages, flipped through them as fast as I could, and I read him my story, from the beginning to the end. As I quieted down, he frowned, staring at me with a wave of silent anger in his eyes, simmering just under the surface. "And the song? The scars?" I didn't need to ask to know he was talking about my suicide attempt.

I felt drained, letting all of that out, explaining the fight at home, the attack on the shop, and how I wasn't even sure if I had a job anymore. Telling him about jail, every bit of it, but in the end, I had left out the scar. "Can I... tell you later?" I asked, my voice breathy, filled with the sobs I'd been holding back. He nodded, and I felt the absence of his warmth as he gently lowered my head to the ground and stood. "I didn't mean to bruise your heart, Kinsley."

I stood slowly, turning to look at him as he grabbed my good hand and pressed it against his chest, right over his heart. There wasn't a need for words, to understand what he was saying.

'I'm still here,' he said, his eyes moving back and forth, studying mine. *'I'm always going to be here.'* I let out a shaky breath, squeezing the cloth on his chest, and pulled him against me, burying my nose against his throat as he hugged me. One hand against my waist, pulling me closer to him, another hand snaking up under my curls, holding the back of my head against his throat as I breathed him in.

I wondered if I had seen it, the way his eyes had told me more, so much more, but at the same time, I was sure I had imagined it. *'My heart isn't bruised,'* I heard whispered in my mind, *'because it's beating for you.'* Maybe, it wasn't his heart that had whispered that, but mine.

I was shaken as he pulled away from me, my eyes wide as I thought about my thoughts. "Let's go," Kinsley said, lacing his fingers with mine. His voice shook me away from the thoughts I couldn't understand. The feelings I had shoved so forcefully away started to leak, to spill outwards, unable to stay contained for much longer. I was silent, as he led me down the stairs. It felt right, to hold his hand.

We drove silently to my house, Kinsley parked across the street under a tree as we stared at it. The front door was closed and there weren't any lights on, everything looked just the same as always. Just goes to show how little you could tell from the outside looking in. "What if he comes here?" I felt like a small boy as Kinsley stared at me, his cerulean eyes lighting up the darkness of the car.

"I'll protect you." How this guy who was even smaller than me thought he was going to be able to protect anyone against my father was beyond me, but I felt the strength coming from him and nodded, opened the car door, and stepped outside. I opened the door easily, whoever had been inside most likely hadn't locked it before they left.

I stood there in the doorway, scared to move, scared to let him into my storm. It was one thing being told it, but to see it was another. Kinsley pressed the palm of his hand against my back, holding it there for comfort. "It's okay, Luke. A house isn't the same thing as a home."

I nodded as I took a step inside, and then another one. I turned around to look at him as he quietly shut the door and turned on the lights to my storm. He was right, a house wasn't the same thing as a home. This was simply a house, but he was my home. I never knew a person could be a home until I found mine.

Kinsley was easier to see now that we were standing in the bright light. He had on his signature black hoodie, his hood fallen, showing off a slight haircut. It wasn't much different, his bangs still hanging in his eyes, but the sides weren't shaggy anymore, they were shorter, cleaner. I wasn't sure which type of style I liked on him better, but in the end, it didn't matter because I still thought he was beautiful all the same.

His eyes held no judgment as he scanned the room, a short look around as he nodded. I leaned down, noticing the paper under my feet, a letter addressed to my mother that had been slipped through the slot. Slowly, I opened it, a frown on my face as I read it over and reread it. I felt my heart drop as I dropped the paper on the floor. "What is it?" He asked quietly, making no move to grab it.

"The landlord sold the property. We have thirty days to find a new house," I mumbled, feeling numb. I should have noticed. All of the wooden signs, all of the moving vans lately. I knew they were wanting to make a mall here, but for a while, I had heard rumors that the landlord wasn't selling and I had forgotten all about it. It seems they agreed after all.

Kinsley studied my face for a moment before giving a sharp nod. "That's fine, Luke. You didn't need thirty days, you already have a new house," he turned to look at the living room, giving another nod. "I'll rent a storage unit tomorrow and have movers here to get the rest for your mother until she gets out,"

He was so uncaring about using his money for others, not even realizing how big of a deal all of that was to someone like me. "I can't, Kinsley, I-" I stammered.

He turned to look at me, his eyes wide as he tilted his head to the side. "You don't want to live with me?" He looked at me with confusion in his eyes.

I gulped, remembering the feel of his lips against mine, about how bad it had been to force myself on him, and the disgust in his eyes afterward. "I don't think I deserve it," I muttered.

Kinsley ignored me, turning around and walking through the house like he owned it. He looked in every room, his eyes glancing over the destruction without care, and I followed him, knowing he was just going to do what he wanted. He walked up the stairs and opened Shawn's room, turning to look at me with raised eyebrows, a question. I shook my head no, walking past him, to mine. I stood there staring, noticing the door was off the hinges, and the room was a disaster. Clothes ripped, mattress torn, broken glass everywhere. "Um, anything you need to take with you tonight?"

I stepped around the glass and grabbed a duffle bag out of the top of the closet, opening up the drawers and grabbing the few clothes that hadn't been ripped. I still had on the shoes I borrowed from Kinsley, but I grabbed another pair out of my closet before turning toward him. "One more thing, but it's in the living room," I said.

He nodded, grabbing my bag from me since I only had one hand and slinging it over his shoulder. We started walking out the door and down the steps when the front door opened. "Are you in here, boy? I see the lights on. I stopped by here earlier and you weren't here." My dad's voice floated up to us. He left the door open as he looked up at us where we were standing. From the front door, he could see about the middle of the stairs, giving him the perfect view of me and Kinsley. "Who is this chick?"

Kinsley had his hood up again, and I knew what it was my father was seeing since I had thought Kinsley was a girl at first too. The smaller body was swallowed by the hoodie, making him look even smaller than he was. The bright cerulean blue eyes, the bangs hanging in his face, and those soft full lips. I shuddered, trying to push the image out of my mind as Kinsley lowered his hood. He pulled out his phone, holding it with the strap of my bag as he aimed it at my father.

"My name is Kinsley Bryant, Mr. Wilson. It's nice to meet you," he said casually as if this was a perfectly normal situation.

My father's eyes sparked with anger as he took a step towards Kinsley and another. Instantly, I bristled, moving to stand in front of him, refusing to let him touch him, but Kinsley touched my shoulder, holding me in place. "You're that faggot boy. I told you to stay away from him. He's over here touching you, fucking disgusting. Did you turn my son too?"

Kinsley held up his hand, showing off the phone. "I'm on a live video, that's instantly being recorded and sent to someone I can trust. Your name, your face, your words, everything is already being recorded and filed away. She's been told to hand the video to the police if something bad happens. I suggest you back away and don't even think of touching either of us."

His voice didn't waver as he stared at my father, and I found myself staring at him in shock, watching my father back away one step, then another. "Also, Luke is straight. Whether I'm straight or not, doesn't matter. It's not like a sickness he can catch by touching a gay person," he rolled his eyes, "Idiot."

My father eyeballed the phone, sweat gathered on his brow as he frowned at it. He didn't like that he'd been shown up. "That won't be held admissible in court since I didn't agree to be videotaped," he said, even as he took another step back, his hands in the air.

"Let's see whose lawyer is better, shall we?" Kinsley asked sweetly with a wide grin, showing off his dimples.

My father growled in frustration, his eyes flashing in anger as he looked at me, then at Kinsley again. He hated not being in control of everything, and I found this situation amazing. To watch him take a step back because of a seventeen-year-old boy. "I don't want trouble, boy," He mumbled, glaring at Kinsley. "Luke has probably told you many lies, he's a liar. I've come to take him home with me. He can't stay here, his mother is abusive and crazy."

I clenched my good hand into a fist, glad it was my throwing hand. It would have been bad if it had been this one that had been hurt. "Don't worry about Luke, I'll take care of him. He's coming home with me. I've already talked to my parents about it. They're waiting for us."

My father clenched his teeth tightly, his jaw popping as Kinsley took a step towards him, making him take a step back towards the front door. "You're just a kid, boy. You can't say you're going to take care of him, you're both just kids. He's underage." He growled. "The money from the taxes I'd get off of him, he has to live with me."

I clicked my tongue against the roof of my mouth, feeling disgusted that this was the only reason he was agreeing to take me. Only so he could make money off of me. "I'll pay you to go away and never come back," Kinsley said quietly.

"Kinsley!" I said, my eyes widened as I took a step towards him.

"No, Luke. I promised I was going to protect you. I know you don't see promises much, but I'm not breaking even a single one to you." Kinsley dropped my bag and tugged his wallet out of his pocket. He maneuvered keeping the phone aimed at my father as he searched his wallet for something. After a second, he pulled a card out, balled it up in his hand, and threw it at my father. He caught it with a frown on his face, opening the card and staring at it. "That's the name of my family lawyer. Call him on Monday, I'll have explained everything to him by then."

My father nodded, glaring at me once more, before turning around and walking away. I stared at his back as he left, feeling the last bit of my child-like hope fading away inside me.

They said kids were supposed to love their parents unconditionally. To have it instilled inside them to always care what they thought, to always seek their acceptance. To want to make them proud of you, to hear them say I love you. But as I watched his back disappear into the darkness, I felt the snap of everything fading away, hardening me. I wasn't going to ever let him hurt me again. He didn't love me, he was never going to be proud of me, and he was willingly walking away without even saying goodbye. He only cared about the amount of money he'd be getting.

I felt Kinsley staring at me and I looked at him, feeling humbled by everything he'd done for me in such a short amount of time. Kinsley studied my face, chewing on his lower lip as his eyes softened, a frown brushing across his features. "I'm sorry, Luke," he mumbled, looking down at his feet.

"Why the hell are you sorry? You didn't do anything."

He shrugged sheepishly, looking up at me once more with flushed cheeks. "I didn't ask your permission for anything, I just took charge. I was freaking scared, I made everything up. I didn't have a video going or anything. I was worried he'd notice," he breathed out, his hands pressed against his sides as he let out a shaky breath.

I blinked at him, a grin spread across my face as I laughed. I wrapped my good arm around him and hugged him tightly. "Thank you, Kinsley," I breathed against him, burying my nose against his throat.

He curled his fingers in the back of my shirt, holding me back tightly. "For what?" he asked, his hair tickling my cheek.

I couldn't help it, unable to stop myself as I pressed a soft kiss against his throat, and another one, enjoying the feel of his soft skin against my lips. I told myself it meant nothing, just a kiss on skin, the same as when Isabella kissed me and Kinsley on the cheek. "Thank you for being my Kinsley," I muttered against his throat, kissing his skin once more before pulling away.

I couldn't look at him, instantly turning away, worried he'd see the way my cheeks were on fire as he coughed and turned his back on me almost instantly. I wasn't sure what to make of that. Did I go too far? I frowned, was he mad at me now?

He cleared his throat, ran his fingers over his face, and grabbed my bag. His eyes were trained to the ground, as if unable to look at me. "Is this it then?"

I walked past him, unsure if I pissed him off or not as I grabbed the bag near the door, the one with his letters and the presents in it, and held it close to my body. "I'm ready," I muttered softly.

He looked at me then, a soft smile on his face that didn't fully reach his eyes as he tilted his head towards the door. "Let's go home, Luke," he said confidently, as he stepped outside.

I glanced down at my bag, awkwardly holding it with my sling as I reached inside it to the small box, dislodging the keys from it, and held them tightly in my hand. I slipped the bag onto my shoulder, keeping the hold on the keys as I looked down at them, then at the door. My keys to Kinsley, to my home.

"I'm coming," I said softly, slipping the keys into my pocket. I turned off the light and closed the door without a single feeling of remorse because Kinsley was right. It wasn't a home, it was simply a house filled with bad memories and broken hearts, and I didn't need it anymore.

Not now that I had found my home.

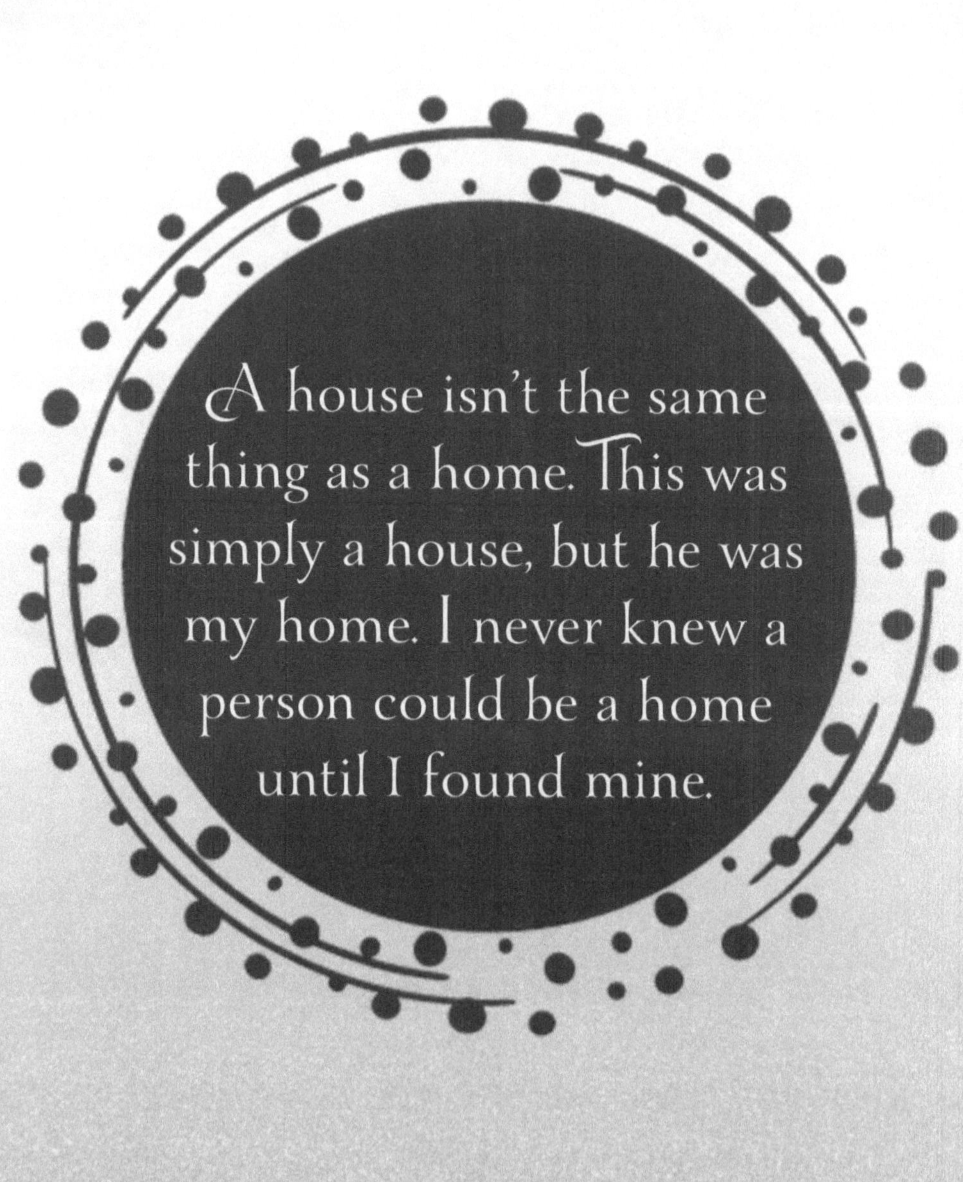

A house isn't the same thing as a home. This was simply a house, but he was my home. I never knew a person could be a home until I found mine.

Chapter 11
Kinsley

"I'm warning you ahead of time, living here with me might end up being a drag for you," I spoke softly.

All around us, the musical sound of the rain hitting the roof and tapping against my windows was heard. Both of us were exhausted when we got home and barely took time to tear off our shoes and climb into bed, before passing out. As always, my parents were gone. We slept through breakfast and lunch, it seemed, and were awoken around three in the afternoon as Kennedy came stomping into the house slamming doors, and screaming at someone on her phone, before taking off again. Luke and I had turned to look at each other, both of us lying on our stomachs, and laughed.

The rain hit hard against the window and I had it cracked just enough to smell the calming scent that lingered in the air. Distantly, I could hear how it was plopping into the pool and I closed my eyes, imagining it. My fingers itched to draw it, the gentle curve just before the drop hit the water, the way the water would spread out, the light blues, the whites, the grays all mixing into a ripple. "Why?" Luke breathed.

We hadn't even bothered to move, even after Kennedy had left. Despite how much both of our stomachs were screaming at us, we lay there, me still on my stomach and Luke rolled onto his back. He was staring at the ceiling, and as I opened my eyes, all I could see was him.

I wondered if this was how it was always going to be. Me lying here, staring at him, watching him see everything else but me. "My parents will exploit you, most likely. You're the son they've always wanted. They'll dress you up and force you to go to parties with us. They might even try to leave me home and make you replace me."

I felt a slight sting of jealousy over the words, but I shoved it away, knowing it was useless. Jealousy over him being what my parents expected, instead of what they got, was useless. "Maybe I'll get to eat decent food," he replied, a smile in his voice.

I grinned as I pinched his side. Luke yelped and rolled onto his side with a grin that mirrored my own. I wondered if he knew how beautiful he was when his green eyes lit up like that, his lips fluttering into such a warm and carefree smile. My favorite kind of Luke.

He had my hand with him, holding it on his stomach where he had grabbed it, making no motion to move or let go. I stared at it, where our hands were. He was lying with his left arm under him, his right arm on top of him, both hands holding mine without reserve. I wondered if he realized he wasn't pulling away and apologizing anymore when he touched me. "The song, Sara by We Three. The scar," I reminded him.

He sucked in a deep breath and closed his eyes. I watched the wind brush against his face and couldn't help but chew on the inside of my cheek in a silent pout. I wanted nothing more than to reach out and brush my fingertips against the soft lashes, to slide my fingers against his curls, and to press my lips against his skin. I never thought I'd be jealous of the wind, but here I was wishing more than anything to be the air just so I'd have a moment to touch him, to kiss him the way I wanted to.

"Kinsley," he breathed, his voice slightly raspy as he opened his eyes. I had to physically stop myself from shivering, goosebumps rising against my shoulders at the sound of his rasp, at the way he breathed my name.

"You won't understand. You won't like me anymore." I never knew a word could feel so underrated until I heard him say the word like. Such a useless word, so silly, so wrong. It wasn't strong enough to explain what it was I felt, it wasn't even close.

I lov- "I promised, Luke. I'm not going anywhere." I stared at him, forcing him to see me, to see what was in my mind, in my heart. To see the words I was too scared to mutter even to myself, let alone to him.

He looked like he was physically in pain as he clenched his eyes tightly, taking deep breaths, before nodding. He looked at me once more, his eyes filled with determination. I could hear the song in my head, having listened to it a million times by now, trying to understand. To understand those who would try to kill themselves.

No matter how lonely I was, no matter how much I wanted a new life, new parents, or someone to simply just love me, I never considered killing myself. I feared the fact that he had tried, and I wanted to know why. I wanted to make sure he'd never do it again. "I did it to see if someone would care about me enough to save me," he spoke after a few seconds of silence.

The eerie way he had said it, the fact that it was supposed to be something horrifying, but he held no emotion in his voice scared me. Made me say the first thing that popped into my head, without thinking first. "Well, looks like someone did, because you're here now," I said with a soft laugh.

Luke rolled onto his back, and I frowned, smacking myself in my mind repeatedly over how stupid and awkward I was being. I opened my mouth, ready to tell him I was sorry, but he scoffed. He didn't have the sling on his right arm, but he had it resting on his stomach as he held my hand with his left, never once letting go of me.

"Yeah," he muttered, his tone filled with sarcasm. He took a breath before he rolled back onto his side, staring at me once more. Despite the sarcasm in his voice a second ago, his eyes were filled with vulnerability that took my breath away. So much pain there, so much sadness.

"I was found the night my mother found out my father was cheating on her. Well, the first time, anyway. I was in eighth grade. Mom had already been pretty messed up for a few years beforehand, and I do not doubt that while that was the first time Mom caught him cheating, it probably wasn't the first time he did it."

Luke was quiet for a moment, his eyes lowered now as if he was too embarrassed to look at me. He fumbled with my finger and my thumb, and I kept my hand relaxed despite the slight tickle I was feeling as he played with my hand. "Shawn was eight or nine, in second grade. He just started hanging out with the Brett kid, and he was starting to stay at his house back then. Mom has always been a nurse, but back then she worked a lot more.

"Nearly every night she worked long twelve-hour shifts most of the time, coming home and crashing in exhaustion. Dad wasn't home much, and that was around the time I started to learn how to cook. My dad was starting to get annoyed with her. The hits were getting worse. He was frustrated she had such a good job, and while I didn't understand it then, I think he was jealous she made more money than he did."

He scoffed at that, and I didn't blame him. If I did end up marrying a woman one day, I wouldn't care if she made more money than me. I'd be there cheering her on, bragging about her, telling the world how amazing she was. Or if I was married to a man, I'd do the same for him too. How could someone be jealous of their partner? It was ridiculous to even think about.

"Dad must have thought I wasn't home that night. He knew I was benched for a few games since he had fractured my right elbow and I couldn't play in the games until it healed. It was a Friday night, a game night, but I didn't feel like going if I couldn't play. Dad snuck his girlfriend in. I heard him stumble in, and I assumed it was just him. I was already tired of everything back then, exhausted.

"I went downstairs and watched him shut the bedroom door behind him. I didn't see her, just him, and thought he was wasted like always. I made some food, but it was tasteless. I remember I kept staring at the door, the closed door, and remembered the past. How we used to have family meals together when I was younger. How he would always stop and rub my head, kiss my forehead, and tell me he loved me.

"He'd call me sport, or bud, he'd give me a fake punch and tell me I was the man of the house and to watch over Mom and Shawn while he was at work. He was... my hero, Kins. And I was forced to watch my hero fade into a drunken abusive loser. I don't know how to explain it, but I felt useless. I was eleven, and I was useless."

Luke closed his eyes, his fingers curled around mine, and all I could do was stare at him. I felt my heart shaking with every word he spoke, every choking sob he held back, every ounce of pain in his voice.

"I told myself, maybe if I died, I could start over again with a life where I was wanted. Maybe in my next life, someone will care about me. Maybe in my next life, my hero won't look like a monster. I took the knife from the counter, went upstairs into the bathroom, and closed the door. I didn't lock it, so that's probably what saved me in the end I guess."

He took a deep breath, his eyes squeezed shut, and I moved slightly closer to him. He had my hand held tightly with his, and I lifted my other hand, sliding it softly down his cheek, sweeping the tears from his skin. He was quiet for a moment, most likely remembering every cut, every pain, every feeling he had, making me feel like a complete asshole for even bringing it up. But I didn't know how else to protect him unless I knew the truth.

The rain plopped softly against the sill, and even though it was the afternoon, it was dark, the angry storm clouds covering the sky. Neither of us had ever thought to move and turn on a light. But there was enough light to see him, to see his pain, to see his sorrow.

Luke opened his eyes, and all I could hear were the numbers. The numbers of the song, the three different times, playing repeatedly in my mind. I wondered if it was the same for him, as it was in the song. If he had sat there staring at the clock, wondering if someone would come, if someone would notice, if someone would remember he existed. I knew what it felt like to wish someone remembered I existed.

He let out a choked laugh, his eyes lifted to mine once more. "Our house had two bathrooms, and my dad had been throwing up in the downstairs one, so the random girlfriend came upstairs and saw me. He must have told her the house was empty. When she came in, I had been lying in the bathtub with the water running, fully clothed, not caring. I had done one wrist and was about to do the other when she came in and stopped me. It's funny, this stranger cared more for me than anyone else.

"Luke, I'm sorry, you don't have to-" I whispered, horrified.

I was breathing hard as Luke moved closer to me, one of his hands lifted to press gently against my lips, silencing me. He left his thumb there for longer than he needed to, spreading a low fire in the pit of my stomach as he slowly slid his thumb down my bottom lip, before pulling away.

"The woman started to scream. She turned off the water and unplugged the drain. I was too heavy for her, and she screamed for my father, but he had passed out by then. She called the ambulance," he said, taking a moment to start laughing. I was horrified by this laugh because it was not filled with the usual happiness that I've come to love so much, but a sarcastic laugh, filled with pain and hopelessness.

"I was going in and out by then. This woman knew nothing. If it was my mom, she would have lifted my hand above my heart to slow the blood flow, and she would have pressed towels against it, but the woman just turned the bathtub back on and shoved my arm under it, trying to wash off the blood without realizing she was making the blood flow out faster.

"I mean, I get it, not everyone is a doctor or a nurse, and she tried her best. But she was still sleeping with a married man, so I can't give her too much credit, I guess," he said with a shrug. He sounded so distant, so uncaring, so masked, that it hurt. I didn't want to hear anymore, but I couldn't bring myself to stop him either.

His voice was raw with pain as he continued, his fingers holding onto mine like a lifeline. "I remember floating, the paramedics carrying me into the ambulance. The woman came with us, she told them all she was my mother. I guess maybe she was trying to get some brownie points in with my dad, hoping when he woke up from his drunken slumber that she'd get rewarded for saving his son.

"I was lucid when we got to the hospital, but I was still going in and out. I had surgery. They stitched the wound, gave me more blood, and saved me. I felt numb, I just didn't care. I was frustrated I was found; I was annoyed I was still alive, still living with these people who didn't give a shit. I woke up to this random woman holding my hand, telling me everything was going to be okay because Mommy was there. She wasn't even my fucking mom, but she was trying so hard to impress my asshole father, and he wasn't even there to see all her efforts."

I shook my head, frustrated for him. "Your parents? What did they do?"

Luke let out a shaky laugh, squeezing my hand tighter before gently petting the inside of my palm with his fingertips. "The ambulance took me to the hospital where my mom worked. I guess at some point my mom must have seen my name on some record somewhere, or maybe she heard my name in passing. The doctor was in the room, talking to this woman about giving me pain meds, giving me papers on therapists, things that should have been given to my mother, and I just stood there holding my bandaged wrist.

"I guess it was kind of my fault too, in a way. I could have spoken up and said I didn't know who this crazy woman was, but I didn't fucking care anymore. The woman held the papers, led me out into the hall, and told me I was going home to see Daddy. She was talking to me like I was five, telling me she'd make me ice cream for my boo-boo, like a freaking weirdo. Then I heard my mom screaming. She had checked my room and was told I was discharged by my mother, but since she was my mother, she came to find out what was going on."

"Oh my God, that must have been horrible," I said, my eyes wide as he shrugged, trying to hide how bothered he was by it.

"They screamed at each other. The woman told my mom she was crazy for disturbing her and her son. My mom told her she was nothing and that she was my mother. They fought, screamed, and I just... I stood there."

He sighed softly, shaking his head at the memory. "The papers with all my info were scattered on the ground and my mother punched the woman in the face. I turned around and walked home, leaving them both there. That night when my mom finally came home, having been fired, she walked right past me and started to scream at my dad. I stood there holding her coat, putting her shoes away, and watched as they yelled back and forth.

"Watched as they hugged, watched as they kissed, and made up. I could have been screaming and they wouldn't have noticed me. I was standing there with a bandage on my wrist and no one cared. They went into their room, and I went into mine. The papers had been left at the hospital, and my mom never remembered to get me another prescription.

"No one tried to sit down with me to see why I tried to kill myself. They didn't bring up a therapist, they didn't ask me if I was okay or how I was feeling. They just... didn't care. It was brushed over, ignored, and forgotten. Just like me, forgotten," he whispered.

I stared at him, his eyes lowered in a soft blush, embarrassed over everything he said. Worried I'd leave still, I'd kick him out, worried I wouldn't care. "No one cared, Kinsley," he said softly, his voice breaking as he lifted his eyes to mine once more. "No one has ever cared."

Attention, I told myself softly. That's what it was. He tried to kill himself for attention. He wanted to be heard, to be seen, and no one noticed.

I wanted to cry with him, but I was worried I'd scare him. To think that a small Luke had tried so hard to be seen and everyone had just ignored him horrified me. He had been so young, and he could have just tried again, and again, and they might not have noticed a second time or a third.

They wouldn't have noticed the first time if it wasn't for some creepy woman saving him. *He wouldn't be here. I could have lost him. I could have never met him.* Those thoughts scared me more than anything else.

The way he was staring at me with his eyes wide, swimming in the wet shine of his tears shattered me. He was scared. Scared I'd throw him away too. Scared I didn't care, that I'd give up on him. I was just scared I'd never be able to move on from him. How could I ever let him go? How could I just give him to someone else?

Remembering what he had said about which hand it was, I took his left hand and pulled it upwards, closer to me, higher, near the pillow. He sucked in a deep breath as I slowly slid his sleeve down, but he didn't stop me. Luke was trembling as I stared at his scar, the deep jagged scar that went from his wrist to the middle of his forearm. I lifted my eyes to him to see him watching me. Gently I scooted my body down, my knees cupping underneath his. I lowered my head against his scar and brushed my cheek against it.

I could feel the ridged bump against my cheek, and I couldn't stop staring at him, overwhelmed by the emotions inside me. I couldn't stop thinking about how this had almost killed him. How I had almost never met him. If he had died, I wouldn't have put my letter in his locker, and we never would have been Sparrow and Green, two souls existing in one heartbeat. "I care. I'm always going to care. *It hurts*," I whispered, trying to keep my voice steady.

I wasn't sure what to say, but I hoped I had said it right, all the same. "Why are you saying it hurts? It's on my body, not yours."

I nodded, feeling his skin sliding back and forth against my cheek. "It marks your body, but it hurts my heart," Luke was quiet, and I frowned, unsure if I had overstepped. "I'm sorry," I mumbled.

I moved slightly, ready to pull away from him, but before I could, he pressed his right hand against the back of my head. He grunted with the movement since it was the shoulder he had dislocated and he had taken his sling off to sleep, but it didn't stop him from touching me. Luke tangled his fingers in my hair, moving them softly back and forth as I relaxed against him.

"Thank you, Kinsley. Thank you for being my best friend," I lifted my eyes to him, noticing how close we were to each other. I could feel his heart beating through his wrist and felt my face flush from the close attention.

Suddenly, a knock on my bedroom door was heard, and as the doorknob started to turn, Luke and I broke apart. Luke fell off the side of the bed as I jumped up and turned on my lamp. Luke clambered into the desk chair and turned on that lamp as well. My father opened the door and was welcomed to the scene of me sitting on the corner of my bed scrolling through my phone, and Luke pretending he was drawing on one of my sketchpads I had left sitting there. "Kinsley? Who... I remember you. What's your name again?"

Luke and I both stood as my dad scratched the back of his head. The look Luke gave me made me remember I had lied to his dad about telling my parents Luke was staying with us. I grinned sheepishly at him as Luke looked at my dad once more. "This is Luke, remember? One of my best friends. His parents moved, so he was going to be staying with us until graduation so he could finish the year here." I lied smoothly.

I was pretty good at lying to my parents, a task I've done countless times. "The football captain," Dad said slowly, remembering. Luke nodded slowly, taking an apprehensive step forward as my father grinned at him. He smacked his hand down on Luke's shoulder and I winced with him, remembering that shoulder had been dislocated a week ago by his father.

"Well, you'll have to sleep in here with Kinsley, but you're welcome to stay, son," he said with a bright grin. Luke let out a breath of relief as my father turned away, before turning back around and holding something out to me. "Almost forgot, Kinsley, but here. Don't forget to fill it up to the line."

I grabbed the damn cup out of his hand as he turned around and walked away, leaving me and Luke alone. I glared at Luke as he pressed his hand against his mouth, trying not to laugh. "You could just say no to drugs, Kins, don't be pressured," he choked out.

I stuck my finger in the air, flipping him off. "Fuck you, Luke," I muttered, trying and failing to hide the smile from lifting the corners of my lips. He laughed, shaking his head at me as I flipped him off once more, walked into the bathroom with the damn cup in my hand, and slammed the door behind me.

How could I ever let him go? How could I just give him to someone else?

Chapter 12
Kinsley

It was quiet, something I wasn't used to much in the art room. Normally, the stoners were in the corner over there, smelling up the room with thick smoke and giggling over the drawings they were attempting to draw to keep up appearances of doing something in the club.

At that point, I was sure they believed Isabella was their club teacher because they liked to come over to her and show her their drawings, standing there all shyly waiting for her to tell them it looked like shit. She was always so blunt and uncaring, and they loved it, like strange little masochists that got off on a hot scary lady telling them their work was trash. I wondered about kids these days.

The stoners never came that day, but I wasn't surprised because I had heard one of them talking about a freshman field trip after school that day. Luke wasn't there either, but he was out on the field, leaving only me and Isabella in our silent solitude to draw in peace. It was colder out, the fall wind sweeping over the town like a giant had decided to stand there and blow, pouring his chilly breath over everyone like a blanket.

Most of the kids had pulled out fall coats, something I refused to wear since I liked my hoodies far better. We still had to leave the windows cracked from the annoying goo smell, but the chill didn't bother me much. Isabella had a little sniffle, and occasionally, her sniffle would break through the quiet in the room, joining in with the scratching of granite against the paper.

I was lost in my thoughts as I drew. I wasn't even really paying attention to what I was drawing, my mind so wrapped up in Luke and what he had said a few weeks ago. It wasn't a four am confession, but it was a confession all the same. The things he'd said about his father, about how he tried to kill himself, were still fresh on my mind even now.

It didn't matter that he'd been living with me for a few weeks now, I could still hear the raw pain in his voice and the quiver in his heart. I hated every part of it.

"How is Luke fitting in with your family?" Isabella asked softly. Neither of us had both of our headphones in, not needing both since there wasn't a group of freshmen giggling in the corner distracting us.

I shrugged, chewing on my bottom lip. To be honest, I was trying hard not to be jealous. I didn't think it would bother me seeing the way my parents were with Luke, but it did a little bit. Dad took him outside as soon as the rain let up and they played basketball together for hours.

Sure, I could have joined, and I knew Luke wanted me to, but there was just something about seeing how my dad high-fived him that bothered me. I wasn't mad at Luke in any way whatsoever. No, it was more frustration that my parents only seemed to care when it was a kid that was doing what they wanted.

My mom went out and bought him a bunch of new clothes and new shoes, and she seemed to be perfectly capable of remembering his size. Dad got him a new phone and set it up, so it let him keep his old number. They were happy, they were excited, and I felt empty.

On one hand, I was glad Luke was getting the attention he deserved. I really was, and seeing him slowly open up was everything to me. He smiled with them, he laughed with them, and it made me wonder when the last time he was able to do that was with his parents. But a small part of me was frustrated, the small childlike part of me that wished I could be remembered too.

In a way, I didn't think my parents were bad. They did try when they wanted to. They just only had one thing in their mind, one small mindset. If I didn't do that one thing, if I didn't obsess over it as they did, then they were just blank. To them, there were two different kinds of people.

The ones who loved sports, got good grades, were the perfect kids, and then there were the others. The ones who didn't love sports, the ones who got mildly good grades, or even bad grades. Hell, I could have been a straight-A student and still been awkward to them because, at the end of the day, they had nothing in common with me.

They revolved around sports, it was how they were raised and how they tried to raise me and Kenedy. The fact that I didn't know them or care about them, made them shuffle away awkwardly. Their solution was I must have been on drugs, to not like sports. I must have been on drugs, to like black clothes instead of bright ones. I must have been on drugs, to like to draw instead of shooting hoops and listening to crowds cheer for me.

I wondered what they'd say when they found out I wasn't straight. Would they just hand me the damn cup and tell me to pee in it? I honestly wouldn't have been surprised.

"He fits in fine," I tried not to have a bitter tone in my voice because I truly wasn't upset with Luke. Despite how frustrated I was with my parents, I was glad he was there.

I wanted him to be there, even though the closer he was, the harder it was for me to breathe. Then again, when he was away, all I could do was hold my breath. I guess in the end having trouble breathing was better than not breathing at all. "My parents love him; they're having fun playing with him. The son they always wanted."

Nice and straight, quiet, not argumentative. Luke was exactly what they wanted, and once again, I wasn't. I wasn't what my parents wanted, and I wasn't what Luke wanted. "How is he fitting in with you?" her eyes lifted, studying me.

I shrugged, tapped my pencil against the paper, and grabbed my soda. Isabella and I knew that Luke was having a double practice that day since there was a game coming up, and we had driven to the closest fast-food restaurant to get something to eat while we waited for him. She had nothing better to do, and I was Luke's ride, so we were waiting for him.

I took a deep sip and she glared at me, a no-nonsense look on her face telling me that I wasn't going to get out of her questions. "I like having him there. I like being with him all the time, I don't have a problem with him at all." I gave her a soft smile, knowing she wasn't going to stop glaring at me.

Truthfully, the past few days had been kind of tense for us. Luke had been freaking out about almost all of it at first. He was worried when that Monday came that I'd be handing his father a shit ton of money, but instead, I drove Luke to my lawyer and had him fill out paperwork to get emancipated. His father wasn't happy about it, but seeing as Luke was seventeen, he had a job and a place to go, and the courts didn't see anything wrong with granting the request.

My parents had to go with Luke to talk to the Judge to promise to keep an eye on him, but otherwise, it seemed to be working out okay. It would take months before all of it was finalized, but for now, his father couldn't come to get him without Luke voluntarily going to him, and that was good enough for me.

He was worried about Shawn, who ignored his texts and calls at first. I was about to drive him to the address and grab Shawn and shove him into the car with us, damn the repercussions, but then Luke started to get texts from Shawn talking about how happy he was now.

How life was better, now that his dad was with his fiance Tina, and they were going to be married as soon as their parents divorced was finalized. It depressed Luke a little, making him think he was the problem all along, but the attention from my parents was counteracting that.

Though now, we'd gotten tense because of the recent conversation with my father. A party, he had said. I knew it was coming up, in about a month for Thanksgiving. It was one of the most important parties my parents threw because it raised a lot of money and made my dad look good.

Dad had told me he had a date picked out for us already and Luke was frustrated about it. I had warned him they'd probably do the same to him as they did to me, but he wasn't happy about it. I had no idea who the two girls were that they were choosing for us, but I wouldn't be surprised if one of them was Lana.

She nodded, seeming to believe me. "Because you're in love with him." I blushed, my face instantly turning red as I dropped my pencil and looked around the room. We had left the art room door open, and I stood up, went over to it, and closed it. I turned to look at her and she giggled, ignoring my glare as she looked down at my paper.

Isabella tapped it, making me look down at it. I wasn't even surprised it was a drawing of Luke, with the amount of time he'd been on my mind. "You going to deny it?" she poked the paper again with a tilt of her eyebrow, telling me there was no point in lying.

I frowned, walked over to the window, and stared down at the field. I could see Luke clearly from there, the bright number one shining on the back of his shirt as he pulled his arm back and threw the ball. I was still impressed by his recovery speed, but then again it wasn't his throwing arm that had been dislocated, thankfully.

"I'm trying hard to get past the feelings, Izzy. It's just hard to see him as a friend when my heart sees him as something more." *When my soul sees him as its other half.* I took a deep breath, forcing myself once more to take all those feelings and shove them down, deep down, hoping maybe this time they'd stay there. They never stayed there.

I turned to look at her, pressing my back against the window with a smirk. "What about you and your boyfriend?" I couldn't help the teasing grin that spread over my lips. She rolled her eyes at me, cursing at me in Spanish as she sat back in her chair angrily.

The biggest frustration yet was the tagger that had been going after her artwork. She was convinced it was a boy because she said the artwork screamed masculinity. The jagged signature, the large S was the only indication of who the art belonged to. Izzy liked to leave behind a bell as her signature. Since the word bell was part of Isabella. The S could stand for anything really, and it frustrated Izzy. She had a belief it was a middle-aged man who lived alone in his mommy's basement only coming out at nighttime to annoy the crap out of her.

The tagger only went after Izzy's work, although occasionally, here and there, a few others popped up. S liked to make drawings that worked against Izzy's. If Izzy drew a girl, the tagger drew lips kissing her. If Izzy drew a hand, the tagger drew another hand holding hers. I thought the two styles were pretty together, but it was pissing Izzy off to no end, something I had to listen to constantly the past week or two.

"Don't call that nasty old man my boyfriend," she grumbled, rocking her chair back for a moment before letting it sit back down on four legs.

I grinned, looking over my shoulder once more as a whistle was heard. The coach was pulling everyone in to make them run suicides, a frown on his face as he threw a football at one of the smaller-looking ones in a helmet and gear. Luke had explained to me once before that if one person messed up, everyone had to run suicides.

I wasn't sure how Luke was still going; he made me join him every morning now for a morning run before school, and then he'd go to practice and run, then practice after school he'd be running, and he never seemed exhausted. He'd go to work, come home, and just stand there smiling like he hadn't run a shit ton of miles all day long.

"You don't know if he's an old man or not, or even a man at all, just saying," I pointed out to her.

She stood up, her chair scooting back painfully sounding against the tile floor as she came to stand next to me. For a few minutes, we stood there together, mildly shivering in the cool chill of the fall air, watching Luke. "The artwork is masculine," she argued lamely.

"Luke said mine was feminine, but I'm a guy. He never suspected I was a boy until he saw me," I reminded her.

She rolled her eyes, reached her hand into my hood, and patted my cheek. "Maybe it's because you're so pretty, all you can do is make pretty things," she teased. "That reminds me, are you going to fix that? Well, I don't think you can fix it. You'd have to redo it," she tilted her head to my destroyed charcoal picture.

My self-portrait, the one Luke had said he loved. He admitted to me he had it saved in his phone and showed it to me, thankful that every picture he had was saved in his iCloud and able to be recovered with the new phone.

The idea of remaking it wasn't appealing to me. The charcoal painting was started before the letters, before Green. Every day was a different emotion, filled with shyness, hesitation, and happiness. The strokes of the charcoal were rough from my parents annoying me, shaky in my fear, curved in my excitement, and rounded in my happiness. I wasn't sure if I could redo that picture to look the same, to have the same result, the same feelings and emotions.

Every angry jagged line, every happy curl, every shy stroke was built from the letters, and I'd never feel that again. Not now that I knew who it was I had been talking to. The mystery, the fear, and the excitement were gone, replaced with the now. "I don't know if I can,"

The whistle blew and the coach started to clap his hands, pointing at the benches filled with water bottles and a little freshman that held towels and ran a table filled with water cups and a large barrel of water. Half of the team collapsed on the ground in the middle of the field breathing hard as the rest trudged towards the benches, grabbing their water bottles for a much-needed break until the coach made them continue.

I watched as some of the players grabbed friends' bottles and brought them over to them, small groups of idle chatter all around the field as they sprayed each other with water and laughed. Luke was looking up at us now, his helmet covering his face making his expression unreadable. I watched as he pulled his helmet off and placed it on the bench, grabbing his water bottle and fumbling with his bag.

Not even a minute or two later both Isabella's phone and mine went off, a group text from the three of us. *'I know y'all are staring at me, creepers. I can feel it,'*

Isabella chuckled as I grinned, and a moment later Isabella's text went through. *'You wish, Curly, but Pretty Boy only has eyes for me,'* she taunted.

I saw him frowning down at his phone, but before he could reply, the coach blew the whistle and they put their stuff down and grabbed their helmets, running back onto the field again. I put my phone in my pocket without adding to the mix, knowing that Isabella was staring at me. "It can't be easy living with him, feeling the way you do, Kinsley," she spoke softly as we watched the players.

I turned around, my back to the window as I shrugged, and slowly slid down into a crouched position on the floor. Isabella wasn't the girly girl type to care about sitting on the dirty floor, and she sat down next to me, her neon tights stretching over her legs as she pulled down her black skirt that covered her bottom half. She had on her signature two studded belts, crisscrossed over her hips as usual, and her dad's army jacket covered her upper half.

Her hair was pulled back into pigtails, a mixture of wavy neon green hair and brown hair pulled together on top of her head. "It's fine, Izzy," I said, trying to smile at her as she studied me. "I like having him near me, knowing he's safe and okay."

Even now, Izzy didn't know everything, but Luke did let her know a little bit. He told her his father was abusive, and his mother had mental problems and was in the psych ward. He didn't tell her about the scar, but I didn't think he would. I had a feeling he'd probably never tell anyone else again unless it was someone who was going to marry him one day.

I guess in a way I felt important to him that he felt like it was okay to tell me, knowing we'd never be anything. He trusted me, more than anyone else, and that meant everything to me. *It's enough,* I told myself firmly. *Knowing he trusts me, it's enough. It has to be enough.*

Isabella let out a soft sigh of frustration and we could hear the coach's loud booming voice as he screamed at someone once more, before the whistle was blown. It looked like they were running suicides again. "But isn't it hard to be near him in the same room every day when you're in love with him? Isn't it hard to be so close but not do anything?"

I knew what she meant because I knew Izzy had liked someone before. Maybe it wasn't true love, but it was important to her. The boy that Izzy loved she met when she was fourteen, and I met him a few times before he left. They were together for a year. She let him in and trusted him. He threw her away like a piece of trash.

She never really talked much to me about it, about her feelings, or the past, but he was probably the reason why she turned down everyone who asked her out, because she had been too young to feel as deeply as she did, and it hurt her. I just had to hope it didn't hurt her beyond repair. I hoped one day she'd find the one who was everything to her, and she'd be happy, and loved, as she deserved.

I had my knees up, and my elbows rested on my knees. My hands were snaked in my hood, wrapped around my neck, linked together as I stared at her. "I just cherish every moment with him. Even if we don't do anything but sit there and talk. The little things," I sucked in a deep breath, letting it out slowly with a soft shrug. "Those are what matters. Just to look at him, to smell his cologne when I sit beside him or lay beside him in bed."

I felt stupid for even saying all of this, admitting it out loud, but it was Izzy, and I knew I could trust her with everything. "When he hugs me, I lose all thoughts. All my worries, all of my fears, all of my insecurities. When he hugs me, I feel like I'm floating. When he smiles at me, I feel like I'm home. Trapped in a house that feels like a prison, surrounded by people who can't stand me, but when he smiles at me, I feel like nothing will ever hurt me." She was quiet as she watched me, her eyes wide, searching.

"I don't need to kiss him," I choked out, taking a deep breath as I closed my eyes. I opened them, letting the breath out slowly, before continuing. "I don't need to kiss him, to touch him, to have sex with him. Just being near him is good enough for me."

We were quiet as the coach blew the whistle again. The cold wind spilled into the windows, blew our hair into our faces, and tickled our noses. The silence was so loud, so judgmental I could barely breathe, my breath slightly raspy as I tried to suck it in and blow it out steadily.

It was a chore to breathe right then, and I didn't understand why. The silence was shattered by the sound of Izzy sniffing, the cold getting to her as she shivered. She ignored it, however, as she sighed, looking at me with wide doe-like eyes filled with sympathy. "If that's true, then why are you crying?"

I touched my cheek, surprised by her words, and felt the wetness coating my skin. "It's enough," I choked out, frustrated at the way my body made me a liar. "It's enough for me."

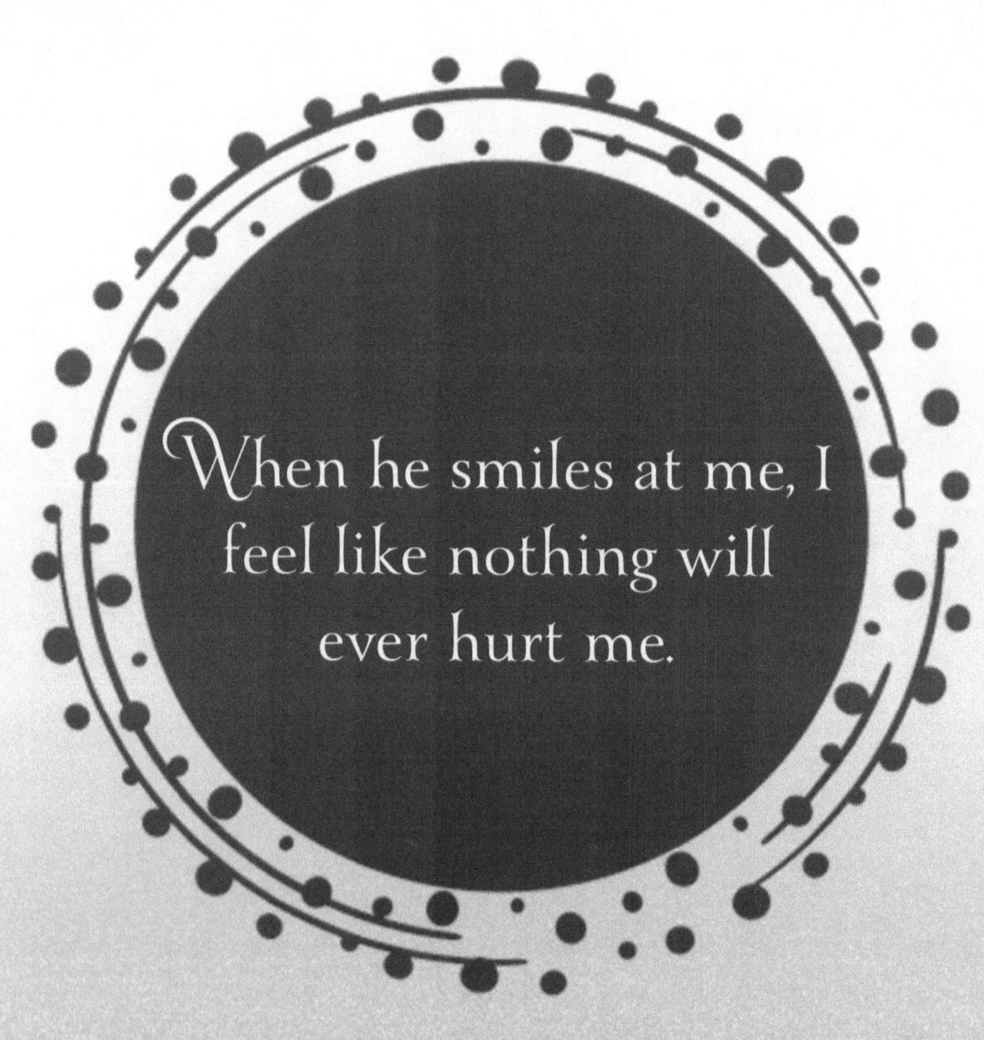

When he smiles at me, I
feel like nothing will
ever hurt me.

Chapter 13
Luke

The past few weeks, I had gotten used to the fact that Kinsley's parents were barely around. When they were around, they were all over me, buying me things I didn't want and doting on me. I was getting used to having bags filled with new clothes and shoes piled in front of Kinsley's door, or boxes of brand-new football equipment ready for me to open. I tried to give it back at first, but Kinsley told me it was pointless.

He pointed to the pile of things in his closet, or the dresser that was now mine, to prove his point, telling me they never accepted the returns, and he would always just push it aside. At this point, I think I had more clothes than Kinsley did. I was slightly uncomfortable, getting all of this attention that should have gone to Kinsley. I could tell it was bugging him, the way he backed away, giving me and his parents space when he walked upstairs and went to his room.

I was just waiting for him to kick me out, to tell me it was too much for him, but while he looked sad watching his parents, he never looked sad when he looked at me. Most of the time, Kinsley's eyes held nothing but slow happiness simmering when he looked at me, only changing when his expression turned into something unreadable before he turned around and walked away.

Before I moved in with him, I thought I knew Kinsley better than I knew myself, and you would think living with him would make us closer, but it didn't. He was more reserved, the pillow that I had placed between us before was back, separating us in the middle of the bed.

His parents didn't see anything wrong with two straight high school boys sleeping in the same bed, since that's what his parents thought we were. It was what I thought I was... Before.

Whenever it was mentioned, Kinsley's father would go on about how he had been forced to sleep in the same bed as another guy all through college, refusing to be in the broken-down dorm room and didn't have the money to afford a two-bedroom or even a one-bedroom house by himself at the time. He'd laugh about it, talking about how he needed to call up his old roommate and see how he was, the good old days before he took over his father's business and made millions off of expanding it.

I found it hard to read Kinsley lately, and it was starting to terrify me. I wasn't sure if it was him pulling away, or if it was me. I wondered, sometimes, if he remembered the kiss. If that was the real reason he placed the pillow between us. I wondered if he felt it, those nights I'd wake up from a nightmare and he was still sleeping. If he felt me leaning there on my elbow, watching him sleep, my fingers dancing through his hair, pushing his bangs from his face, sliding my thumb against his lips, wondering.

I had always thought I was straight. The idea of even looking at another guy was never something I'd wanted, and even now as I thought about it, I couldn't help but feel repulsed by the idea of liking another guy.

I had taken chances here and there, glanced at guys in the school of all types ever since the first time I tried to check out Bobby. Skinny guys, smaller guys, larger ones. There were all kinds of naked guys around me in the locker room walking around without care or shame of their naked bodies, but none of them did anything to me.

Then there was Kinsley, who had slipped his hand into my pocket the day I kissed him, brushed his finger against the inside of my leg, and set every part of me on fire.

'Faggot,' my father's voice spat through my mind, making me curl away from all of the thoughts, all of the feelings, shoving everything deep deep down inside me. I was scared of that word, scared of what it meant, scared of anything to do with it. Scared of the way Kinsley slept with his mouth slightly open, his full lips looking so inviting. I wasn't sure if it was me pushing Kinsley away because of my conflicting feelings, or if he was pushing me away.

Sometimes I wanted to ask him if he remembered the kiss, but fear kept me silent. How could I ask him if he remembered something that seemed to gross him out? I could still remember the look on his face as I pulled away from him that night. The more I thought about it, the more I wondered if that was what it was. The distance, the unreadable expressions, the pillow placed in between us.

Despite the pillow, however, we were the same, mostly. We still went out every few nights after I was finished with work, and we still tagged buildings. I won't say I was getting better at it, but I was getting better at grabbing everything we were using and running with it. Isabella promised to stop wearing flip-flops if I promised not to carry her again.

After school, we'd drop Isabella off at home, then I'd drop Kinsley off at home, and then I'd drive to work. I had gotten my permit, part of a necessity to get emancipated, and while I was supposed to be driving with an adult for a year, no one ever really seemed to give a shit that I wasn't.

My boss wasn't mad at me, despite everything my dad had done. He was annoyed he had to drop the charges, but because the police didn't believe that it was my father, he was worried if he didn't drop the charges then I'd be the one convicted for the damage.

I was surprised he still let me work there, but when I went back that first day to apologize to him about my father, he simply threw over some overalls and gloves, handed me a box of parts Kinsley had ordered for me, and told me to get working. I was about halfway finished fixing my car, doing it in my free time, and I was excited about it. Kinsley's parents wanted to buy me a car, calling me their charity case whenever we went somewhere, but I refused, telling them I already had one. They were never around to see if that was true or not.

As I drove through the gate and down the long pathway to Kinsley's house, I felt content, knowing that everything was going okay. It was weird, everything that was happening lately, but I was safe and that was all that I needed to focus on for now. One step at a time.

My phone buzzed when I parked Kinsley's car in the garage, and I paused, looking down at it to see a text from Shawn. It was a picture, of Shawn and my dad sitting down and eating dinner together at the kitchen table. They were bent over a textbook and they had the evidence of laughter on their faces as they pointed at something. *'Tina took this and told me I should send it to you since I haven't talked to you this week. We're doing good, how are you doing?'* Shawn asked.

He was so formal now, so clipped-toned, so distant. I missed my little brother who would sneak into my room during the middle of the storms and hide under my blanket with me. I would pull out packs of Oreos and try to distract him. Then again, that was when he was in elementary school, and now that I thought about it, he hadn't done that in a while, even before the separation. Maybe this was just what it looked like, seeing your little brother grow up. *I'm doing good too, bro. Just got home from work, I'm glad you're happy,'* I replied.

No questions about how work went, where home was, or how the people I was staying with were. Just a reply of a thumbs up, and nothing more. No time for me anymore, it seemed. I sighed and scratched the back of my head with a frown.

I noticed Kinsley's dad's car was in the garage, which was kind of unusual for a Friday night. Then again I didn't have a game tonight, so maybe Kennedy didn't either. Basketball and football were two different sports, on two different wavelengths, but most of the time their games were scheduled around the same days. Usually, it was the reason why the coaches didn't let us do both of those particular sports since they would clash.

I didn't think about it as I grabbed the doorknob and placed the key into it. I had gotten used to the silence that came from Kinsley's house, the beautiful prison as Kinsley called it. I had gotten used to it either being empty or the sound of Kinsley's parents joking around with Kennedy in the living room when they were home, and Kinsley upstairs drawing, always away from the others. But I didn't think I'd ever have to walk back into a storm.

I should have realized that even beautiful prisons were filled with their horrors if you dug deep enough.

"Get back here! I'm sick of your fucking attitude! There's nothing wrong with you joining basketball!" Kinsley's dad shouted.

I stood there wide-eyed, the doorknob in my hand, and all I could do was tremble. I hadn't been emotionally ready to see this, to hear this once more. Kinsley walked past fast, his hood up, his hands clenched, and his body shaking. He was walking to the stairs, and his father was looming behind him, hovering.

It was as if everything was pushed back into my mind even though it was weeks since the last time. All I saw was me standing there, my father hovering, the growl in his voice, the rasp. Even though he wasn't here, that slur was there, his voice spilled into my mind, louder than ever before.

Kinsley's father grabbed his arm, yanking him backward, tearing the hood off of his face as he glared down at him. I felt small, so very small as I watched them. It wasn't the same as when Roan was hurting him. Roan was a teenager, he was young like us, but

Kinsley's dad was the same size as mine, the same age, and the same fear. I tried to tell my body to move, to help, but I was frozen in the storm.

"I'm not going to do it! I don't care if this is my last year of high school, I won't join any sports again, I already told you this! I can't play when Roan is there! I don't want to!" He shouted.

I blinked, seeing the differences, the reality. I would have crumbled, I would have fallen to my knees, I would have raised my hands above my head and waited for the blows. Kinsley was strong, his body poised, his head up high, determined. He was arguing back, loud and angry; his father wasn't hitting him.

I took a step into the room, closed the door quietly behind me, and pressed my back against it as I slowly slipped off my shoes. Everything I did was slow, the feeling of escape deeply embedded inside me.

Families fight, I tried to tell myself. *Not everyone has a parent that'll abuse them.* Despite this, I was scared nonetheless. Scared for Kinsley, scared for me, scared of the memories it was invoking.

"Why are your eyes red? Are you on drugs?" Kinsley's father grabbed his chin and tilted his head back to look at him closer. It was probably the only thing that hurt him, the way his father craned his head back, but at the same time, it wasn't on purpose. His father was just so much stronger than him.

It was weird to see such a big, strong adult who wasn't hurting his son. He could just punch him, shove him, and Kinsley would fall. He could hurt him and make him do as he wanted, but he didn't. I wanted to know why Kinsley's father didn't hurt him, but mine hurt me.

Kinsley slapped his father's hand away from his chin, and I flinched, pressing back into the door again, waiting for his father to hit him, but he didn't. "It's called crying, Dad, emotions. Being a human, having a heart! Not that I'd expect you to know what that feels like!" Kinsley took a step back as he tugged at his hoodie, adjusting it. "You don't even care that he tried to kill me!"

I knew then why he wore the hoodie constantly. All those years of Roan beating him up, and now that Roan wasn't touching him, he still wore it around the house to hide his tattoo. A songbird in a cage. I thought it was fitting, the way Kinsley called this home a beautiful prison, and then got that as his tattoo. It was like Kinsley was calling himself the songbird, trapped in the beautiful prison, sitting there all alone, singing to himself, waiting for someone to come with a key and free him.

"Go pee in the cup," Kinsley's father growled, obviously angry. He had his hands clenched, his eyes wide, anger pooling through him, and I was confused because he didn't swing at him. I was confused, but I was still scared all the same. The fear of the past bubbled inside me, triggering something I was worried I'd never get over. If I ever considered going to therapy, I already knew what they'd tell me. PTSD, anxiety, perhaps. I wouldn't be surprised if I had depression as well.

Kinsley threw his arms up in the air, his eyes wide, frustrated. "Oh my fucking God, Dad, I'm not on drugs!"

His father was unrelenting, as he pointed at the stairs, making me flinch as his hand raised over Kinsley's head. "Right now!"

Kinsley was breathing hard, his face red in embarrassment and anger as his eyes fluttered around the room. I could tell he was thinking of arguing back but when he saw me he faltered. He lifted his hand to his hood and yanked it over his head. Without a word, he turned around and walked up the stairs, his father throwing his hands in the air as he started to mutter something under his breath.

He turned towards the kitchen, not even noticing me as I slowly walked up the stairs after Kinsley. The crinkle of the grocery bag I had in my hand was all I could hear for a moment in the large house until I heard his father talking angrily on the phone in the kitchen. I looked down at the bag, wondering if I should even follow Kinsley to his room right then. I had changed out of the greasy clothes, the dirty ones in this bag since I didn't want to get his car dirty, but I still needed a shower and I was hungry.

I stood frozen, unsure if I should go into the kitchen and face his father, or if I should have followed Kinsley. I realized I wouldn't be able to be near his father right then, not with how scared and jumpy I was, and Kinsley was probably off crying somewhere. I walked up the rest of the stairs, noticing his bedroom door was closed. I was pretty sure that was the first time I had seen him close it when I wasn't in it, and it spoke to me.

I hovered in front of it, worried, but as I heard a crash coming from Kinsley's room, I turned the doorknob and opened it. I had been worried he had fallen or hurt himself, but as I stepped into the room, the first thing I saw was Kinsley standing there in the middle of the room. His hands were clenched into fists, and across from him was the remains of his lamp, broken and shattered pieces thrown against the wall and landed on the carpet around it.

He didn't even seem to notice me as I closed the door and took a few steps toward him, terrified. I knew I shouldn't have been surprised. His father might not have hurt him, but he was still acting like an asshole. Kinsley had tried talking to his parents about Roan for years, but they didn't care. They told him to man up and work out more. He tried telling them he was not interested in playing on teams, but they kept trying to push him anyway. They didn't understand him, and instead of trying to do things he liked to try and connect with him that way, they just kept trying to push their ideals on him.

Realistically, I shouldn't have been surprised to see Kinsley so angry, so frustrated. He was only human after all, and his dad was pushing his buttons. But it was Kinsley, my quiet and calm Kinsley. He grabbed the second lamp and ripped it out of the wall, making the dim light that had been lighting the room fade and cascade everything into darkness.

It took a second for my eyes to adjust to the darkened room, the moonlight slowly spilling into the opened windows. It was enough light for me to watch Kinsley slam the second lamp against the wall, fear spilling through me once more. I didn't want to see this Kinsley. I didn't want to ever see this Kinsley again.

He was shaking, a growl of frustration spilling from his lips, and I accidentally dropped the grocery bag on the ground. The noise was louder than it should have been, or at least that's what I was thinking as I took a step back from it. Kinsley turned sharply to look at me, and there was something about the anger in his eyes and the fact that he'd just been destroying things, that made me flinch away.

I fell to my knees, took a deep breath, and another, trying to calm my heartbeat. I felt so small, so tiny, so weak, and I hated every part of it. *This is Kinsley*, I tried telling myself. My mind was having problems separating my fear from my rationality. "Pl-please," I stammered, unable to help myself.

I felt as broken as the pieces of glass that were littered around his carpet floor as he dropped his hands and faced me. It was stupid, being scared like this. Kinsley wasn't as strong as me, but just the physical act was enough to bring it all back, every bit of it.

In an instant, Kinsley fell to his knees in front of me. He gripped my shoulders, reminding me I needed to breathe. I felt my vision swim and wondered briefly if this was what a panic attack felt like. I hated myself for making his anger and frustrations with his father about me, but he didn't seem to care.

His cerulean eyes were shining in the darkness of the room as he peered intensely into my eyes. "No," he shook his head back and forth. "I would never," a promise, the rage from before already gone.

I whimpered, trying to force myself to take a deep breath and another. He pressed his hands tightly against my cheeks, forcing me to look him in the eyes. I had forgotten the last time I was this close to Kinsley's face and for some reason, it made me just as breathless as before, only this time for a different reason. "I would never hurt you, Luke. Never."

I was shaking as he pulled me against him. My hands clutched his shirt tightly, wrapped around his waist as he moved closer to me, as close as he could. I held onto him as a lifeline, breathing in the scent of his neck as his face pressed against my hair. He had his fingers in my curls, brushing them off of my forehead as he pressed a soft kiss against my temple.

I breathed in his scent again and again, his body wash calming me, helping me get past the pain in my chest, letting me breathe again. "I will never hurt you," Kinsley's voice was deep, a whispered promise as he squeezed me tighter against him.

It was strange, all the times that I had heard those words, those promises, this was the first time I felt like I could believe it. Because it was Kinsley, my Kinsley, and I knew I could believe him. At least him, I knew I could trust.

I could forgive the world for all of the wrong things it gave me, because at least it did something right when it gave me him.

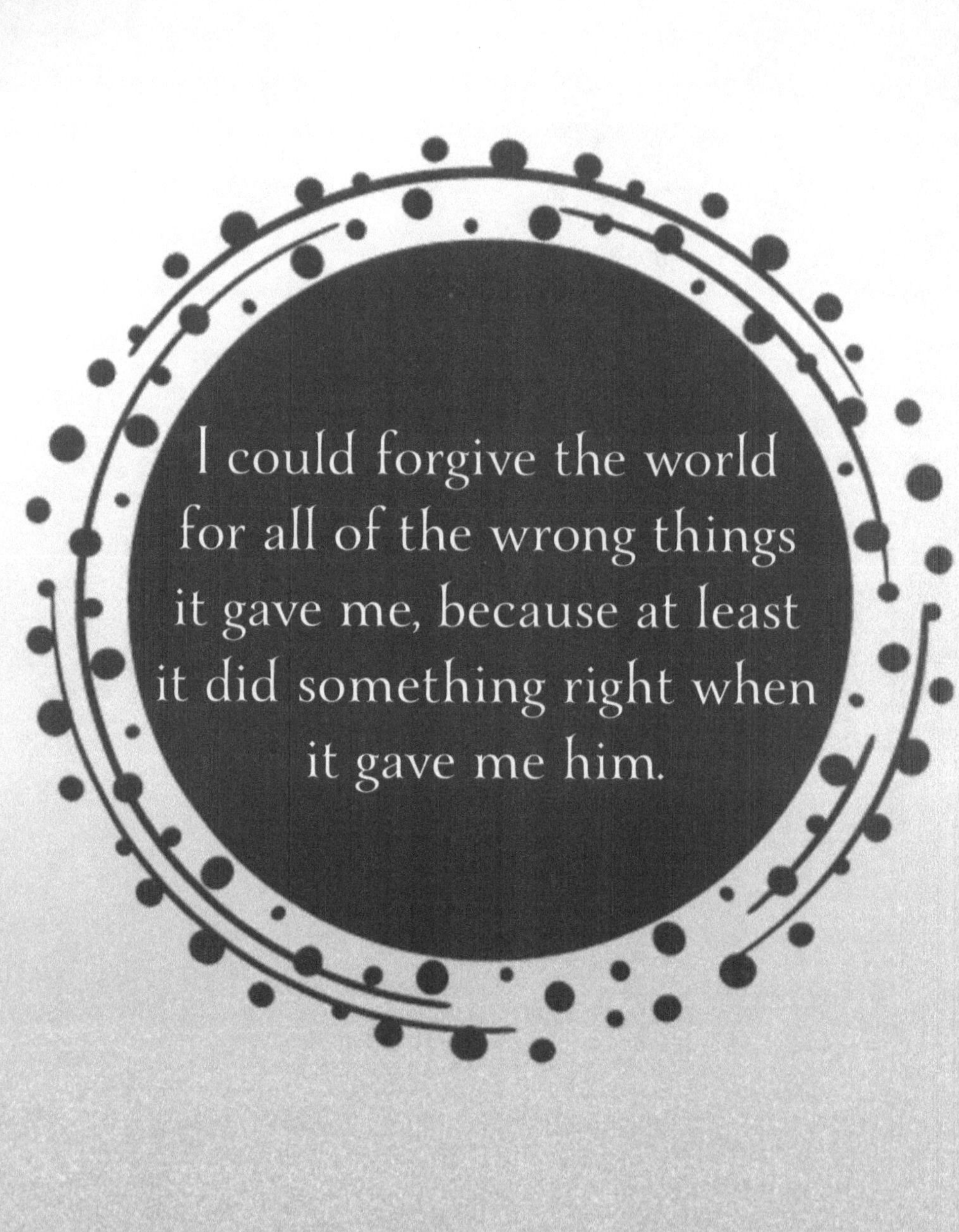

I could forgive the world
for all of the wrong things
it gave me, because at least
it did something right when
it gave me him.

Chapter 14
Kinsley

My favorite thing in the world was to lie next to him. The second best thing was when it rained, but it didn't rain much anymore. I could hear the howl of the wind outside, it was getting colder. Today was Thanksgiving, and the party was tonight. I lay on my back, looked off to the side, and stared at my window. I couldn't see if it was snowing or not, and I was too lazy to get up and look. I kind of doubted it, we were more likely to have a tornado than snow for Thanksgiving, but it didn't stop me from hoping. I kind of liked the snow.

The pillow that I had placed in between Luke and I must have been moved at some point during the night, and my hand had snaked underneath it, searching for him, for his warmth. I wasn't even surprised to feel his fingers laced with mine. It was like no matter how much I tried to tell myself I needed to stop feeling like this, my heart would pop out of nowhere and laugh at me.

I should have moved, pulled my hand away, and rolled over, but I didn't want to. It seemed my heart was stronger than my willpower. I felt Luke's thumb gently moving back and forth over my fingers and closed my eyes as I enjoyed the small tingles that moved up and down my hand at his touch. I could hear his heavy breathing and I lifted my free hand, placing it behind my head.

I knew without needing to look that it was four in the morning. After so many months, I had become attuned to it. My body had gotten used to waking up then, my ears poised to hear his voice, to hear his whispered secrets that came only when no one else was around. Our little world, his and mine, and I wanted it to last forever.

I thought about everything that had happened between us since he moved in with me. It had been harder being near him than I had anticipated. I needed the pillow to remind myself of what I would never have. Boundaries, because he was straight and he would never be mine. I didn't want him to wake up accidentally dry-humping me again and feel embarrassed. But at the same time, I wanted nothing more than to rip the pillow out of the way and scoop him into my arms, to run my fingers through his curls, and to breathe him in.

I thought about the way he had had a panic attack not too long ago. There were small dents on my wall now. My parents had never even noticed I had killed the lamps, never heard the noise, never noticed the glass in the trashcan. I felt stupid for acting out like that, even though I was human and even I had a breaking point.

Still, I felt like an asshole for throwing things, I felt like a child for having such a tantrum, ashamed. It made me wonder how his father could be a grown man who threw things, screamed and yelled, and not feel stupid about it afterward. I guess it was true in a way when people said everyone was wired differently.

I held Luke's hand tighter, just a little bit, feeling comfort in his touch. I had been trying so hard not to touch him because I was scared if I did then I wouldn't be able to stop. I could still feel his skin against my lips when I kissed his temple, and I wanted to do it again. I wanted to do so many things, just thinking about it was making me feel like I was burning. I let out a soft shuddered breath, closed my eyes once more, and counted to ten.

Trying to think of other things, anything really, then the feel of his skin against my lips. Sometimes I hated the fact that I was a teenager, not that I was making it easier for myself. I just kept touching him. I just kept surrounding myself with him, knowing it was too much for me, I couldn't stop myself. Even in my sleep I was touching him, drawn to the other half of my soul. It was hard to get over the one that gave me a reason to keep going.

"Kinsley?" Luke surprised me, his voice deeper, raspy from sleep. I blinked, turning my head to look at him, seeing him staring back at me. His light green eyes looked so dark, almost like the leaves before they started to change, reminding me of a forest. I could almost smell the pine and the grass as he stared at me like that, and I found myself turning my body towards his, wanting to be as close as I could. Neither of us pulled our hands away from each other, as we turned onto our sides, staring.

"Did I wake you?" I wondered although I wasn't sure how I could have. I wasn't being loud and wasn't moving around much.

He hummed, his free hand moving to my wrist, pressing against my vein. He did that a lot, I realized, though I wasn't sure why. "No, I think it's because of how used to this time my body is. It's our time, I guess."

I nodded, understanding. He was right; this was always going to be our time. He was silent for a while, both of us staring unabashed, not needing words to speak to study each other. During times like this, I wondered what he was thinking. "Why did you put the pillow between us?" his eyes lowered, resting on the pillow that was dislodged from me slipping my hand underneath it.

"My dad." It wasn't fully a lie. He asked if I wanted bunk beds, but I didn't want a new bed. I wanted to be next to Luke, where I could see him, where I could hear him. He wanted us to sleep top and tail then, and I refused, not interested in the idea of sleeping with my face near someone else's feet even if it was someone I was in love with. I told him about the pillow, and he agreed, saying the bed was big enough for that.

In a way it didn't matter, he'd never come in here to see it anyway, but I wanted it because I couldn't trust myself. I was failing miserably at it though, obviously, since I had been touching him in our sleep.

Luke blinked a few times, and I wondered what he thought the reason for the pillow was. He was looking at me again, his eyes wider, and for a moment I thought I saw a small coral color splash against his cheeks, before fading away. "Oh, okay," he mumbled.

Was I imagining it? It sounded like he was happy as he spoke those words. Maybe I was more tired than I thought I was. Nothing made sense at four in the morning.

I don't know why I asked, to be honest. Maybe it was because of the setting in the room, or the feel of his fingers laced with mine, or his other hand pressed against the vein on my wrist. I don't even know why the thought popped into my mind, to be honest, but before I could think about it, I spilled the question out of my mouth with a pause. "Do you believe in marriage?"

He frowned, his eyebrows knitted in confusion, and I was annoyed with myself. Four in the morning was a dangerous time for me; I needed to learn how to think before speaking. "Um," his head tilted slightly into the pillow, confused.

Despite his confusion, I could see he was thinking about the answer, really giving it attention, and I found myself wondering what he'd reply despite how strange and random the question was. "No," he said finally, a sharp pain poking me in the chest at his words. I didn't know why I felt pain from that, it wasn't like he'd ever marry me.

"It never works out right. I mean, look at my parents, for example. My mother and father were happy when they were first together. He was nice, she was happy, and we were happy. I don't know what started everything. I was so little, too young to understand. All I know was one minute everything was perfect, and the next, a storm."

I grabbed the pillow with my left hand, setting it behind me as I scooted closer to him. He wasn't stopping me, wasn't letting go of me, his eyes were silently watching me as I moved from my pillow to his, inches from him. "What about mine? They're creepily in love," I couldn't help but laugh softly even as I shrugged at the thought.

He knew by then how my parents had acted with each other. Despite how little they seemed to care for me, they were all over each other like two teenagers who'd been dating for only six months. It didn't matter that they'd been married for years, they would probably always be in their honeymoon phase.

Luke scoffed, rolling his eyes slightly. I could feel his breath against my chin and couldn't quite stop myself from pressing the side of my hand down on the bed near his chest. He didn't move, allowing me to rest my hand against the side of his bare chest. Ever since I saw the scar on his wrist, he hadn't been trying as hard to cover it from me. It didn't help that the house was almost like an oven, the heat set high for the chill outside, making both of us end up sleeping shirtless most nights.

I felt his heart beating slightly fast against my hand and sighed, feeling calmer with his heartbeat pounding against my hand. Maybe in a way, he was doing the same for me when he laid his fingers against the vein of my wrist. "Your parents are rich. Mine were almost considered poor, there's a difference, Kins,"

I blinked, confused. "How is that a difference? What does money have to do with any of it?"

His eyes softened as he scooted even closer to me, our foreheads almost touching as we stared each other in the eyes. Maybe this was a strange position for most, but we were friends, best friends, and it was perfect for us. Maybe some would argue that best friends didn't sit there listening to each other's heartbeats, that they didn't whisper to each other at four in the morning their secrets they couldn't speak during the day, but for us, this was normal.

"Because yours are constantly in a good mood not having to worry about finances. I remember a lot of my parents' earlier fights were because of finances. First, we didn't have enough money, but then my mom got a higher nursing title. Then my dad was pissed off she was making more money than he was. Most of their earlier fights were about money, and then the abuse. After that, she'd accuse him of cheating, but she always just stayed. Took the blows, took the pain, took everything. Maybe she thought it was for us? I don't know how she seemed to justify that to be okay. I don't know if I'll ever understand."

In a way, I was glad he wasn't hiding any of his past secrets from me anymore, now that I knew everything. I knew about his deepest darkest secret, and it didn't change anything. But at the same time, I wished I didn't have to hear it, only because I wished he didn't have to live through it. Every time he talked to me about his past, my chest ached, wishing I had known him sooner, so I could have taken him away earlier. I wondered briefly if a little Luke would have been willing to take my hand and lead him away. Maybe I'll never know.

"I don't know what my future holds, I might end up about as poor as my parents are. Some poor person might get stuck with my broke ass and then what, I tie them to me?" he let out a dark chuckle, and I frowned, watching the way the pain flickered in his eyes. I remembered once, something he had told me. How he didn't want me to think about him the way he thought of himself. I just wished he'd see himself how I saw him. "It's a recipe for disaster."

I leaned forward, my forehead against his. "Money doesn't solve everything, Luke. It's just something assholes hide behind to pretend they're smiling." He hummed, his eyes closing, and I stared unabashedly at him as he started to drift to sleep. I wasn't surprised, knowing that there had been so much going on that day, that we both needed to get back to sleep to deal with it all.

Neither of us had been looking forward to the party, knowing that my parents were just going to be showing us off. Kennedy would have been pampered with her boyfriend Wyatt attached to her hip, grinning and smiling at everyone. They had been bragging to all of their rich friends about how awesome they were for taking in Luke, their charity case. They liked to show off the talented football captain, bragging about how if it hadn't been for them he would have lost everything, even though they hadn't done anything but give him more useless things he didn't need to begin with.

Then there was me. The only time my parents smiled at me and touched me was when others were looking. They bragged about trophies I had never received, talked about scholarships I had never been given, and colleges that hadn't begged for me as they would pretend. I would have been forced to stand there smiling through their lies, knowing that deep down inside they must have been disappointed in me, to have to make up such elaborate lies to pretend I was good enough for them.

Then there were the dates. I had been so tired of them setting me up with all of these little pampered rich girls. I had a feeling Luke wouldn't have cared as much, but that was understood, I guess. He was straight, he shouldn't have had a big deal about being given some pretty girl to walk around with. I, on the other hand, had already been in love with someone else, and while I had been trying desperately to force myself to look at the girls my father threw at me, none of them had been anything remarkable to me.

I had a feeling that when all of this was over, I'd be perfectly fine finding some really poor person and marrying them, despite what Luke said. The idea of living with money, knowing I'd have to deal with the pompous rich people that went with it for the rest of my life, horrified me.

I turned my hand, pressing it flat against Luke's heart, enjoying the warmth of his bare skin against my hand. As for Luke, I had to believe it wasn't true. I didn't want him to be alone for the rest of his life. While a selfish part of me wanted him to stay by my side forever, I tried to push down the selfish part of me, wanting nothing more than for him to be happy.

I wanted him to see that not every relationship was the same as our parents'. I wanted him to love, and to be loved in return. While I wasn't sure if anyone would ever be able to love him the way I did, I hoped he'd have it, anyway, because he deserved it. Even if I wasn't the right gender for him, he deserved to be loved by a girl the way I loved him, the way I understood him.

It hurt, but I had faith that he was going to find someone beautiful, someone who saw him the way that I did. Someone who deserved him and was so much better than me. He'd find a nice girl, and he'd marry her. He'd love her with everything he had. I just hoped he'd still be my best friend, I guess.

I was there, standing beside him. Maybe he would make me his best man, and I would try my best to smile, to be nice to the woman who was getting everything I wanted, and me? I would just... I would watch. I would smile, trying to hide how much I would be breaking inside, knowing it could have been me; if only I had been the right gender for him.

I didn't know when it was I drifted off to sleep, but I wasn't surprised to be woken up by the sound of pounding on the door. I also wasn't really surprised to have Luke pressed against me, his mouth parted like a silent kiss against my collarbone, and his fingers tightly pressed against my back, holding me even closer to him.

I had my right hand tangled in his curls, my left hand on his lower back, pressing our bodies flush against each other. To say my body was aching would be an understatement. Luke sleepily groaned, lifting his head. His nose brushed against mine as I looked down at him, watching him blink a few times, before realizing just how close we were to each other. As his eyes widened in surprise, the pounding sounded again, making both of us jump in surprise.

"Hurry up! Your mother wants you both downstairs for the tuxes!" Dad shouted, before stomping down the hallway.

We split apart from each other quickly, both of us with cheeks painted red, clutching the blanket tightly to make sure it hid things we were embarrassed to show. "I'm sorry, I guess we forgot to put the pillow back," Luke looked down at his hands.

I took a deep breath, I was disappointed for some reason. Maybe it was because I knew he was embarrassed to be pressed close against me. Embarrassed to be hard, when I knew it meant nothing to him. All boys woke with morning wood. Mine was throbbing for an entirely different reason, but his wasn't, I already knew. His wouldn't be for the same reasons as mine.

"It's fine, Luke. I know it's nothing. All guys get morning wood, it's natural. It doesn't mean anything. Come on, we got to get dressed." I chuckled softly, trying to ease the tension.

However, I still had to try and prepare myself. With a deep breath, I closed my eyes, I chewed on my lower lip for a moment, before standing. I grabbed the extra pillow, held it against the front of my sweatpants, and made my way to the bathroom. "Yeah," Luke mumbled softly. "It doesn't mean anything," I stopped walking for a moment, feeling a pain shooting through me but brushed it away. I nodded in a pained agreement with him as I stepped into the bathroom and shut the door.

To be honest, I wanted to cry as I pressed my back against the door. Slowly, I lowered myself down against the floor. I curled my knees against my chest, my arms wrapped around my knees, and took deep breaths. *Push it all down,* I told myself. *Take all of your feelings, and shove them down into the box, deep down where you won't ever have to feel them again.* I wasn't sure how to make them go away when they were every part of me.

I could hear him moving around in the bedroom, and I forced myself to get up, knowing he'd want to come in here too eventually. It was freaking hard peeing when I was like this, but it helped make it go down in a way, so that was a plus. I washed my hands and brushed my teeth, running a comb through my tangled hair.

I was glad my cheeks weren't painted cherry red anymore as I finally opened the bathroom door. Luke's eyes moved to my bare chest before slowly rising to my face, chewing on his lower lip as I nodded at him. "All yours," I mumbled, feeling slightly self-conscious under his scrutinizing gaze.

He had already grabbed a long-sleeved shirt and was slipping it on his head as he looked at me, tugging it down over his hardened abs. I was finding it hard not to look at them, glad he was covering them. "Okay," he replied, his head lowered as he walked past me.

This was another reason for the pillow. Mornings, when we woke up tangled around each other, were so freaking awkward. It always made me feel like he was disgusted, waking up touching me, knowing I was attracted to his gender. I could still remember the way he didn't want to be friends with me at first, and while he said he wasn't homophobic, I wondered if there were times he was hesitant about it all the same when he got all awkward like this around me.

I pulled a long-sleeved shirt over my head, keeping the sweatpants from last night on, knowing I'd have to change into whatever new suit my mother had gotten us in a few minutes anyway. Ever since that one party when I was first paired with Lana, she decided that I couldn't dress myself and started to do it herself. She always got a variety, making us change as she picked the shirt that matched us the best, the tie that worked the best with it, and the perfect suit.

The only time she ever looked at me longer than five minutes was when she was trying to make sure I looked perfect for their stupid events. The bathroom door opened as I turned to look at it, Luke came out with a shy frown on his face.

"Ready?" I hoped we'd get past this strange awkwardness before the party. I needed to make sure not to move the damn pillow out of the way again. It was just because it was four in the morning, and when it was four in the morning I felt so much braver than I should.

"Yeah," He smiled softly at me. "Maybe they'll let us eat breakfast before they start making us try on enough clothes to clothe a homeless shelter," he pressed his hand against his stomach jokingly.

I grinned, excited that he'd changed the subject and the tension between us was fading away. "Probably not, to be honest. But there would be lots of food at the party."

He opened the bedroom door and held it open for me as well. With a tilt of his head, I slid past him, unable to help brushing my shoulder against his collarbone as he sucked in a deep breath. I looked up at him for a moment, and it was back again, thick in the air, the unending tension between us. "That food sucked ass," he said after a few minutes of staring awkwardly at each other.

I let out a deep breath, moving away from him as he shut my bedroom door behind us. "Yeah, it does," I agreed. I wasn't looking forward to this party at all, but to be honest, maybe it would be nice to get out of my room for a bit. Anything to step away from this awkward ever-growing tension.

Our little world, his and mine, and I wanted it to last forever.

Chapter 15
Luke

"This is awful. I had requested the steak to be medium well, not medium," I wanted to smack my face against the table, repeatedly, as I listened to her obnoxious voice.

The waiter was flabbergasted, and I couldn't blame him. "Ma'am, this is medium well, as requested. Just a little bit of pink, no blood in the meat at all."

Honestly, I wasn't sure if he was allowed to argue with her, but he was right. Plus, he was probably mentally complaining about how annoying she was in his head. Every five minutes, she had been calling him over for something or another. I was half tempted to make him sit here with her, and I'd take the food to the back so I could get away from her. Lana started to screech loudly about how awful he was and argumentative as he apologized, and I pulled my phone out of my pocket, writing a short text but not sending it.

'Save me,' I wrote, before angling the phone towards the waiter.

He looked down at me, his lips curling into a smirk as he tried to hold back his laughter while Lana continued to screech like a pterodactyl. I wasn't entirely sure what the hell had happened to her; she was always annoying, but she hadn't been this bad before.

Of course, the waiter couldn't reply to me. Instead, he grabbed the plate from Lana and walked away, in the middle of her rant, as Kinsley's father came over to us. I could see the little vein in his forehead bulging, and I couldn't help but flinch, hoping no one noticed as he moved to Lana. "I'm sorry about your waiter, Lana. I'll make sure he's fired, and a new one comes back in his place with the proper food."

Lana blinked at him, her eyelashes fake and way too big for her face as she fluttered them at him. "Thank you, Mr. Bryant." I wasn't sure if I was impressed with her ability to go from screeching one moment to flirting the next, or if I was horrified she was flirting with a married older man. As Kinsley's father walked away, I sent the text message to Isabella just for the hell of it. I could have sent it to Kinsley but I didn't know how to feel about him at this moment.

This wasn't the first event I went to since I moved in with Kinsley, and it wasn't the first time I saw him paired up with some rich girl to make his parents happy. It still annoyed me, even as it did before I moved in. Though this was the first time it felt like my chest was breaking, and I wasn't sure what to think about it.

I was vaguely aware of the fact that Lana was talking to me, but honestly, if there was one thing I was good at, it was giving this girl nods and grunts to make her think I was listening to her, as I had done during most of our relationship anyway. It seemed that Kinsley's mother had found out Lana and I had dated before and thought it would be romantic if we, in her words, *found our way back to each other again.*

Plus, it didn't help that Kinsley had disturbed her with something he had said to her before, and she refused to even talk to him now. The word diarrhea floated around, but I wasn't curious enough to ask him what that was all about. That meant Lana was given to me, and Kinsley was given to someone else entirely. I didn't like the way that Kinsley had been over there laughing with her this whole time and never once looked at me.

My phone went off, and I looked at it, Lana making a frustrated noise as I opened it. *'No way in hell am I stepping foot into that building of glitter and nasty ass fancy food,'* Isabella replied. I chuckled, shaking my head as another text came through. *'I'm sure Kinsley feels the same. He hates these things, and his parents give him girls every single time to date. If he's dealing with it, you can too. Suck it up, Curly.'*

"Who are you texting? Another girl?" Lana nearly screamed at me.

I looked up with flushed cheeks to notice some of the tables were looking at me, including Kinsley. Why the hell the first time he decided to look at me was when Lana was accusing me of talking to some girl was beyond me.

He had an unreadable look on his face, and I tried not to think about how cute he looked with his hair all slicked back like that, a few strands of his blond hair falling into his cerulean eyes. I let out a shuddered breath, realizing I just thought of him as cute. A boy... cute. But it was Kinsley, and he was different from everyone else.

Kinsley looked back at his date, and I frowned, studying her. I vaguely knew her. She was one of the popular girls only because she had a lot of money, but she kept to herself as Kinsley did. They were kind of the same in that aspect. She also wasn't one of the rich kids who liked to flaunt it with designer clothes, choosing instead to wear regular jeans and shirts, baggy coats, and headphones.

The more I looked at her, the more I realized she was kind of the female version of Kinsley, except not, in a way. I remembered after a while she was on the swim team. "Who's she?" I asked, pointing at the girl Kinsley was with.

Lana was annoyed, and I realized I probably interrupted her rant about some makeup or nail polish that was coming out recently. I thought it was funny she kept hinting I was going to be buying her things just because I was being forced to spend time with her. "Serina Chang. She's a swimmer." Lana spit it out like it was disgusting. I wasn't really surprised; the cheerleaders and the swim team ladies didn't seem to like each other for some reason. I never paid much attention to the cheerleaders when they complained about it.

I studied Serina; she was pretty. She was different from the other girls in here too, and I could tell by the way Kinsley's mom kept looking at her with a pinched look on her face that she was unhappy with the way Serina was dressed. She had on a dress like the other girls, something pretty that went to her knees, but she had on a pair of black leggings underneath it. It kind of reminded me of Isabella since she tended to wear black leggings under her shorts and short skirts constantly. She had on black combat-type boots too, and that was not something any of the other girls around here were wearing.

Serina's hair was long and black, but as she lifted it and put it down again, I was surprised to see a little bit of red dye peeking through as if she had the underneath of her hair dyed a dark red color. I knew by looking at her that she was Asian; her warm honey-colored eyes were fluttering around the room as she pointed at everything, saying something that was making Kinsley laugh.

I realized I hadn't texted back Isabella and sent her a fast reply. *I don't think he's as upset about it as you thought he would be, at least tonight. He seems to be enjoying his date.* I tried to ignore how clipped and annoyed my reply was as I sent it.

"Why are you asking about Serina? She's a freak. Look at her over there with those boots. I wouldn't be caught dead wearing those. He's a freak too though, they can have each other. They match."

I glared at her, my hands tightening around my phone. "Don't call him a freak." I nearly growled at her. I was so done with her voice, and she could tell too, by the way her eyes fluttered in surprise.

When my phone went off again, I gladly turned to it, not wanting to look at her any longer. *'Yeah, I'll believe that when I see it. Kinsley has been being paired up with that awful Lana girl lately; he's been whining about it every time.'*

Without really caring what Lana was going to think, I turned towards Kinsley and Serina again, angled my phone towards them, and took a picture. It seemed I had taken it at the right time since Serina was laughing at something Kinsley had said and Kinsley was grinning, his dimples showing as he scrunched his nose at her.

It was a good picture of him, a really good picture, the only problem was she was in it too. I sent it to Isabella and went into the picture, cropping it so only Kinsley was in it, and saved it. I wasn't sure why I was doing this, to be honest. Why I was caring, why I was frustrated, why I was saving his picture in my phone.

My phone went off as Lana started to ask me why I took a picture of them and I ignored her, looking at the text. *'I don't know her. Who is she? Damn, they look cozy together. That isn't a look I see on my pretty boy often. It's nice seeing him smile.'*

I gripped the phone slightly because of her choice of words. *He wasn't hers, he was mine.* I mean… ours. I took a deep breath, feeling exhausted and the event had barely started. A new waiter came out and made sure to baby Lana the way she wanted, cutting her steak for her and showing off the inside, cutting the rest of it and decorating it on her plate for her.

Kinsley's parents stood up in the middle of the room, clicking their glasses with a fork softly, the clink echoing through the room. Everyone quieted down, and I found myself staring at Kinsley as he turned to look at his parents. He was running his fingers through his hair, clearly annoyed by the feel of the gel in it, and I felt my fingers twitching in response.

I wasn't even really paying attention to what his parents were saying, to be honest. Serina had pulled her phone out and was tapping Kinsley's shoulder, getting his attention. He turned to look at her, his cheek pressed against hers as she pressed buttons, pointing at something. He pulled away from her for a moment to stare at her with wide eyes, a slow smile spreading over his lips before he moved closer to her again. I felt my chest throb as I watched them, the flutter of wings sliding through every part of me.

My phone went off again, pulling me away from the scene I was horrifiedly watching. *'Are you being jealous of our pretty boy and the cute girl together?'* Isabella asked, an emoji of a tongue sticking out.

I frowned down at it, everyone clapping around us at whatever Kinsley's parents said. There was a flutter of movement, a lot of adults standing and moving towards them, and I knew it was something about the charity they were throwing this whole party for. It made me wonder briefly why we were having steak during a Thanksgiving event, but I shoved the wonder away as I texted Isabella back. *'Why would I be jealous of her? He's not interested in her, he doesn't even know her.'*

I looked around the room, trying to force myself not to look at Kinsley because there was too much frustration about them being together like that. I wanted to stand up, to get away from Lana. I wanted to go over to Kinsley grab his wrist and yank him away from here. I was done being here, I just wanted to go home.

"Are you interested in Serina? I think she's single, but looking at the way that freak- I mean Kinsley, is looking at her, I don't think she will be single for long. Who knows, maybe they already got together," Lana was saying.

I felt ringing in my ears, her words farther away than they should have been as I gave a strained chuckle and shrugged. How the hell was I supposed to explain to her why I was annoyed when I didn't even understand it myself?

My phone went off once more, and I looked at it, noticing it was simply an emoji from Isabella with a smirking face. Since it was sent by itself, it was fairly large on the screen, and I stared at it, not entirely sure what it meant. *'What? Why the smirking face emoji?'*

As I waited for her reply, I tried not to look at Kinsley again, but I was failing. Every time I looked over there, they were looking at something on Serina's phone, and I could tell by the way his father kept glancing at them with a smile on his face that he was happy about whatever was taking place as well. Kinsley's mother looked torn, and the way she kept looking at the boots Serina was wearing, I could tell that she mostly just didn't like Serina's fashion choice.

The waiters all came back as the lights dimmed slightly, the sun outside had set, and candles started being lit around the large elaborately decorated room. Again, I wondered why this event was located on Thanksgiving when there wasn't anything about Thanksgiving here. There weren't turkeys, pies, or any of the normal holiday food here. The decorations were lots of gold and sparkles, elaborately placed around the large room.

The steps were curved, leading up to other rooms. I didn't know what they were for, probably private rooms for conversations. The stairs were roped with gold tinsel around the railing, and honestly, I would have suggested that this was an event for Christmas instead of Thanksgiving, with how it was decorated. But no one else seemed to care, so I tried to pretend it wasn't confusing me. Maybe this was a rich thing, and I was trying not to show off how poor I was.

It didn't help that I was already annoyed with this suit and tie. I wasn't sure how people could button things so close to their throats, but I didn't seem to be one of those people. I felt so stiff and uncomfortable sitting there, listening to Lana go on and on about cheerleading triangles. I was glad when the waiters started to put out the dessert in place of the dinner we had just been served.

The dessert was probably the best part of the whole meal, in my opinion. I tried to focus on it instead of Kinsley, who was still over there leaning over Serina's shoulder while she pointed at something on her phone. I struggled not to go over there and throw Lana at Serina to deal with and drag Kinsley back to this table with me. There was something wrong with me, and I wasn't sure what it was. I felt so frustrated.

My heart raced, my palms were sweaty, and my chest was painful. I had this unsettling feeling inside me, ripping through me. I had never felt like this before. I tried to focus on the desert in front of me because I was slightly worried I was having a heart attack and I was pretty sure I was too young for that.

"This looks awful!" Lana started to screech as the new waiter walked over to the table to fix whatever she was flipping out about. I looked down at the desert, noticing it was like a mini chocolate ball with a small pitcher of melted chocolate in it. I looked at the other tables and noticed they were drizzling the melted chocolate on top of the ball and copied them, poured it over the ball, and watched in amazement as it melted, revealing a fairly small but elaborate cake inside.

I was kind of curious about what the point of spending thousands of dollars for fancy decorations and food was when you were asking people to spend money for charity. Like, couldn't they have taken the money spent on this whole event and donated it themselves?

But I shoved all of that thought process away and took a bite out of the cake, trying not to cringe over how sweet it was.

My phone went off again and I almost didn't get it, worried that whatever Isabella was going to say would be something I wanted no part of reading. I made the mistake of glancing at Kinsley again, the pounding pain in my chest returned as he handed Serina his phone, and she handed him hers. They tapped on the buttons, turned the phones towards themselves, and took selfies for the contact photo. I was horrified that they were exchanging numbers, and the fact that his father was right there grinning like an asshole over it didn't help either.

I wasn't quite sure why I was having difficulty breathing, but I stood up, pulling at the tie. "I'll be right back, I need air."

I had already put a cigarette in between my lips before I even made it out the doors. A few tables of rich families looked at me with horror on their faces, as if only poor people smoked. I did not doubt that half of this room probably did, even if they were going to pretend they didn't. I lit the cigarette as I walked through the doors, breathing in the thick smoke so fast I nearly choked on it as it burned down my throat.

The cigarette dangled from my lips as I put the lighter away and fished my phone out of my pocket with one hand, nearly ripping the tie off my neck with the other. I looked at the time before the text, feeling annoyed that it was still another few hours of being forced to watch Kinsley and Serina together before I could go home.

I sat on the curb, pulled the cigarette out of my mouth, and blew out the smoke, letting the calmness from the nicotine wash through me. "What the fuck is wrong with me," I muttered, before putting the cigarette back in my mouth again.

Vaguely, I realized sitting here was probably bad. Kinsley's mom was going to yell at me for getting the suit dirty from the curb, but at that moment, I couldn't bring myself to care. I opened the text from Isabella, and as I read it, dread washed over me. I knew I wasn't going to like what it said.

'I asked if you were jealous of them being together, Luke. I didn't ask if you were jealous of her. I wonder why it is that you automatically assumed I was talking about you liking Kinsley. Interesting.'

I felt like someone had punched me in the stomach as I read and re-read her text. She was right, though. I skimmed through the texts and realized she was right. I had automatically assumed she was talking about Kinsley. Because I was only thinking about Kinsley from the start. *'I'm straight,'* I texted Isabella back, almost desperately as my fingers shook on the keys.

I could hear it, a slow pulse in my head, the sound of my father's voice, the feel of his spit against my face, and shuddered. My phone vibrated, but since I hadn't closed out of the text screen it popped into place, and my eyes were automatically drawn to it. *'Paper, cardboard, string, noodle,'*

I was confused, my head tilted to the side as I took another drag of the cigarette, letting the smoke billow around me slowly as I blew it out. *'Why are you ranting off random words?'*

She replied with a laughing emoji, and I wanted nothing more than to find her and shake her, this crazy girl. Only a few seconds later she replied with words. *'No reason, just saying a list of random things that start straight, but could be curved as well,'*

I had to admit, it took me way too long to figure out what she was talking about, and I closed my phone feeling stupid and frustrated as I slipped it into my pocket without replying to her.

She was telling me that no matter how much I claimed to be straight, there was a chance I wasn't. The more I thought about the pain in my chest and the way it physically hurt seeing Kinsley smiling at Serina, the more I started to wonder if Isabella was right.

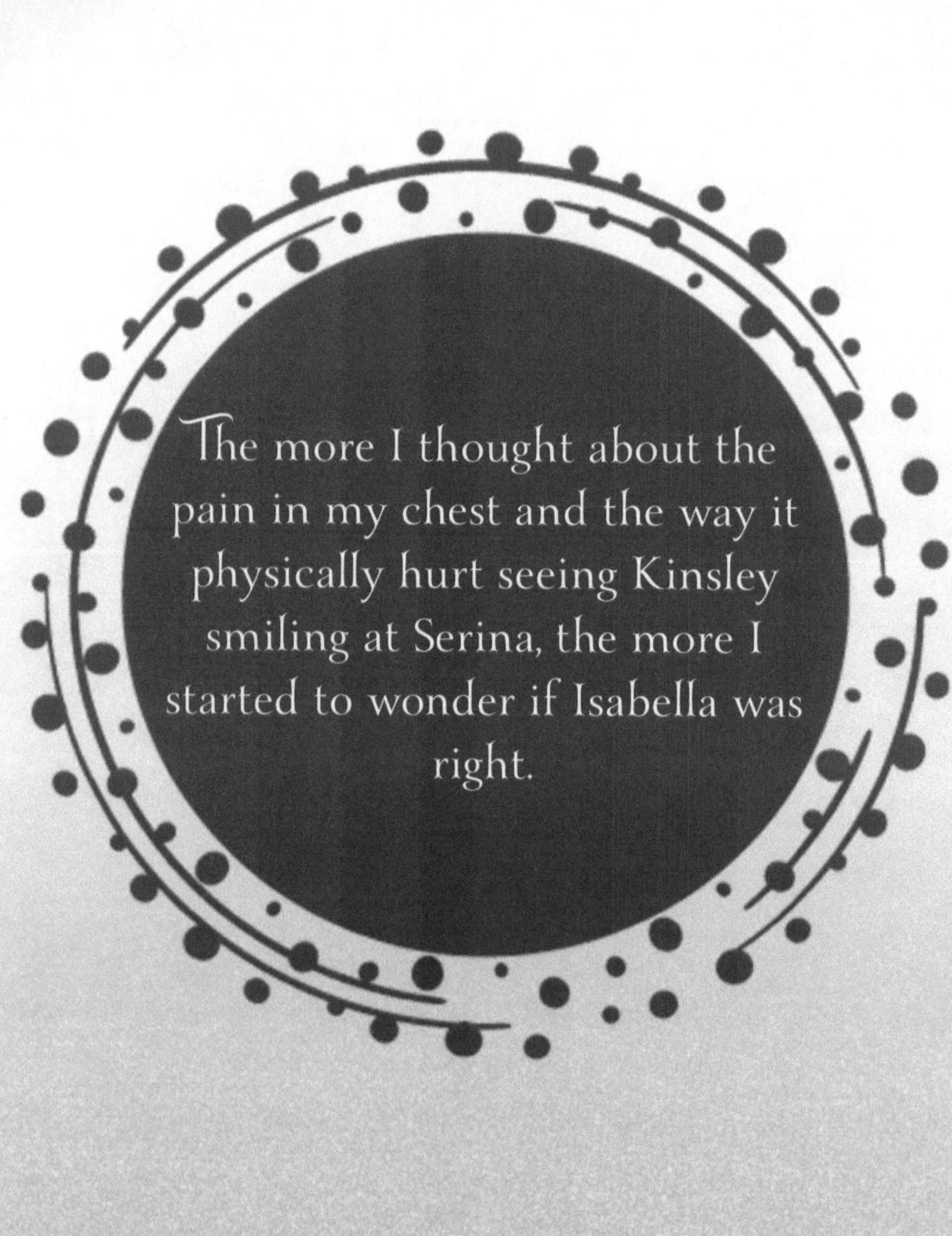
The more I thought about the pain in my chest and the way it physically hurt seeing Kinsley smiling at Serina, the more I started to wonder if Isabella was right.

Chapter 16
Kinsley

"So you're telling me that you've been in the same school as me since freshman year? How did I never notice you?" This wasn't the first time tonight I'd asked Serina this question; I just couldn't wrap my head around it.

When my father dragged us to the party earlier than most of the other guests, he made Luke and me stand to the side and told us our dates would be there soon. I tried to pretend like I was throwing up on Luke so both of us could leave early, but my mother wasn't having any of it. Well, I blamed Luke for that, to be honest; he could have tried to look disgusted. It was hard to believe I threw up on him when he was laughing.

Then Lana showed up, and I nearly wanted to throw my body off of the roof. I asked Luke to shove me out the window, but before he was able to reply to my depressed moment, my mother pushed Luke towards her instead, surprising all of us. Then it was Luke's turn to look at me like he wanted a push out the window, and all I could do was stare.

The way she was with Luke was different than with me. With me, it was obvious she was just trying to be kind since her parents told her to. My mother went off about how sweet they were together, how Romeo and Juliet they were to be on separate sides of the poverty line and to break up, only to be given a chance to meet again.

Lana was acting her normal snobby self, but Luke smiled at her, and she blushed. I wondered if she still loved him. If he ever loved her. He told me he remembered her, and he used to date her, but he never told me if he ever loved her or not. His first love, his first kiss was her.

After that, I felt like I was going to be sick for an entirely different reason. It was hard watching them like that, how natural they looked together. When it came time to order drinks, he remembered her order, and she was so excited about it. I wanted to walk over there and tell her he remembered how I liked my drinks too, but then what was the point? How childish that would be. She could just rip off her clothes and prove to me then and there she'd always be above me since she was the gender he wanted.

I was surprised by Serina. She wasn't what I expected, and I had a feeling she wasn't what my mother expected either. When she walked in looking badass with her half-dyed hair and her combat boots, my mother's jaw dropped to the ground.

"Well, I'm not much different from you, Kins," Serina shoved her shoulder into mine with a laugh. "I tend to wear hoods too. I'm not the only Asian girl in school, but there's not a lot of us. The few Asian girls that are there are fully Asian, and my mother is white. They don't like me. It's not easy being mixed. The Asians don't like me, and the white kids look at me like I'm an alien, and I don't belong anywhere. So I just keep quiet, you know?"

I thought the whole judging people based on race or gender was stupid. I wasn't sure why we needed to have categories anyway. We all bled the same color on the inside, and we all had the same colored organs- well, at birth, anyway. I couldn't claim that as true for those who killed their organs with alcohol abuse or cigarettes or such.

I never understood why colors mattered. So Serina's eyes were a different shape, but they were still beautiful. So her hair was black when she was born, and mine was blond. Why did skin color matter when hair color didn't? Were we all going to start categorizing each other as the brown-haired people, or the black-haired people, and so on? Why did skin color get categorized but hair color or eye color didn't? Whoever first started segregation was probably the stupidest person in the world, in my opinion.

"But you're on the swim team. Surely you have some friends there, right?" Though the moment I asked it, I could tell she didn't. Serina flinched but tried to cover it with a shrug and a laugh. She was strong, really strong. The way she pretended like nothing bothered her. There was something so similar between Serina and me that made me see right through her. An easy-going grin, a calm interior, and an unbothered personality to hide just how bothered we were. We were so similar it was scary.

"Same stupid girls who don't feel comfortable with me. They don't even want to touch me to high-five me when I beat a record. I don't get invited to go eat after practice or games, I tend to just go off by myself afterward. It's fine, I don't need them. I don't need anyone."

I felt awful, knowing this. Here Isabella and I were, thinking we were the only outcasts in the school, and then we just started collecting them. I felt like maybe I should change the name of the art club to the outcast club because Luke ended up pretty much joining, and here was Serina, in need of decent friends. It made me realize that no matter how much we thought everything was okay and everyone was happy, there was always someone out there hiding, always someone who felt alone.

"But you're an artist," I reminded her. I was mildly surprised to realize I liked Serina pretty much from the beginning. Well, not the very beginning, she was kind of a bitch at the beginning. But then she opened her phone, and I saw her background was for SayWeCanFly, one of my favorite bands, and the moment I started to gush over it, everything about her changed.

For a while, we had been going back and forth, her showing me a bunch of bands she had on her phone, and then she'd tease me about concerts she had snuck out to see since I was never allowed to. We were caught up laughing about almost all of them, remembering the funny things the singers did on stage, or certain signs that the fans had held up that night.

I had never been to a concert, wasn't allowed, but I watched pretty much all of my favorite bands' live concerts over YouTube videos and such to try and get the feel of it as much as I could. Just another thing about Serina that was so cool, how she just casually shrugged and said she snuck out like it wasn't a big deal.

As she was showing me pictures of the last concert she went to, I was surprised to see a drawing in her camera roll. It was something simple, something pretty, an old pine tree she said was behind her house. The detail in it was fantastic, and I was completely shocked when I saw it. "Why haven't you joined the art club?"

I wished she would have, from the beginning. How cool it would have been to have Izzy and Serina as my friends in freshman year. Serina shrugged, looking embarrassed. "Because the swim team has practice pretty much every day after school, and on the days it doesn't, I'm forced to go home and practice. I don't get a day off, even on Sundays. My father had won a few medals when he was in college, and he's determined to have me do the same. He's very strict. There's no saying no to my father."

I wondered if she was forced into it like my parents kept trying to force me into basketball. In a way, I felt a kinship with Serina. The more she talked, the more I felt like in a way she was the female version of me. "Did you even like swimming?"

After dinner, Luke had pretty much vanished and so did Lana. I didn't want to think about it, to be honest. There were a few times Lana was screeching about something, but most of the time when I looked over at Luke he was either texting or nodding and smiling at something Lana said. It didn't help the fact that Lana seemed to be texting when Luke was, and when he'd nod and smile she'd look at him, almost like they were texting each other.

I felt a throb in my chest, so painful, because why was it her? Why did it have to be her? I was trying to see the good in her since I trusted Luke with every part of me and if he liked her then there had to be a reason for it but she wasn't good enough for him. He deserved someone better, so much better. *Someone like me-*

"I guess so," Serina said, cutting through my thoughts like a butter knife slicing through butter. Honestly, it was probably for the best, since my thoughts were going to a dark place I wanted no part of. I didn't think Serina would be happy to see me crying right then.

"If I had more time with it, I'd probably like it better. But if I'm not swimming, then I'm playing the cello. It was the instrument my mother played in high school and college. If I'm not doing that, then I'm learning Chinese or studying college-level math equations. Dad wants me to be above everyone else. The schedule he has for me is pretty rigorous."

I frowned, feeling bad for her. "So it's okay that we're walking like this? You don't have anything scheduled after dinner that you're going to get in trouble for missing?"

She chuckled, throwing her arms wide as she walked, the sound of her combat boots slapping down slightly hard on the pavement. When Luke and Lana vanished, so did Lana's car, so I had a feeling wherever Luke went, he was with her. After dinner, Serina had told me she wanted to show me something secret, something she'd never shown anyone else before, and we left my car parked out front since Serina promised we weren't going far.

"They're happy I'm talking to a boy, one they think is so handsome and rich. They won't say anything about me missing my schedule for the night as long as I'm with you. Maybe I should hang out with you more often. It feels so nice not having to worry about doing this or that, and what's coming next." She let out a wistful sigh, and I couldn't help but want to help her.

"Sure, I don't care. You have my number, and I don't have a job or anything. I might have to get a ride if Luke has my car, but otherwise, I can hang out with you whenever you want." I didn't mind helping her have some breathing room, and she was fun to spend time with, so that helped.

I stared at her from the corner of my eye and wondered if maybe I could love her one day. I wasn't stupid, I saw the way my parents looked at us, and walking after dinner together probably gave them the wrong ideas.

She was a lot like me, but not at the same time. Her parents were attentive to her, overbearingly so, while mine constantly forgot I existed and only paid attention when they felt like arguing with me or checking to see if I was doing drugs. I guess in a way she was like Luke too, in that sense. She was like me but not, and he was like me but not as well.

It seemed that parents could be assholes whether they were attentive or not, and while they did different things, they were still hard for us to deal with. In the end, Serina would graduate from college early most likely, and be something amazing like an astronaut or a scientist or a doctor, and she'd have her parents hugging her and loving her for it. Me? Even if I did go to college for something with sports, I doubted I could save my relationship with my parents.

It made me wonder, what if I had dated Serina? Sporty, swim team Serina. The swim team and the basketball players were close; the girls always dated the basketball guys. It would have made sense if we had gotten together, in that way at least. Maybe if I could have loved her, I could have joined basketball, and I could have made my parents happy.

But as soon as I had thought about it, I frowned. Just the idea of it felt wrong to me. I wasn't sure if I would ever be able to love someone else, not like Luke; and that scared me. "So who is Luke? My parents said you had a little sister, but the way you talk about him makes it sound like he's living with you."

I blinked at her, surprised. "Luke Wilson, you don't know him? The football captain?" I wondered. She shrugged, and I grinned, shaking my head at her. "He isn't related to me, but my parents took him in when his parents left town. So he could finish his high school life here instead of trying to transfer somewhere else," it was kind of the truth if you ignored the stuff I left out. Both of his parents were currently not in town, his father had moved to another one and the psych ward Luke's mother was staying in wasn't here either.

She nodded, understanding. "I see, so like a brother to you, even if he's not."

I flinched, rubbing the back of my head. There was no way in hell I would ever see Luke as my brother. "So what is this secret thing you need to show me?" I wondered, hoping to not only get some answers but to change the subject. I didn't want to think about Luke right then. About what he could have been doing with Lana, now that they were older and he wasn't a scared virgin anymore.

If Lana wasn't busy squeaking like a crazed lady, she was pretty. Big breasts, a curvy waist, a tight body from years of working out for cheerleading. The type of girl who wore her uniform to school, constantly to show off her belly button and her abs, the type of girl who had her hair pulled back and tightened in a high ponytail, making sure it was perfect at all times. I guess she was the type of girl Luke was interested in. Even if I was a girl, I wouldn't be his type, I guess.

Serina lifted the bottom of her dress to reveal shorts on top of the leggings. She pulled a scrunchie out of her pocket and lifted her hair into a messy bun on top of her head, showing off the red underneath her hair. "It's a secret, Kins," she pressed her finger against her lips and winked at me. I grinned, shaking my head at her as she giggled at me. "Don't ruin the secret."

I pressed my hand against my chest, pretending to be sad. "I'd never," I muttered, making her laugh once more. Her laugh reminded me of Luke's, in a way. Or maybe it was just the fact that her laughing made me miss his. Things were so weird, so tense and strange between us, that I didn't remember the last time Luke had genuinely laughed. I looked down at my hands with a frown. I wasn't happy about that realization.

"Okay, close your eyes!" Serina ordered as she snuck behind me and slid her hands around the side of my neck, pressing her hands against my eyes. She wasn't as tall as me, but she was pretty close. My five-foot-eleven frame, I'd say she was around five-foot-seven or eight. It wasn't that much of a stretch for her to put her hands on my eyes.

I let out a nervous chuckle because yeah, she was pretty cool and everything, but she was pretty much a stranger still and had been leading me down a dark alley in town that I'd admittedly barely been paying attention to, and anything could happen. She could pull a knife on me. Not that I thought she was going to, but she could if she wanted to. "Okay, surprise!" She shouted as she moved her hands from my eyes.

I blinked, my eyes adjusting to the dim light from the blinking street lamp that was close by, and I realized I knew this place since Isabella and I had frequented it recently. I recognized my freehand spray paint drawing of a large dandelion flower. Luke's drawing of a dog, or a cat, whichever honestly, was pretty close to mine. I wasn't going to tell him I wasn't sure which animal it was he was trying to make.

Then there was Isabella's, and her art on the walls always looked better than mine and Luke's because my medium was paper and pencils, while she excelled at spray paint and all kinds of paints. Her stencil being premade and not something she came up with at the last second helped as well.

Isabella had made a variety of flowers, the reason I had my idea to do a flower, to begin with. In the middle of her flowers was a little girl, hunched over and holding a flower in her hands, almost like she was breathing it in. Isabella had just done this drawing a week ago, and I was glad to see how well it came out now that it was dry. However, there was a new addition to it, and I sighed, knowing Isabella wasn't going to be happy about that.

Standing beside the little girl was a little boy, staring at the little girl with a look of admiration and happiness on his face. It was well done, and I could see what Isabella was talking about when she said it looked masculine. Always drew the opposite of what Isabella drew, the stronger lines while Isabella's and mine tended to have more curves and soft strokes. This one was wilder, harsher, more masculine; and right there underneath it, a hairsbreadth from Isabella's bell, was the S.

I looked at Serina, the way she was grinning, looking at the picture with a look of admiration and happiness on her face, and then at the picture once more. *S.* I thought to myself, tilting my head to the side. *S for Serina.* "You're a tagger." There weren't any accusations in my voice, or anger, no disgust, just simple curiosity.

She seemed surprised by my tone, or maybe it was the fact that I wasn't either in a state of awe or disgusted. I mean, one of my pictures was up there as well, so it made sense I wasn't disgusted about it. "You don't seem freaked out, why aren't you freaked out? I've never shown this to anyone before, I assumed if I ever did they'd, I don't know, freak out?" She let out a nervous laugh. "I expected more of a reaction than that, to be honest."

I laughed softly, because what else was I supposed to do? "It's hard to be disgusted about it when my drawing is up there too," I grinned, flashing my dimples at her. Now it was her turn to look all wide-eyed and surprised, and I couldn't help but laugh out loud at her expression.

She let out a shaky breath, moved to her drawing, and then to Isabella's. "This one?" She wondered, her warm honey-colored eyes fluttering over my face, searching me for answers.

I moved closer to the pictures. "This one," I pointed at my flower. She nodded, her head tilted to the side.

"I noticed the differences. There have always been two different ones, but in the past six months or so there's been a third one. If you count it as something," She mumbled, trying to make it so I didn't hear the last part.

I couldn't help but grin because yeah, I knew Luke tried his best, and it was really cute how hard he tried, but that boy couldn't draw. I wasn't going to stop him from trying, though. The way he bent over the paper with his pencil, the concentration on his face, and the happiness that shone when I told him I liked it was worth every bit of it. "I'm not telling you who did the other pictures. It's not my secret to tell."

She stared at me, chewing on her lower lip, before letting out a sigh. "I guess that's fair. It tells me something about you though, Kinsley." She said with a smile on her face. "It tells me you are someone that can be trusted. Do you want to know my secret?"

Serina slid her fingers over the curves of the bell, tracing it over and over again. "Sure, if you want to tell me. I don't tell other people's secrets," I told her. *I don't even tell my secrets.*

She grinned as she tapped her finger against the bell. "This person, whoever they are. I'm in love with them. How silly it is, right? Being in love with a drawing style? But ever since the first time I saw it, how perfect it is, and how well it compliments mine, I have been in love with it. I studied their drawings. The things they make and the stroke style tell a lot about someone. The flowers tell me soft, and fragrant. The little girl tells me sweet, kind. The girl smelling the flower tells me curiosity, and the act in itself tells me brave, determined, and skilled," she stared up at the picture in admiration.

I watched her, my hands crossed over my chest, wondering if she cared that the person she claimed to be in love with was a female. "You don't know them. How can you be in love with someone you've never met?"

"I don't need to see them, to love them. I feel them here," she pressed her fist gently against her chest. "Do you understand?"

All of a sudden, everything came back to me, leaving me breathless, weak in the knees, and shaky. The feelings of the letters, and how excited they made me. With every new letter, I loved Green more and more, without knowing their gender, their appearance, or anything. I didn't need those because I loved their soul. I knew that no matter who they were, what their appearance was, what race they were, I'd love them because I fell in love with their soul. "I understand," I told her truthfully, my voice slightly breathless.

She studied me, a soft smile fluttered over her lips as she gave a sharp nod. "I believe you."

I wasn't sure if I would ever be able to love someone else, not like Luke; and that scared me.

Chapter 17
Luke

I sat next to Kinsley and watched him draw. I didn't have work that day, and there wasn't school because it was Thanksgiving break. I pulled my knees up to my chest and wrapped my arms around them. I wanted to be a small little ball, to be so small I could be invisible. So small I could disappear at any given moment.

The feelings that were inside me felt like I was a boat at sea, in the middle of a storm. The waves crashed around me, licked up and down, and pulled me one way and the other. I wasn't sure if I'd survive the storm, or if it would tip me over, drag me down into the ocean, and drown me.

There was something vulnerable about learning that everything about me that I'd always known was wrong. The thought of going from one sexuality to another, realizing that I was different than I'd always thought I was, was scary. I felt like I had ripped off all of my clothes and was standing in the middle of the mall, everyone looking at me, pointing at me, judging me.

Kinsley leaned over his paper, his body graceful, poised. His parents weren't home and he had the sleeves of his sweater rolled up to his elbows, showing off his tattoo. The sweater was white and fuzzy, and he looked so soft and tiny in it that I wanted to wrap my arms around him and pull him against me, to hold him and never let go. But then I couldn't help but think about last night, and everything just faded away.

I had stayed outside and smoked for a lot longer than I expected I would. When I got that text from Isabella, it was like everything was right there, smacking me over and over again in the face. The possibility, the feelings that were so forbidden, so foreign, were right there spilled out of the box I had tried so hard to shove them in. I sat there and smoked cigarette after cigarette, lost in my thoughts as I tried to run away from my father's voice. If he could see my thoughts, if he could hear the way my heart beat when I was near Kinsley, he'd kill me. I had no doubt he'd kill me.

Lana had come out to talk to me, to see what was taking me so long and when she saw me smoking she got all pissy and demanded I quit. I told her to back off and she ended up driving home, pissed off that neither Kinsley nor I was interested in her or her bullshit. I ended up walking home, despite how far it was.

I didn't call a cab even though Kinsley's parents gave me a credit card for emergencies, the card that sat in my wallet that I doubted I'd ever use. I just wanted to walk, to feel the cold air against my heated body, and to think. By the time I got home, I assumed Kinsley would have been there since I had walked for a good hour or so, but he wasn't. I had taken a shower, hung the tux up on the side of the closet that was mine, and waited; he still wasn't home. I was stubborn, I knew I should have texted him, but the more I thought about it the more scared I was.

His parents came home, changed their clothes, and left. Kennedy came home giggling and shushing her boyfriend as she led him into her room and shut the door, and I waited. I lay there in the bed, staring at Kinsley's side of the bed, and I wanted to cry because what if Isabella was right? What if I wasn't straight? What if I liked my best friend?

I stared into the dim light from the lamp and grabbed the extra pillow to put between us. I rolled over, my back to the pillow as I stared at Kinsley's dresser. I needed to think, but at the same time, I was scared of my thoughts, and I wasn't sure what I was supposed to do. How did not being straight work? Was I born like this? Or did Kinsley turn me? Is it even possible to be turned?

I had a million questions piling through my mind, most of them stupid as I panicked silently, and then he came into the room. I closed my eyes and pretended to be asleep as he stared at me. I could feel him looking at me, but then his gaze faded away, and I opened my eyes, watching him from under my eyelashes. He was smiling, and I felt like I was dying. He whistled softly under his breath, a happy tune as he pulled his tux off and threw it on the ground without a care.

I stared at his back as he pulled his shirt off, and studied the way his shoulder blades popped out of his skin, his broad back, and his muscular form. My eyes trailed down his back as if my eyes were fingers. I could almost feel his skin as I clutched my fingers tightly in the blankets and let out a soft silent breath. I realized as he pulled his pants off and stood there in boxers, that maybe I had never been straight because I've never felt like this before for anyone. Just him, it had only ever been just him.

He grabbed some clothes and went into the bathroom, the water turned on for a shower, and I slid my hand down my body, finding the place where it was throbbing, and fixed it; unsure what it meant, or what I was. "Luke, are you okay?" Kinsley asked, snapping me out of my thoughts.

I blinked, coming face to face with Kinsley as he turned towards me, a soft smile on his face as he chuckled at me. His ash blond hair hung in his cerulean eyes and I wanted to run my fingers through it, to push it out of his face, and kiss him. *God, I just want to kiss him.*

"Yeah," I choked out, my cheeks reddened at my thoughts. Kinsley was so perceptive, and I was scared he knew what I was thinking. "Just a little tired."

It wasn't a lie, to be honest. I had barely slept last night. He had gotten out of the shower and stood there on his side of the bed, like he had just been staring at me, or the bed, at the pillow, at something. Then he had pulled out his phone, sent a text, received a text, and was softly laughing. My phone wasn't going off, but that didn't mean he wasn't talking to Isabella without the group texts. But a part of me couldn't help but feel sad, thinking that it wasn't Isabella.

I knew he exchanged numbers with Serina. I knew that while Kinsley wasn't straight, he wasn't gay either. Even after he had fallen asleep, I was still awake. I had rolled over to stare at him from across the pillow and I wanted to cry, because Kinsley had never really slept on his side, always on his back or his stomach, but he had his back to me last night. I had never felt more distant from him, seeing his back turned to me like that.

He hummed in response, his eyes lowered to his picture as he smiled down at it. "Hey Kins?" I was quiet, shy even. He hummed once more, his pencil scraped against the paper as I took a deep breath and let it out slowly. "If you're not gay, and you're not straight, does that mean you're bisexual? What exactly is your label?" I asked, unsure how all of this worked.

Kinsley lifted his eyes to me with a confused look on his face. "Um," he stammered. He put his elbow on the desk, his head resting against the palm of his hand as he stared at me. Why did he have to look so pretty no matter what he was doing? "Why?"

In the distance, music was playing. It wasn't too loud, so we could talk to each other. We had it playing on his stereo since no one was ever home.

I shrugged, unable to explain. How could I tell him that I was on the verge of breaking down, that I might have had feelings for him and I knew he had feelings for someone else? How could I tell him I might not have been straight after all, but I had no idea how any of this not-straight-ness worked?

Was I something now? Did I have a title or a label? Was there a bunch of boxes set up somewhere in the universe where someone picked everyone up and categorized them according to sexuality? "Just curious how not being straight worked, I guess,"

His lips fluttered for a moment, and I was blinded by his smile. His dimples flashed as he laughed at me. "How not being straight worked?" he choked out, finding what I said hilarious. I must have frowned or something because he quieted down, let out a final laugh, and flashed his teeth at me as he smiled.

"It's not like a job that you have to have training for, Luke. It's just something you're born with. Sometimes people figure it out pretty early in life, sometimes people don't figure it out until they're in high school or college, and sometimes people don't figure it out until they're a lot older. I heard of sixty-year-olds figuring out they've been in love with their friends after so many years and finally getting together. It's hard to come to terms with it, the older you are. It's hard telling those around you, especially if you're surrounded by homophobes. I guess that's why I never really said anything about myself to anyone except you and Izzy."

I couldn't help it, I smiled, because he didn't say he told Serina. He trusted me more than her. Then again, why would he tell her he wasn't straight if she was a girl? Would he even need to tell her? I felt my smile fade away once more as he kept talking, oblivious to my thoughts. "As for my label, I don't have one. I guess in a way the world started with three, right? Gay, straight, bisexual. Then more labels started to pop up, pansexual, demisexual, and asexual, and it was hard to keep track of them all now.

"It seems like there's a label for almost every type of feeling, to explain how one person is different from the other. I researched for a long time trying to figure out where I fit in, but nothing ever felt right. So I guess I just gave up. I don't need a label to love someone. I don't need a label to define me. I'm just Kinsley, and I'm fine being unlabeled."

I nodded, and he watched me for a few seconds, before going back to his drawing. Something was reassuring in what he said. I had been worried, trying to figure out what I was, and where I fit in, but I guess in the end it didn't matter, right? Who I loved, what I felt, it didn't need a title. I didn't need a title to tell me I had feelings for him. Whatever those feelings were.

"Though some people start to think that they're possibly part of the LGBTQ+ community and they explore, only to figure out later on that they're straight. And that's okay, as long as no one gets hurt by it. It isn't easy figuring yourself out," he added a few seconds later as if it were an afterthought.

I frowned, because what if that was me? What if I was straight, and I was just confused? Kinsley was really pretty, he had done so much for me and saved me in so many ways. He was a light, my light that pulled me out of my darkness. Maybe I was mistaking admiration for something more? What if I tried to kiss him when we were both sober and I ruined everything? I shuddered, remembering once more the look on his face after I had kissed him. I was scared to see that expression again.

I decided then would be the best time to change the subject because I felt like the longer this went on the less air I was getting in my lungs, and then I'd have to explain to Kinsley why I randomly passed out in the chair next to him.

"You're like a bad boy, with that tattoo," I said, nodding my head at it.

Honestly, I had no idea why that popped out of my mouth, but the challenging look that flashed over Kinsley's face was worth my embarrassment. "So what, you jealous?"

Before I could even reply to him, he grabbed my hand with one hand and a Sharpie with another. I blinked in surprise as he pushed up my sleeve and ran his finger over my scar before putting the top of the Sharpie down on my skin.

It felt weird, the Sharpie on me. The way it slid over my skin, marking me. I realized I wasn't even trying to pull away because it was Kinsley, and he could do whatever he wanted to me. I think I was fine with being his, even if he wasn't mine. At least we were touching, we were talking, we were smiling, and that was enough for me. It had to be enough.

"A key?" He pulled away and grinned at me. I stared at the key, at the arm he had chosen, and how it covered my whole scar. For the first time in years, I was able to look at my wrist without feeling disgusted with myself, and I couldn't quite help feeling vulnerable. "It looks nice," I mumbled quietly. I never really thought I'd get a tattoo when I got older, but the longer I looked at it, the more I realized I wanted it. This one, his drawing, his work. I wanted it on my body to show the world how amazing he was.

I wondered if he noticed that when we held hands my key would be pressed against his birdcage. I wanted to be the key to free him. I stood up to get my phone from my nightstand and took a picture of it as he stared at his drawing. I wanted to keep it, to show it to a tattoo artist, to have them do it when I got old enough. I didn't want it to ever fade away.

I stood in the middle of the room, my head tilted to the side as I smiled. I moved to Kinsley and grabbed his hand with a grin on my face. "This is my current favorite song. Dance with me?" Kinsley grinned as the beginning chords of the song Better by SMYL came on. He dropped his pencil and stood up without any hesitation. I grabbed his waist as he wrapped his arms around my neck, smiling shyly at me as we moved slowly back and forth to the soft sultry sound of the song.

There was something about this song that pulled at me; the words were so deep and meaningful, and it made me feel like I could do anything, be anything. But then I realized this was probably wrong. What if Kinsley was right and everything was just a phase for me? What if with every close touch, I was ruining everything?

Kinsley was everything to me, and the idea of losing him was horrifying. What if I got too close and it was a disaster? How could I keep going if he was gone? I stopped dancing, and Kinsley frowned. "We shouldn't do this, I'm not... gay," I chewed on my bottom lip as I averted my eyes.

Kinsley, who always seemed to take everything in stride, lifted one of his hands from around my neck, clutched my chin between his finger and his thumb, and turned my head so I was looking at him once more. I stared into his piercing gaze, the tension thick in the air. I forced myself to stare at his eyes, instead of at his lips like I wanted to.

"Why does dancing have to be gay? Besides, I'm not gay either. That's a stereotype, Luke. I'm just a guy, who happens to be standing across from another guy, and we're dancing. Nothing gay about dancing. Why does it matter what gender we are to dance?"

His thumb ran up and down the side of my jaw as I felt myself starting to calm down. There were so many thoughts right then, so much panic, it was making me go mental. "You're right. It doesn't mean anything. Just two friends dancing."

He let go of my jaw and lowered his eyes as I wrapped my arms around his waist and pulled him even closer to me. He let out a soft sigh, both of his arms around my neck once more as he pressed his head against my collarbone, his breath fanned my skin that peeked above the collar of my shirt. "Exactly, it doesn't mean anything."

I felt like I had a hundred birds inside me, scratching at my heart, fluttering against the inside of my stomach. It wasn't a fun feeling at all and I tried to ignore it. Another tug had him pull him even closer to me, his chest pressed against mine. I ran a hand up his back, slid it back down again unable to stop myself despite how intimate it was.

"Want to know a secret?" I breathed. He nodded, his nose pressed against my throat for a moment before he lowered his head once more. "You're my best friend." Kinsley chuckled against me, his laugh vibrating his body against mine as we rocked back and forth.

I wasn't sure if this was called dancing. It was more like we were hugging while standing and swaying side to side. But I wasn't complaining, and neither was he. His voice was deeper than usual as he replied, a soft shudder ran through my body as my cheeks heated up at the deeper timbre. "You're my best friend too."

I was scared he would notice my shudder, and I let out a laugh, trying to disguise it by saying something. "Damn, don't tell me that. Now I have to keep it a secret otherwise Isabella will kill me." I joked. I mean, kind of joked. Izzy was scary when she was angry.

Kinsley smiled, and I smiled, because even if I couldn't see him, I could feel his lips curved against my skin. I pressed my hand to the back of his head and ran my fingers up the back of his neck. I tangled them in his hair, before sliding my hand down his back once more. I just wanted to touch him, every part of him. I didn't think I'd ever get tired of touching him. "Are you scared of Izzy?"

I snorted because that shouldn't even be a question. "Damn right I am. She's terrifying, especially with her shoe."

Kinsley chuckled, and we were quiet for a moment. "She's my best friend too, but you're more. More best, in a way. You're the bestest," he pulled away a little as he spoke, to look me in the eyes with that intensity that blazed in his cerulean eyes.

My eyes searched his, my fingers clutched onto his waist tightly, holding him like a lifeline. "You're the bestest for me too, Kinsley," I breathed.

I didn't know how to explain the warmth that flowed through me, the realization that slowly slipped through me as I stared at him. It was like everything that scared me, everything that worried me, everything that I tried to understand wasn't important anymore. None of it was important. Just him, just this, just us.

If I tried to kiss him again, would he pull away? God, but I wanted to.

The doorknob started to jiggle, and we broke apart fast. Where we had been standing, the bed was the closest, and I flung myself onto it, my back against the headboard as I grabbed my phone. Kinsley ran over to his desk, grabbed the back of his chair, and sat in it as the door opened.

We were both flustered with red cheeks as we stared down at the things we were pretending we were doing moments before the door opened. I realized my phone was upside down, and I flipped it as I lifted my eyes to the door. Kinsley's dad was there, a bright grin on his face as his eyes swept around the room, passed over me, and found Kinsley.

"Hey, champ!" he walked over to Kinsley and clapped him on the shoulder. I winced with him because while his dad wasn't physically abusive like mine was, his dad was really strong and painful most of the time, even if it wasn't on purpose. I noticed Kinsley had his arm pressed down against the desk, hiding his tattoo. I slowly pulled my sleeves down, glad he hadn't noticed me.

"Hey, Dad, what's up?" he stammered, confused. I couldn't blame him; this was probably the first time I'd ever seen his dad be nice to him when there weren't people around us.

His dad grinned, and when he turned to look at me, Kinsley pulled his sleeves down. He looked at Kinsley once more, looking like a happy doting parent. It wasn't a look I saw on him often, and never directed toward Kinsley.

"Your mother and I had dinner with the Chang family this evening, and you were mentioned quite a bit. You left an impression on them. We invited them all back here for drinks, so I can't stay up here long. But Serina came as well, and she's waiting for you at the gazebo."

Kinsley perked up, a smile sliding over his lips as he nodded his head. I felt my heart shatter into a million tiny pieces, because damn, how stupid was I? I had been considering kissing him five seconds ago. I was glad his father had stopped me, that would have been horrible. "Really? Sweet, I'll go say hi to her." Kinsley's dad stepped back so Kinsley could get up, and Kinsley flashed me a smile. "I'll be back in a little bit."

I nodded because what else was I supposed to say to that? Don't go? Stay with me? He wasn't in love with me, he liked her, it seemed. His dad grinned at him, messed up Kinsley's hair that I had my fingers in only minutes ago, and Kinsley smiled softly at him under the attention he had never really gotten from him before. No, there was no way I could say anything to him, not seeing how happy he was.

"I'm proud of you, champ," his dad said as he wrapped his arm around his shoulder and pulled him towards the door.

I stared at the door for a heartbeat after they left until I forced myself to stand. I stood still in the middle of the room for a moment before moving toward the window. From up there, I could see the gazebo. It was dark out, but there were lights on outside, white fairy lights that were wrapped around the gazebo, lighting it up for a romantic setting.

I realized, as I watched Kinsley run out of the house and towards the gazebo, just why my heart felt like it was getting stabbed over and over again. She stepped into the light, and Kinsley wrapped her into a hug, her body smaller and softer than mine would ever be. I realized exactly what this was.

With my forehead against the glass, I felt the warm trickle of a tear slide down my cheek, my chest ached, and I couldn't exactly breathe as Serina stood on her tiptoes and kissed Kinsley's cheek. He wrapped his arm around her shoulder and pulled her with him towards the gazebo, both of them sat down next to each other on the bench inside.

The bench I sat on, the gazebo I stood in with him when we watched the rain falling around us. I couldn't do much more than laugh as I turned and pressed my back against the window. I pulled my feet up onto the window seat and buried my flushed face into my knees.

Back then, even then, I felt this. I didn't know what it was until now.

It felt like every part of me was breaking, and there was no point trying to gather up the pieces, to fix it, because what was the point? I was inescapably in love with him, but he was never, ever going to be mine.

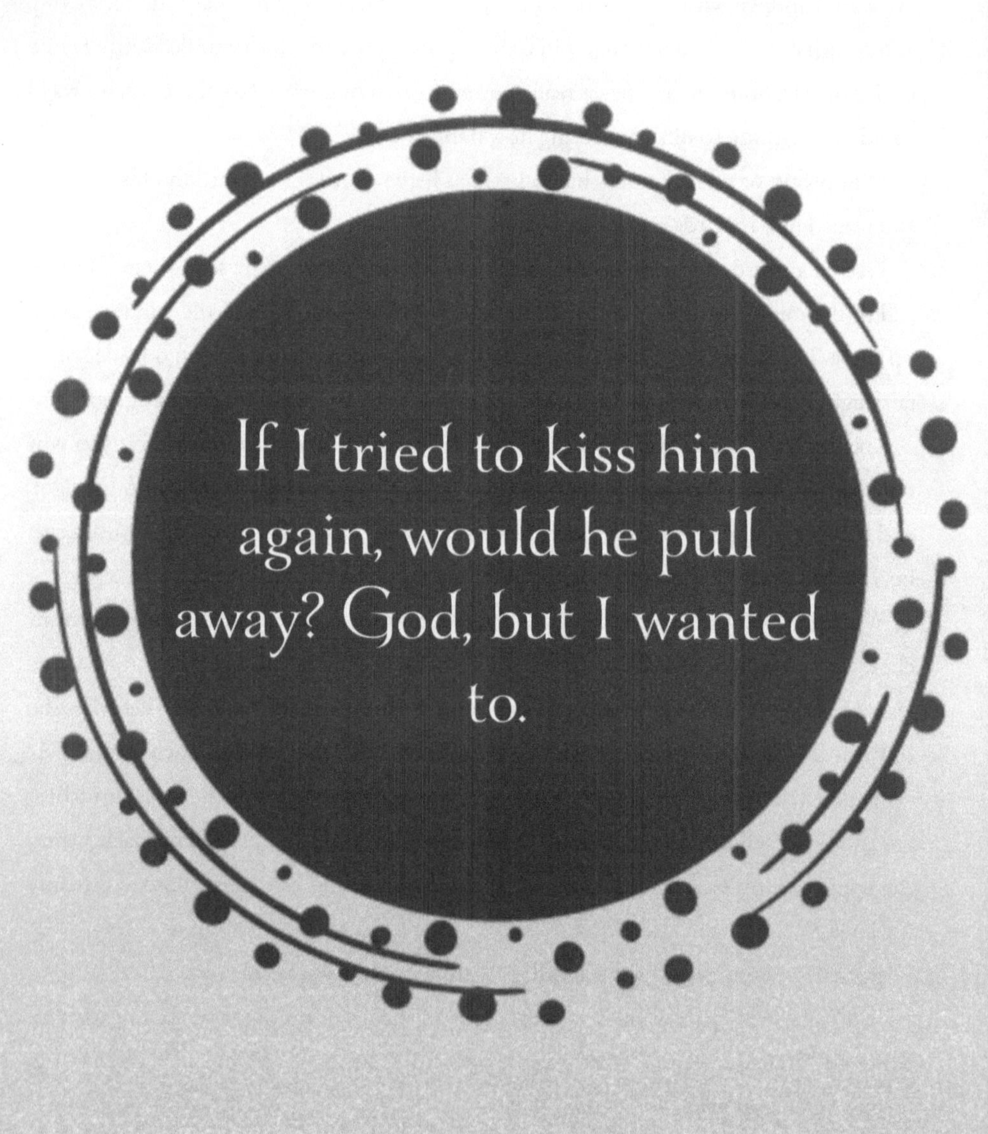

If I tried to kiss him
again, would he pull
away? God, but I wanted
to.

Chapter 18
Kinsley

"Hey Kins," Serina laughed, nudging her shoulder into mine as she sat down next to me. "My parents like you. They think you're a gentleman and keep going on about how handsome you are."

I rolled my eyes because I didn't think of myself as a gentleman. "Why, because I drove you home? Was I supposed to let you walk alone in the dark?"

She puffed up her cheeks, crinkling her nose at me at the same time. It was quite a hilarious look, to be honest. "You think I can't handle myself? I can kick their ass if they try to touch me," she lifted her fists and punched the air to show her point.

I held up my hands, laughing. I didn't have it in me to tell her I had taken a few years of karate lessons, and her hands were not positioned right. "Oooh, scary." Serina blushed in embarrassment and punched me in the side. "Sassy," I mumbled, earning myself another punch.

"I was hoping you could show me some of your drawings. While you're not my mystery lover, you're still really good at drawing," she said after a few minutes of us laughing.

I hummed in response, my arms draped over the back of the bench as I turned around and looked up at my window. It was tinted slightly from there, and while I could make out a shape, I wasn't sure what it was. *Possibly the curtain*, I thought with a shrug.

I thought about Luke, and about what happened before my father had come in. He had been so different the past few days, and I wasn't sure what to think about it. I wondered if he had been disgusted with me last night after what had happened the morning we both woke up pressed up against each other. It had been the first time Luke had put the pillow there himself and I was sad about it. I had been so worried he didn't want to be my friend anymore, that I was surprised and happy when he stuck by me all day.

Then there were his questions. He wanted to know my label. Was that his way of trying to figure out whether or not I was going to jump him or something? I guess in a way all straight guys, no matter what they said, were scared of their non-straight best friend falling for them.

He said he wasn't vain enough to think I did, and I thought it was laughable because I was completely in love with him, just hiding it so he didn't feel uncomfortable. He said he was straight, and I was going to do my best to respect his sexuality, even if deep down inside all I wanted to do was cry.

I pulled my arms in, wrapping them around me, and tried to hide the redness in my cheeks as I thought about the way he had held me. His fingers ran up and down my back, tangled in my hair, and left every part of me breathless. I had wanted nothing more than to turn my head, to kiss his throat, his jaw, his lips. It was hard to understand, the way I felt for him. So strong, so fierce, so endless.

Loving Luke was like falling into a bottomless pit, with no ending in sight. I was afraid I was too far away from the surface to crawl myself out of it, but at the same time, I didn't want to either. Maybe one day, I'd find someone else who made my heart flutter with the mere twitch of their lips, someone who made me forget how to breathe when they looked at me with that intense gaze.

Maybe one day I'd find someone else who could press their fingers against the pulse of my wrist, stare me deeply in the eyes, and speak to my soul. But not now, not tomorrow, and not next week, either. I had a feeling I was going to be drowning in everything that was Luke Wilson for a long, long time... and I was slowly starting to accept that.

I had always wanted to know what it felt like to fall in love, and some might say it wasn't worth it for all the pain and heartbreak. But then he smiled at me, pressing his fingers against the pulse of my wrist, and I pressed my hand against his chest, and we became one all over again.

It was worth it, every part of it, and if I had a chance to go back and do it again, I would. Repeatedly; no matter how many times it shattered me.

"My Luke is in the bedroom if that's okay. I don't mind bringing you up there to look. It would be fun to introduce you to my friends."

She tilted her head to the side, the red underneath her hair spilling through as she narrowed her eyes, curious. "YOUR Luke?"

I repeated what I had said over again in my mind and felt the splash of red trickling across my cheeks at her query. "My best friend, Luke, I meant," I mumbled, shuffling uncomfortably in my seat.

She hummed, but she was looking at me in a different light now; studying me, trying to figure out my secrets. "I'm scared to meet your friends, knowing one of them is the one that drew that." She lowered her head and looked down at her hands.

I stared at her, chewing on my bottom lip. "You don't want to meet them?"

The way she flushed was cute, the embarrassment not only lighting up her cheeks, but it devoured her neck and her ears, a full-on blush that covered probably a lot more of her body than I was able to see with her clothes on. She was dressed the way I usually did, wearing all black, and I guess I must have just lumped her in with the emo kids in school throughout the years if I ever did see her.

Serina had on a black leather jacket, the hood halfway over the back of her head, as if she had it pulled up at some point but it had been slowly falling, her hair spilling out underneath it. Her jeans were black and decorated in holes that while parents probably assumed they were hand-made, I knew they came like that since I was wearing a pair similar as well.

Once again I was comparing us, seeing how similar we were, and I smiled. I hoped I would be able to be friends with her, as I was with the others. "I did, but I didn't at the same time, you know? I guess I was just scared. What if they didn't like me? What if they saw me and thought: *'Oh, it's that weird Asian girl,'* Or they called me a lesbian slur or something?"

I cringed because I understood more than she probably thought I did. I had been so scared to meet with Green, scared they thought I was a loser because of Roan. Scared that they thought I was gay or with Isabella. But I lucked out with Luke being Luke. Even if we did have a rocky start, we worked out for the best. Well, maybe not the best, but close enough. It was close enough for me. It had to be. "I see," I looked down at my hands with a frown.

"I think you know more than you're letting on, Kins. Is there someone you're in love with?" I was silent for a while, and she leaned over, placed her hand on my knee, and patted it gently. "You don't have to tell me," she added, almost like an afterthought.

I nodded, rubbing my hand against the back of my throat as I once more looked up at my window. If the curtain had been in the way before, it was moved now because there was nothing there now. Maybe it had been Luke, looking down at us, but I doubted it. Why would he care? Maybe he had been curious. "Yes, I am," I whispered, trying to keep the broken sound out of my voice and failing.

"They don't love you back?" she asked quietly. "Do they know?"

I took a deep breath as I leaned forward, my elbows resting on my knees right next to her hand as I pressed my face into the palms of my hands. "No, to both questions."

She patted my knee once more before she pulled away. "Then problem solved, Kins, you just got to tell them! I'm sure they love you too."

I chuckled weakly, and even I could hear how sad it sounded as I turned my head to the side, resting my cheek against my hands, and stared at her. "That will never happen, Serina. Because he's straight."

I watched her curiously, knowing that what I had said was a big deal. I didn't go out of my way to tell people I wasn't straight, but because Serina claimed she was in love with Isabella despite not knowing who she was. I figured I should throw it out there. If she was homophobic, at least she would be homophobic to me. I'd rather take her scrutiny than allow her to be mean to Izzy.

Her expression went through a few different emotions, and it was as scary as it was entertaining, to say the least. Confusion, as she mouthed what I had said, trying to figure out why it was different from what she was expecting before she figured it out.

I gave her time to comprehend everything. She looked up at the window, then at me. I knew she had figured it out. "Your Luke?" She wondered, sadness in her voice.

I sat up, my hands pressed against my knees as I gave a sharp nod. "It started with letters, and the wrong locker," I let out a soft laugh as I started to slowly tell her my secret. I didn't try to romanticize it, but as I described to her how I had sat there watching, waiting, how I had felt so crushed when I saw who it was, she let out a soft breath.

As I explained to her what had happened in the art room, how he had turned me down, she leaned over and grabbed my hand, lacing her fingers with mine, and held my hand in her lap. It was hard, talking about the beginning, the middle, and the present. There was no ending, but I hoped there never would be. I hoped Luke would always be there, somewhere close by.

I wasn't stupid, I knew he would grow up and go off to college, and I would go off to college. He would forget all about me, but I would never forget him. I could never forget the one who had made me whole.

Once I was finished, we sat there and stared at the flickering lights that surrounded the gazebo. I felt vulnerable. I had explained my life to someone I had just met, but I felt like I could trust her. Maybe she was right, about the artwork. How it spoke to you, how it made you feel.

Her drawings were filled with promises, as if she had seen Izzy's hopeful soft pieces and was answering them in turn with a promise. A promise to be there, each step of the way, watching. A promise to always complete everything Izzy started, even if neither of them knew who the other was. A good person. Serina was a good person, and I could tell even more when she scooted closer to me, laid her head on my shoulder, and sighed.

She wasn't disturbed by my secret, by my sexuality. The more I got to know her, the more I wanted to tell her who Izzy was, but I wouldn't. I couldn't tell Izzy's secret, if it was meant to be, they'd find a way to each other on their own. "Are you straight?" I asked her after a few seconds of silence. She stiffened on me, and I couldn't help but chuckle as I shook my head. "You don't have to tell me. You and two others are the only ones who know about me."

She giggled softly as she swung her legs back and forth. Serina was tall enough to touch the ground but she must have lifted her toes to make herself feel smaller, like a little kid trying to touch the ground. "I'm bisexual. I never dated girls before, but I dated a boy once. I just know I'm attracted to both, so I'm not picky about the gender. This country sucks for people like us. I always thought when I got older I'd move far away, get a job somewhere in a big city, become a millionaire on my own, and throw the magazines of my success in my parents' faces."

I couldn't help but laugh with her because this seemed to be a theme for those of us outcasts who were trapped inside the prison of the small town. "Honestly, I'm tired of money. I won't care if I move into a small little shack somewhere in the middle of the woods and grow a beard. Just be poor, as long as I get away from my parents."

The way she laughed was loud, her head thrown back, and I couldn't help but laugh as she snorted, embarrassingly pressing her hands against her face at her outburst. "Oh my gosh, I snorted," She giggled, as we burst out into another fit of laughter. "I can't see you with a beard, please don't ever grow one. You're too pretty for a beard," she choked out through her laughs.

"Grandpa Kinsley," Serina breathed as we clutched our stomachs, lifting our fingers to our eyes to wipe at the tears.

I couldn't help but grin at her face. Her eyeliner was running down her cheeks and I lifted my sleeve to her eyes and wiped at it, a thankful nod as I cleared the smudged black from her eyes. I loved how she had her makeup, the dark eyes, the ruby red lips, and different colors of eyeshadow. I didn't know girls could do more than one, but I guess there wasn't a rule for it. She had different shades of red, lighter that gradually went darker, matching the color of the underneath of her hair.

The back door opened and we both turned to look as my father poked his head out. He had that smile in his eyes that he had earlier and I couldn't help but smile in return, despite knowing the only reason for it was I was doing something they wanted for the first time in a while. Although I couldn't pretend like it didn't make me feel better, a little bit.

Maybe if I was good, they'd like me again. I missed the way it felt when my parents liked me. My mom's hugs, my dad calling me champ, telling me he had been proud of me. I had missed being important to them, instead of just being the disappointment they had called me after I had refused to do sports anymore.

I let go of Serina's face and he smiled even wider at me, making me think he had probably thought we had been kissing. "Let's start wrapping it up, you love birds. The Changs are going to be leaving soon," He had even thrown in a wink.

He shut the door, and within seconds we started to laugh, both of us holding each other as we tried not to let each other fall. "We're love birds, did you notice?" I had to choke out the words as I had wiped at my tears.

Serina had giggled as she had run her fingers through her hair, the red had spilled out onto her hand as if it had been bleeding. "No offense Kins, but you feel like my long-lost brother,"

I grinned. "I feel the same way. Like you're my sister from another mister," After another round of laughter, we had quieted down for a while, the mood had turned fairly fast without us noticing. Both of us had been lost in our thoughts. While Father had said to wrap it up, I was fairly sure they would take forever, probably in there talking about our wedding. Serina had been born from a rich family lifestyle as well and had made no movement to hurry, both of our parents had been so similar.

All around us, the wind had softly blown, reminding me that it had been getting colder. While Serina had had on a thick leather jacket I had only run out there wearing my sweater, and it hadn't been as warm as I had wanted it to be. The wind had whistled with a promise of snow coming soon and I had smiled, wondering if it would come before Christmas, or after. It had been hard to tell there. While it had always snowed every year, it had never been consistent as to when it would. A few times it had waited until February to start, as if the snow had slept in, and had decided to rush to make up for its tardiness.

"We should pretend we're dating," she said suddenly, out of the blue. I looked at her, confused. "Your parents want you to date someone, right? I overheard your father saying it to my mother. He's been trying to force you on pointless dates with the girls of all the rich families, and I guess last night was my turn with you. If I was with you, my parents would ease off on me. Just because of last night, I've got two days of no lessons, and it's been marvelous."

Serina had her hands pressed on either side of her, holding onto the seat, looking forward as a small blush spilled over her cheeks in embarrassment. I guess I could understand that. It wasn't every day you offered to be a fake girlfriend to your new friend; it made sense she was embarrassed.

"You help me get some break from my parents' overbearing schedules, and I help you not have to deal with any more dates with snotty rich girls. Just two friends hanging out, telling everyone we're dating to make our parents happy. Then we graduate from high school, and honestly, we'll both probably be applying for the same colleges anyway with the way we drew. We can just tell them we broke up; we'd be hours away, and they couldn't do anything about it. We would be free then. What do you say?"

I thought about it, wondering if I could do it. What she said sounded awesome, to be honest. She knew I was in love with someone else, and I knew she was infatuated with the idea of someone else. Neither of us was expecting to be with each other romantically, and we had good chemistry together for it to be believable for our parents.

I hoped, in a way, it would make Luke believe it as well. The way he'd acted lately, I wondered if my being with someone else would make him feel more comfortable around me. It wasn't easy sleeping next to someone who wasn't straight when you were, and maybe the idea of me having a girlfriend would make him feel more comfortable.

I guess if it got too much, I could ask Dad for bunk beds again. He probably wouldn't care about it. While I wanted to be as close to Luke as I possibly could, I had to respect that he was straight and that he wasn't in love with me. He'd never be in love with me. There was, however, someone else I was worried about.

Izzy was a conundrum. She wasn't very good at keeping secrets, and I knew if I told her about Serina she'd get pissed off for so many reasons. She would like the idea of me dating her to appease my parents. Honestly, if it hadn't been for Serina being the tagger that was going over her work then she'd probably like her. But Serina didn't want to meet my friends, she wasn't ready for it, and I understood that. I knew if I told Izzy, she'd probably tell Luke, and then he'd be uncomfortable all over again with me.

"Can we keep it a secret from others? Luke. I think I'm too much for him. He knows I'm not straight and while he said he's not vain enough to think I'm in love with him, he's gotten distant from me pretty much ever since we moved in together and he's forced to share a space with me. He even put the pillow in between us himself last night, and usually, it's always been me putting it there. I know he's not homophobic but I think it worries him that I don't care about gender. If I'm dating you, maybe he'll feel more comfortable around me."

She placed her hand on my shoulder with a nod. "I told my cousin once, that there was a possibility I liked girls. I was younger, but she wasn't. I was around thirteen when I told her. She was around seventeen or eighteen. She looked so disgusted. I made the mistake of telling her when she was having a sleepover, a weekend sleepover for a holiday so a bunch of girls were over for four days in a row.

"The girls didn't want to go anywhere near me, they kept squealing about how I would try to touch them while they were sleeping, they were so uncomfortable around me. It was awful. By the time the slumber party was almost over I had gathered them all together and told them it was an assignment for class, I had to say something untrue and record how those around me handled it.

"Once being told I was straight the girls all rushed to hug me, suddenly I wasn't disgusting anymore to them. So, I get it. Straight people suck sometimes, they do. I'll keep your secret. You're keeping mine, after all, it's only fair,"

I felt relieved as I grinned at her. "And you have to try and consider meeting my friends. When you're ready. I'll be with them all day in school, and we all go to the art club after school. Well, besides Luke, he has football. But he shows up at the art club when he's done since I'm his ride."

She smiled, both of us stood up as the glass door slid open once more, and her mother called for her in Chinese. Her mother was white, and you could tell she wasn't fluent in Chinese, but she did a good job, in my opinion. Not that I could be a good judge of that, of course, since I had no idea what she was saying.

Serina looked at me with a bright smile that showed off her teeth. "Maybe one day I'll have enough courage to go tagging with you guys, instead of waiting for you to be done and answering back my lover's drawing."

I couldn't help but think it was funny, that Serina thought of Isabella as her lover, while Isabella thought of Serina as a middle-aged older man living in his mother's basement. I wasn't sure if the two of them would ever get together, with this rocky start, but who knows? At least neither of them was straight, so maybe it would work out for them.

I wrapped my arm around Serina's shoulder and grinned at her. "Come on, girlfriend. Let's go tell our parents and get the squeals over with," I said with a smirk.

"Ew, parents," she said, screwing her face up in disgust. The both of us were laughing once more as we walked inside.

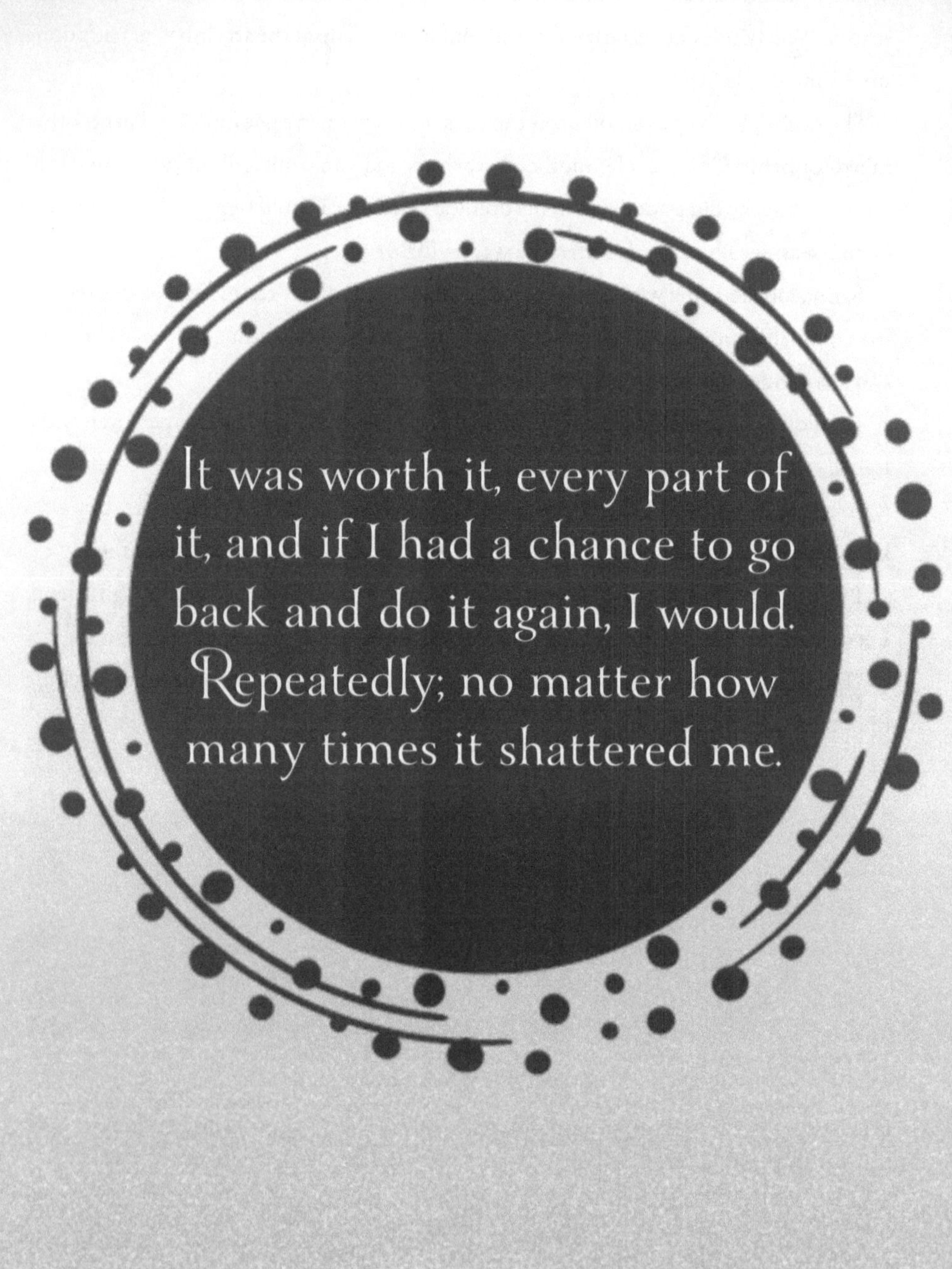

It was worth it, every part of it, and if I had a chance to go back and do it again, I would. Repeatedly; no matter how many times it shattered me.

Chapter 19
Kinsley

"What's up, my hoes?" Isabella asked, grinning at us through Luke's window. I was shocked for a moment because it had only been a few days since the last time I saw her, and there she was sporting her lovely dark brown hair with bright pink highlights in them.

It didn't even register to me what she had said until Luke replied to her. "We're your hoes now? Are you our pimp?" the corner of his lip twitched in amusement. He was sitting next to me in the passenger seat and Isabella was leaning against the window sill, her arms crossed in front of her as her chin rested on them. She had on her father's old army jacket again, her signature jacket she wore pretty much every day unless it was so hot she was melting underneath it.

It didn't surprise me she was wearing it now, we were all wearing a coat of sorts. I had on my black hoodie, and Luke was wearing one of them as well, surprisingly. Normally he wore his bright red football jacket, but I guess he was in a mood that day. He had been a little off for a while now, to be honest, and it was worrying me.

I hated lying to him, but I had to hope the news of me and Serina being together would be enough to snap him out of it. I was worried, given his background of suicide, and I wasn't able to stop myself from watching him. Worried at any moment I was going to lose him. "Yes, I'm y'all's pimp. Now get the hell out of my seat, please, and thank you, Curly," Isabella punctuated her words by unlocking Luke's door through the open window and opening it for him.

She even made a grand gesture of bowing slightly as she held onto the door, her free hand pointed outwards as if she were a butler leading someone down the hallway. Normally this would be when Luke would glance at me, when we'd hold each other's gazes and try to stop ourselves from laughing. Instead, he stood up, ruffed Isabella's hair, and earned himself a whack against his ass with her shoe as she shoved him in the backseat with a growl. I frowned, lost in my thoughts as I tapped my fingers against the steering wheel.

After Serina and I walked into the house last night, we wasted no time telling our parents about us. Kennedy was downstairs too, her boyfriend sitting on the couch with her as if she couldn't be away from him for even one night.

All six of them - my parents, Serina's parents, Kennedy, and Wyatt - sat there waiting and talking as we walked in. It was strange how all six of them had their eyes narrowed in on where Serina and I were holding hands, and the whole time I thought it felt strange to hold her hand when all I wanted to do was hold Luke's. Holding Serina's tiny and soft hand was like holding Isabella's, and I found my eyes searching the room, searching for him, always for him.

Luke had been standing there at the top of the stairs, holding a plate of cake in his hands as we walked in. He stopped halfway, his eyes fixated on mine and Serina's hands then lifted to my eyes. I couldn't watch him as Serina told my parents the news about our fake relationship. I couldn't look at him as they celebrated. All six of them stood up and cheered as they wrapped us in hugs.

I turned to look at Luke once more and he was smiling. He gave me a thumbs-up and walked up the stairs, leaving me alone in the middle of the celebration. I thought it was strange. Now my parents were happy with me, loved me, were excited for me, and I felt more than ever like I was trapped in a cage.

It was fitting that I had drawn Luke a key because I guess a part of me hoped he'd use it to free me. Instead, he smiled and walked away. He left me all alone with a family full of strangers when he was the only one I knew.

My parents were ecstatic, and all I could do was hide my sorrow behind grins and nods, because at least my parents were happy with the gender of the person holding my hand.

The car ride consisted of Isabella and Luke bickering. Luke teased her about her pink hair and she screeched at him. Apparently, it was supposed to be red, but she messed up and made it pink instead and now she was stuck with it for three months. If you dye your hair too much, it'll damage it, and she tended to wait three months in between. I wasn't sure if that was the way it worked or not, but I wasn't going to argue with her. The number of times Luke grunted in pain from her smacking him with the back of her shoe against his head was not something I looked forward to, even if it was slightly hilarious to watch.

I thought back to last night, to Luke. He had been awake when Serina and her family left. We were so awkward. He didn't ask me any questions, and I didn't want to answer them anyway. I promised him I'd never lie to him, and I guess a part of me hoped if I didn't directly look him in the eyes and tell him I was dating her, then I wasn't technically lying to him.

I was scared he'd bring it up, even a casual lift of his shoulder as he said, *'So, Serina, huh?'* would probably be enough to make me fall apart and cry to him. I'd spill all of my secrets, and I was glad he didn't. I was scared once I admitted it was fake, everything else inside me would tumble out, like word vomit, and I'd be left sitting there on my knees shaking with tears sparkling down my cheeks as the truth of my feelings for him poured out of me.

He hadn't said a word about it to me. He had smiled, his eyes lowered, looking to the side, away from me. Distance, as always, was there. I was slightly confused because I thought knowledge of me being with a girl would be enough to bring him back to before he moved in with me. But it was still there just as much as the pillow that never moved from between us or the vision of his back as he faced away from me. Maybe he needed time to get used to it, to see Serina and me together, and maybe then he'd stop being apprehensive about me. Otherwise, I wasn't sure what to do. God, I hope I didn't ruin us.

This morning wasn't much different. Soft smiles, quiet glances, and awkward tension. He made sure not to touch me, something that tore at me more than anything because, in a sense, touch was a part of us. No matter what our sexualities were, Luke and I always communicated by touches and stares. The feel of his hand as he twined it with mine, his fingers as he gently ran them down my arm and pressed them against the pulse of my wrist. I didn't know what to do with myself without his touch, and now when I looked him in the eyes, I couldn't read him.

My phone went off in my pocket and the car quieted down. It was Serina since the only other two people I talked to were sitting in the car with me. Luke stared out the window, his mouth shut with an audible snap, and I realized he had been in the middle of a sentence when my phone went off. "I'm sorry," I slid my finger down the side of the phone to stop the ringtone. I could still feel it vibrating against my leg. "Continue your conversation, I didn't mean to interrupt."

Luke was angry, I thought. His jaw clenched, his eyes hardened, and his lips tightened as his hands clenched tightly on top of his knees. It made me feel like a complete asshole for not silencing my phone before getting into the car, and for not paying attention to what it was they were even talking about. Lost in my thoughts, maybe it was something really important, that he was angry just from the mere ring of my phone interrupting their conversation.

"Who's that?" Isabella asked, her eyes wide as she looked at me.

I looked at Luke once more, confused. If they were talking about something serious she wouldn't look so hyper and uncaring that their conversation had been interrupted, but she was acting like nothing was going on. So why was he angry?

Though just as confused as before, a second glance at Luke through the rearview mirror showed a very different Luke from moments before. He had relaxed his body, his forehead pressed against the glass, his eyes lowered. Luke grabbed his hat out of his backpack, slipped it over his head, and lowered the bill over his eyes. "Our pretty boy has a girlfriend, Izzy," Luke mumbled, his fingers still holding onto the bill of his hat, hiding his face from my view.

Isabella squealed as I parked the car, and as I held my hand over the joystick I stared at Luke in the rearview mirror, wishing he'd move his hat, so I could see his expression. His voice with those words, all of it was wrong, every part of it. I felt like I was going to be sick. Then he lifted his head and I could see his eyes. Luke's lips curved into a soft smile as he nodded at me in the mirror. "Sorry, I told her before you could,"

I didn't give a fuck he told her first, I just was trying to recover from the way I felt like I was going to die and throw up at the same time. I guess I thought maybe if I moved on it would be easier. Not with Serina because she's infatuated with the idea of love for a drawing style. But if I had gotten another person, boy or girl, and tried to move on, I thought maybe it would be easier between us.

However, just seeing his smile, and hearing the sound of those words on his lips, how uncaring he was. How natural he sounded when he said it, destroyed me. I guess a part of me wanted him to be affected by it. A part of me wanted him to be angry, to yell, to scream, to fight for me. But here he was smiling. Though he had said multiple times he was straight though, so what did I expect?

I looked away as I turned the car off, and before I could look at him again he was out of the car, leaving me alone with Izzy. She knew my parents had been trying to force dates on me, but she also knew I had declined all of them. For me to have accepted one, that told her I had liked someone. She knew I wouldn't let my parents bully me into actually dating someone without wanting to, especially after what happened the last time I tried, with the letters in the wrong locker.

Isabella knew I had been planning on just going on pointless dates miserably until I turned eighteen since I didn't have much of a choice otherwise. Of all the things she knew about me, she would be surprised that Serina and I had come up with such a plan. I grinned sheepishly at her as we both got out of the car.

We barely had time to shut the doors and tug on our bags before Serina pulled up beside me. Izzy and Luke stared at the car in confusion because normally people didn't park next to me. Everyone knew my car by now, and I liked to park off to the side anyway to stay away from the front rows where Roan and his friends and the other rich kids liked to park.

I could see the mechanic in Luke eyeballing the car, taking in how expensive it was, studying it. I wondered if he knew who it was just by the look of the car. I knew who it was because I had a feeling that even though Serina said she didn't want to meet my friends, she wouldn't be able to resist once she started to come to school.

Besides, how could she be my girlfriend if we didn't hang out together during school, right? Both of us had kids who were friends with our parents and used them to gather information about us. If we were going to fake it, we needed to fake it right.

Serina stepped out of her car and pulled the hood of her black leather jacket down on her head, leaving Isabella the only one out of all four of us not wearing some sort of black coat. Maybe if I was going to change the art club to the outcasts club, the black coats should be part of a uniform requirement.

She looked slightly scared, but I didn't say anything because it was her decision. She didn't have to come over here to meet them, I wasn't making her. I was proud of her for being brave, however, especially so soon. I waited weeks to see Luke when I thought he was Peyton, and even after knowing he wasn't Peyton, I still waited about a week to see him. I couldn't blame Serina for wanting to do the same.

Isabella automatically took a step toward Luke, and I was surprised when Luke slid his fingers down her arm and laced their hands together in the way normally Isabella initiated. I realized I was staring at their joined hands for too long, as Serina cleared her throat, making me snap my eyes up to look at her. She had a sad look on her face, knowing what I was looking at, what I was thinking, and she was probably thinking the same.

If I only had two friends and there were two other drawings on the buildings, then these two were the others, Serina was thinking. That meant one of them had the drawing style she was in love with, and seeing them holding hands told her they were together. They weren't, but I still didn't like seeing it either.

"Serina, this is Isabella Reyes, and Luke Wilson, my best friends. Guys, this is Serina Chang–," *my girlfriend*, I tried to say, but failed, looking into Luke's beautiful sea-foam green eyes.

Thankfully I didn't need to say it, because everyone seemed to understand. "The girl from the picture," Isabella said with a nod. I frowned, my eyebrow raised as she looked at Luke, a silent exchange going on between them that made me both uncomfortable and unhappy at the same time.

While Luke seemed to have trouble touching me, he held her hand perfectly fine. While he had trouble looking me in the eyes, he had no problem staring at her. I was frustrated about it. A dark, horrible part of me wanted to blurt out to him that once upon a time Isabella kissed a girl herself, but I didn't want him to be uncomfortable around both of his best friends if he was struggling with it with one.

The bell went off in the distance, and Serina slipped her fingers against mine, lacing them together naturally. Luke and Isabella looked at our hands, then at each other, and while Luke looked away, Isabella grinned, mouthing to me something that looked like: *'I'm interrogating you later.'* I rolled my eyes because I didn't doubt it for a second.

It felt like the whole school was staring at us as we walked in the doors. Honestly, it wasn't; that was such a dramatic way of saying it, but I could see why people felt like that in movies. There were a lot of eyes looking at us though, staring at me and Serina holding hands, staring at Luke and Isabella holding hands, making silent assumptions.

They were used to seeing Isabella holding hands with both me and Luke at that point, but Serina was a new addition to the group. The doors opened up to the first-floor hall, filled with kids roaming around their lockers, trying to hurry and grab their books before the late bell went off. I had my books in Luke's locker, all three of us sharing all three of our lockers at that point, and wondered if I should risk it or just let it be, with how weird he was being. Then again, that year Luke, Izzy, and I had a lot of the same classes together and I knew he needed to go to his locker anyway.

Serina's cheeks were flushed under the attention, but she looked slightly excited as well, not that I could blame her. She said she hadn't had friends before, and I squeezed her hand a little for encouragement. Her eyes moved around me to study Luke, to study Izzy, as she tried to figure out which one it was she was in love with, I guess.

If I didn't feel like I was going to throw up, I'd tell her she was being cute. Did I look like that too when I was infatuated with the letters I was receiving from Green? "What's your first-period class?" She asked as we all headed up to the second floor. Isabella and Luke stood behind me and Serina since all four of us couldn't stand side by side on the stairs.

I felt eyes staring at me and assumed they were Isabella's. Probably scrutinizing me, trying to figure out what was going on. I knew I should have called her last night, but it was so fresh, so new, and I was still trying to figure everything out. It's not easy trying to come up with lies when the only people I've ever really lied to were my parents and Kennedy.

"We all have the same first period, English class," Last year Isabella and I were in Math class for our first period. Luke had his English class for the first period last year too, and he said the only thing that made it tolerable was the fact that we were in it with him this year.

We had pretty much all of the same classes this year since this school let their seniors pick the classes they were going to take and write down the order we wanted them. Of course, they had to run our requests through a system to make sure there was room for them, but pretty much we got what we wanted. Isabella and Luke had Spanish, and I had Italian, and while Isabella and I were in gym class this year, Luke was in weight lifting, but other than that, we were all pretty much the same. She nodded. "I'm in Math class for my first period. Text me your schedule, okay?" Her eyes tried and failed to not flicker over toward Isabella and Luke as he slowly opened his locker for all of us.

I smiled at her as she stood on her tippy toes and kissed my cheek, causing a few of the kids around us to ooh at us. "Damn Kinsley, did you get yourself a girlfriend? Maybe you're not a fag after all," Roan said, standing close enough to me that I could feel the heat of his skin against mine. He looked intimidating as he peered down at me, his eyes wide, and his mouth set into a wide grin, looking Serina up and down. "Serina," He nodded at her in greeting.

Roan took another step towards me as I gently shoved Serina out of the way. My back pressed against the locker behind me as I clenched my fingers against the metal, waiting for the blow. Before Roan could touch me, Luke punched the locker right next to my head. His eyes flashed with anger as he turned to look at Roan. Luke's body was stiff with anger and tension as he stared him down. Roan laughed as he took a step back and held up his hands. Despite his easy-going laugh, there was fear in his eyes as he slipped his hand to his face, seeming to remember the feel of Luke's fist against it at the end of last year.

Without a word, Roan turned and walked away, shoving one of his teammates away from him as if he had said something to piss him off. Luke turned to look at me, the anger in his eyes still there for a moment before they settled. The dark green shifted back to the sea-foam green I loved more than anything.

We stared at each other, and all I wanted to do was clasp his cheeks, brush my fingers against the soft skin, and hug him. To touch him once more and never let go. But then the bell rang, and Izzy shut Luke's locker. She had all three of our textbooks as Serina watched me and Luke with wide eyes filled with wonder.

Luke backed away fast, almost like someone had smacked him. He grabbed all three of our textbooks from Isabella as he grabbed her wrist with his other hand and yanked her away from us and down the hall towards the classroom. I let out a deep shaky breath as I turned to look at Serina, her head tilted to the side as she watched me.

"He's not the one I'm in love with, is he?" She wondered. I closed my eyes. I felt drained already even though school had just fucking started. I shook my head no, even if that meant I had exposed Isabella without actually saying it out loud. I was tired of being filled with so many secrets, they were slowly spilling out of me faster than I could breathe.

Serina's wide smile surprised me as I opened my eyes. "Good." With another kiss on my cheek, she waved goodbye and walked off. I have to admit I stood there longer than I needed to as I tried to comprehend everything that had just happened while kids ran screaming and laughing at each other towards their classrooms, even if we were all probably already in trouble for being late.

I shook my head, confused as I forced my legs to walk, despite how much they felt like jelly. I could still feel Luke's breath against my face, his eyes so close to mine, and I closed my eyes in the middle of the hallway as kids wove around me, pressed my face against the palms of my hands, and all I could do was silently scream.

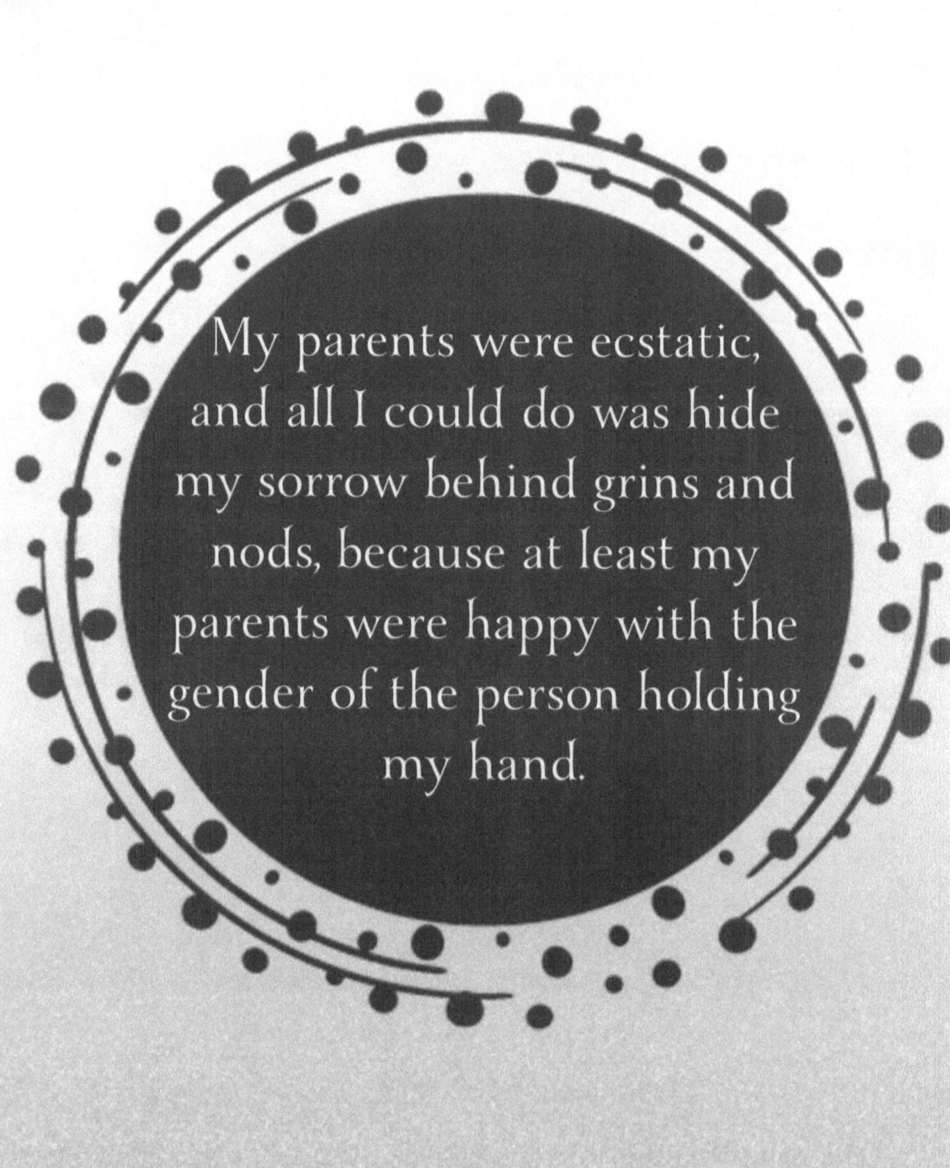
My parents were ecstatic, and all I could do was hide my sorrow behind grins and nods, because at least my parents were happy with the gender of the person holding my hand.

Chapter 20
Kinsley

For the first time in my life, I wondered if I was gay as I stared down at the little folded triangle in frustration. If I didn't think girls were attractive too, then I would have believed it because right now I was having a full-on drama queen moment as I stared at the little folded triangle. I couldn't help but wonder who decided it was okay to invent something so incredibly pointless as the concept of folding little fucking triangle notes.

I took a deep breath, then another, trying to calm myself down. It was just a note. I could do this, even if Isabella was pissing me off even more with how she was sitting there, her legs jumping up and down a mile a minute and her hands clasped across her desk. I could feel Luke's leg brush against mine, and I tried to hold in the shudder, contemplating whether or not I should move my leg or not, and decided it would be fine to leave it there. He wasn't moving either, and I was glad he hadn't noticed. Even this small touch, I craved, having been thoroughly deprived of it recently.

Luke and I sat side by side at a joint desk, which I never would have expected for English class, but I guess senior year was different than the others. There were a lot more group projects than before, and the main project required two people to work on pretty much for a whole semester or two for a final grade during the last quarter. At least I wasn't going to be forced to move around, thankfully, since Roan was in this class as well. He was currently sitting in his chair with only two legs balancing, and I kind of wished I had a straw so I could shoot a spitball at him and make him fall over.

Some boy who kept looking at Isabella and doing the sign of the cross whenever she started to draw was sitting next to her. It was funny at first. Isabella would sit there drawing things that horrified him, making him start bringing a bible to class, and when he wasn't looking, she slipped a crude drawing of a little red satan into it, making him miss school for almost a week. However, now she mostly ignored him, only paying attention to him when she felt bored.

I could feel Luke's breath against my ear since this teacher forced me to have my hood lowered, making sure we weren't hiding headphones in our ears. I was glad English was one of my best subjects because I had trouble concentrating when all I wanted to do was look at him. He was leaning close to me, most likely waiting for me to open the letter. Normally when Isabella threw them over here, they were for both of us, instead of just me. However, I had a feeling this one was just for me, and I was dreading what it could say.

As I started to unwrap the triangle, Luke's fingers pressed against my wrist for a moment, sending a tingle through my body as the hair on the back of my neck stood up. I looked at him in confusion and realized it wasn't anything. Of course, it meant nothing to him. He had just been trying to stop me silently as the teacher looked over at us. I waited as the teacher watched us. The pressure of his fingers against my wrist made me wish I could be brave enough to slide my fingers with his in the middle of the classroom without having to worry or care what everyone else thought.

There was a girl who was lying on her boyfriend in front of us, and I hated how they were leaning, how they were holding hands, whispering, giggling, and kissing. No one batted their eyes at them, but if it was two guys, the whole school would flip out. Finally, the teacher moved on, turning around to write on the board. I was still focused on the feel of Luke's fingers on my skin and not the letter as I opened it. I didn't even look at it until Luke pulled his fingers away from my wrist. I had to read over it three times to see what it was she wrote, as wrapped up in my feelings for Luke as I was.

'So, tell me all about Serina Chang, and don't think that just because I'm excited that I'm not pissed off at you for not telling me earlier.'

I heard Luke sigh, but I tried not to think about it as I tapped the lead of my pencil against the paper. Luke was doing something, and with a glance at him, I noticed he was doodling something on his paper. He had a frown on his face, his eyes down in an almost sad way as he focused on the paper, and nothing else. I shook my head, unsure why he was acting like that, and felt the absence of his knee against mine as he pulled away from me.

I guess I was just confused. I thought everything would get better once I agreed to be Serina's boyfriend, but it seemed like everything was just as tense as before. Maybe he just needed some more time to believe it. Maybe he needed to see us together more often. If he saw us acting like a couple, he wouldn't be worried about it anymore, I was sure of it.

'Serina is fun, I think you'll like her. She likes the same bands as me. She's pretty much a genius. She knows Chinese, and she dyes her hair like you do,' I wrote. I wanted to gush about Serina to her, to make sure that no matter what was going on, Isabella could see how awesome Serina was. I didn't want Isabella to hate her, knowing that Serina was just like me, in a way.

I could see myself in her, in the way she stared at Izzy's drawings with a happy lovesick look on her face, or the way she stared at Izzy, her eyes following her once she found out that if it wasn't Luke who had been drawing the pictures, it was Izzy. They were both bisexual, I was fairly sure since I never really asked Izzy, and I hoped more than anything that while I wasn't ever going to get my happy ending with the other half of my soul, at least maybe she could. Even though I just met Serina, she was so important to me already. Like the sister bond I never really had with Kennedy. She was someone I wanted to protect, to help, to be there for. I just wanted everyone to be happy, even if I never truly would be.

Luke chuckled softly under his breath and I looked at him in surprise. "Of course she knows Chinese, Kins. It's her heritage. Just like you and Isabella are being sneaky getting by using the languages you already know to be your four language credit classes for college."

It bothered me that he was smiling. That he was reading about me talking about someone else, and he didn't care. I let out a shaky breath as I folded the paper into a normal square and threw it at Isabella when the teacher wasn't looking. I was quiet, Luke was quiet, and I wanted nothing more than to lean over and lay my head against his shoulder. I was exhausted already, and I just wanted to go to sleep.

"It's good, Kins," Luke said softly, his lips resting above my head, his breath tickling against my cheek. I hadn't even realized I had put my head down until he spoke and my cheeks flushed, knowing I had been lost in my thoughts staring at him.

Everyone had gotten used to the weird sudden friendship of me, Luke, and Isabella, and seeing us together never really caused any sort of oohs and awes as it did when Isabella was alone with one of us. No one ever saw two guys and thought about how they might be together. No, everyone always assumed everyone was straight until said otherwise, and then they'd just look at the guys like they were disgusting and move as far away from them as possible. Or in Roan's case, they'd beat the shit out of me for something I couldn't even control.

"It's good that you have things in common with her. She seems nice," his voice was barely a whisper as he looked to the side while he spoke. Mostly, I was distracted by the way he had looked at me. The look in his eyes, how they held something unreadable. I wanted to ask him what it was he was thinking. For so long I knew Luke by sight, and I had been able to tell what he was thinking just by the way his eyes peered into mine. I didn't know this expression and it startled me.

His fingers rested on his desk, his pinky finger brushed against my elbow, and I didn't move, because even that small touch was enough to send fire burning through every part of me. I wanted to move my elbow closer, to feel him slide his finger against my hoodie, or to slide his hand up my clothes, to touch every part of me. I sucked in a soft breath, shifting my body slightly, annoyed by my sudden thoughts and what they were doing to me, uncomfortable.

He struggled to smile, and then the smile slowly slipped into a frown, and sat up. I pulled my arm back, my pinky finger resting beside his, neither of us moving them. He was looking at his finger, and I was watching him, wondering if he was fine with touching me, or if he was trying to figure out how to pull away without being rude.

"Why are you-" I started to whisper before my pocket vibrated. I had my leg pressed up against the bottom of the desk from when I was shifting around, and it vibrated the wood, making Luke flinch in surprise just as I had done.

He jerked his pinky finger away from mine, and I stared sadly down at my finger, my lonely finger, burning for the feel of what had been, and what I wanted more than anything again. I felt like no matter how close I was to him, I was so far away, and I worried I'd never find my way to where I belonged.

I knew it was either Serina or Isabella. However, I had a feeling it was Serina since she had told me to text her my schedule, and I did so when I first sat down. I pulled my phone out of my pocket and peered down at it, feeling Luke do the same since where I had the phone sitting was half on my leg and half on his. While I enjoyed the fact that we were so close, it was torturous as well. So close, but not close enough, never close enough.

'Hey, Kins! We have three classes together, and we never noticed!' she texted with a laughing emoji after the words. I smiled because there was just something so fun about Serina, about her excitement to have a friend, and to be friends with me. I guess since she grew up feeling like she hadn't belonged with much of anyone, it must have been exciting for her to finally have someone she could talk to, to be herself with, someone who understood her.

Another text popped up, and I felt Luke's breath against the side of my neck. I wanted to turn my head, to press my lips against his, but I forced myself to take deep breaths, calm my raging teenage hormones, and concentrate. *'My parents probably already talked to your parents about this, so don't be surprised to go home and see them having clothes ready for you, but there's a party at my house tonight.'*

I raised my eyebrows at that in surprise, my head tilted to the side as my forehead brushed against Luke's cheek. He let out a soft startled noise and moved slightly. Not enough for him to be unable to read the next text that was coming in, but enough that he wasn't touching my forehead. It seemed like when Serina was excited about something, she was the type of person who texted short texts, one after the other. I could just see her sitting there poised, ready to send message after message before I could even reply to one.

'It's going to be strange since my parents arranged it for me, but they won't be there. I guess they wanted to set me up with all of the rich boys out there, the same your parents were doing to you, but they didn't expect me to get a boyfriend before the party happened. They can't go back on the invites now though, and all of the rich kids are coming.'

I rolled my eyes. I wasn't looking forward to going to a party filled with a bunch of the richer kids in this town all sitting around staring at each other or making out with their boyfriends or girlfriends while some ridiculous classic music played in the background and everyone sipped martinis.

I frowned as I started to reply to her. *'That sounds boring as hell, Serina. I don't want to hang out with a bunch of rich assholes. you're the only one I like, plus Roan will be there messing with me and it just sounds like it'll be awful.'*

Luke sighed beside me, and I knew he had still been silently reading our texts. Maybe someone else would have been annoyed by the lack of privacy, but I had mostly just wanted him to move closer, to lay his head on my shoulder. Besides, if I had been forced to go to this party by my parents, then he had been too. I had known he hadn't been working tonight, his boss had taken off an extra week for the holiday to go visit a friend somewhere he had said, and the shop had been closed for another week because of it.

It wasn't even a second or two later when she replied. *'I know, Kins, trust me. I don't want to go either when I think about all of the rich asshole kids that'll be there. But then I had an idea, and I think you'll like it. My parents aren't going to be there. They're flying to China for the week to visit family there and left me behind for the party. I have the butler who's supposed to be watching me, but I paid him off so he'll give me the night of freedom. Do you want to know my idea? I'm excited, and you need to be excited too!'*

I let out a soft chuckle as Luke moved back closer to me and rested his cheek against my temple once more. I wondered slightly what this must have looked like to people, but those behind us could tell by our position that we were both looking down at my phone. They probably thought we were playing a game together or something to pass the time.

'Yes, tell me your idea.' I wasn't that interested, to be honest. I was more focused on Luke touching me, something he hadn't done much lately besides when I drew on his arm and he danced with me.

I was so focused on my thoughts of dancing with Luke, of feeling his fingers sliding up and down my back, tangling in my hair, that I jumped when the phone vibrated again. Luke snorted at me as I nearly dropped it.

His breath tickled my neck as he breathed out a whisper to me. "Careful, Pretty Boy." I felt the blush spread fast over my cheeks, my ears, and down my neck, and imagined the rest of my body was covered so fiercely in the red that adorned my cheeks that I would have resembled a tomato at that point.

He called me pretty boy, something I was so used to Isabella calling me, but never Luke. I sucked in a deep breath and forced myself to chuckle when I wanted desperately to look at him and beg him to say it again. To see what his expression was when he said it.

I closed my eyes, counted to five, and opened them, trying to cool the blush as I looked down at her text again. *'I figured, screw it, right? I printed out flyers for the party and slipped them in everyone's lockers a few minutes ago. I got permission from the teacher to go to the library. So who knows how many people will be there. Cool, right? My first party! You'll be there, right? With Luke and Isabella?'*

I didn't reply, because I was waiting for Luke to say something. I knew I'd have to ask Isabella, she'd have to ask her mother first, but at least Luke who was sitting next to me reading over my shoulder could reply. "I guess. It's not like I'll have a choice, she's right. Your parents probably have clothes laid out just waiting for us to come home and put them on." He whispered. I wanted to tell him that we could just run away. Just us, all alone, forever. But obviously, that wasn't going to happen.

Instead, I replied to her. *'I'd have to ask Isabella, but Luke said he was fine with it.'*

'Sweet! I got the idea for the lockers from you, I hope you don't mind. You know, about how you told me about how you and Luke became friends? Except this time, it's not the wrong locker since I put them in everyone's lockers.' She said with another laughing emoji.

I smiled, replying to her that it was fine, that I didn't mind her using my idea and a laughing emoji. I was still smiling as I slipped my phone into my pocket and looked up at Luke, who was so close to me I could feel his breath against my cheek. My smile slipped, however, taking in the expression on his face.

"You told her? About the lockers, the letters, all of it?"

I nodded slowly with a frown on my face because I wasn't sure why that mattered. "Yeah, we talked about a lot of things recently. I told her how I met you, Isabella, and everything. She's not going to tell anyone, you don't have to worry, I trust her."

He was quiet as he stared at me. He pulled away slightly to sit back in his chair, twirling his pencil around his fingers as he turned to look at it. I wasn't sure why he looked upset. Maybe it was because he didn't know her and I told her about the letters without really asking him if he was okay with it. I didn't know it was a big deal, but maybe it was, to him. "I'm sorry-" I started to whisper as he lifted his head, and gave me a soft smile.

"It's okay, Kins. She's your girlfriend, after all, it's understandable you don't want to keep secrets from her."

I stared at him silently as he turned away from me. He looked down at his paper once more, and I sighed, lowering my eyes to mine. *Girlfriend,* I whispered in my mind. I was starting to wish I had never agreed to any part of it. I just wished he hadn't been so uncaring about it, while I felt like I was dying.

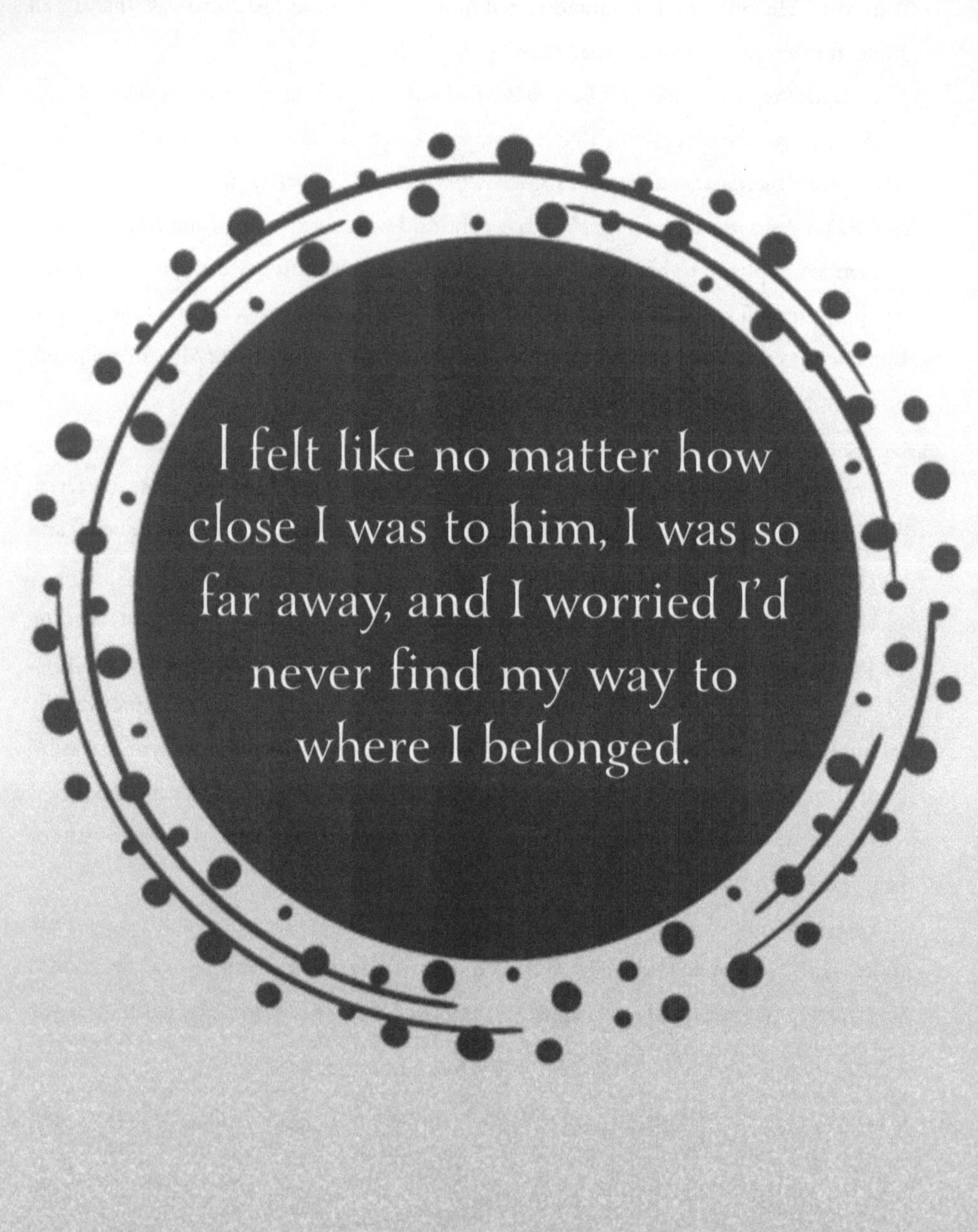
I felt like no matter how close I was to him, I was so far away, and I worried I'd never find my way to where I belonged.

Chapter 21
Luke

My head throbbed as I stood there, watching Kinsley put his phone and wallet in his pants pocket. I tried as hard as I could to not check him out, but wearing the tux and dress pants his parents had forced both of us into made it hard for me not to stare at him. It was kind of funny how now that I had accepted I was in love with him, I couldn't stop myself from staring at him, from wanting him.

The differences between what I felt for him and the two girls I had dated in the past were startling to me. *He has a girlfriend, he's not interested in you, and you're going to end up losing him and ruin everything if you don't calm down.* I told myself firmly. I let out a soft breath, closed my eyes, and counted to ten. I leaned against the doorframe, my arms crossed, as I tried to tell myself it was going to be okay when I wasn't sure if it would ever be okay.

"Are you okay?" Kinsley asked.

His voice was soft and close, and I opened my eyes fast, nearly having a heart attack over how close he was. He had moved so quietly that I didn't hear him coming near me, and now he was so close that I could lean over and kiss him. I licked my dry lips almost as a reflex as he pressed his hand against my forehead, causing me to flinch and jerk my face away.

I looked down in an attempt not to see how I had hurt him, but why couldn't he see that the more he touched me, the more I wanted to beg him not to stop? I felt like I was ready to fall to my knees and beg him to choose me, to love me, but he wasn't interested in me. Ever since the beginning, he had only ever wanted to be friends. I had been forced to ask someone out, resulting in the letters.

'Maybe we'll end up hating each other. It doesn't matter anyway though, because no names, right?'

I let out a deep breath. My jaw clenched as I curled my hands into tight fists at my sides. "I'm fine, just tired," I forced out, hoping he'd buy it. I wasn't able to look him in the eyes when his hair was off his face like that and his eyes were so bright and so startling blue I was afraid I'd get lost in them and he'd notice.

What if we ended up hating each other in the end? The letters might have been over, but we were still there, just an advanced form of the letters. There could still be an ending, right? Friends split up constantly for the most stupid of reasons. Tony stopped talking to me when I started being friends with Izzy, telling me he had a crush on her and it wasn't cool that I was dating her. I told him I wasn't even dating her and he didn't believe me. It didn't bother me all that much, but if it was Kinsley who left, it would have destroyed me.

It was simpler back then when all I had to worry about was whether there would be a letter in my locker or not. Now I was worried about everything, and I felt like if it kept going like this I'd end up having an ulcer. Kinsley was frowning. I didn't look at him, I couldn't look at him, but I knew he was frowning all the same.

I wanted to ask him if Serina could feel his happiness radiating from him as I could. If she could sense when he was upset, if she'd ever seen him at his lowest breaking point, or how even despite him being so angry he was able to throw all of that anger away just to hold me and make sure I was fine.

I wanted to ask her if he would ever do any of that for her, but I already knew the answer. She was the one he was interested in romantically, not me. It had never been me from the start. Kinsley was quiet, seeming to sense my mood as his mother walked up the stairs and clapped, excitement in her eyes as she looked at us.

'Or maybe...just maybe...we'll end up falling in love. Maybe we'll be the type of romance that's talked about, the type of romance that everyone envies and wishes they could have,'

I wondered about that, so quietly in the back of my mind, remembering the words Kinsley had written almost like an afterthought. Compared to his other letters, the first one he had written was shaky, like he had been scared, despite the words he said sounding so confident. A romance that everyone envies. I laughed quietly, and Kinsley looked at me as his mother's fingers straightened his already straight tux, her fingers messing with his already jelled hair.

I doubted anyone would envy the desperate way my soul longed for his, just to watch him love someone else.

"Maybe I should come with you guys. The Chang family and ours will be joined together one day, after all. It would be nice to get to know them more."

I looked down at my hands, wondering if there was a way I could have felt more lost than I did then, and I felt it then. The way Kinsley felt, trapped in a beautifully decorative prison. It had been so hard to breathe, standing in this hallway listening to Kinsley try to shush his mother, to tell her maybe she could invite them over another time. Listening to Kinsley and his mother talk about the woman I guessed he would possibly marry one day. It reminded me of the time he and I had talked about marriage.

Kinsley believed in marriage, and I was just lost. I doubted he was that serious about her yet; it had only been a few days. But wasn't that how it worked? His parents were proud of him, and he was happy. He was happy with her, in a way he'd never be with me. I wasn't sure if I could handle being his while he was someone else's, but my heart didn't seem to care about that. It beat on the same wavelength as Kinsley's, no matter how painful it was.

'Maybe I should try again,' the little voice popped back into my head.

I flinched, noticeably, as I clenched my hands into tight fists, trying to hide the shaking. It had been so long since I had that thought, that little darkness inside me, pulling at me, begging me to touch it once more. Kinsley's mother must have left at some point, having been convinced to leave and not come with us, because the next thing I felt was his arms wrapping around my waist, his head nudging mine to lift just enough for him to scoot his nose under my chin, tucked inside my embrace where he belonged.

The way I held him was so desperate, filled with so much longing that it nearly took my breath away as he touched me. I was shaking, my heart was quaking, and I was scared more than anything he could feel it. *Why can't you feel how desperately I love you?* I wished he could read what I was too scared to say out loud.

Kinsley pulled back enough that he could look at me, his hands gripping my waist tightly, neither of us pulling away. I chewed on my lower lip, watching the way his cheeks pinkened, as if a paintbrush had danced across his skin, lighting up those dimples I loved so much with their beautiful shade. His eyes were so bright and sparkling, so luminescent that I licked my lips, feeling my breath fade away.

"Kins, I-"

"Alright, boys, no drinking, no drugs! Don't forget there'll be a cup for both of you on the counter in the bathroom when you get home! We'll be heading out as well, an emergency at the office. Use condoms!" Mr. Bryant shouted, a deep chuckle rumbled from him as Kinsley and I broke apart. I could hear his mother smack his father and his father chuckled at her while Kinsley scoffed, rolling his eyes.

I felt like I was an open book, my body shaking and my heart racing. What the hell was I about to do? What the hell was I about to say? I almost ruined everything. "What was it you were about to say?" Kinsley asked, his voice soft as he stared at me.

Kennedy walked out of her room, digging in her oversized bag. "I was just going to tell you we were going to be late," I muttered quietly.

He frowned but nodded, and together we walked past Kennedy, who was cursing under her breath, searching for her keys to lock her bedroom door. The ride to Isabella's house was quiet and filled with tension. I ended up sitting in the backseat, not because I didn't want to argue with Izzy but because I just couldn't be so close to him right then. I was embarrassed over what I had almost said, my fingers wove paths in my curls and pulled at the gel, making it a mess as I sat there thinking.

What if he knows? I stressed. *What if he finds out? What if he hates me?* I wanted to jump out of the car every time he looked at me. His alluring full lips were pressed into a tight line as he stared. Every red light, every stop sign, he tried to understand what I was hiding. Too perceptive, he was too much sometimes, and I felt like I couldn't breathe.

By the time we got to Izzy's, I felt like I was naked, sitting back here with a sign on my forehead screaming out at the top of my lungs on repeat how much I loved him. I tried to distract myself by staring out the window, looking in wonder as we approached a house that was bigger than Kinsley's. I wondered if that meant the Chang family was even richer than the Bryants were and if that was the main reason why they were sucking up to him so much.

I wanted to scream at them that gender didn't matter, but in the end, who was I to say anything? Before I realized I was in love with Kinsley, I was closed off, unsure of my feelings, of my identity. I was scared to touch him, scared to dance with him, scared to do anything that would perceive me as gay.

Now I didn't care. I just loved him, and that's all I cared about. Even if I was in love with the him that wasn't in love with me.

I could feel the music before we even made it down the large and intricate driveway. Everyone seemed to be smart at this party. I've been to one before, Lana dragged me to it, and after that, I refused any more. At Lana's party, there were cars everywhere, piled up and squeezed together to the point where most had to wait for others to leave, to be able to leave themselves. Here, the cars were to drive up to the front, where a handful of butlers were standing and waiting. For us to give them our keys, to park our car for us.

It was smart because we'd have to get our car from them to leave. The man standing to the side with a machine in between his legs and a book in his hands was enough to tell me she had a breathalyzer ready, so they could check to make sure no one was driving home drunk. I hated that Serina was kind, to know she was a good girl, that she cared and she was smart. It made me sick in my stomach because while I wanted to hate her, I couldn't. I just felt numb.

Kinsley parked, leaving the car on, and slipped out as the butlers opened all of the doors for us. I was reminded again of Lana's party where everyone had to show off their invitation, but here they didn't seem to care. The butlers just bowed and pointed the way inside. The music was too loud to even hear unless we were pressed against each other screaming into their ears. It was pounding so hard I felt the pain in my chest, the throb of the drums beating through me. The screech of the guitar and the rasp of the singer.

We walked into the strangest scene I've ever been a part of. There was a variety of those whose parents forced them to dress nice like Kinsley and me, and those that were as slutty as they could be. Almost immediately the rich kids were throwing their tuxes off to the side, a pile of them scattered near a rack that did have a few hung up neatly.

As the lights pulsed around us, the girls took off their dresses and stood uncaring in their bras and panties. The boys hooted and hollered at them as they begged the ladies to stay half-naked. Some of them obliged, but some of them grabbed the dress shirts off of the guys closest to them. They slipped them on and danced around in their dress shoes, their arms in the air as they shook their hips side to side to the beat of the music.

I already wanted to go home. I couldn't breathe, the air was thick with pot smoke and cigarettes, reminding me that I hadn't smoked since the night I chain-smoked outside of the Thanksgiving party. For some reason, the smell of smoke made my stomach churn now as if I had smoked so much I felt disgusted by it that night.

But Kinsley was grinning, and that alone made me stay still. His eyes moved around the room as he took everything in, the cerulean color glowed in the dim pulsating lights as he yanked his tux off and threw it at the pile on the ground. Serina seemed to appear out of nowhere, her eyes wide and rimmed with red, a drunken haze had her eyes glazed over as she wrapped her arms around Isabella's shoulders and kissed her on her cheek.

"Hello, gorgeous!" Serina screamed, and I nearly chuckled as Isabella looked at me for help with flushed cheeks. She wasn't sure what to say, and I couldn't blame her. A girl I didn't recognize ran up to me, her fingers quick to grab at my white shirt under my jacket, ripping it open and making the buttons break off.

I gasped, my eyes wide as I looked down at my chest in surprise. The girl giggled, turned around, and ground back against me. I was shocked by the sudden motion of this stranger and I pressed my hands against her waist to stop her as I looked at Kinsley.

I couldn't read his expression, his jaw clenched as he stared at her, at me, and then turned his back to me. He grabbed Serina's wrist as he tugged her towards the dance floor and she lifted her hand in the air, pumped it up and down, and cheered.

Isabella grabbed the girl touching me by the hair and yanked her off of me, her face screwed up in disgust. "Ya nasty! Get that dirty thing off of my Curly!" Her eyes were flashing, her heel already in her hand as she glared at the girl menacingly. The girl gasped, her hands in the air as she stared at the shoe and ran off, leaving me and Isabella alone.

I sighed in relief as Isabella grabbed my shoulder to use me to balance on one foot so she could put her shoe back on. I leaned over and pressed my lips against her ear so she could hear me. "Thank you, I was slightly traumatized,"

I pulled away as she laughed at me. She looked gorgeous in her dress. Not slutty like most of the other girls, and not expensive and unnecessary either. She had on a spaghetti top dress that had belt loops, her signature two studded belts draped over each other as her skirt flared around her knees. It was a black dress but there were colors on it like she'd taken a handful of different paints and flicked them onto the dress, glow-in-the-dark paint that was making her stand out in the dim light. She had black webbed tights on underneath the skirt and black heels, the pink in her hair standing out as well.

"Let's dance!" She shouted with a tug on my wrist.

I pulled my tux and my shirt off and threw them to the side, not caring about them anymore since they were both ruined. It was too dark in there for anyone to see my scar unless they had decided to grab my wrist and hold it under a light. I tried to ignore the scar, forget about it, and relax.

It wasn't like I was the only shirtless guy around there anyway, and as Isabella pulled me into the middle of the dance floor I wasn't surprised to watch Serina pull Kinsley's shirt off as well. I frowned, as she slipped it onto her shoulders as if in an act of ownership, and it pulled at me. Seeing her smaller body in his shirt, the way he threw his head back and laughed at her churned my stomach at the sight.

Isabella put my hands on her hips, and for a while, I was lost dancing with her. My eyes closed, I felt her body against mine, and I just danced. I didn't want to think about Kinsley and the way I wished I was dancing with him instead. I wished he was wearing my clothes instead of giving her his. I wished he was wrapped in my arms instead of holding her against him.

Every time I opened my eyes, I seemed to see him staring, watching me. My cheeks were on fire, and I was confused. As Isabella handed me a cup, I stared at it for half a second before I ended up dumping it upside down onto Serina's hardwood floor. Isabella was too drunk to notice by now that I wasn't drinking, and I felt like it was my little act of rebellion against Serina. By spilling the harsh-smelling liquid onto her floor, even though it wasn't the first spill there and wasn't going to be the last.

I didn't know how long we danced before we stepped away. Isabella seemed to make herself my date, and I didn't mind because she was scary enough to keep the other girls away. Everyone seemed to think we were dating anyway now since Serina was with Kinsley, and that left me and Izzy to mock. The number of rumors I've heard of them thinking Kinsley dumped Isabella for Serina, or Isabella left him for me and Serina was his rebound.

For some reason, they all thought Izzy was a player, going back and forth between us, and she just kept laughing because she never dated either of us. It didn't help that when someone asked her who kissed better, me or Kinsley, she said I did and winked at me. I highly doubted that, to be honest, since she had kissed me in a drunken haze and I didn't even move, but it was enough to keep the rumors going.

"Paint!" A chant went throughout the room as Isabella pulled me back onto the dance floor and I watched in confusion as Serina and Kinsley were both standing in front of a table filled with buckets of paint. Both of them had mirrored looks of mischief on their faces. I didn't know when the table or the paint was placed there, but others went up to it, helping them open the cans as the lights dimmed even more. The paint glowed in the dark. Serina stuck her hands in the paint and wasted no time sliding it down Kinsley's chest, leaving behind lines of blue.

Kinsley had his hands buried in the green as Isabella dragged me over to the table, a grin on her face. She grabbed a pink paint bucket and started flinging handfuls of paint at the girls that were close by. Shrieks blended with the music as ladies complained about their dresses while others rushed to the table and got handfuls of paint, chasing everyone around.

Kinsley was suddenly in front of me, a glimmer in his eyes as he slammed his hands onto my chest. He slid his fingers down my body and tugged at my pants, yanking me against him as his stomach brushed against mine. I stared at him with wide eyes as he grinned at me with a mischievous look on his face.

I pressed my hands against his waist to steady myself for a moment, then moved my fingers, wet with the blue paint, as I cupped his cheeks and tilted his head higher. I wanted to kiss him in a way I'd never wanted to kiss anyone before, and even though I hadn't drunk anything, I felt drunk under the dim lights. The glow-in-the-dark paint lit us all up, and the music pounded in time with my heartbeat. I stared at him, my heart racing, but before I could say or do anything, we were shoved apart by people who wanted to get to the paint on the table.

The paint had hardened slightly on my skin as Isabella appeared out of nowhere and tugged me against her, dancing with me. Her head was thrown back as I twirled her, but my eyes were on Serina and Kinsley, dancing. I didn't know why I could see them so clearly through the bodies of glow-in-the-dark paint, everyone mostly naked now as they danced. The lights moved and lit up random people, leaving the rest of the room darker, lit up with the colors of paint splattered over everyone.

I winced as a spotlight moved slowly above me. My heart was racing as I watched Serina laughing. She tripped over something and slammed into Kinsley as he grinned down at her drunken self. I stood still, my blood pounding in my ears as she cupped his cheeks and rose on her tippy toes. Her lips pressed against his, and I stopped breathing. My chest tightened painfully as I gasped, my eyes wide, frozen in shock.

Hands pressed against my eyes, masking me in darkness as tears slid down my cheeks. The feel of lips against my ear as I let out a quiet sob. My body was shaking, I had to struggle to draw in a breath. "Did you figure it out yet?" Isabella breathed. "Your feelings?"

I pulled her hands off of my eyes and looked into hers. Even though she was drunk, she looked sad, watching the way I was breaking. She tried to stop me from looking, but it was too late. I wiped my eyes and looked up to see Kinsley and Serina pull apart, and Kinsley's eyes found mine. I felt the frustration build as I looked down at Isabella as I pulled away from her. "I'm going home," I yelled at her so she could hear.

She nodded, glanced at Kinsley, then at me, and nodded again. "Go ahead, I'll crash here for the night. I'll make Serina take me home."

I nodded and she leaned on her toes to press a soft kiss against my cheek. I thanked her once more for being my friend, and for understanding me, and then I walked away. I felt anger spill through me as I moved past the sweaty, paint-splattered bodies. It was irrational, the anger.

Regardless, I was angry that he put his damn letter in my locker and made me feel like I was someone important. Angry that he opened me up, that he came into my life. That he saw me when no one else did. Angry that once again I just wasn't enough.

I shoved the doors open so hard the butlers jumped in surprise. They paused for a moment before rushing to me. "Going home, sir? What was the number you were given? Or would you like me to call you an Uber?" The one with the breathalyzer asked.

I frowned, unsure because Kinsley had it. Kinsley who was probably going to stay here and lose his virginity that night. Another shudder of anger raced through me as the doors opened behind me. I closed my eyes because even before he spoke, I knew it was him. "Number forty-eight," Kinsley said as he reached around me to hand them the paper. The man made me breathe into the breathalyzer and turned to Kinsley, who I was surprised to hear hadn't drunk anything either.

"You don't have to leave because of me, Kinsley," my voice was clipped, I was unable to keep the anger out of my voice as the man pulled the car around. "Stay with your girlfriend," I tried so hard not to sneer, but I was so angry I could barely breathe.

Kinsley sighed. I couldn't look at him as the man stepped out of the car, leaving it running for us. "I'm going home, Luke. I had already paid for a cab for Izzy, she didn't want to leave yet. Just, come on."

I was surprised when he slipped into the passenger seat since it was his car, but I didn't question it and got into the driver's seat, gripping the wheel tightly. We lit up the inside of the car with our different paint, and if I wasn't angry, I would have thought it was funny, the choice of colors. Since Kinsley was blue, light blue like his eyes, and I was green, like mine. "Just drive home, Luke,"

I felt like crying again as I silently pulled out of the driveway. My hands shook as I sucked in a deep breath and let it out slowly. *I was home the moment you held me. The moment you looked me in the eyes and smiled. I just wish I could have figured it out sooner.*

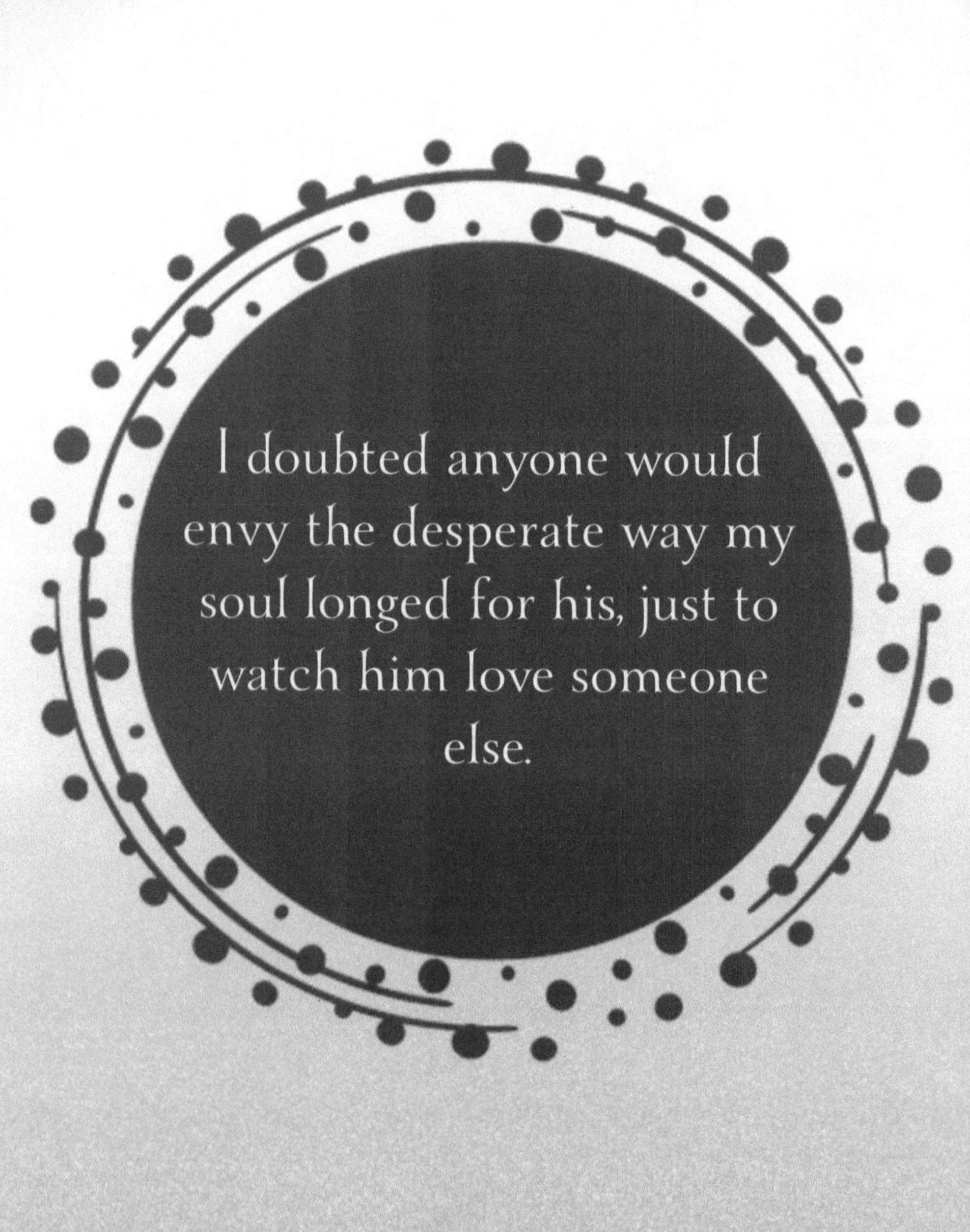
I doubted anyone would envy the desperate way my soul longed for his, just to watch him love someone else.

Chapter 22
Luke

The ride home was silent. We didn't try to play any music, no laughter or grins tonight. The dashboard read around two-forty in the morning, and I wondered where the time went. I parked in the garage, sat idly as the car ran, and slowly went through the motions of putting the car into park.

"What now?" Kinsley's voice was laced with exhaustion. I couldn't look at him, afraid all I'd see is his eyes, how they closed, her lips, how they touched his, and how he hadn't pushed her away.

She was his girlfriend, why would he push her away?

I tapped my fingers on the steering wheel, my teeth tugged at my bottom lip as I looked at my wrist. I couldn't see it in the dark of the garage even with the lights of the car and my glow-in-the-dark paint lighting us up. I couldn't see the scar, but I knew it was there. "We're not exactly dressed properly to go into your house, Kinsley."

My voice was sharp, angry, like daggers and I could see him flinch as if I stabbed him with every word. I couldn't stop the anger from spilling out of me. I knew it was unjustified, he wasn't mine and I had no say in what he did or who he did it with. I knew this, but I couldn't stop the jealousy from overtaking me.

All I could see was the way he looked pressed against me, the smell of his skin, the taste of his lips as he pressed them against mine. All I saw was him, all I felt was him. Now someone else knew him as I did.

Before that night, I had felt like I was inside the storm, and Kinsley had been the calm that kept it from touching me. But right then, I felt like I was toxic. Maybe I should have just left. Maybe I had been the storm all along, and Kinsley had just been trying to make me still. I had felt like I was already lost, a black hole opening up and swallowing me whole.

"Remember? They had said earlier that something was going on at the office. Kennedy left too when we were leaving, so you don't have to worry,"

I was probably silent for too long because he tried to talk to me again. "Luke, I-" I turned the car off and got out before he could say anything more. His silence was so loud as he followed me.

He was quiet as we took off our shoes and moved through the house. The house was lit up by the lamps all around that always stayed on, no matter what time of day it was. The soft dim lights lit the way enough for us to not need a light switch turned on, and as Kinsley started to head to the stairs, I turned to the kitchen. "What are you doing?" he asked as he turned to follow me.

I grabbed a bag of chips from the cabinet. I didn't even see what kind they were, I didn't care, I just needed something to focus on. Something I had control over, even if it was something simple like food. "I'm hungry, Kins, is that okay?" My voice was laced with anger.

He took a step back and I felt everything slowly drain away. The anger had been so unnecessary, and he was scared of me. He shifted from one foot to the other, unsure of what to do. I wanted to apologize to him, but I was trapped in my guilt. Was this what my father had felt the first time he scared my mother? Or did he like it, the sick bastard? Kinsley grabbed a soda from the fridge and left without another word.

I guess this is what Kinsley meant when he said I wasn't like my father. While I felt like shit, watching his shoulders slump down as he left, my father must have thrived on it, to do it again and again. I didn't want him to feel like this, knowing I had caused it. I didn't want to ever be like this again.

I left the chips on the counter unopened and followed him. I didn't want to be near him right now, not while he was covered in paint made by her fingers, his lips red from her touch, but I needed to apologize to him. Maybe once I was done I could take a shirt out of the drawer and head outside. I hadn't even realized it was almost winter now, considering the chill in the air. I didn't know if Kinsley even felt it, but I hadn't.

Kinsley left the door open, and I wondered why he always left it open if I wasn't in there, but closed it if I was. Even when the house was empty, he closed the door, as if putting us in our own little bubble of safety and peace away from everyone else.

He sat on the edge of his bed, his head lowered as his hands rested against his face and I nearly crumbled.

I wanted to fall to my knees and stare up at him, to press my hands against his cheeks and tell him everything was going to be okay. But how could it be okay when he was with her? How could it be okay when right now she was covered in paint dancing in Kinsley's shirt, with his kiss on her lips, and the feel of his hands against her waist? How could any of it be okay?

"I'm sorry," my voice came out in a strangled whisper, like someone had cut open my throat and squeezed my vocal cords.

I moved past him, unable to stare any longer. The room was dark, except for a single softly dimmed lamp he had turned on when he entered the room. Parts of us glowed softly, but it wasn't dark enough for us to be fully glow-in-the-dark. I tried not to notice that underneath his sorrow was a lean figure hunched over, his skin tight over his muscles. I tried not to imagine crawling on the bed and wrapping my arms around his waist, pulling his back against my chest, and kissing the soft tender skin under his earlobe.

"No, Luke, god, I'm sorry-" I stopped walking towards the dresser and turned to him, confused.

"The hell do you have to be sorry for?" I couldn't help but stare in astonishment. He went to reply as he stood and stared, but I cut him off. "Don't, Kins. You didn't do anything wrong. I was the one who got angry, I was the one who left early, I was the one who took it out on you. I'm sorry. I'm just going to grab some clothes and sleep somewhere else for a few days, okay? Maybe I need some space to cool down."

I turned my back to him as I moved to the dresser and went to open a drawer. Almost instantly, the dresser was slammed shut, Kinsley's body pressed against mine as he stared at me, his eyes crackling with anger. "Why are you going? What the hell are you even angry for? Where would you go?" Despite how angry he looked, his voice was laced with panic.

I was shaking as his eyes darted back and forth, studying me. He was too close, the heat of his body warmed mine and made me ache all over. I wanted to touch the paint on his cheeks, to press my fingers against it, tilt his head up, and kiss him. I shoved him away from me and tried to open the dresser once more as he held it closed. "To my house, Kinsley," I spat out in frustration.

"It wasn't there anymore, this is your house,"

I sucked in a deep breath because he was right. It wasn't there anymore, it had been knocked down to become a mall. And this was my home, because he was my home. Even then, there was nowhere else I wanted to be than right there, with him.

But I couldn't, because I was the storm, and I didn't want to break him. I was the broken one, I didn't want to shatter him along with me.

"I'll go to the rooftop," Our rooftop. I remembered Kinsley's birthday, how he had laid on my lap and I played with his hair.

Even then, I loved him, even then.

I tried to move past him toward the bathroom to try and get some of the paint off of me as Kinsley grabbed my shoulder and turned me towards him. Slowly, I took a step back, then another as he advanced on me.

I realized, absently, that while he was angry, while his face was red and his hands were curled into fists, I wasn't scared. I wasn't scared of Kinsley. He had promised he would never hurt me, and I trusted him. "What's wrong, Luke? Just fucking tell me already,"

Fear slipped through me, and I wondered if he could see it. If he could see the way my heart beat for him. *Can you see the way my soul calls for yours? Can you see how much I love you?* I was terrified he could see through me. "Leave me alone, Kins," my voice was weak as I tried to move around him.

"Stop trying to run away and talk to me!" He grabbed my shoulders and pressed my back against the wall.

I felt it then, coming back in full force, the anger. The anger and the fear that moved back and forth between us, with the secret that was so close to the surface, pressed against the tip of my tongue as it waited to ruin everything. I was breathless, I wanted more than anything to just fall to my knees. I wanted Kinsley to wrap his arms around me and hold me while I cried.

I was vulnerable under his scrutiny, and as I spoke my voice was softer than I expected it to be, with a broken rasp of unshed tears. I grabbed his shoulders and flipped us, pressed his back against the wall as he stared at me without fear, calm. Kinsley had always been calm.

"There's a storm, Kinsley," my eyes searched, begging him to see through me, to understand what I was too scared to say. *Look at me, just me. I love you, Kinsley. Even if you love her, I'm in love with you.* "There's a storm raging inside me. It's painful, and I don't know how to fix it."

I didn't want to cry. I was tired of crying, and I blinked a few times, trying to hold it back. I felt like I was a book and he was reading me, opening up the middle, getting to every part that defined me, that made me who I was. The part of me that was Kinsley.

His touch burned like fire, leaving a flaming path in its wake. His finger lingered on my cheek and he didn't pull away like I thought he would. I didn't want him to, but I needed him to. I needed him to stop making me feel like I was the only one he saw, when it clearly wasn't true. "You don't need to fix anything, Luke."

Despite how calm he sounded, I could see he was nervous. His hand shook on my cheek. He slid his finger under my chin to rest against my throat. My head slid down, it felt like a million pounds of weight was lying on my shoulders as I pressed my forehead against his and peered into his eyes. I shook my head no, my fingers curled around his waist, and pushed him back against the wall once more as I moved closer to him.

"There's something wrong with me, Kinsley," I glanced at my wrist, barely visible where I had it but I could see it all the same.

He looked down and I knew he understood what I meant. Only Kinsley could make sense of the logic in my fucked up brain. "I can't do anything right. Look, I couldn't even fucking do this right!" I shouted as I pushed him back against the wall once more.

It was a struggle to breathe, and while I tried desperately not to cry, I felt the wetness on my cheeks. Almost angrily, I wiped at it, furious it was there. Kinsley pressed his fingers against my cheeks and turned my gaze back to him. I took a deep breath, and another. He was waiting for me to focus on him, to calm down, to listen.

"Of all the things you do right, Luke, I'm glad you screwed up that one."

One of his hands moved to grab my wrist. His fingers curled around the skin, and the palm of his hand rested against the scar, hiding it from my view. Not that I could have even looked at it, when he was this close, when he felt this right, and when he was looking at me like that.

Kinsley lifted my wrist to his face. He twirled his fingers to press the palm of his hand against the back of my wrist, and leaned his cheek against the front of it, right over my scar. Gently, almost like a feather pressing against my skin, he turned his head and closed his eyes to press his lips against my scar.

A shudder ran through me, and a small fire slowly built warmer and warmer inside me. He turned his face once more to press his cheek against the scar, the intensity in his gaze left me breathless. "My life is so much better, knowing you," he breathed, a soft smile lifting the corners of his lips.

I couldn't explain what it was inside me that snapped. I knew he wasn't mine, that he belonged to her. I knew I should just nod and take a step back. I should tell him I'm sorry and go take a shower, go back to lying next to him. That fucking pillow in between us, to keep us away from each other. The same routine, repeatedly.

I knew it was what I was supposed to do, but the way he looked at me right then, all I could think about was Sparrow. As Kinsley's cerulean eyes peered into mine, lit up like a sparkle in the dimly lit room, I thought about the letters. I licked my lips, a shudder ran through me as I thought about them, about him, about everything. *'Be brave like Sparrow,'*

I thought about Isabella, and her words to me the first time she'd ever seen me cry. *'It's okay if he makes you strong,'*

Or what I had said to Kinsley. *'If it wasn't for you, I wouldn't be as strong as I am right now. Hopefully one day, I'll be as strong as you,'*

I needed to be strong. I needed to be me.

I slid my face down the side of his cheek and rested my forehead against his collarbone as I kept my left hand on his cheek, and my right hand on his waist. It was like I was holding a treasure; my lifeline. I was scared if I let go of him, he'd run away. *Is this going to be the last time he'll let me touch him?* Despite that thought, I couldn't stop myself, not anymore. I wasn't able to hold myself back anymore.

"Kins," I breathed against his skin. He shivered, his fingers curled around my shoulders, holding me against him encouragingly. "I know you're with her. I know you love her, I know you chose her. But I can't stop myself anymore. I'm so fucking tired of hiding everything from you. I'm tired of holding back, of keeping secrets, it's so draining," my voice strained under the fear of my words.

Kinsley shuffled from foot to foot, something he did when he was scared and nervous. "What are you talking about?"

Of course. How would he know, unless I told him? My truth. The story of when my life began, starting with a letter that was placed in the wrong locker. "I know you're with her, and I'm not going to stand in your way. I'll give you space, I'll back away, and I won't make you feel uncomfortable. But I just can't hide this anymore, Kins," my hands shook as I stayed pressed to his collarbone. I was too scared to look at him, not for this. Maybe I wasn't brave enough to look at him, but I was going to be strong enough to say it. At least I could do that.

"Luke," his voice was strained.

I shook my head no, silencing him. "I absolutely hated the girls, Kinsley. The girls you were forced to date. Every time you talked about going out, I waited impatiently for you to say that it was awful. I wanted you to hate it, to hate every part of it, and I wasn't happy again until you did. But then Serina came, and I can't do it,"

I had to pause as a broken sob slipped out. "It's different with Serina. You like her, and she's apparently perfect for you, and I just, and I-" I took a deep breath, and another. I could feel Kinsley's heart beating through his collarbone. The sound calmed me and encouraged me. Almost as if it was telling me to keep going, not to give up.

Just tell me, Kinsley's heart whispered.

And so I did.

"I'm in love with you, Kinsley." I breathed.

Kinsley was shaking. His nails sunk desperately into my skin, and I felt something wet in my hair as I pulled away, to look at him. His eyes sparkled as tears slipped silently down his cheeks. "I... what?" He stammered, clearly thrown.

I sighed as I let go of him. I took a step back from him as he let go of me. "I won't get in the way, and I won't push myself on you. I know you're with her, I know you love her. But I can't hide it anymore." I tried as hard as I could to smile.

"I'm in love with you," I repeated, softer this time as I stared him in the eyes.

He sucked in a deep breath, his hands wrapped around his stomach as he held himself, almost as if he had been punched. I wanted to touch him, to hold him, comfort him, but that wasn't my job. It wasn't ever going to be my job.

"Luke," his voice was filled with pain. "It wasn't real. From the beginning, none of it was real."

I frowned in confusion. "What? The letters?"

He shook his head no as he let out a soft laugh. Why the hell was he laughing? "Serina is amazing, Luke. We talked all through dinner because we liked the same bands," he looked like he was in shock as he rambled, his eyes so wide and filled with wonder. My eye twitched in discomfort as my jaw clenched. I took a step away from him.

"I said I wasn't going to get in the way but I don't want to listen to you talk about her either, that was just fucking torture,"

He surprised me by grabbing my shoulders. All of a sudden my back was pressed against the wall, his body pressed against mine, and he was smiling. *God, that smile.* It wasn't fair that he was using that against me right then. My arms were against the cold wall as his hands pressed against my biceps, holding me in place.

"Then I saw something, Luke. A drawing," he continued as if I hadn't even interrupted him to begin with. "I have to tell Serina's secret so you can understand, but you can't tell Izzy, okay? That's for them to figure out." I nodded, just kind of going with it at this point.

"That night, Serina and I went for a walk after dinner. She wanted to show me something. The drawing, Luke. The fourth drawing. The tagger that had been stalking Izzy. It's been Serina from the start."

I was shocked. My mouth fell open in surprise. "The fuck?" I stammered. "I mean, okay, I didn't expect that. But I'm still kind of confused about why you're telling me all of this."

So they bonded over their love of tagging? Was that what he was trying to tell me? "Serina has been following along after Izzy's drawings, not because she wants to ruin them as Izzy thinks, but because she saw the drawing and it spoke to her. Serina fell in love with the way Izzy drew. Serina had never loved me from the start, and I had never loved her either. We had agreed to date to keep our parents off our backs, but neither of us loved the other. She's in love with Izzy, Luke, not me."

The words, the way he said them, the excitement in his voice. I knew he wasn't lying to me, and I felt suddenly shy. I felt so stupid knowing I had confessed everything I was feeling for no reason because he wasn't even really with her. It was smart, a cover for both of them. Even I had fallen for it. But the kissing, the touching, it made it feel so real. "Then why did you kiss her?" I had to fight to keep the jealousy out of my voice.

"The sucky part of being rich is all of the rich families like to get together and pretend they're all friends while they compete constantly. That means the parents get info about their so-called friends' children to use against them. We both have kids who talk to their parents, and those parents talk to our parents. The touching at school, the hanging out, is to make it look real. Plus, once you get to know her she's actually really cool. She's so much like me it's scary," he let out a soft laugh as he shook his head at the thought.

"The kiss was nothing, Luke. She was drunk, and I knew it meant nothing. She even muttered Izzy's name before she kissed me. I didn't kiss her back, I mostly was holding her so she didn't fall over. She should have known not to wear heels if she was going to get drunk. I'm not in love with her, we're just friends, nothing more."

I chewed on my bottom lip and wished I was anywhere other than here. I exposed my secret for nothing. He wasn't in love with her, but that didn't mean he liked me either. We were friends, best friends, and I probably just ruined everything. "Oh," my voice was so small as I pressed my lips together tightly.

I knew I was blushing; my cheeks felt so warm as I looked down at the floor, unable to look him in the eyes any longer. "I, um. I'm going to go take a shower," I moved to the side as I tried to get away from him. Everything felt so awkward now, and I felt vulnerable under his gaze. Telling him my feelings, confessing to him. I was stupid for even causing all of this drama to begin with.

However, Kinsley wasn't done with me quite yet. He grabbed my arms and pushed me back to the wall once more. I felt so defeated as I fell to my knees and slipped onto my butt. Kinsley lowered himself right in front of me as he kept ahold of my arms. "Is this where you kick me out?" I let out a soft, pained chuckle as I stared down at the ground.

Kinsley pressed his fingers against my cheeks and made me look him in the eyes. All of a sudden, Kinsley looked shy, his cheeks painted with a deep cherry red color. Despite how shy he looked, however, his voice was clear and strong.

"I'm not in love with Serina." I nodded, or tried to, since my head was being held tightly in his grip. "I'm in love with you."

My body stiffened in shock as I stared at him. He was higher than me, and while he was on his knees I was sitting on my butt, and it felt kind of strange to be looking up at him. To be honest, I wasn't sure if I had heard him right, because surely he hadn't said what I thought he said.

"What?" I whispered. My fingers slid to his waist, and my thumbs moved softly over the tight skin, pieces of dry paint crumbled off of his skin and down his body onto the carpet. "What did you say?"

He moved closer to me, his fingers sliding into my curls, tangled in them as he pulled my head back just a little bit more. His face lowered, a mischievous smile as his eyes danced in mirth, his lips resting a hair's breadth above mine. "It's better if I show you."

I closed my eyes as his lips pressed against mine. I moved my hands to his lower back to press him closer to me as he sat down on my legs. I breathed him in, inhaled him, every part of him. His cheeks blazed such a bright red as I pulled him closer to me and kissed him back without hesitation. I had missed this taste, this feeling, this touch.

Before Kinsley, my life was nothing but a giant mess. A puzzle outline, and nothing more. The pieces of me were piled in a circle, and I had been slowly trying to put them together, but failing. I found pieces, slowly as time went along, but by the end, I was left with a hole, right in the center; a missing piece.

Kinsley and I pulled apart for a moment, both of our hearts raced as we stared at each other. I couldn't help but laugh as I pulled him back against me and pressed his lips against mine once more. I couldn't help but smile, because the missing piece I had searched for all along, ended up finding me, instead. All because of a letter, and the wrong locker.

I'm in love with you,
Kinsley.

Chapter 23
Kinsley

I kissed three people in my life. My first kiss was with Isabella when we were fifteen. We were in her hometown, sitting in her cousin's basement. He was barely twenty and wanted to be a tattoo artist. He had his setup and was only supposed to be using it to tattoo on fake skin. We decided to volunteer. Getting drunk was her cousin's idea, and we decided it was probably a good idea since we were scared out of our minds. Izzy's tattoo was a drawing she drew herself, of a dandelion. She had it in the middle of her back, the stem going up her spine, and it looked like someone had blown it, the pappus blowing around her left shoulder blade and up her shoulder.

It was a big piece, daring, and I was still surprised her mother hadn't found it yet. Though one of the things I loved best about her mother was how accepting and sweet she was. She didn't care that her daughter dressed the way she did, her body covered in various bright colors, her hair whatever color she chose for that month.

Our kiss was silly, it meant nothing. Izzy kissed everyone when she was drunk, she even tried to kiss her cousin. We weren't awkward afterward, despite how strange the situation was, we were fine. Izzy and I were always going to be fine.

My second kiss, with Serina. Serina was barely there and talked the whole time about how gorgeous Isabella looked. She slipped my shirt onto her shoulders intending to breathe in Isabella's perfume that had rubbed off on me when she hugged me. The kiss was nothing, I hadn't even moved my lips, just stood there waiting for her to stop, holding her up so she didn't fall. I doubted she'd even remember it, or much of anything tomorrow morning.

The third was a kiss that tasted like oxygen.

The third was a craving that I knew I'd have for the rest of my life. The feel of soft skin gliding over mine, his tongue dancing against mine to a rhythm only we would ever know. Every time his tongue slid against mine, my heart beat to the same rhythm as his. Luke's fingers curled at my waist, and pulled me even closer, as if it were possible. I could be breathing him into my body and it wouldn't be close enough. As his fingers slid up my bare back, the rough pads of his fingers pressed against my scars, I knew with every beat of my heart that I was home.

'I found you,' Luke's heart whispered into my mind.

A soft hum came from him as he slid his hands to my waist once more, tracing a path only his fingers would ever touch again. *'Welcome home,'* My heart responded.

We pulled apart slowly, both of our eyes closed as we imagined every touch, every taste, every feeling again, and again. It was silly, how we desperately tried to cling to the memories as if they were feathers that would blow away in the wind. He was far from a memory. Luke was like a tattoo, engraved forever in my heart. Even if I tried to erase him, he'd always be there, embedded into my soul.

He spread his legs as I sat down between them, looking up at him once more with an almost shy demeanor. He kept his eyes closed, they moved back and forth under the lids as his eyelashes danced back and forth against his tanned skin. I wanted to kiss that skin, to kiss every part of it, but I was shy now that we weren't kissing. All of my bravery faded away, and all that was left was fear.

What if he didn't like it? Kissing a boy was a lot different than kissing a girl. What if he had just been curious, and now that we did it he was done? I was scared he'd open his eyes and tell me he was sorry. Terrified he'd stand up and walk away.

He had his fingers curled around my wrists now, and I wasn't sure if he was holding me to anchor me to him or if he was trying to make sure I wouldn't touch him again. My heart was racing, my breathing faltering, and I wished desperately he'd just opened his eyes and told me where we stood.

He already knew I wasn't straight, but he has always claimed he was. All of this might be new to him, a new realization, and I was scared I was just his test subject. As his eyes opened, I tried to coach myself to smile, to tell him it's okay and we can still be friends. Sometimes people experiment, and I was determined that if this was that, I'd made sure he knew I was still here, that I was always going to be here.

Luke's eyes were darker in the dim light, the green looked more like a soft forest breeze, the way they moved back and forth as he studied my expression. I had no idea what my expression was. I was terrified he was reading me, learning every part of me. What if he didn't like what he saw? Was he finished with my book now? Was he going to shut the page and walk away, or was he going to turn the page and keep reading?

Amidst my inner panic, what I didn't expect was for him to smile.

"So worried," he whispered, the corner of his lip lifted as he studied me.

I let out a soft breath because, of course, he could tell my emotions. Of course, he could see what I was thinking. Before I could say anything, however, he spoke again. "That was much better than the first kiss,"

I had no idea why we were whispering. We were so close to each other, in a darkened room, behind a closed door in a house that was always empty, a decorative prison. But whispering felt like we were telling secrets, and I didn't need to look to tell it was almost four in the morning. Our time, our hour. It was always going to be ours. "There was a first?" my lips lifted into a soft smile. "Did you attack me in my sleep?"

He laughed, his head leaned back against the wall as his Adam's apple bobbed, and I was entranced by the tight skin over his throat, and how much I wanted to lean forward and slide my tongue against the skin, and feel him unravel underneath me. He looked at me once more, and I wanted to be closer, always closer, never close enough.

"When we got drunk, during my birthday party. I kissed you," he gave me a sheepish shrug as his fingers tightened slightly around my wrists.

I pouted because I felt like I was robbed. A blush slid easily across my cheeks as I tried to remember, but no matter how hard I tried, I barely remembered anything from that night. I wanted to know what his expression was when he touched me, I wanted to know what his eyes said after he pulled away, or how I had reacted. I wanted to know everything, but yet I didn't.

"Doesn't seem fair," I mumbled as his smile grew even brighter, his teeth a dull shine in the dim light as he stared at me in humor. "That you remember it, and I don't."

Luke leaned forward and hooked his pinky fingers in the waistband of my dress pants. I was fairly sure I made some sort of noise in surprise as he pulled me closer to him, so close my chest hovered over his. As Luke stared down into my eyes, his hands moved gently over the curve of my ribs, his fingers tracing each one dangerously slow.

The rough pads of his fingertips lifted over my pecs, slid over my collarbone, and up my neck. He wrapped his hands around my throat, his fingers laced behind my neck as his thumbs slid back and forth over my jawbone. Gently he lifted my head even more, his forehead pressed against mine, and he smiled at me.

"You'll remember all of the rest," he promised as he pressed his smile against my lips.

I clung to him, our mouths moved in a soft rhythm that was so natural it seemed unrealistic. To touch him, to hold him, to kiss him. A feeling that felt so new, but so familiar at the same time. Knowing there would be more humbled me, but at the same time, it made me confident.

He loves me, he said.

I love him, I told him.

As simple as that, but yet it wasn't at the same time. Three small words that could be spoken so easily, were the hardest ones I've ever had to say. Now I could say them freely, without fear, because he felt the same. The same as me.

Luke's forehead pressed against mine as he stared, a soft smile that brushed across his lips in a way I never wanted to stop. That stare was for me and me alone. That kiss was for me and me alone. Those eyes, that soft gaze, it was the only one that I'd known, hopefully until the end of time.

"So, the birthday party." I teased as my fingers brushed against his hip bones. I had to admit, I enjoyed the shudder that ran through his body, and the way goosebumps rose on his shoulders from my touch. "Was that when you started having feelings for me?"

I stood up and pulled him with me, because as comfortable as I was in his embrace, I was uncomfortable in the paint that was hard and dry. It flaked off of my skin and left a strange blue and green mess scattered on top of my carpet.

Luke seemed to understand what I was thinking, not that I was surprised. He grabbed my hand without hesitation as he pulled us over to the dressers to get clothes for showers. Luke hummed in response, his eyes darted to mine over and over again, making him miss the handle of the drawers as if looking at me was too important compared to seeing what it was he was doing.

"Before then. I just didn't understand." A smile fluttered across his lips as he watched me. He cursed under his breath as he closed the drawer on his finger, an embarrassed blush painted across his cheeks. "You?" His voice was slightly muffled as he pressed his hurt finger against his lips and lightly bit the end of it, trying to smother the pain.

I shut my drawer with my bundle of clothes held out away from my dirty, flaking paint-covered body as I turned to look at him. He was hard to look away from. The way he stood there in dress pants that hung low on his hips. His body was flawless, his muscles pronounced, and his upper body bare, except for the paint my fingers had slid down his body.

I could see where I had grabbed his pants and pulled him against me, speckles of dried blue mixed with the green, blending us together in the small little trail of hair under his belly button leading down into his waistline, disappearing under the fabric.

He smirked as I lifted my eyes to his, telling me he had known I was checking him out and was determined to argue with me if I tried to deny it. Instead, I smiled and answered him honestly. "Since the beginning,"

Luke's tongue darted across his lips and he ducked his chin as a blush crept up his neck. "You can take a shower first, I'll wait," he mumbled, his eyes shifted to his feet as he shuffled back and forth in embarrassment.

I moved closer to him. He looked at me, a shy smile on his face as I reached up without hesitation and pressed my lips to Luke's. I loved how something so new felt so natural, so perfect, as if it had been practiced for years instead of a few kisses that spanned over the last half hour. "I'll hurry," I promised.

We took fast showers, and even though both of us had grabbed sweatpants to sleep in, neither of us put them on as we slid under the blankets. To be almost fully naked under the blankets, with only our boxers on, felt dangerous, but in a good way. Shy, both of us were shy, but it was four in the morning and we were brave when it was our time.

We lay staring at each other, but it wasn't awkward. His gaze was one I knew by heart, and the way we stared was enough to speak without needing to move our lips. The extra pillow had been thrown off the bed, and we lay there close but not close enough, staring.

Slowly, I lifted my hand to press against his heart, to feel the way it sped up under his skin. His eyes closed for a moment as if he was savoring my touch, before opening with a drunken gaze that I hoped would never go away. He took my wrist and wrapped his fingers around it as his forefinger pressed against the pulse, to listen to my heartbeat as well. "If Izzy was here, she'd be laughing at us,"

His voice was deeper, slightly raspy as he looked at me through hooded eyes and I had to force myself not to feel his voice slide over my skin. "She'd say: *'Boys are stupid,'* and then smack us with her shoe," I flashed a tight grin, my nose crinkling as we both laughed.

Luke's eyes searched mine as he bit his bottom lip, thinking. "Can we tell her? Both of them?"

My head tilted to the side in wonder, my hair halfway dry as it brushed against my forehead. Luke brushed my hair out of my eyes, gently pushing my bangs behind my ear, before letting his fingers rest absently on my cheek. "Tell them what?"

He slid his hand down my cheek to my throat, his eyes followed the trail for a moment before he met my gaze once more. I watched in wonder as his neck started to redden, like a slow trail that slid up his neck, over his ears, and splashed across his cheeks. When he replied, his voice was shaky. "That you're mine,"

I closed my eyes with a smile as I replayed those words, his voice, over and over again in my mind. I moved closer to him, my hands mo over his body to his neck as he slid his down to my waist, holding us close together. Touching him, and how he touched me, had always been natural for us.

Maybe we had been together since the letters. We fit together like two pieces of a puzzle. As if we had been together in another lifetime, just two souls finding each other once more. Maybe we just didn't realize, and now that we knew our feelings, it wasn't awkward, it wasn't strange. Just another turn of the page, another path both of us were going to go down, together. Always, always together.

I pressed my forehead against him, breathing in the scent of his body wash as his drying curls tickled the side of my forehead. "I had always been yours," *since the beginning*.

Luke let out a soft breath, his nose sliding back and forth against mine, a soft kiss all on its own. His fingers pressed gently against my hips, ran soft lines up and down the taut skin, and sent shivers through my body. "I never liked kissing," he admitted, his eyes open, searching mine. I felt a frown slipping over my face as he smiled, a slow smile.

"But it's different with you. I don't want to stop kissing you. Even after the first time, I craved you. I constantly woke up in the middle of the night to stare at you. I had to pull myself away because I was afraid I'd touch you and never want to stop."

I laughed softly. God, I was so stupid. "I thought you were going distant because you were disgusted to be sharing space with someone who wasn't straight. I thought if I got a girlfriend, it would make you feel better, safer, or something." I mumbled, annoyed at myself. He was laughing as well, both of us stupid in our ways. "But it seems you're not straight either. Because I am a guy if you haven't noticed."

"I noticed," he replied with a deep sensual voice, his eyes shifting down between us. His fingers slid from my hip to my chest, a soft heated trail down my chest, over the curve of my abs, to rest against the waistband of my boxers. "Definitely."

"So what does that make you? Bi? Gay?"

He was quiet for a moment, studying my face as his fingers slid slowly back and forth across the top of my boxers almost absently, teasing me despite not realizing what he was doing. "I'm just Luke," he said with a shrug. "I don't need a label to tell me I love you. I don't need to waste time trying to find one either. I'm just Luke, you're just Kinsley, and I love you, all the same."

I pressed on the back of his head to pull him toward me, my fingers tangled in his curls as I slid my tongue against his bottom lip, waiting. His lips parted easily, and his tongue slid against mine, curling my tongue into his mouth as he slowly and softly sucked on the appendage.

Warmth spread through me. I gasped at the sensation as his fingers gripped my hips firmly, and my body rolled onto my back as his hovered. My back involuntarily arched as my body sought out more of his touch. Luke's fingers teased against my stomach once more, in between us. His lips were hot as he slid down my cheek to find a purchase just below my ear. I closed my eyes tightly, enjoying the sensations.

"Luke," I breathed. His fingers slid down my stomach and ghosted over my skin as they curved and dipped with my navel. He played with the soft trail of hair under my belly button, his finger slid down the trail, to rest against my waistband once more.

Luke's lips lowered slightly, arresting the flesh under my jaw with a light suckle. I let my head fall to the side, baring my throat for him as he hummed in appreciation against my skin. My fingers ran up the curve of his neck, tangled in his hair for a moment, to slide down his neck and grip his shoulders as I tried to pull him even closer to me.

It just wasn't close enough. My thighs were nudged apart as he placed himself between them, his weight held up with one arm while the other rested on my waist, fingers sliding back and forth tauntingly. His fingers were soft, hesitant as he slipped them just under the waistband, to stay at the top as they pressed against the skin. Asking a silent question, one that I found I was too speechless to answer.

I inhaled sharply as his fingers pressed against the skin, and he lifted his head to stare into my eyes, a flustered heated expression on his face as he frowned. "Kins, I'm sorry-" He stammered, both of us breathing heavily. "I- should I stop?"

I studied him, his hand pressed against my body, and knew with every part of me I wanted him, this with him. I was always going to want him. Luke left a mark on my soul, and I never wanted him to let me go. I pressed my fingers against his cheeks, my eyes darting back and forth as I stared into his, to read every part of him.

He was my favorite story, from cover to cover, the only one I'd read over and over again for the rest of my life no matter how worn and torn it became. "Never," I breathed.

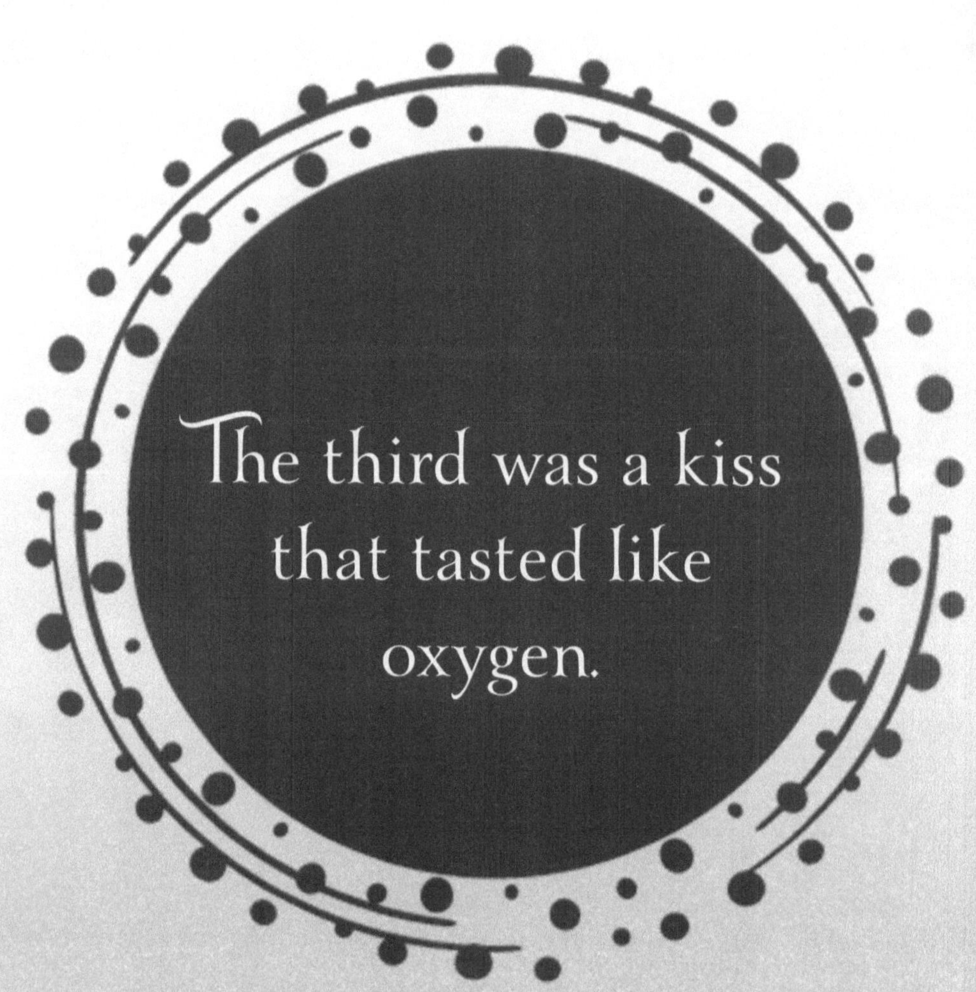
The third was a kiss
that tasted like
oxygen.

Chapter 24
Luke

I awoke to the soft chirping of birds. *Kinsley hates those birds*, was the first thought that popped into my mind. Kinsley complained about them for days when we first started to be friends. Now, however, they didn't seem to bother him. Nests made by one group, left behind for more to come and lay more eggs, to be hatched and raised over and over again as the seasons passed.

It was Saturday, I had the weekend off, and I could sleep in if I wanted to. Honestly, I felt wide awake but I was scared to move because I didn't want to open my eyes and see that everything that happened had been a dream.

I felt something soft pressed against my body. Something soft that was tucked under my arm, held against me, safe. For a moment, I thought it was that damn pillow again and my heart sped up in fear, begging me to open my eyes, to see if everything that happened last night was real, or if it had been a dream. I was scared to move, to open my eyes.

The warm soft thing moved, a soft groan slipped out, and I subconsciously wrapped my arms tighter around him and smiled. No pillow, not a dream, reality. Kinsley squirmed in my hold as I pulled him even tighter against me, my nose shoved into his hair as I breathed him in. His hair tickled inside my nose. He smelled like jasmine and lavender. Soft and warm, and mine.

"Luke," Kinsley whined, his voice deeper, the rasp stirring a low fire inside me. To want someone like this, to want them and keep wanting them, was so new to me. I never wanted the girls I was with before; it was just him that I couldn't get enough of.

"Lukeeee," Kinsley rolled around in my arms, his fingers pressed against my chest as he slid his nose under my jaw, to nuzzle against me. His legs slid against mine, tangled with them, reminding me of the lack of clothing both of us had.

Back and forth his nose slid against the soft skin under my jaw and I ran my fingers up and down his back gently, like a soft caress, enjoying the way he shuddered under my touch. I found his scars, traced over each one, the softness of the raised skin as I slid my fingers back and forth over them, loving every part of him. They were his flaws, but they were perfect because they were a part of him. "Let me go, I have to pee, and you have to feed me," he whispered against my throat.

I chuckled and let go of him as he rolled away to the other side of the bed. I raised my eyebrow at him. "Why do I have to feed you? You are capable of making cereal all on your own, Mr. Bryant."

He crinkled his nose, his eyes moved down to the blanket, back up to me, and down to the blanket again. I watched as his cheeks started to redden, embarrassment crept across his face as he brushed his fingers up and down the blanket softly. Nervous, he was being nervous, and I found it adorable. "I don't think I can walk up or down stairs right now."

I couldn't help my grin or the fact that my ego was slightly larger hearing that than it probably should have been. I scooted closer to him and wrapped my arms around him once more, to press a kiss to his forehead. "Do you need me to carry you like a princess?" I whispered in his ear. He replied by punching me in the stomach.

I laughed through the pain as he kicked me and shoved me until I rolled off the side of the bed in a heap of blankets. Even as I tried to untangle them, I was laughing. Kinsley must have managed well enough because a second later, I heard the bathroom door slam. I grinned as I sat up and peered at the closed door.

"I love you!" I felt elated. None of it was a dream, absolutely none of it. I could say those words to him without fear, without worry, and he'd say them back to me.

Kinsley opened the door, a small crack as he slipped his hand out and flipped me off, before promptly pulling his hand back inside and closing it once more. I chuckled softly as I winced. I guess he wasn't going to say it back this time.

I located my boxers, slipped them on, and grabbed the sweatpants I had originally pulled out of the drawer earlier to wear before we both decided to go to bed without them. Since Kinsley was in the bathroom pouting, I went down the hall and the stairs, ignoring the way everything was always so quiet and empty.

New paintings leaned against the living room couch, along with some golfing equipment to be set up in the backyard as well. Unnecessary, honestly, since they were never home to play it.

I rolled my eyes as I went into the kitchen. With a quiet good morning to the maid, she moved past me with another box, something else they must have ordered to decorate their barely used house. I could see why Kinsley's tattoo made so much sense. Kinsley was like a bird. He was beautiful and trapped inside a fancy decorated cage, ignored most of the time, and showered with useless things that he didn't want or need.

All he wanted was to be free. I was determined to be the one to free him. Originally, I had wanted to take Shawn away from here when I graduated, but from the texts and the calls, it seemed like Shawn was doing fine, so much better without me there. But Kinsley, I was going to do everything I could to make him happy.

I considered making Kinsley a full-on breakfast with everything I could think of, but in the end, I settled for his favorite cereal. I already teased him enough for this morning, I wasn't interested in starting off our relationship with him being angry at me. However, I realized he made me see a new side of myself. With my exes, I never felt so unnerved, so antsy to please him. I liked the idea of spoiling him.

I wondered if he'd be the type of guy who liked dates, or if he'd rather just stay home and cuddle. We'd probably start dating now, right? Where would you even take a guy out on a date? I was starting to panic as I grabbed both of the cereal bowls and walked up the stairs with them. I wasn't sure how to be in a relationship with a guy, it's not like I've ever had much practice with it. Then again, I wasn't that great with a girl either, considering I never liked them.

As I walked back into the room, Kinsley walked out of the bathroom wearing his boxers and a pair of sweatpants as well. He was barefoot, his back arched slightly into a graceful curve as he stretched, and I found it hard to look away from him. He was covered in red marks, small little bruises I had made on his skin, and I shuddered, swallowing hard as I tried to force myself to look away.

I wasn't sure if I could trust myself around a naked or half-naked Kinsley, not now that I knew him in a way no one else ever had. It was hard to stop my thoughts from straying, from wanting to do it again, and again. It was annoying, being a teenager sometimes, a struggle trying to go against all of the urges.

Kinsley smiled, his cerulean eyes sparkled in the sunlight as it came pouring in through the windows. I handed him both of the bowls and pressed a kiss against his temple, before walking past him into the bathroom and shutting the door. I didn't take long, brushing my teeth and running a comb through the tangle of curls, but I did take a second to admire the bruises that were scattered over my skin as well. I pressed my finger against each one, ran the tip of my finger over each spot, and smiled. I liked the idea of having his marks all over my body.

Kinsley was sitting on the window seat eating his cereal. I took a second to grab my phone since it had gone off and sat down across from him. Both of us leaned against opposite sides of the large window with our bowls of cereal in the middle of us. Kinsley had one leg bent, his foot tucked under his other leg as it hung over the side and I copied his pose, flipping open the phone.

'Are you okay, Izzy? Did you get home safely?'

It didn't take long for Izzy to reply with a thumbs up and Kinsley shrugged, closed his phone, and slung it back towards the bed. I copied him, I didn't feel the need to have my phone right then. I just wanted to spend time with him. He leaned backward, his back resting against the window sill as he gave me a lazy smile. "Hi," his voice was soft, filled with wonder.

I squeezed his knee softly, before sitting back and grabbing my bowl. "Hi," I replied, flashing my teeth at him for a second before proceeding to shove food into my mouth. For a few minutes, we settled into our comfortable silence, our eyes lifting to find each other over and over again, to share soft blushes.

More than once his toes slid up the side of my foot, and I returned the touch. It was a simple touch, but it was one of curiosity and it meant everything to me. Wanting to see where we stood now that everything had happened last night. I understood how awkward it was, how surreal.

It was me who made this awkwardness, after all. Kinsley had never claimed to be straight, so it was understood he was comfortable with this. I could see it every time he studied me as if he was waiting for me to change my mind. To stand up and walk away, or tell him I wanted to go back to being friends.

I don't think he understood just how awakened I felt. I had a strange vulnerability now, as if I had pulled my heart from my chest and handed it to him, hoping he'd keep it safe and not shatter it. I was happy, I felt lighter and free. I wasn't just experimenting, this felt right, absolutely right. I just needed to make him see that.

"So, babe. Baby? Dear? Honey? I swear there's another one," We had both finished our cereal a few minutes ago, and the bowls moved to Kinsley's desk. Kinsley looked at me like I grew a third head, his head tilted to the side as he tried to hold back laughter. "Sweetie?" I added, trying to fight the grin that was spilling across my face.

"What the hell are you doing, you weirdo?" Kinsley asked, letting out a soft snort. He pressed his hand against his mouth in embarrassment and I grinned, mostly just happy he was smiling. His dimples were pronounced in the sunlight and I wanted to slide my fingers up and down the deep grooves.

I shrugged. Kinsley lifted his knees to his chest and wrapped his arms around them while he stared at me. "I've never been in a relationship with a guy before, just trying to figure out what I'm supposed to be doing. Are pet names a thing with two guys?"

He pressed his face into his arms and for a second I thought he was angry until I saw his shoulders shake in silent laughter. I scooted closer with a grin, slipped one leg in between the back of his feet and his butt, my other leg draped over the side. I was never close enough to him. It was almost scary how obsessed I was. Up close like this, I could see small light brown freckles dance against his shoulder, lit up by the light coming in from outside. I traced a small path between each freckle while he contained himself until he looked at me once more.

"I don't think there's a set of standard rules each type of couple has to follow. Whether they're a same-gender couple or an opposite-gender couple, I'm pretty sure they can do whatever the hell they feel comfortable with. You can call me whatever you want, Luke," he replied, a smile on his face contrasting with the blush.

I pressed my forehead against his. "I think I'll call you mine, if you're fine with that." I paused for only a second to watch his cheeks light up with that soft red tint before I kissed him. I had wanted to kiss him all morning but was scared to. It wasn't dark anymore, it wasn't four in the morning anymore, and to kiss him and to be kissed back was a scary thing in the light of a new day. It spoke of unspoken things, of wants and needs that I had and that I hoped he had as well.

It was a normal kiss, not too rushed and not too slow. The type of kiss that spoke words, telling the other person not to worry, because there would be more. Hoping that he wanted there to be more. I wasn't sure how to ask about a relationship. I kind of assumed we were already in one, but maybe I was supposed to formally ask as well. Everything was new to me, and as scary as it was, it was exciting. God, how I had been waiting for this chapter, even if I almost didn't realize it in time.

If it was possible to get any redder, he was succeeding. The way his cheeks lit up from the inside, the sparkle in his eyes as he blushed, it was magnificent. I made it my secret vow to always make him look like this, feel like this, no matter what.

"I'm fine with that," he unwrapped one of his hands and pressed it against my heart. I smiled at the familiar touch, the familiar gesture that seemed to be ours. I wrapped my fingers around his wrist, to press my finger against the pulse there. To listen to his heartbeat as it gently thumped against my finger. "I've never been with a guy before either, you know. It's all new for me too," he spoke after a few seconds of silence.

"Well, I guess I've been in a kinda-but-not-really relationship with a guy for almost a year now, just been too stupid to notice," I said as he barked out a laugh.

"I guess that makes two of us,"

I wondered how my heartbeat felt to him right then, as I stared at him with a shy swallow. "Um, I mean, this a relationship, right? I mean-" I blew out a small breath of air as I tried to put together my words. "Do I have to ask you to be my boyfriend? Or do you ask? How does this work with two guys?"

His eyes were alight, the sparkles danced with mirth as he smiled brightly at me. Such a pretty smile, for such a pretty boy. My pretty boy. "I mean I'm kind of already someone else's boyfriend—" he started to say, his eyes filled with humor as I gave him a soft shove backward.

He shoved me back, and both of us pushed against each other, the laughter rang out into the empty room as I fell backward off of the window seat with Kinsley wrapped in my arms. He lifted himself, one leg on either side of my stomach as he sat down on me. His fingers slid up and down my chest, silently studying my body.

I closed my eyes and enjoyed the feel of his soft fingers against me, tracing every curve and every line that was his. "I would love to be your boyfriend." I opened my eyes and noticed the soft blush across his cheeks as his hair fell into his eyes. Ever calm, it was nice seeing him so frazzled sometimes. I cupped his hips, holding him against me as he traced a soft pattern in the hair under my navel. "I love you, Luke."

I slid my fingers up his hips as I lifted my upper body to meet his, wrapped my arms around his neck, and pressed his lips against mine. The softness of his mouth, the taste of him was everything, and I knew I'd never get tired of the way he felt in my arms. I pulled away from him with a soft hum, leaned back down, and my hands slid down his body to rest on his hips once more. "I love you, Kinsley."

Kinsley went back to silently studying me, and I chewed on my bottom lip. I figured there wouldn't be any problem just asking him. Sure, he wasn't an expert on two-guy relationships since he'd never been in one before, but I already knew from last night he'd researched at least somewhat, to know what to do and the right things we needed to make it happen. "So um, am I supposed to take you out on a date now?" As I spoke, Kinsley lifted his eyes to mine with surprise.

He leaned forward, his chest pressing against mine as he placed one elbow on either side of my head, to shift in just the right way to make me suck in a deep shaky breath. "A date?" He seemed to know exactly what he was doing to me as he pulled his legs together and separated mine, to slide himself even closer to me.

I tried to hide how breathless I was, to hide the sounds that gathered in my throat as he smiled mischievously at me. "A date. Like, dinner and a movie, or a picnic, or anything you want," I muttered, my words fading away with a soft moan as he smiled wider at me.

Automatically my legs wrapped around his and pulled him closer to me. It was never close enough. Kinsley kissed a heated trail down the side of my cheek, his teeth tugged on the underneath of my ear as he nibbled it, before breathing a soft growl into my ear. "Just you," he breathed, making goosebumps rise all over my skin. "I just want you,"

I shook slightly in anticipation as he held himself up with one hand, the other slid up and down my abs, lower each time, teasingly slow. My cheeks swelled as I blew out a long shaky breath, and I smiled through hooded eyes filled with excitement. "I think I can give you that,"

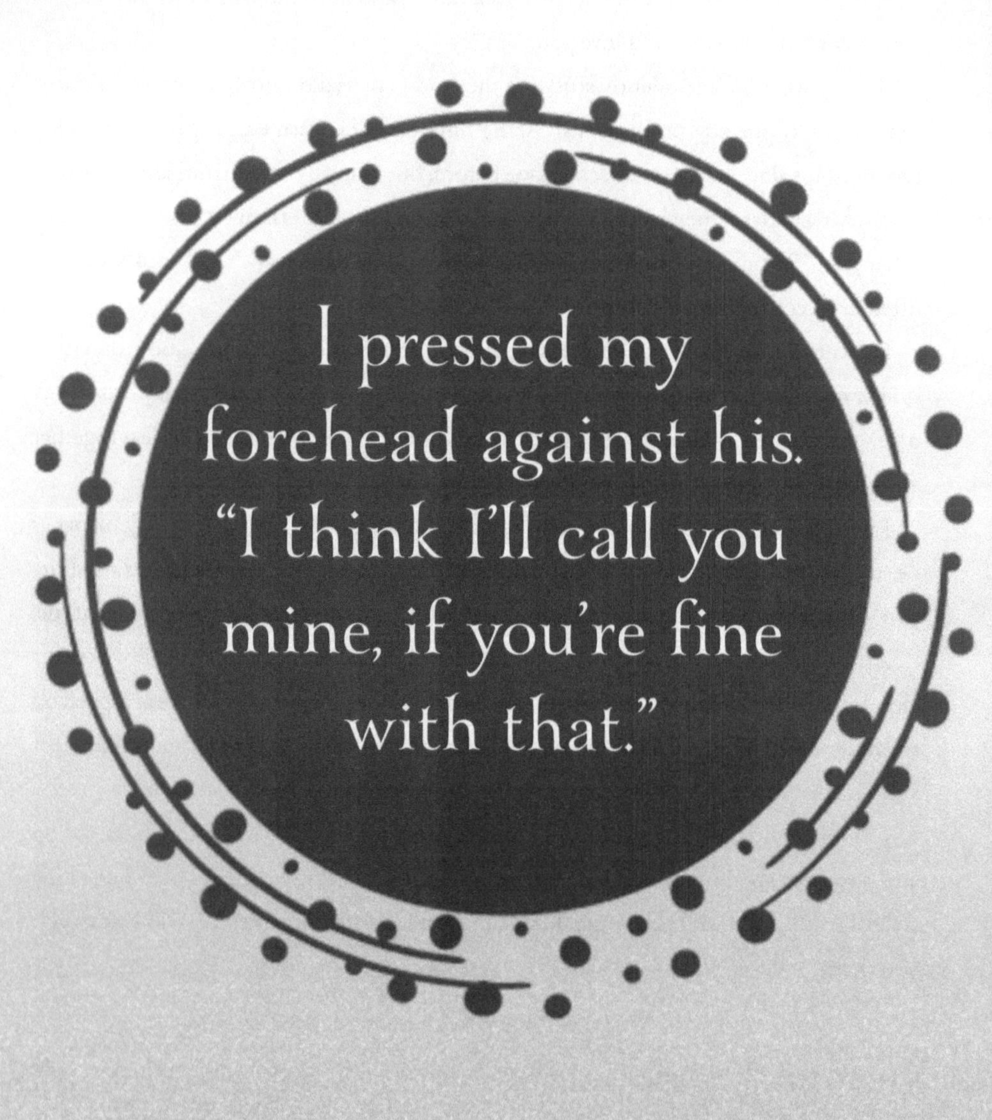
I pressed my forehead against his. "I think I'll call you mine, if you're fine with that."

Chapter 25
Kinsley

"Are you okay, Izzy?" I asked quietly. She had said her hellos as she normally did, but she had been slightly distant all weekend and didn't once mention tagging anything. Luke and I were so wrapped up in our newfound relationship to not notice, and I felt like an awful friend. Especially when she was acting off like this. Luke was the one driving us to school that day, and while Izzy sat up in the front seat as she normally did, I was out of my seat belt in the middle of them, leaning on the armrest as I stared at her.

I was trying to hide how flustered I was because, while we had both agreed not to be obvious with each other until we talked to the girls at lunch, Luke wasn't cooperating. With my hood down, he had one hand on the steering wheel and the other buried in my hair, combing through the few knots I didn't care enough to brush through that morning. I wouldn't even be surprised if he wasn't doing it on purpose, so used to touching me over the weekend without reservation that he found it hard not to touch me now.

"You should be wearing a seatbelt, Kins," despite the scolding, his words held no heat when he had a smile in his voice.

I turned to look at him, watching the smile light up his face as his fingers slid from my hair to my cheek, to trace a soft circle. "You should be driving with an adult since you only have a permit,"

He glanced down at me for a second, his eyes dancing in mirth as he looked back at the road. "Brat," he mumbled, the right side of his lips lifting into a smirk.

I chomped onto the tip of his finger, and he hissed in surprise as I turned back to look at Isabella. It was strange, the fact that she wasn't even paying attention to us. Something was very wrong. I mean, she was smart and perceptive, and Luke and I were failing at hiding any sort of feelings we had for each other. She should have called us out a while ago, to be honest. I poked her shoulder, trying to get her attention. "Izzy?"

Luke's hand moved to the back of my neck and gripped it slightly, stirring a feeling inside my stomach that had a small fire building inside me. He was torturing me, but I loved every part of it. Isabella turned to look at me, pulled out of her thoughts, and smiled. "I'm good, Pretty Boy. What are you doing to his neck?" She narrowed her eyes at Luke. "You better not be bullying our pretty boy."

"I would never bully my pretty boy," he flashed a wide smile at her as I sat back fast to avoid the blow I knew was coming. The shoe slapped against Luke's arm with a soft grunt mixed in with a chuckle. I couldn't stop the smile that stretched almost painfully across my face as I stared at the back of Luke's ear. I watched the different shades of red it was painted as it deepened, stilled, and faded away, like the sea foam at the sea as it slowly moved across the sand before retreating.

He said, *my pretty boy*. He claimed me as his. I kind of understand now why those little twelve-year-old girls would giggle and kick their feet during the cheesiest scenes in the movies.

I pressed my warm cheeks against the tops of my knees, wanting to squeak like a little girl. I wasn't sure how I was going to contain this feeling. I wasn't sure how I was going to have to pretend to the school I was dating Serina when the only one I wanted to hold hands with was the tall handsome quarterback.

None of them would ever understand; they'd probably never accept it. I couldn't wait to get out of that town and… I sighed as I looked out the window. Of all the things we'd talked about over the weekend, the future wasn't one of them. Colleges, towns, cities, countries even. Now that we were together, were we supposed to start talking about that? Did he think this was just for now until we graduated and went our separate ways? Or was he going to sit down with me and start filling out college applications to the same places as me, hoping we'd get in somewhere together?

Chewing on my bottom lip, I stared out the window, lost in my thoughts this time. I must have been quiet for too long because Luke seemed to notice. Fingers slid against the side of my knee, pulling me out of my thoughts. I lifted my eyes and caught Luke's worried gaze in the rearview mirror. He leaned back and slid his finger over my knee for a moment before he pulled his hand to the front seat again. Isabella was looking out the window once more, ignoring us.

We didn't need to speak for me to hear what he was saying. *'Are we okay? Is this still okay? Are you having doubts or regrets?'*

I could hear his questions with every breath he took. For someone so big and muscular, Luke was surprisingly sweet and gentle. I flashed him a reassuring smile as I leaned forward and slid my finger down his shoulder. The leather of his jersey was slightly cold under my fingertip as I pinched his elbow through his jersey. *'It's okay, it'll always be okay. We'll always be okay.'* As I thought that, his shoulders dropped in relief and he smiled, already focused back on the road.

All of my worries about the future faded away. Tomorrow meant nothing, compared to today. All I needed to worry about was today. Tomorrow would come and go, a future unknown and unconcerned compared to today, and every today that would come to pass. Worrying about the future was a waste of time.

Luke was here now, he was mine now, and I wasn't going to waste time worrying about what could happen. There was no point trying to read the pages at the end for answers. I needed to slowly turn the page one at a time, and live in the now.

I was lost in thoughts of Luke as we pulled into the school. By then, everyone was used to seeing the three of us together. However, as Serina pulled in next to us, I knew that while the relationship between Serina and me was still new, they were expecting that as well. High school was all about new gossip, and we were still new enough to be talked about. At least until someone got pregnant or dropped out or broke a body part, and then we'd be old news.

As we all got out, I grabbed both my backpack and his, shutting our doors almost at the same time as I handed him his bag. Luke had a mischievous grin on his face as he slid his hand down the back of mine. He took extra time to touch me before he grabbed the bag from me. I sucked in a deep breath as I pulled my hood over my head to hide my expression. I had a feeling he was going to torture me with small soft touches all day, and I was glad to have a hood to hide under.

In a way, I thought it was fun how secretive we were. A secret only we knew, that the world around us didn't, if at least for this brief period. Then again, it kind of sucked ass that we couldn't just be us. I thought it was counterproductive that people were so ready to tell us how to live our lives when most of them didn't even know how to live theirs.

Serina had sunglasses over her face, her hood pulled up, and her head down as she moved closer to me. When she spoke, her voice was slightly strained and soft. Pained almost, as if she was struggling to make herself speak at all. "Good morning, boys. Morning, Isabella."

I automatically moved closer to her as was expected of me and frowned. With a glance down her face, I could see that under her sunglasses, her eyes were swollen, as if she had been crying. "Let's get to class, guys," Isabella said with a clipped tone as she grabbed Luke's hand on impulse and nearly yanked his arm out of his socket, dragging him away.

Alright, that was strange. She was angry. Serina hesitantly laced her fingers with mine, and I squeezed her hand softly. She lifted her eyes to mine as I touched her cheek. "Are you okay?"

"I'm fine, Kinsley. Let's get going, okay? The bell is going to ring soon."

I looked at the school, only to see Luke looking back at me. His green eyes were darker than usual as they moved from my face to my hand, a flicker of annoyance in his eyes. I tried to hide how strangely happy it made me to see him jealous, now that I knew what a jealous Luke looked like. All weekend long we'd reconnected, telling each other pretty much everything we'd been hiding from each other this whole time. I felt kind of stupid that I never noticed how jealous he was before.

With a parking lot full of either cars or kids walking up from the road or the bus stop, a couple of girls from the swim team called out for us to get a room. Serina's cheek felt warm under my hand from the scrutiny, and as Luke turned around to follow Izzy into the building, I couldn't help but wince. He was definitely annoyed.

I dropped my hand as we both chuckled awkwardly. Serina wasn't her normal chipper self and I felt bad for it, I couldn't help but wonder if it was my fault. I was supposed to take her on dates so her parents wouldn't bombard her with so much, but the moment Luke told me he loved me, no one else existed in my world.

Maybe her parents thought it was weird she wasn't going on a date the first weekend she got a boyfriend. I was kind of sucking at this fake boyfriend deal. "How did the party go after I left? Sorry I kind of left you with all of that," All of that paint, all of that trash, and she had to handle all of it herself.

Serina shrugged, and I was glad to see her eyes light up as she laughed. She scooped some of her hair out of her eyes and pulled her sunglasses down slightly to look up into my eyes, a grin on her face that fit her so much better than her earlier sadness. "My butlers were horrified, but they cleaned everything. My parents were gone the whole weekend, so they didn't see any of the damage. There was glow-in-the-dark paint everywhere, the maids were laughing over it."

Despite what she said, however, there was clearly something she wasn't telling me. Serina shifted her eyes away from me, her bottom lip tugged in between her teeth as she picked at the skin nervously, and I wondered if she was lying. Though to be honest, I didn't know her well enough to know if she was or not. I tried to give her the benefit of the doubt and to believe her. Just as I did with Luke, I was only going to believe what she said. If there was something she wanted me to know, she could tell me, but I wasn't as good at reading her as I was Isabella.

"I'm so glad you weren't in trouble. What about the day after? Were you flooded with annoying teenagers whining over hangovers?"

Another flash of something in her eyes before she pushed her sunglasses back up to hide her expression. "I, um, stayed in my room for a while. However, I did instruct the maids to set out hangover remedies and to have various bottles of Tylenol and Advil on hand for anyone who needed them when I was setting up the party. I didn't see the outcome of the party until later on when everyone was gone."

I wanted to ask her why it looked like she was crying, but I knew it wasn't my place to ask. I felt bad that I had told Luke her secret, but I knew it was necessary so he'd understand. "You know we're all your friends, right? Luke and Izzy don't know you all that well, but they don't seem to have a problem with you. You're not alone. You were always welcome with us. Actually, I wanted to ask you if you wanted to eat lunch with us today. Luke and I wanted to talk to you girls about something important."

As we walked up the stairs to the lockers, I noticed Isabella and Luke were gone, so I figured they must have already been in the classroom. "Sure, I guess it's fine with me. Meet you at the cars for lunch?"

I opened Luke's locker, but my textbook was gone, so he probably grabbed it for me. I shrugged and closed the locker, then spun around and pressed my finger against her nose as she crinkled it at me. "See you then."

We parted and I headed to the classroom, and I couldn't help but try to figure out what it was she had looked so upset about. Maybe I should have pressed her on it. I kind of hoped I wasn't already failing over here to be her fake boyfriend. However, when I saw Luke sitting there in our normal seats, all thoughts of Serina faded away. I sat down and leaned close to him, a shy smile on my face. "Hi."

He already had both of our textbooks opened to the page written on the board, his binder opened to a new page that he had just started to work on. As I spoke, he looked at me with a smile creeping across his lips. "Hi." Though a second after he said it, his smile faded and a small pout started to appear in its place.

Gently, he smacked his knee into mine, and the cap of his pencil tapped against the desk as he hummed in frustration. "Gotta pee?" I teased.

The bell rang, and the teacher walked in, hands filled with things as we all talked quietly, waiting for the class to start. Luke moved closer to me and pressed his lips against my ear so no one could overhear. "When you're with her, I just want to grab you, throw you against something, and kiss you. To show everyone who you're really with," he whispered, his deep voice sending a shudder through my spine.

I let out a breathless gasp, my eyes wide as my cheeks flushed, my heart racing in my chest. He pressed his knee against mine as he laid his arm down beside mine. With joined desks, our arms were flush against each other. Gently, he slid his pinky finger against mine. I looped my pinky around his slowly, to not attract attention. The girl in front of us sat back, and her long curly hair brushed against our hands, but we didn't move, allowing it to cover us.

I glanced at him from under my eyelashes. I kind of expected him to be squirming and blushing with how daring that statement was, but instead, he had a smug look on his face, happy to see how I was reacting to his words. "You have no idea how much I want you to," I whispered.

Luke slid his tongue across his lips, wetting them. "One day," he promised.

The teacher started telling us what to turn our pages to as if we hadn't already done so. Then again, with the way most of the class was moving around and whining, it looked like Luke and I were the rare few who had our books already opened properly. I grabbed my notebook, trying to keep the smile off my face as I pulled it out. I made sure not to let go of his pinky, immensely glad that he was right-handed since I was left-handed, making this possible. Maybe it was childish to hold hands under the cover of some girl's hair, but I didn't mind being childish if it meant I could touch him.

The teacher started calling out the assignment as I wrote a quick note to Isabella, telling her the four of us were eating lunch together. It was kind of hard folding with one hand, and Luke watched me with a wide smile, not even trying to help, the asshole. I shook my head at him as I finally managed to fold it and throw it at her. I wanted to ask her what was going on with her to make her so absentminded but figured she'd tell me when she was ready, whatever it was.

Izzy blinked a few times before acknowledging the note. For a few minutes, I started attempting to do the assignment. I was amazing in English class, but Luke turned his hand palm up and slowly slid it under mine, kind of distracting me. He moved slowly, trying to make sure we didn't disturb the girl's hair. His fingers gently curved with mine, lacing together in a way that felt more real, more natural than any other person I'd ever held hands with before.

He had a sparkle in those resplendent green eyes that were peering at me from under his eyelashes. *'Behave,'* I mouthed to him as he grinned at me.

He gave my hand a little squeeze that sent warmth through my arm and left me craving more. *'Make me,'* he dared.

I started to weigh the pros and cons of saying fuck it all and kissing him right there and then, but thankfully Isabella distracted me by throwing the note back onto my desk. I was glad she did because otherwise, I would have ended up ruining everything with Luke, Serina, the school, and our families. I let out a soft breath as I looked down at the note and frowned because it was folded normally, without any sort of tiny unnecessary triangle that she was so well known for.

I glanced at her and noticed that instead of messing with her seatmate or drawing, she was staring absently at the clock as if she was counting down the minutes until the end of school. She looked exhausted with dark circles under her eyes, and only one of her usual two studded belts holding up her pants. She was wearing her father's army coat, the buttons buttoned up to her throat in a way she never really wore it as she lifted the collar over her nose and breathed it in, a sad look on her face. I wished she would tell me what was bothering her.

I looked down at the note and opened it. *'Sounds great, Pretty Boy.'* I could almost hear the uncaring voice she had used in her head as she wrote this.

Normally, she would have teased me and said something about Luke that would have made me embarrassed and want to try and hide the note from him. But it was so short, so uncaring. I pursed my lips as I tapped my eraser on the paper. Luke had to work tonight, and I wondered if Isabella would be more open with me if it was just us.

No matter what was going on, whether I was with Luke, or if we ever broke up, I never wanted to lose Isabella. She was more like family to me than my own was, her and Mami both, and it would have destroyed me if I had ever lost her. I wrote down a short message, determined to try and figure out what was going on. *'We were gonna go tagging tonight, okay? Just you and me,'*

I threw the note back and watched her read it. There was a small smile on her face as she read it, and I nearly breathed out in relief because maybe everything was okay after all. She gave me a thumbs-up and we both sat there for a good minute grinning at each other like lunatics until our teacher told us to pay attention.

Even being reprimanded, I squeezed Luke's hand with a smile as he shook his head at me with a chuckle. We could have been okay, like this. All of us. We could have lasted like this, I was sure of it. We just had to get past the school year, and then we would have figured out the after. For now, all I wanted to do was feel this, be here, in the now.

As I glanced at Luke, he smiled at me, not even embarrassed to be caught looking at me. He lifted his hand from mine and gently traced a heart against the palm of my hand before clasping our hands together once more.

It made my heart swell as I remembered how he had had that nightmare about his father, and I had traced *'I love you'* on his hand after he had fallen asleep.

'I love you,' I mouthed to him.

Luke pressed his lips together as he ducked his head, his eyes averted as the tips of his ears reddened. After a second, his eyes slid to mine once more, and I smiled, reading the reply in his stare. *'I love you too.'*

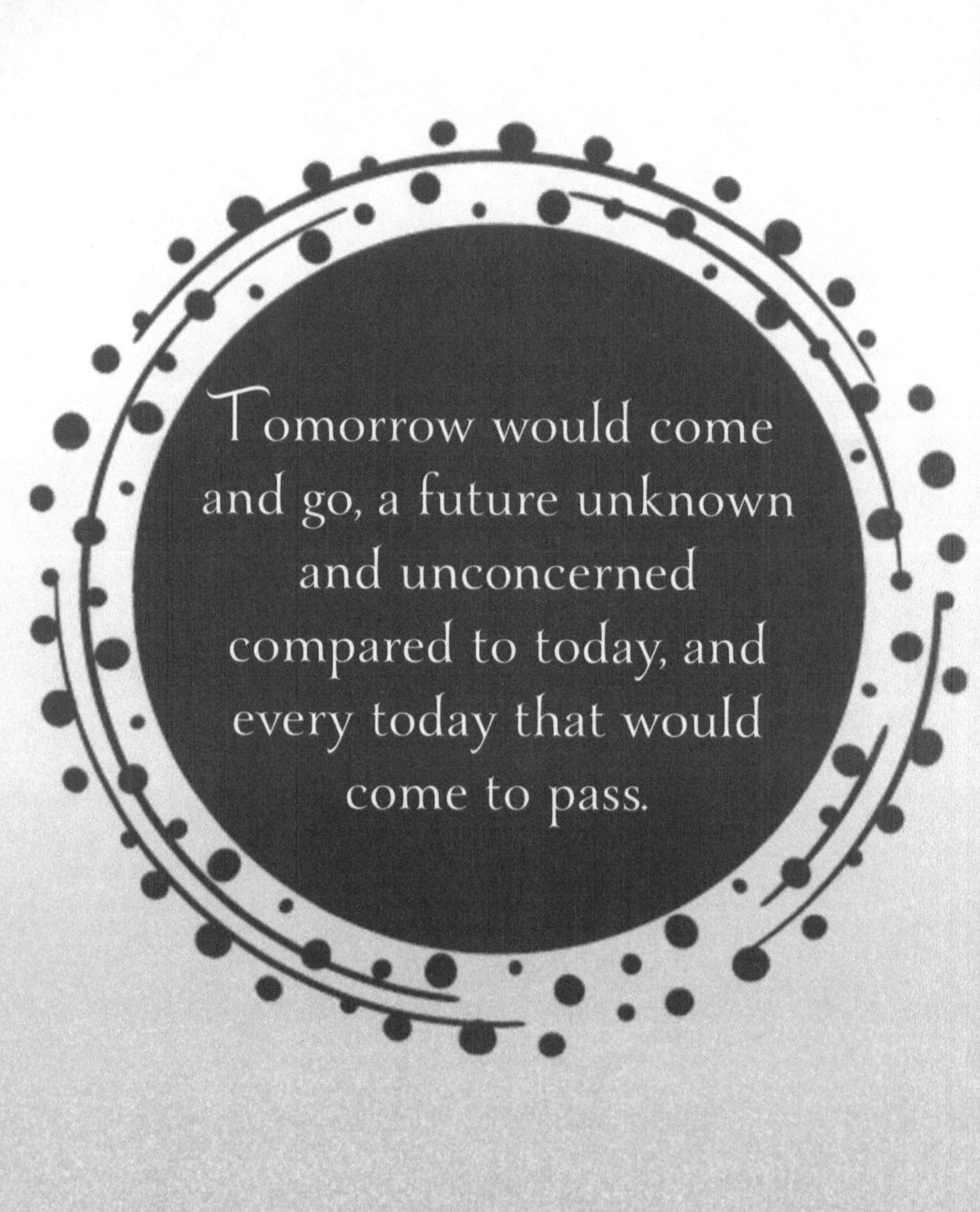

Tomorrow would come
and go, a future unknown
and unconcerned
compared to today, and
every today that would
come to pass.

Chapter 26
Luke

I sat next to Isabella in Spanish class, and even if Kinsley hadn't been staring at her all morning with a confused and concerned look on his face, I would have noticed something was up with her. I kind of thought it was funny how just a year ago everywhere Isabella and Kinsley went, they were oohed and awed at, the two loners that stuck together. Now, the oohs and awes were for me and Isabella.

I didn't need a cover as Kinsley did, but then again, if Isabella was going to go along with it, then I might as well. Maybe that would get Kinsley's parents to stop hounding both of us. Ever since Kinsley and Serina told them they were a couple, his parents were on my case, trying to hook me up with Lana again. Honestly, I thought it was sad that her parents threw her at anyone with money, not concerned with how she kept getting rejected and embarrassed. Maybe they should consider helping her fix her personality before shoving her on people all the time. "I didn't know you were such a player," the girl sitting next to me whispered.

I looked around the room, confused, as Isabella continued to tap her pen on the edge of her desk and stare at the clock absently. Another thing that showed there was something up with her since she always was drawing. I looked at the girl on the other side of me, trying to remember her name, as she glared at me. "What?"

Isabella snapped her head lazily towards us. She started to fumble with her bag, the crinkle of a gum wrapper as she pulled some out of her bag. "They were always together, you know. Since the beginning of high school. You just come in and steal her away from him, I thought you guys were friends."

I looked back and forth between the girl and Isabella and pressed my lips together in a tight line. In front of us, Roan turned his head to look at us, curious about the random conversation going on behind him. The number of times I wanted to just kick the back of his head and slam it down onto his desk was uncountable.

The teacher droned on about the difference between different fruits in Spanish as I frowned at the girl. "Who even are you?" I wondered, causing Isabella to snort into her hand beside me.

"She's one of your cheerleaders," Isabella whispered to me as she laughed. I narrowed my eyes at the girl as she blushed a deep blush, clearly embarrassed that I didn't know her. Was I supposed to know all of the damn cheerleaders? I didn't care about any of them.

Isabella leaned forward, and I already knew she was about to do or say something fucking crazy. "So what, you jealous? Do you wanna join?" She looked the girl up and down with a wink.

My mouth fell open in surprise as the girl sputtered, and Isabella started to laugh softly, clearly amused. "What I do with Luke is none of your business, get your jealous panties out of a twist and find some other jock to torture."

The girl huffed, clearly annoyed as she leaned over and started to gossip with her friend next to her. I rolled my eyes, smirking at Izzy as she grinned innocently at me. "Love you, you weirdo,"

She batted her eyes at me. "Love you too, boyfriend," She held out the d at the end for a few seconds, exaggerating it as she laughed at me.

We were quiet for a few minutes, and I groaned, wishing the time would go faster. It was lunch next, and I was scared out of my mind to tell the girls about Kinsley and me, but at the same time, I just really wanted to see him. We'd pretty much been together without realizing it for a year, and now suddenly it felt painful to be away from him.

I wondered when it was someone could consider us together. Maybe back when the letters were going back and forth, back when we both were falling in love with the other, despite not even knowing who each other was. I didn't need to see him, to know him, I just knew he was the other half of my soul, all the same.

I looked at Isabella with a frown. She was drawing at least, instead of staring at the clock, but a small spiral wasn't what she usually drew. "Are you okay?"

Isabella glanced at me; her bottom lip tugged in between her lips. She averted her gaze for a moment before looking at me once more. Slowly, she pulled out a blank piece of paper and started to write on it. She slid it over to me hesitantly, scared almost.

'I did something bad, unintentionally,' she had written.

My first thought was: *Why are you telling me? Why aren't you telling Kinsley?* But then I started to think about it and nodded. All three of us were best friends. While I was drastically closer to Kinsley than I was to Isabella, we were still there for each other. If it wasn't for her, I might have never figured out my feelings for Kinsley. That or I would have just pushed him against something and made out with him, feeling like I wanted to die for attacking him afterward.

So I smiled softly at Isabella because she was my friend, and I was there for her whenever she needed me. I wasn't sure if I'd ever feel as close to her as she was to Kinsley, or maybe I had my own Isabella out there somewhere that I just hadn't gotten close to yet. But that didn't mean I wasn't going to leave her hanging.

Before I met her and Kinsley, I had thought there was no one real out there. Just a sea of fakes, but here I was, learning that they weren't all fake, not really. There was Kinsley, the most real person I'd ever met, and Isabella. Maybe even Serina. I needed to get past my dislike for her. It was all there from the beginning because I was jealous. She probably was just as amazing as Isabella was.

'No matter what it is, you can tell me. I won't judge you, I promise,' I wrote, pushing the paper back toward her.

She stared at it for so long that I started to write the homework down on a piece of paper. I tended to do my homework at the shop since there was a lot of downtime in between fixing things. My car was almost finished now, thanks to Kinsley, and I was just waiting for a couple more parts to arrive to finish it. I was excited to finally get it done, to finally have something that was mine, something that couldn't be taken away from me.

Isabella sighed as she pushed the paper back to me. *'Then I can't tell you, Curly. Because I don't want to make you a liar.'*

I stared at her, then at the paper, confused. What the hell did I say wrong? Was this a girl thing? Was this a period thing? I kind of wondered if it made me an asshole to be glad I was with a guy and wouldn't have to worry about Kinsley having mood swings once a month. I was about to reply to her, anything, something, but before I could, the bell rang.

I didn't know who was more relieved, to be honest, her or me. She grabbed the paper and shoved it into her pocket. I followed her silently as she walked down the stairs and to the cars. I wasn't the right one to do all of this helping, to be honest. Advice, the right words, that was more Kinsley's thing. I guess I made a crappy friend after all.

I was trying so hard not to be sad that Isabella didn't trust me with her secrets, but the moment I saw Kinsley everything just faded away. He leaned against his car, his elbows on the hood as Serina sat next to his arm laughing about something. I looked at them and wondered what it was others saw when they saw them. Did they look at Kinsley and Serina and think about how well they matched? Did they look like they matched each other?

Maybe it was the jealous part of me, but I didn't think Kinsley looked good next to anyone, except me. A couple of girls on the swim team walked past and hooted at Kinsley and Serina. Serina lowered her head, her sunglasses propped on her face as she blushed. I frowned, not particularly liking the way she blushed over girls hooting at her and Kinsley, and Kinsley obliviously just flipped everyone off without a care.

As Isabella moved around them to sit in the front seat of Kinsley's car, I came up behind him. I couldn't help but smirk as I pinched his butt, making him jump slightly as a blush spilled over his cheeks. "L-Luke!" he stammered, as Serina got off the hood of the car and moved towards the backseat.

"I didn't do anything, you have no proof," I muttered, peering down at him.

Kinsley's eyes sparkled with humor. "You better stop," He warned quietly, his lips twitching as he tried to keep a straight face.

I leaned close enough that my lips could ghost over Kinsley's ear. "Gonna spank me if I don't?" I whispered, before pulling away.

He struggled not to laugh as his eyebrow twitched. He looked down my body, then back up again, his tongue darted out and slid slowly across his lips, wetting them. The challenge in his eyes made me take a second to check my breathing. Surely I had stopped at some point while he gazed at me like that, undressing me with his eyes.

"Come on ladies! Any day now!" Isabella screamed out the window as she smacked her fist onto the horn.

I slid my pinky finger against Kinsley's as we moved to the same side of the car. He took the keys from me as I sat down next to Serina, both Serina and Kinsley gave me strange looks as he shrugged and sat behind the wheel. I knew he was mine, and what was going on with him and Serina was fake, but I needed time to stop seeing her as someone I was jealous of. And if that meant I needed to sit next to her to make sure Kinsley didn't, then I was willing to be that childish.

"Where to?" Serina sat back against the seat as she pulled her seatbelt on. She was practically glowing, her eyes wide and curious as she looked everywhere, excitedly. I wondered if she was just excited to spend time with people, and started to feel bad about being jealous of her. She wasn't the one Kinsley loved, I was. Kinsley said it, and I trusted him more than anyone else.

"I kind of just wanted to go somewhere close. Like the drive-through, and we could take the food to the park across the street? I wanted to talk to you guys," Kinsley's voice wavered slightly, a hint of worry in it as he spoke.

Isabella looked startled, her eyes wide as she studied him, and I wanted to reach forward and brush my fingers against his to tell him everything was going to be okay. They already knew he wasn't straight, and I guess in a way I was the one who should feel freaked out, having to reveal my sexuality to them, but I wasn't. I was anticipating it. I wanted to run down the street and tell everyone I was in love with Kinsley Bryant, but I wouldn't because I wasn't crazy. Plus, I didn't have a death wish.

"Why?" Isabella squeaked.

Kinsley was so perceptive, but it seemed like he didn't notice her discomfort. He grabbed her hand as he smiled at her. "It'll be okay, Izzy," Isabella opened her mouth, closed it, then gave Kinsley a soft nod and turned away. Serina sighed beside me, and I frowned, unsure of what was going on with any of them anymore.

We loaded the car up with our bags of food and drove to the park. If it had been another time, I would have been arguing with Kinsley for him just paying for it all himself, but I was antsy and wanted to get this over with. I knew how important Isabella had been to him, how important she had been to me, and even Serina had started to be important to Kinsley. The idea of them being angry and leaving our little group was starting to worry me.

We found a sunny area since it was pretty chilly. All of us were wrapped in coats of various kinds, even Kinsley had on a black coat over his black hoodie, refusing to trade his hoodie for a winter coat. I had on my jersey and a long-sleeved shirt underneath. Isabella had on that old army jacket, and Serina was probably the only one wearing an actual winter coat. I was the only one who stuck out, my bright red jersey like a sore thumb against all of their dark clothes. I was surprised when Isabella sat next to me.

I assumed she would sit next to Kinsley, to be honest, but I was starting to think maybe she was avoiding him. Not too much, she didn't pull away from him in the car when he held her hand, but she walked near me, held my hand, and dragged me around. I had a weird feeling in my stomach and hoped I wasn't right. If she had a crush on me, that would be bad. I didn't want to hurt her.

I looked at Kinsley, who was across from me, and waited for him to say something. He looked just as unsure of what to do as I felt. I took a deep breath, trying to find the courage to just say it. Serina was staring at Isabella, and Isabella was looking at her food, trying to decide which to eat first, I guess. "Kinsley, just-" *Say it.* I shot him a helpless look as he stared at me.

He gave me a tight nod as he took a deep breath. He took a sip of his soda, and set it down in the grass in between us, watching the others from under his eyelashes. "I have to tell you something, both of you," How he was always so sure of himself, so ready to just say it, was beyond me. I was a coward. I just sat there and waited for my boyfriend to out me because I didn't have the courage to say it myself.

Kinsley looked at me, and all of my worries faded away because he was there. He understood me and knew what I was thinking and feeling. It was Kinsley, he was always going to understand. My fingers twitched, searching for the stick that I would usually grab and place between my fingers. The nicotine that I would use to reduce the stress I was feeling, but I had quit the night of the gala and hadn't smoked once since.

"Did you get pregnant?" Isabella's voice was light, but it didn't quite hide the sadness in her tone.

Kinsley had to pause to laugh, his head shook back and forth rapidly as he crinkled his nose at her. "Luke and I confessed how we felt for each other. We were together, guys."

Kinsley looked at me, and for a second, we just stared back and forth as if there was no one else around us. To say it to ourselves was one thing, but to say it to others was a whole other thing entirely. My heart was beating fast. It was as if I could hear what he was saying, without him needing to say it. *Is this okay? Still okay?*

Now that the girls knew, I wasn't going to hold back. I moved our things out of the way and scooted until our knees were pressed against each other and grabbed his wrist.

Kinsley sucked in a deep breath as I watched him, a soft smile on my lips as I felt his heart beating through his pulse.

"Still okay, always," I whispered. Kinsley's cheeks flushed a dull coral color, his blond hair tickled his nose as he smiled at me.

Isabella was the first one to make a sound. Her laughter rang through the empty park as we turned to look at her like she had lost her damn mind. I did notice, however, that whatever had bothered her was long forgotten; her face lit up with happiness. I looked at Serina, wondering if she'd be angry, but she had a smile on her face as she looked back and forth between Kinsley and me and clapped.

"So, when did this come about? No, no, first question first. Who did the poking?" Isabella asked, her eyes narrowed at us.

I felt my cheeks light up as I shifted back and forth, unsure how to even answer that question before Kinsley beat me to it. "Which time?" He taunted, cocking his eyebrow at her.

Kinsley was laughing as I leaned forward and punched his shoulder, while both of the girls started to laugh at us. "Vers, I knew it," Isabella sang, doing a small little shimmy in the middle of the grass.

"What is a vers?" I wondered, unsure what the hell she was even going on about.

Kinsley leaned forward, grabbed the collar of my shirt, and pressed his lips against my ear. "When a guy both likes to give it and receive it," he had a sly grin on his face as he sat back down.

I averted my gaze, my cheeks lit up like fire as they all laughed. "Shhh," I muttered, making them all laugh even louder.

Isabella wrapped her arms around Kinsley's shoulders and kissed his cheeks as I grabbed his wrist and pulled him closer to me, sticking my tongue out at her as she tried to tug him back again. "Ladies, no need to fight over me," Kinsley choked out as we all laughed again.

Finally, we started to calm down, this time Kinsley and I sat next to each other, side by side as Isabella and Serina continued to sit across from each other. "So, why don't you care?" Isabella asked Serina with a confused look on her face.

Serina shrugged, taking a sip of her drink. "Because we weren't together anyway. Kinsley and I knew from the start we weren't in love with each other. I wanted to get my parents to stop hounding me to date guys and to stop their ridiculous schedules, and Kinsley was tired of getting girls like Lana thrown at them. We figured we could just pretend we were dating each other, that way they'd give us some slack. Then we'd turn eighteen and go off to college and pretend we'd broken up, and they couldn't do anything about it."

I noticed the way she was looking at Isabella was far from nonchalant, as she was trying to act. "It was all a lie? And you all knew?"

I felt the pain in her voice like a smack across my face, but she was looking at Kinsley when she said it. "I didn't tell Luke either. I thought he was being distant from me because he was uncomfortable with me not being straight. I thought if I got a girlfriend, he'd relax near me again. I was worried if I told you, then you'd tell Luke."

Isabella took a deep breath, her bag gripped tightly as she stared at him in disbelief. "I wouldn't have told him anything! Not if you told me not to!" She nearly shouted, her voice breaking.

"I have been there for everything with you, watching you try to get over Luke, and then I had to watch Luke starting to realize his feelings while you were with Serina. I could have just told him if I had known it was all fake! But I thought you had moved on, and you didn't tell me anything! And I was so scared I did something bad, and I–"

She stood up and took a step back from us. "Izzy," Kinsley said, his voice breaking as he stared at her.

She held up her hand as she shook her head no, glaring at him. "No. Don't Izzy me, *estúpido*," she spat at him, her accent more pronounced than ever. Kinsley went to stand up but she took another step back, clutching her bag tightly. "No, Pretty Boy, no. I love you, and I'll always love you, and you too Curly, but I needed a minute to breathe,"

"Isabella," Serina whispered, going to stand up.

Isabella glared at her, shocking the crap out of me because as far as I knew Serina did nothing to her. "*Hell no*." She said, before turning around and walking away from all three of us.

We watched in disbelief as Isabella disappeared inside the school, anger radiating from her. I looked at Kinsley, who sat there with tears in his eyes, trying to hold them back. Gently, I cupped his cheeks, making him look at me. "Give her a minute, Kins. She'll be okay." I whispered as I pressed my forehead against his.

Kinsley gave a soft nod as he closed his eyes. He wrapped his fingers around my wrists, to hold me against him, like a lifeline. "I hope so."

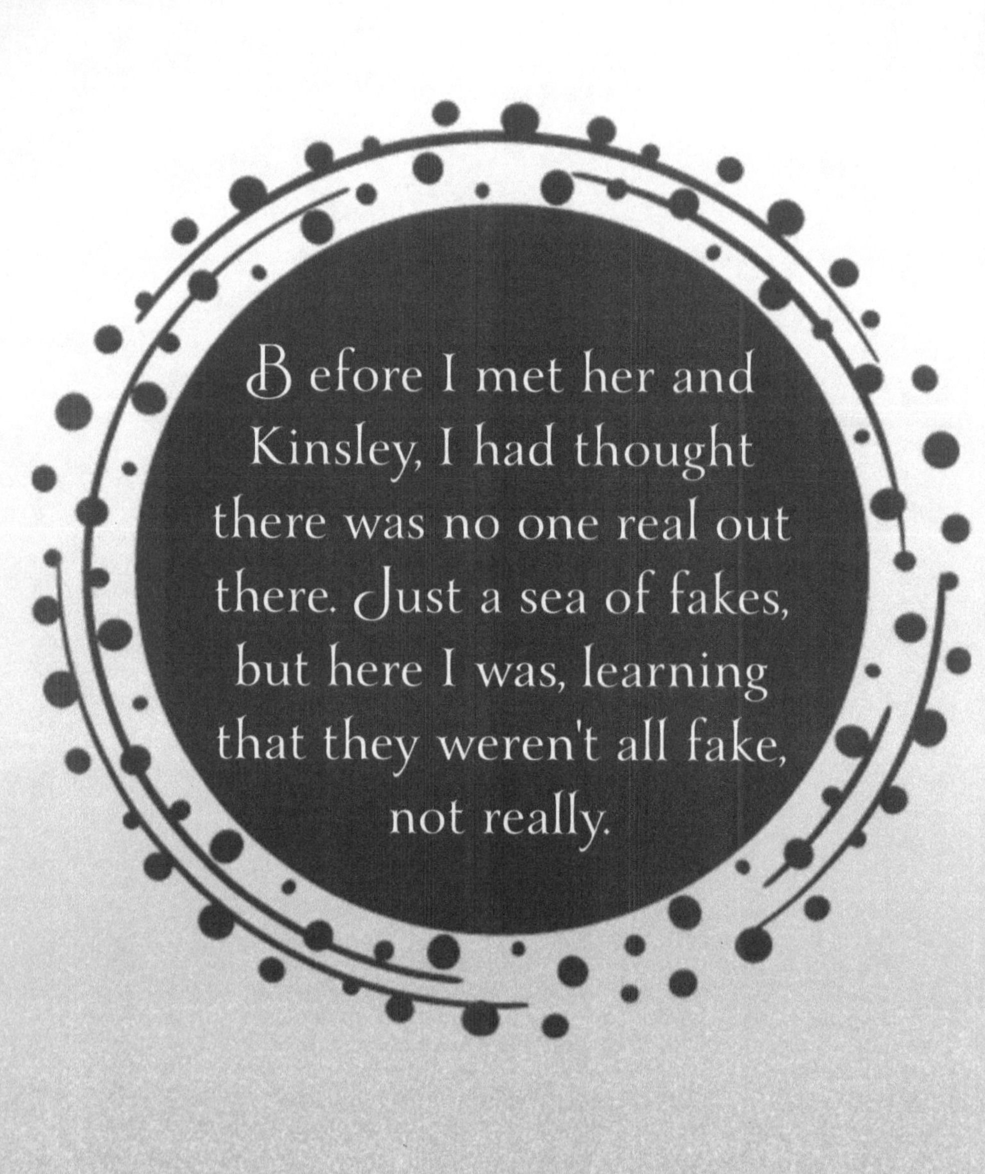
Before I met her and Kinsley, I had thought there was no one real out there. Just a sea of fakes, but here I was, learning that they weren't all fake, not really.

Chapter 27
Luke

The rest of the day was off, ever since lunch. I wanted to enjoy the secrecy of sneaking around torturing my boyfriend with little touches and glances that had him blushing for the rest of the school day, but I couldn't when he looked like that. He was visibly depressed, and Isabella was ignoring both of us. After school, I went to football practice as usual, while Kinsley went up to the art room to wait for me. It was our routine, and then the three of us would go home afterward, or Kinsley would drop me off at work if I needed to work that night.

Usually, Isabella and Kinsley walked up the stairs together, but Kinsley was all alone as he slowly trudged up the stairs. It was a struggle for me to go to practice, seeing him so torn. I wanted to go into the art room with him, to pick him up and curl him against me, to hold him and promise him everything was going to be okay.

But how could I protect him from this? How could I promise him something I wasn't sure of? He hadn't told me it was a fake relationship either, but I understood why he did it and I wasn't angry with him for it. Isabella, on the other hand, also had a legitimate reason to be angry. She had been best friends with him since they were fifteen, and he should have trusted her with the information. It was a large circle of things I understood but couldn't do anything about. In the end, all I could do was watch the two of them silently cry on the inside, offer them both comfort if they wanted it, and wait, hoping they'd get past it and the group would be okay.

I was silent as Serina walked beside me; she was going to practice as well. I never thought I'd be alone with her, and I knew I needed to give her a chance, but I was still slightly hesitant with her because of everything. It was fake, but she still kissed my Kinsley. "I know you don't like me," Serina said after a few seconds.

I flinched, wondering if she was a mind reader. "I don't hate you, I just don't know you," If I could ignore what happened with her and Kinsley, she seemed nice. The way she responsibly handled the party was something to admire about her, and she genuinely seemed like she just wanted to have friends. But was she real like Kinsley and Isabella, or was she fake like everyone else seemed to be?

Serina shrugged, lowering her hood as she absentmindedly pulled her long shiny black hair into a ponytail. I could see the red underneath it more now and wondered how she got away with that if her parents were so strict. Then again, she always seemed to wear it down unless she was doing sports and it was hidden under a cap for meets, maybe she had just been able to hide it this whole time so far. "I'm not in love with him, I'm in love with–"

"I know, Serina. Don't talk about that here," I muttered as I glanced around the hallway. It was mostly empty, but a few others were walking toward the gym as well. In front of us, most of my football players were together shoving each other and laughing. I used to be there standing with them, pretending to smile, pretending I cared about the shit they said, but ever since I started hanging out with Kinsley, I stopped going through the motions of pretending. I wasn't even surprised that none of them seemed to care.

Serina looked off-put and I frowned, wondering if I was about to screw up another friendship for Kinsley. "He had to tell me, to make me understand it was fake. I won't tell her anything, I promise." God, that day was just getting worse and worse.

I was tired of all the secrets. I never wanted to keep anything from those I cared the most about. It was starting to get exhausting. Serina, thankfully, seemed to understand. I was worried she'd start getting mad at Kinsley too, and I wasn't sure if Kinsley could handle everyone hating him at the same time.

Kinsley was so brave and strong, but deep down inside he was just a boy who wished he was more important. While he was the most important person to me, he didn't feel important. Hopefully one day he'd see just how important he was to me, to Isabella, and possibly even to Serina. He needed to see how amazing he was.

"I understand."

We were silent for a moment as we moved toward the gym. We walked through the doors and hovered in the middle of the two locker rooms awkwardly. The girls' changing room was on the opposite side of the boys' and we'd have to split up to get where we were going.

"I just, I don't know. I saw her art and it was like a calling for me. I don't know how to explain it. I saw it, and I wanted to keep seeing it. The more I saw the art on the wall, the more I searched for it. I got so excited seeing each new piece and drawing next to it, like a reply. I didn't know who Izzy was, or what gender she was, I didn't care. I just saw the art and I felt deep in my soul, like it was the other half of me. Does that make sense? I don't know how else to explain it," Serina looked down shyly, her feet shuffled back and forth as she slid a piece of her hair out of her face and behind her ear.

I stared at her in a new light. Maybe it was how she said it, but it reminded me of the letters. It was so long ago since they happened, but they were everything to me. More than once over the last year, I cursed those letters. Cursed how they ended up in my locker, the wrong locker. But at the same time, they meant everything to me. They helped me discover who I am and what I want. Because of them, I was able to find Kinsley.

'Maybe...just maybe...we'll end up falling in love.' I smiled softly as the words from Kinsley's first letter popped into my mind. Before when I had read the letters, I didn't have a voice to them, but now it was his voice I heard when I repeated the letters over and over again in my mind. The words that saved me more times than I could count.

Serina looked embarrassed to have admitted that to me, but I was glad she did because it helped me see her properly. It helped me see that in a way, she was just like us. She knew who Izzy was now, while Izzy didn't know who she was, and I guess in a way, this was Kinsley all over again. I could see why Serina and Kinsley hit it off so well from the beginning because they were the same, while Isabella and I were the ones who needed a little extra push to see that everything we'd always wanted was right there in front of our faces the whole time.

I smiled at her, watching her blink in surprise as I let out a soft laugh. "I understand." We moved slowly, making our way to the wall, trying to put off separating as long as we could while we talked.

Serina's brown eyes shone, tears shimmering on the surface as she realized everything was going to be okay with us. To have friends, more than one friend. Maybe she was like me as well, in that sense. I could see that it was all she wanted. To have people who understood her, who were real, not fake, and to pine away after a certain stubborn someone who hopefully one day would understand. It was funny how I started not liking Serina, and here I was thinking maybe she could be my Izzy. It would be nice to have my own best friend since I couldn't exactly count my boyfriend as one anymore.

Suddenly, I was pulled away from Serina, flung backward as my back pressed against the wall with a strong elbow pressed against my jugular. "Isabella's not enough for you? Do you have to flirt with this one too? What the fuck is wrong with you, Wilson?"

I choked, my eyes wide as Roan's dark brown eyes filled with anger and frustration peered into me. His elbow pressed so tightly against my throat that I couldn't breathe, and I tried to tell myself I needed to stay still and not fight back. However, I couldn't help the internal panic that was causing me to lift my fingers to his arm and try to dig into his skin as I tried to pull him off of me.

It had been a while since I punched him in the face, and I could tell he'd bulked up a little more since then. We were probably even now when it came to strength. I was going to have to start lifting more weights again to make sure I was stronger than him, just in case he tried to hurt Kinsley again.

"Get off of him!" Serina punched Roan in the side and kicked the back of his knee as he held me. "What the fuck is wrong with you!?"

As Roan folded in on himself, I remembered Kinsley talking about middle school and when Roan started being a dick to him. Because Kinsley broke his knee, and even though he was healed and given the okay, it was always going to be a little bit weaker for the rest of his life. He'd have to wear a brace on it when he played, and getting kicked the way Serina had kicked him made him buckle instantly, surprised by the sharp pain in his knee as he let go of me.

I fell to my knees trying to suck air back into my lungs as Serina took a step in front of me, her hands on her hips as she stared Roan down. There was a small group gathering now, people curious because Roan didn't normally bully the athletes and they wanted to see what was going on.

"I never knew you were such a player, Wilson. Did you befriend Kinsley to get with all of his women? You took Isabella from him and now you're going after Serina? What the fuck is wrong with you that you want someone else now that you have Isabella?" Anger flashed in his eyes as he nearly spat at me.

I felt dizzy as I struggled to stand, the oxygen slowly flowing through me as I took deep breaths, trying to calm myself back down again. I thought about what he said, moving it around and around in my mind, confused slightly. "Do you have a crush on Kinsley?" I wasn't even jealous, it was more like surprised. How fucked up would it be that he'd been bullying Kinsley this whole time, calling him slurs and nearly killing him, all because he was secretly gay himself?

Roan's whole face contorted in disgust and anger as he went to charge at me, but Serina stood her ground as he came face to face with her. I jumped towards her, not about to let her get beat up for me. A few of his basketball friends seemed to agree with that thought process as they ran forward and held Roan back, pulling him away from her. "There's no way in hell I like him, that disgusting little faggot!"

"Did you forget Kinsley's dating me?" Serina yelled out, flipping him off as he was pulled backward more. Roan was pulled against the opposite wall as the coach went to talk to him because while Roan usually seemed to get away with bullying those who weren't that important to the school, the football players and the swim team members were a whole other story. We were winning teams, we were important for boosting the school's popularity and getting more sponsors and income for the school. There was a chance Roan might be in trouble this time.

Serina looked around and made sure we were alone before she cupped her hands over her mouth and wiggled her eyebrows at me. "Kinsley is my brother from another mother, you don't have to hate me, Luke. I'll never want him, I promise," she whispered.

I crinkled my nose at her, laughing softly. "Oh my God, you can't say brother from another mother, where did you even get that from?"

She put her hands on her hips, a challenging look in her eyes. "Your boyfriend said it first. He said I was his sister from another mister." I couldn't help but laugh out loud at that.

"I swear, I'm going to tease the shit out of him for that-" I started to say before reality settled back into place and I frowned. "I mean, not right now."

Serina seemed to read my mind, a frown on her face as she took a step towards me. "Luke, she'll come around. I know I'm new to the group but I've seen Kinsley and Isabella around all the time together. They are best friends, the bestest, and they'll be okay."

I shrugged because I hoped she was right. "I just wish I knew what she was trying to hold back. Even in the classroom earlier today she said something was wrong but when I tried to get her to tell me she shut down. And then she said during lunch she thought she did something wrong. Maybe that's part of why she's so angry," I hated feeling so helpless.

Serina watched me, her eyes skimmed over my face as she bit her lip. "Um, I-" she started to say before her swim coach called for her. "I got to go, I'm sorry."

I wasn't sure if what she was about to say was even something important or not, but I shrugged, going into the boys' locker room and changing. I felt like I was in a better place now that I'd talked to Serina, and I hoped it meant I could help Kinsley more instead of acting like a jealous twat. I just wished we were all passed this, the four of us happy, friends, and everything was okay.

A year ago I was just going through the motions, wondering if I should try to kill myself again, but here I was trying desperately to help everyone else live. I never knew I'd have even one person who was more important to me than air itself, but here I was struggling to hold on to everyone, wanting to keep this little group alive and happy.

I practically floated through football, my head in the clouds the whole time, but I seemed to have done it all right since no one yelled at me. Before I knew it, I was dressed and showered, heading up the stairs to the art club. I hoped more than anything that when I opened the door, Kinsley would be talking with Isabella, and everything would be fine. That the fight was passed, and everyone was happy again. But as I opened the door, all I could hear was the giggles of the stoned sophomores in the corner, a slightly bigger group this year since they recruited new freshmen to hang out with them and *show them the ropes.*

Kinsley was off to his side alone, and the place Isabella usually sat was empty. I tugged the chair across from him out and sat down. I remembered this seat, this position, like a flashback. The day I had first discovered who Kinsley was. He had sat down across from me and drew me a butterfly, to prove that he was Sparrow. So much had happened since the last time I had sat across from him in this art club. So much sadness, and so much happiness.

Kinsley was lost in his drawing, his lips turned down into a frown, and I noticed he was drawing Isabella. I didn't want to interrupt him when he was so distracted, so lost in his thoughts, but I pressed the tip of my finger against the top of his paper and slid it against the soft smooth surface, getting his attention.

I waited until he looked up, pulling his headphones out of his ears as the soft sound of SYML blared through the headphones. The stoners started to laugh over something that had to do with the word: *'Moist'* and I leaned forward, close enough for Kinsley to hear me.

"I love you."

Kinsley blinked a few times, a soft blush spilling over his cheeks as he chewed on his bottom lip. A small smile fluttered over his lips as he looked down shyly. "I love you." He slid his pinky finger up the paper and pressed the tip of it against mine. I didn't want to ask him about Isabella, but he seemed to want to talk about it. "She didn't show up, won't answer my texts. She hates me, Luke."

I wrapped my hand around his wrist as I felt his heartbeat beating steadily under my fingertips. "She doesn't hate you, Kinsley. She just needs a minute. She probably called her mother to come to get her. Maybe everything will be okay tomorrow. And even if it isn't, maybe it will be okay the day after. Give her a chance, okay? She just needs to breathe."

The door opened and I flinched in surprise but watched in mild amusement as the group of stoners started to sing a song together and stomp down the hall, leaving us alone in the room. "Fucking weirdos," Kinsley muttered as I choked out a laugh.

Kinsley pulled away from me to put his stuff in his bag, and I watched him as he slid his headphones into his pocket, stood up, and went to the door. He locked it, then came back over to me. I watched him in silence as he pulled my chair back a little, just enough so he could have room as he straddled my waist and sat down in my lap. His chest pressed against mine as he wrapped his arms around my neck and pressed his forehead to my collarbone.

I sighed against him because having him in my arms was everything I'd been craving since the moment we had to leave the house. Nothing felt right unless I was holding him or he was holding me. To feel his skin against mine, not even in a sexual way. Just to touch him, to make sure he was still here, still mine, was everything to me.

As he kissed my collarbone, I closed my eyes, burying my nose in his hair, and breathed him in. I wrapped my arms around his waist, pulling him even closer to me, snuggling us together into our world. We didn't need words to speak, not when we were this connected.

'Don't ever let go,' Kinsley's heart whispered to mine.
And I wouldn't.

'Don't ever let go,'
Kinsley's heart whispered
to mine.

And I wouldn't.

Chapter 28
Luke

I didn't want to leave him like that, but he had wiped his tears and dropped me off at work, promising me he was going to be okay. I knew he had made plans with Izzy to go tagging with her, but I doubted she'd do it now. He probably felt the same way, but knowing him he'd still drive over there and wait, desperately hoping she'd show and forgive him. As Kinsley left I pulled out my phone and dialed Izzy's number. Honestly, I was surprised when she answered me.

"What is it, Curly?" She sounded exhausted. I blinked a few times in surprise, before blurting out the first thing that popped into my mind.

"You don't hate me?" I pressed my fingers against my mouth and shook my head at myself.

She gave a soft chuckle as I mentally scolded myself. "I don't hate any of you. But you don't know, Luke, you didn't do anything wrong. Sure, you found out before me, but I can't blame you for not telling me as you were in the middle of wrapping yourself around him. Literally," she teased.

I blushed, imagining all of the ways I'd been wrapped around Kinsley all weekend, and all of the ways I wanted to do it again. But then I frowned because there was something else everyone but her knew, something much bigger. Who Serina was, and how she felt for Izzy. I felt sick to my stomach keeping that secret, knowing how much this one affected her. I wished I could just tell her, but it wasn't my business to tell. "He's a mess, Izzy," I kicked my feet against the ground.

"As he should be." She snapped. Isabella sighed, and I knew she felt bad.

I opened my mouth and closed it, unsure of what to even say or how to help. Kinsley was the nice one, he was the one who always knew what to say, but I needed to be strong for him. "He loves you, Izzy. He just wants everything to be okay. He never meant to hurt you. He didn't want to force you to keep a secret from me."

"I don't understand why you're not angry about it. He lied to you too, and if he hadn't pretended it was fake, you wouldn't have even gotten so jealous and upset about it."

I nodded. I glanced at the garage and I could see Paul, my boss, pacing as he glanced at the clock, probably wondering where I was. "Without the jealousy, I wouldn't have had the courage to confess to him. Maybe somewhere down the line I probably would have thrown him against the wall and kissed him or something when it got to be too much, but then how long would that have been?

"How much missed time? We've already missed almost a year together as it is because I was too stupid to see, and now, how much is left? We're going to graduate soon, are you going to keep hating him then? What about all of your plans on getting a place together in New York? Is everything just broken now?"

I hadn't thought about it before, but what about us? It had always been Kinsley's dream to go off and get a place with Isabella, but what about now? Was he automatically including me in it? Was there even anything in New York for me? I didn't think this was just a casual fling for either of us. Growing up, turning into adults, it was so fucking scary sometimes. Isabella sighed, and I could just see her pinch the bridge of her nose in frustration. "Why do you have to put it like that?" She mumbled, her words sharp as she tried desperately to hold onto her anger.

She was so stubborn, but I knew she was just as hurt as Kinsley was. "Give me a day to be angry, okay? Just one day, and I'll be fine. Pick me up tomorrow."

As she hung up, I stared at the phone, blinking a few times, before letting out a soft laugh. I guessed one day of anger was allowed, considering everything. I admired Isabella, how strong she was, how sure she was.

I decided to send Kinsley a small text, knowing he wasn't happy and I wanted to make sure he knew he wasn't alone. *'I love you, Pretty Boy.'*

Kinsley's reply was pretty much instant. *'Missed me already?'* I grinned because I could just see his cocky expression, his hand on his hip as he raised his eyebrow at me. *'I love you too, Lukie.'*

I put my phone in my pocket, feeling lighter than ever as I walked into the garage. His nickname he had only ever called me once, back when he was drunk. I didn't think he remembered it, he probably would have said something to me if he suddenly remembered the kiss, but it still made me smile hearing him call me that.

Although Paul was pacing in a way that told me he was waiting for me, he was also looking pretty distracted. He was on his phone typing something when I slid past him. I made my way to the few lockers in the back and slipped my shoes off, my clothes following. I used to just wear whatever and slide the overalls on top without care, but ever since I started to live with Kinsley in his pretty house filled with expensive loneliness I started to feel self-conscious about all of the grease on my shoes and my clothes.

I started to leave a handful of t-shirts and jeans there, dirty steel-toe boots I didn't care to keep getting grease on, and left them in the locker. Paul had a washing machine and a dryer there, albeit a cheap one that I needed to fix every once in a while, but it was good enough for me to wash my greasy clothes in when I felt like they were getting too dirty.

As I slipped the dirty jeans on, my boss scared the crap out of me, coming up behind me and touching my shoulder blade. "Dang, son. Got yourself a girlfriend? Those are some scratches," he said, making me jump and twirl around with wide eyes.

"I um," I stammered, shuffling my feet as I quickly buttoned my jeans, tugging on my bottom lip. I wasn't sure what to say to that. This town was so judgmental, and I wasn't sure where Paul stood with all of it. Was it okay to tell people I had a boyfriend? Would I be okay? But in the end, I couldn't do it, not just yet, because I was scared; I wasn't ready. Not yet, anyway.

"Something like that," I felt like a coward. Would Kinsley have agreed to it? Would he have stood there and corrected him? For the first time, I realized maybe instead of being brave like Kinsley, I should start being brave like Luke. I just needed to figure out how.

Paul slapped my shoulder with a grin as I finished dressing. I apologized to him for being a tad bit late, since it was only about ten minutes and we didn't look busy, but he waved his hand before I could finish my apology, surprising me once more. Normally he was adamant about me being on time.

As I grabbed a bandana, I followed him into the main area of the garage while he started to bite his inner cheek distractedly. The smell of oil was thick in the air, and I automatically breathed it in as I slid the bandana onto my head, making sure to tie it tightly in the back to keep my curls off of my forehead.

Maybe it was strange for me to love the smell of oil, the smell of grease, and the feel of the machines under my fingers, but this was what I loved, what I enjoyed. Maybe, just maybe, I should take a minute later to look up colleges in New York for mechanics. I'm sure it wouldn't be hard, I could probably apply to just about any school for it, most of them had the basics at least. To be near Kinsley, to at least try to be near him, to give him the option that I wasn't going to go away unless he wanted me to. I wanted to at least give him that. I didn't care where I ended up, what state I was in, or what country even, all I cared about was being with him.

This wasn't a casual fling for me. It was more, so much more. I was scared of how much I felt for him, but at the same time, the thought of breaking up, of leaving each other, terrified me even more.

'Do you believe in marriage?' Kinsley's voice popped into my head, stopping me cold as I looked down at the ground and simply stared. I was glad my boss was even more distracted than I was because he didn't seem to notice as I stared down at my ring finger, my thumb sliding over it repeatedly, contemplating things I'd never once contemplated before.

"There's something I need to talk to you about, Luke," Paul said, snapping me out of my thoughts.

I gave him a soft nod at how serious he looked as I grabbed a pair of gloves, sliding them into my back pocket in case I needed them. I could see a box sitting over near my car and wondered if that was a piece I'd been waiting for. Normally I'd have walked right over to it, excited over the new box, but I could see by the way my boss was looking at me with a guilty expression on his face that I needed to focus on this, whatever this was.

"Are you firing me?" I blurted out as I started to wring my hands together. I was waiting for it, to be honest. The shit my father pulled those months ago. I was still surprised every day I came in here and he just waved me toward the newest cars to work on. Just waiting for him to tell me to get out, that he didn't want the son of a monster in his shop, or anywhere near him.

Paul blinked, his head tilted to the side as he frowned at me, crossing his arms over his chest. "Of course not, Luke,"

I studied him, taking in his nervous stance. He had longer hair than mine, his down to his shoulders, the reason I started using bandanas was that he did as well. His hair was a dirty blond, and when it was caked with grease and dirt it looked brown, as it did now. His body was about as muscular as my dad's, if not more, which was kind of normal for this type of job. It was hard, lifting tires and such, most of these car parts were heavy and the muscle helped.

Even though he was an older man, muscular and strong enough to hurt me, I wasn't scared of him as I was of my dad, or as I have been of Kinsley's dad. Maybe it was because I'd been working for him since I was fifteen, and I knew him better than I knew my father. I knew he was a good man, and I knew he wouldn't hurt me.

"Come sit down, son. I need to tell you something," he said, guilt strong in his voice as he led me toward the back of the garage.

He had his little office area in the back, a dirty table that had more grease on it than anything else. Stacks of papers off the side that needed to be signed and filed, were thrown to the side without a care. His winter jacket was laid against the back of the chair as I sat down on the stool that was across from the desk. Paul leaned over and opened the small mini fridge he had under his desk, pulling out a couple of sodas and handing me one. They were rootbeer, the kind in the glass bottle and I had to take a second to get the top off of it before I could take a sip of it, enjoying the way the cool liquid felt on my dry throat.

"Look, I don't know how to say this, Luke. You know I've never been one for small talk, I don't give a damn about the weather or the state of the local football team. So I'm just going to say it, okay?"

I gave a tight nod as I realized he was waiting for me to reply something, and as he nodded back I put the bottle down on the desk, wondering what it was that he was getting so worked up over. If it wasn't about him firing me, I doubted he'd be promoting me. We were the only two in the damn shop after all. Maybe he was going to tell me he was hiring someone else and I was getting fewer hours. "Your mother and I have been in contact since she was placed in the psych ward," he spat out, surprising me entirely.

Of all the things I was expecting him to say, anything about my mother wasn't one of them. "After you got out of jail, I found out the info about the psych ward. She said she didn't want any visitors, but she let me come see her. She felt bad about you and said she should have backed you up, but she wasn't in her right mind. She was terrified, still is,

Luke. I'm not going to tell you that she was in the right not sticking by you when you told the cops about your pop, but she was scared. Being a victim, it's not easy."

My hands clenched into fists, my cheeks spotted with embarrassment because he knew. He knew how weak I was, how I couldn't protect my mom or anyone. "I, um," I stammered, unsure what to say to that.

How to make your thoughts move, the way you want them to? My mind was blank, trying to think of a reply, but I was lost. Lost in the rush of everything coming back to me. That night, the feel of getting slammed, my shoulder cracked against the frame, his breath in my face as he spat at me, punched me, kicked me. My mom's tiny useless blows on my body, watching her get dragged away. All of it was like a rush flowing through me, and I grabbed the trash can beside his desk and threw up.

I didn't realize I was crying until I snapped back into reality and found him rocking me gently, his strong arms wrapped around me as he shushed me, patting my back almost awkwardly. We didn't do this, not us. We had known each other for so long, but we didn't hug, we didn't cry, and we didn't open up to each other. It was awkward, but he didn't leave as I sobbed, clutching the trash can tightly in my hands.

"Luke, I'm sorry. I didn't want to bring it up, I was just trying to explain. There's more to explain," he said, his voice filled with sadness.

I nodded, letting go of the trash can but keeping it close by as he passed me my root beer. I took a sip of it, my nose crinkled in disgust at the taste of it all mixed, and swished it around my mouth, spitting it into the trash can in disgust, before taking another sip and swallowing it. "It's okay, I'm okay," I stammered, my teeth clicking together as I tried to calm my racing heart. More than anything, I wished Kinsley was here. Kinsley with his touch that calmed me. Kinsley, the calm to my storm.

As Paul sat back, giving me a little space, we both found ourselves sitting on the ground without caring about moving to the chairs. I turned to look at him almost shyly, feeling strange having cried in front of him like that. I wiped my hand across my cheeks, trying to hide the evidence as if that was going to make what happened fade away. "I've been visiting your mother, talking to her, and she's told me just about everything. She's been taking her meds and getting better. She got out, Luke. A week ago, she's out."

I watched him pick at some dirt that was caked onto the bed of his nail as he chewed on his bottom lip, nervous. "Where did she go?" I asked, trying to keep the hurt out of my voice. I hadn't changed my number, after all. Why didn't she try to call me? Kinsley had given the keys to my mom's storage unit to the desk of the psych ward when I had handed them her things, so she'd have them when she got out. Did she take everything out of the storage unit? Did she get a home somewhere else? "Why didn't she call me?"

My boss patted my shoulder with a heavy sigh. "She feels guilty, and she knows you're in a much better place now. She knows you're living with the Bryants, and she didn't think you'd want her to disrupt your life. But I felt like you should know, so I told you. She, we..." he stammered, looking at his desk, at the ceiling, at the floor, anywhere but at me.

"We're dating. Taking it slow, you know? She moved into my house with me. You're always welcome to come to visit or to stay as well if you want. She misses you. You can come live with us. Anytime. I know I'm not your father. I wouldn't want to be that motherfucker– I mean, I won't try to replace your father, Luke, but I do intend to marry her one day if she'll have me. I won't hurt her, I'll never hurt her, or you. I know it's hard to believe, given what you've been through, but I promise. I would never lay a hand on any of you."

I think I was in shock, my eyes wide as my boss handed me a paper with his address on it. It was so much information, so much to handle, so much I hadn't expected. My mom was better? All I could see was the faint images of her smiling, the way she'd take my hands and dance my little toddler body around the kitchen, or pull the stool up to the counter so I could lick the whisk. We used to sing along to the little radio on the counter as she baked. The hugs, the kisses, the smiles. Was it possible she could return to that? Could I?

I wasn't sure what to think about his offer. To live with her again. To see her kind, to see her happy. I wanted to see that again, but... Kinsley. I was shaking, as I folded the paper and slipped it into my pocket. Paul stood now, his hand held out as he smiled softly at me. Gently, I grabbed his hand, allowing him to pull me up to my feet. "You're more of a father than my father has ever been."

His eyes went wide as I thought of the few times my father had been kind. Taking me fishing, how he'd hold me and kiss my forehead, call me his boy, and tell me he was proud of me. So long ago, so few, and drowned under all of the yelling, the fists, the fighting, the screaming.

Paul opened his mouth, closed it, and I decided then and there, it was time to be strong. Strong like Luke. "I'll visit, I promise. But I don't want to move in. Not because I have a problem with my mother, or with you. But because I want to stay where I am. To stay with Kinsley. My boyfriend. I want to stay with my boyfriend." I let out a soft shaky breath.

My heart raced as I stared at him. I pressed my fingers over my mouth, scared. I was shaking as he stared at me, his mouth hanging open like a fish, before snapping it shut once more. I wondered if this was okay, to say this now. To tell him like this, to tell him at all. I didn't even know why I did it, to be honest. He wasn't my father, and now maybe he wasn't going to be. Would he still want to marry my mother knowing his future stepson was dating a boy?

I immediately felt mad at myself, wondering why I had let it slip out like that. To be strong, but I shouldn't have said it, not like that. What if I ruined the small bit of happiness my mom had been craving all along? What if I ruined everything? I took a step back, my eyes wide as he stared at me.

Maybe I just wanted to have someone older, someone like a father, who would tell me everything was okay. That they were proud of me, no matter what. Maybe I just wanted a little bit of that happiness too.

"I, um," I felt vulnerable under his stare. Was he going to fire me now? Kick me out, take back his address, tell me to never come back? Was he going to hurt me too? I curled my arms around my waist as his hand came close to my face, fear racing through me.

But instead of the blow that I expected to feel against my face, instead of the grip of fingers against my body as I got shoved to the wall and punched, he patted my shoulder gently. I was shocked as he pulled me against him, hugging me a little less awkwardly than before. I realized this was the first time I had come out, besides Kinsley. It was terrifying. "It's okay, son. I understand. Have you told anyone else?"

I knew what he was asking. *Does your dad know? Does your mom?* But he said it was okay, and that little bit of hope flowed through me as I shook, my teeth clattering in my mouth even though I wasn't cold. "No, besides Kinsley, you're the first one I've told," I said. Serina and Isabella knew, but Kinsley had told them, not me.

He was quiet as he patted my back, then he let out a hum of acknowledgment. "You were always welcome in my house, you and Kinsley both."

And I shattered, all over again.

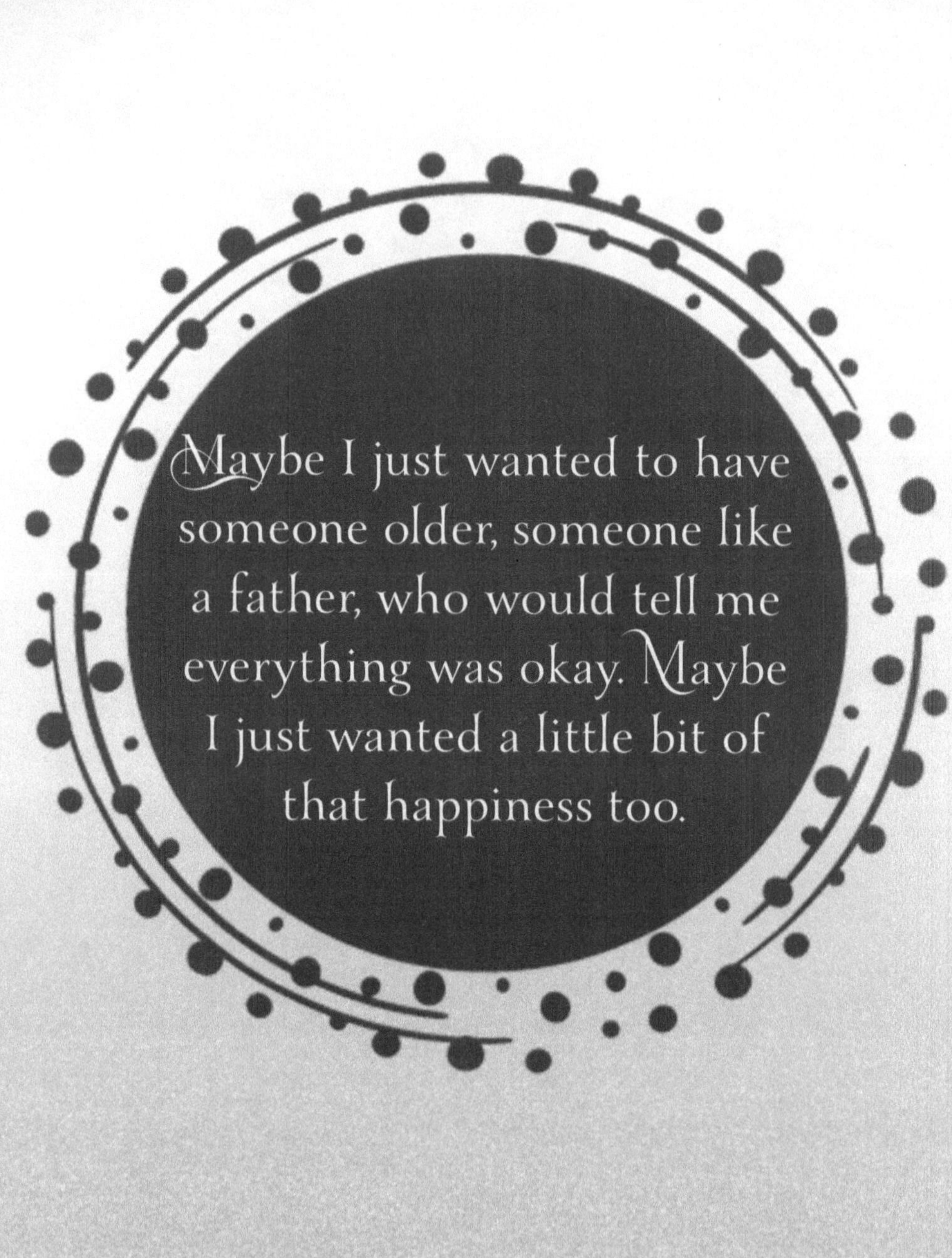
Maybe I just wanted to have someone older, someone like a father, who would tell me everything was okay. Maybe I just wanted a little bit of that happiness too.

Chapter 29
Kinsley

I was lost in my thoughts until Luke came through the door. As always, I left it open for him, even though he had a key. I didn't want him to ever feel like he wasn't welcome. He was covered in grease, his curls pressed down under the weight of it. Stains patterned over his cheeks and his throat. His nails were caked, but his clothes and his shoes were clean, indicating he changed at work before coming home. He gave me an exhausted smile before heading into the bathroom.

I stood up and grabbed some clothes for him out of his dresser, following him into the bathroom. On nights like this when he worked late, his boss drove him home, or at least up to the gate. I always told him to call me and get me to come to get him, but he said he liked to walk sometimes, even if it was just from the gate to the house.

I tried to hide my sadness. I had a soft light blue blanket wrapped around my shoulders, holding it tightly against me not for warmth, but for security. Isabella hadn't been there. No matter how long I waited, she wasn't there. I parked at the graveyard and stared at her house, but Izzy never came out.

I was snapped out of my thoughts as Luke's lips brushed softly against mine, like a whisper, before pulling away. I smelled the sharp smell of grease on his tanned skin as he stared at me, a smile fluttered over my lips despite the turmoil I felt inside me. "I like the mechanic smell," I blurted out as my cheeks started to heat up, unsure why I had even said that.

Luke peered at me from under his eyelashes as he started to grin a slow grin, to which my heart responded with wings fluttering around inside my chest. "Good." His voice was a rumble, clearly thrown by what I said as he took a step back to yank his shirt off of his body. He threw it into the laundry hamper we both shared and I watched his body as his muscles moved under his skin.

My finger darted out and traced a line down his abs absently. Luke sucked in a soft breath as he looked back at me. "I'm dirty," he muttered, his cheeks a soft glow as I put his clean clothes down on the sink counter and started to fumble with his belt.

"I don't care," I whispered.

He pressed his lips to my forehead, before taking a step back, out of the way of my exploring hands. "Give me a few minutes, then I can hug you, okay? I don't want to get you dirty," he said with a soft chuckle. "You look so cozy like that, I just want to hug you,"

I pouted as he turned on the shower and stubbornly sat down on the bathroom floor. I leaned against the doorframe as he chuckled at me. He must have accepted that I wasn't going to go away and he shrugged, undressing the rest of the way. He wasn't shy as he moved around naked in front of me, but I wasn't surprised, he did tend to dress in a locker room almost every day with about thirty other guys.

Luke stepped into the shower, his body slightly obscured by the tinted glass, and closed my eyes, laying my head on my knees. I wrapped my arms around my knees as my blanket curled me into a small ball, and I tried as hard as I could not to hold onto the sadness that was choking me. "She hates me," I mumbled, loud enough that he could hear.

Luke opened the shower door a crack and a small trickle of water slipped down the side and tapped against the ground. I opened my eyes to watch it slowly form into a small circle, to sit there, slowly accumulating. "She doesn't hate you. I talked to her today, Kins. She just needs a little bit of space. She said for us to pick her up in the morning."

I sighed in relief because while I knew what I had done was wrong and she was still going to be upset about it, I was glad she wasn't going to stop being my friend. It's always been Kinsley and Isabella, and I couldn't imagine a future without her by my side. "Is this your first fight with her?"

I had to strain to hear his words over the sound of the water slapping heavier than before against the shower floor. Luke's elbows were raised as he scrubbed at his curls, the water falling around him. "The second one," a soft chuckle spilled from my lips as I remembered. "She got pissed off at me for letting her get so drunk she got a huge tattoo. She blames me for her indulgent ways, it seems. Now she has to be careful around her mom at all times. Mami would kill her if she ever saw that."

Luke was laughing as the shower turned off, the smell of the orange soap he used to get rid of the grease was tangent in the air as he opened the shower door all the way and grabbed the towel hanging close by. I watched him as he dried off, his curls wet and bouncing on top of his head as he shook it, the towel sliding up and down his body to dry off as much as he could.

Noticing the little circle of water, he threw the towel on top of it and stepped on it, drying the floor. Luke grabbed his boxers and pulled them up as I scooted close to him and wrapped my legs around his ankle. I wrapped my arms around his knee, holding his leg in a tight grasp against my body.

"Kins, I need my leg to put my pants on," he said as I shook my head stubbornly, not caring that I was acting like a baby. He sighed, a smile on his lips as he walked awkwardly into the bedroom with me clinging to his leg.

"Are you being a koala tonight, baby?" he asked, his voice slightly breathless from the strain of walking with my weight on his left leg.

My cheeks were red as I buried my face in his leg, the hairs softly tickling me as my heart thumped faster and faster in my chest. Despite how sad I was over Isabella, I couldn't help but smile, hearing him call me that. So casually, so calmly, with no hesitation.

"Your Koala," I muttered. Luke leaned down and placed his hands under my armpits, lifting me off of his leg and holding me against his chest. I wrapped my legs around his waist as he carried me the rest of the way to the bed. He sat down and scooted back, his arms around me, holding me against him. Neither of us was in a hurry to let go.

I felt warm in his embrace, my face pressed against his collarbone as I inhaled the smell of his body wash on his throat. The water from his curls slowly dripped down my face and slid down my nose to his collarbone, molding against both of our chests as we pressed them tightly together. I wrapped my blanket around both of us as he pulled me even closer to him, warming every part of me from the inside out. "My mom is out of the psych ward," Luke's voice was soft, hesitant.

I sat up, my forehead pressed against his. I chewed on my bottom lip, worried. "That's a good thing, right? That means she's taking her meds correctly and trying to get better?" I wasn't entirely sure how it all worked with a psych ward.

Luke shrugged. "I guess so. I mean she'll still have to go to therapy, she'll still have to take the meds. But I guess they helped her get past her manic episode and put her on a proper path. It's not the first time she's been in a psych ward but I guess this time it'll be different. She moved in with my boss, I guess." He said, his gaze on my cheek. I felt water slide down it and he lifted his finger to it, rubbing softly against the water from his hair, smearing it into my skin.

"I knew my boss always had a crush on my mom, I just didn't know it would ever get this far. He said they've been in contact, and they're dating now. Taking it slow, you know? He gave me his address. Said if I wanted to move in with them, I could."

I tried as hard as I could to keep my breath even, telling myself that even if he left, that didn't mean he was leaving me. Would his feelings for me fade away if he wasn't living with me anymore? I didn't want to believe that was possible. I swallowed down my insecurities as I took a deep breath. He was staring at me, waiting for me to say something, anything.

I wasn't going to be selfish and told him he couldn't leave, that he couldn't go live with his mother. He wasn't my property. "That's awesome. He's a good guy, right? She's been through so much, I'm glad she's dating someone who knows about what happened and still wants to be with her. Are you going to go?" I tried to keep the strain out of my voice.

It was only fair that he knew it was all his choice. I wasn't going to hold him back if it was what he wanted. Luke studied my expression, and I hoped desperately he wasn't able to read my mind. "I don't want to go. Not to live there, I mean. I told him I'd visit."

I was surprised because he had chosen me over his mother. It wasn't even going to be a choice; I would have never made him choose. "You can go if you want to. I'm not going anywhere. I'll still be with you, as long as you want me to be. I don't want you to think you have to stay here to stay with me."

I cupped his cheeks, his seafoam green eyes moved back and forth as he watched me. Both of us were filled with unspoken thoughts, thoughts of worry and fear, of things we shouldn't even be worried and scared of. Then again, I guess that's what being a teenager meant in the long run. They should probably write that in the dictionary under the word teenagers.

"You're my home, Kinsley. Where you are, is the only place I will ever want to be." He said, his voice deep as he watched me. I cupped the back of his neck, our noses pressed together as I sucked in a deep breath of surprise. But it seemed he wasn't done surprising me, not yet.

"I told him, Paul. I told him you're my boyfriend." His cheeks danced a lovely coral color in embarrassment as he looked down, his skin under my fingers warmer to the touch and I wasn't sure what to think about what he had just said. He told his boss? "Sorry, I guess I kind of outed you," he added as an afterthought.

I wasn't even angry. I felt elated. I was happy that he'd said it out loud, that our relationship was important enough to him to want to tell someone important to him. Of all the times he'd told me how brave I was, he had been braver than he thought he was. "Are you okay with this? He'll tell your mom, and then your mom will know. What about the future? What if she hates you?" I felt slightly breathless, my heart pounding with worry. *What if you regret me?*

He was quiet as his fingers slid down my waist, lifting the soft material of the black shirt I had on, lightly tracing his fingers up and down my sides. It was because my parents were home that I was even wearing a shirt. But Luke had locked the door when he walked in, and I wasn't worried about them walking in and seeing us.

"If she loves me, she'll accept me for who I am. Who I am, is connected to you. She can't love me if she can't accept my love for you." He lifted his eyes to mine. "As for the future? I spent my break looking at colleges in New York. It's yours and Izzy's dream to go there, right? My dream is to be with you, wherever you go."

I felt a knot in my throat as I stared at him, overwhelmed by his words. I had been worried about the after too, but I had tried to hide it, unsure what was going to happen once we graduated. I let out a soft shaky breath as I smiled at him, my thumbs brushed up and down the sides of his neck, toying with the curls around the nape of his neck.

"So we're all moving to New York then? You're going to live with me and Izzy? You'll be fine with that kind of future planning?"

"You're not getting rid of me that easily, Kinsley Bryant."

I grinned, unable to stop myself from teasing him. Every day, he seemed to be surprising me more and more than the last. "Careful," I taunted, flashing my teeth at him. "If you don't watch it, someone will think you're proposing."

Luke shrugged, his eyes lowered to my lips, before raising them to my eyes once more. "I mean we've kind of been together for a year without realizing it, so I guess it's long enough to propose, right? The wedding would have to wait until later though."

As I stared at him in shocked silence, his nose slid up and down the length of mine, and a soft hum of contentment spilled from his throat. "I thought you didn't believe in marriage?" I whispered. All I could think about was the conversation I had with him one night. Where he said all marriages ended up like his parents, and he'd never want to force someone to go through that with him.

Luke cupped my cheeks, pressing his fingers against the soft skin, his eyes filled with a seriousness that told me he wasn't kidding anymore. The way he was staring at me was filled with promises of things I never thought I'd have, things that I wanted desperately. "I believe in you, Kinsley," he said, his eyes searching mine.

Without another word, I pulled him closer to me. My lips pressed against his with a desperation I didn't think was possible. He leaned back, my legs straddling him as he lay down on the bed. As I pulled the blanket over our heads, we were lost in each other, lost in the one place we forever wanted to be.

We were woken up by pounding on the stairs and screaming. I had never had a storm in my house that wasn't centered around my parents yelling at me, standing together as a team as they attacked me verbally. I froze, wrapped around Luke's arms, my face buried in his chest. I was startled, listening to my parents screaming at each other. Luke let out a soft whimper, indicating he was awake, and I sat up fast, staring down at him. My heart raced as he pressed his fingers against his face, his knees pulled up to his chest, fear pouring out of every part of him. "No," he whimpered, his voice broken as the storm raged on.

I stood up, grabbed my boxers off of the ground, and pulled them on, going over to the door and pressing my ear against it. I wanted to double-check that it was locked as I listened. I could hear little snippets of their fight through the closed door and clenched my teeth in disgust, determined to never be that, to never do that. To never fight like that.

My father accused my mother of letting a client touch her inappropriately, and instead of sitting down and discussing it like rational adults, they both slurred their words, spitting cusses and insults at each other. It was clear that they were both drunk by the sound of their words.

I heard glass shattering, my father's loud booming voice and Luke stood up fast and got out of the bed and slipped on his boxers. His breath came out in fast pants as his eyes widely stared around the room, searching for an escape. I didn't have a ladder connected to my window like his did, and a soft sob slipped from his lips as he stared at the closed bedroom door.

I walked over to him and pressed my hands against his cheeks, forcing him to look at me as his body went rigid, the need for flight making his body tense. "Luke, look at me," I said, my voice strong, filled with the anger I was feeling at my parents. "Don't focus on them, focus on me." A soft whimper spilled from his throat. His cheeks were coated in wet crystalline lines that glittered from the moonlight pouring into the window.

Luke was breathing harder, his hands clenched in fists at his side, and I was scared he was going to have a panic attack again. Quickly, I grabbed my comforter off of the bed and wrapped it around his body, the blanket covered most of his curls as I held it closed over his chest, covering almost all of him from view.

His eyes were wide as he clasped his hands around the blanket, pulling it even closer against him like a security blanket while he stared around the room, and I tried once more to get through to him. I grabbed the blanket where it was around his head, pulling his face down to mine as our foreheads pressed together, forcing him to see only me, just me.

"Baby," I whispered, watching his eyes flutter in response. "Don't listen to it, don't think about it, don't see it." My hands shook in anger. "When you think no one sees you, I see you. When you think no one knows you, I know you. You're not alone, I will always be here with you."

Luke let out a soft ragged breath, his body shaking under the blanket as his eyes focused on me. "You're my calm in the middle of the storm," Luke whispered, his eyes searching mine.

I nodded at him as I took a step back, going over to my desk. As the sound of glass shattering filled the house once more, I grabbed my headphones and my phone. I slipped the headphones over his ears and held the phone in my hands for a moment as I stared at him, watching him for a moment, before replying to him. "You'll never have to worry about the storm with me," I promised, before hitting the play button on my phone.

I was angry as I left my room and nearly ran down the stairs. I didn't care that I was only wearing boxers. By the time I found my parents in the middle of the living room surrounded by broken glass, they were too drunk to notice my tattoo anyway. Before I knew it, all I was doing was yelling at them.

"What the hell is wrong with you? There are kids in the house. Behaving like this is unnecessary. You're both drunk, go to sleep and talk it out in the morning. What will this achieve? What does this help? It does nothing but scare everyone around you! Not that I expect you to care about your kids. Your daughter is probably going to be a teen mom with the way you let her sleepover at her boyfriend's house all the time. She's only in middle school.

"You never check on me, never ask me how I am. Do you even know how many times I've sat there waiting for you to care about me? To remember I exist? But you never will, will you? Because I'll never be good enough to fit into your picture-perfect world. All you ever care about is yourself, even now, throwing a tantrum like two-year-olds in the middle of the night. If anyone in this house needs to be disappointed in anyone, it's me disappointed in you."

My parents were too drunk to probably remember any of this, but I let them have all of my feelings, screaming at them until there was nothing left to come out. Then I grabbed my father and shoved him onto the couch. I grabbed my mother's arm and guided her to their bedroom, tucking her into bed as I came back to the living room to throw an extra pillow and blanket at my father's blank expression.

The maid wasn't here, that would be strange if she was randomly here at this time, but even if she was, I wouldn't have made her clean their mess like this. I grabbed a trash bag and started cleaning it myself, grumbling here and there at my stupid father who kept lying there blinking blankly at the stupidly unnecessary tall ceiling until he passed out.

I was surprised when I finished to see Kennedy standing at the top of the stairs watching me, silently staring, before turning around and going back into her room. By the time I got back up to my bedroom, it was late. Luke and my kind of late, our promised hour. He was on his knees, but the blanket was still wrapped around him and my headphones were blaring in his ears. I was glad he looked calmer, and as I sat down in front of him, he turned off the music and silently pulled the headphones off of his ears, staring at me.

"I'm tired of being broken," he whispered, exhaustion in his voice.

I could see it, too. How tired he was, how frustrated he was. I sat cross-legged in front of him, reaching into the blanket to press against his chest, my eyes never leaving his as I felt his heart fluttering against the palm of my hand. "Silly," I breathed out a soft laugh as he threaded his eyebrows at me in confusion.

Luke grabbed my wrist, the rough pads of his fingertips finding my pulse and pressing against it gently. "How is that silly?"

I took a deep breath, my lips curling into a soft smile. "You're not broken, Luke. You're a half, and I'm a half, and together we're whole," I whispered, feeling the truth in my words as his heart sped up against my hand. "You were never broken, Luke, and neither was I. We just needed to be with each other, to be complete."

He let out a soft shaky breath as his Adam's apple slowly bobbed up and down, and I watched as his lips twitched and he smiled.

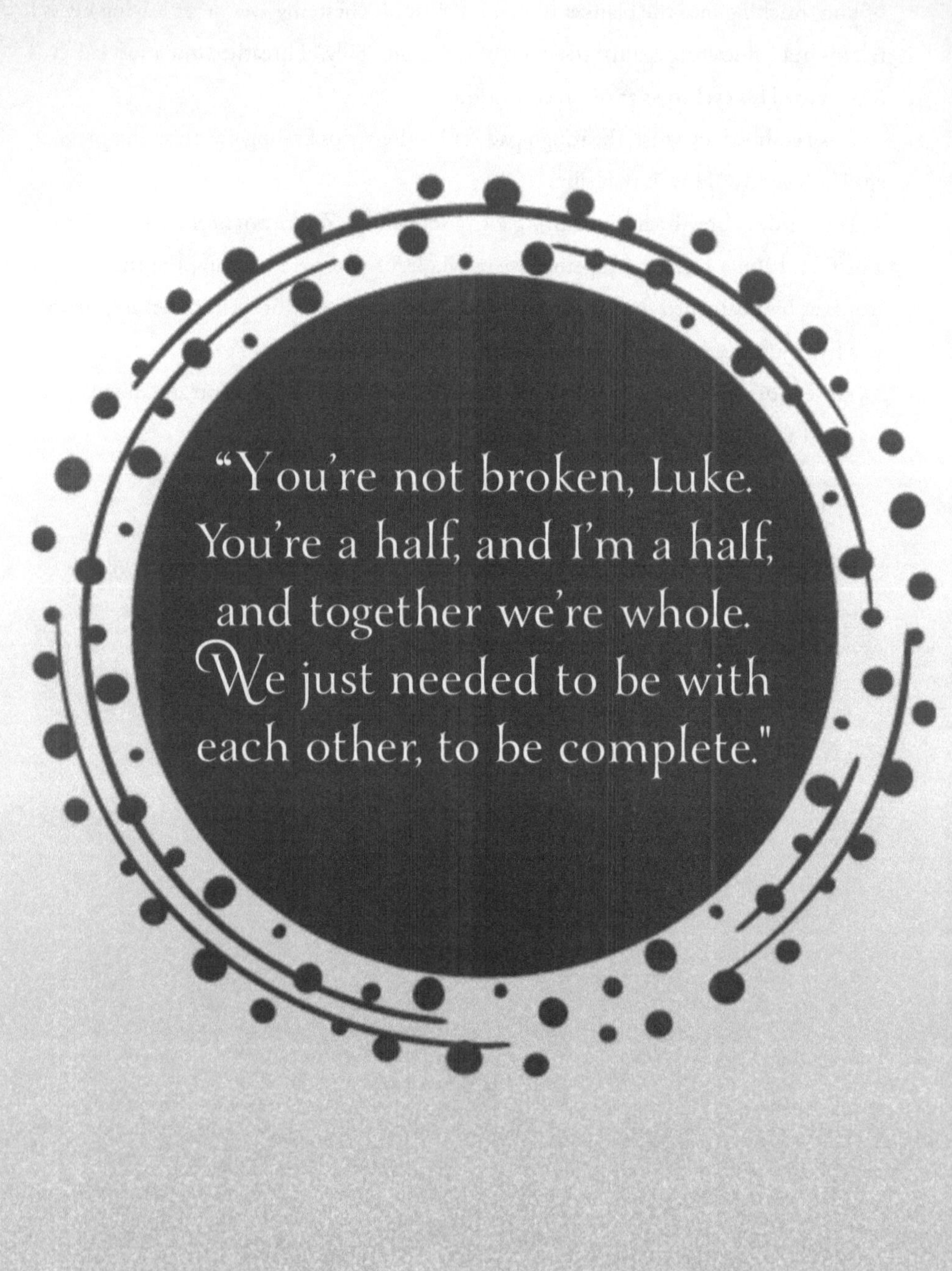
"You're not broken, Luke. You're a half, and I'm a half, and together we're whole. We just needed to be with each other, to be complete."

Chapter 30
Kinsley

I woke up three minutes before the alarm went off and lay there the whole time just taking in all that was Luke. He was lying on his stomach, his arms lifted under the pillow and raised above his head, his fingertips brushing delicately against the headboard. The blanket was pooled at his waist, showing off his upper body for me to just hungrily stare at. My eyes skimmed over every line, every curve, in a way that I never would have had the courage to look before.

But he was mine now, and there was nothing wrong with looking at the lines and the curves that my hands had memorized again and again. Luke was like a puzzle, and I found myself slowly tracing every curve, my fingers sliding over the soft tanned skin on his back as he sighed in contentment. I placed his pieces back together over and over again with every dip and every touch; every kiss.

Even as I stared at him, however, I couldn't stop thinking about last night. How broken he sounded, how sad. Every sob, every clenched fist, every strained word was etched in my mind and it shattered me over and over again, knowing that my boy had gone through that; such pain. I couldn't help but wonder how many broken synapses had held him together. How long it would take before every scream, every bang, every hit melted into silence; his storm to finally fade away. I wanted to take care of him, to be there for him, but I knew I wasn't enough. I wished I knew how to be enough for him to breathe the way I desperately wished he could breathe.

Of all the things they taught you in school, they didn't teach you how to love someone that was broken. They didn't teach you how much it tore into you, mind, body, and soul. How worried those who had to watch and see were, how horrifying it was to listen to the sobs that were broken in ways you didn't know quite how to fix, no matter how hard you tried.

I turned towards the phone and checked the time, turning off the alarm before it could go off, and told myself five more minutes before I would wake him. I fluttered my fingers through his curls, watching them bounce softly around his forehead as his nose crinkled from the tickle of the hair on his skin.

There was something peaceful about the way his freckles dotted soft little paths from one shoulder blade to the next, a path I was certain I was the only one who ever took time to appreciate. Like the flutter of leaves spilling over his skin, he was covered in beauty so grand I was reluctant to look away but knew that I needed to. As much as I would love to lay here and memorize every breath, every sigh, every soft groan of his body stretching, we had to go to school.

I sat up and slipped out of bed quietly because I wanted to give him five more minutes before he was woken from the safety and the security we made together. How someone who thought he was broken could come into a broken prison and make everything feel right, feel whole, was remarkable. I didn't care how big this decorative prison was, I just cared that he was here in it, with me.

Home, Luke had said. *Home is where you are*. As I stared at him, I couldn't help but smile because he was right. Home was wherever he was, for me as well. *Home*. I really liked that word. *Maybe home could be our always.*

I slipped into the bathroom and brushed my teeth, staring at the circles under my eyes because I didn't sleep much. Maybe a few hours, but I had been too scared as he lay in my arms crying, his body stiff with fear. Even after my parents had fallen asleep, he whimpered, trapped in the nightmares that I had tried so painstakingly to erase.

Every whimper was met with a brush of my lips against his forehead, my fingers sliding up and down over the skin between his eyebrows, trying to smooth out the wrinkled frown. Every sob was met with my lips pressed against his cheeks, drying the tears that were slowly but surely sliding down them, even in his sleep. I wanted him to feel how safe he was with me, and if that meant I didn't sleep, then it was worth it to see that he had.

I took a second to relieve myself, staring at the wall behind the toilet as I squeezed my eyes shut, and opened them wide, trying to wake myself up and smile. It would be okay, we would be okay. I would make sure we would always be okay. I finished up, then went back out to Luke. He hadn't moved, his body in the same position as he rested easily, and I watched him for a moment with a fond smile.

He said I was the calm to his storm, and I wondered if he realized he was the same for me. There would never be a moment in my life that I wouldn't crave him, and while I couldn't possibly see into the future to say this with certainty, I felt that certainty there all the same. There was no one like Luke Wilson, not for me. He was always, always going to be my Green.

My home.

I climbed up the end of the bed, my knees on either side of his feet, and slowly crawled over the bedding. The blankets dipped where my knees pressed, pulling tautly over his legs as I slowly climbed up his body. Luke barely moved as my elbows pressed into the soft material beside his armpits, my arms stretching out, lifting, moving until my fingers were ghosting over his. I laced the palms of my hands sliding against the backs of his, curling our fingers together. I laid my nose against the skin underneath his ear, sliding my nose up and down the softness, breathing in everything that was Luke, my Luke.

He groaned, his fingers slowly gripped mine back and pulled me closer. "Morning, babe," I whispered in his ear as I pressed a kiss to the skin right in front of his lobe. There was a soft prickle of hair that grew overnight.

He was smiling. Even though I couldn't see it, I could feel it from the way I was touching him, from the way his soul was touching mine. "Can you wake me up like this every day, for the rest of our lives?" he asked, his voice a deep rasp that made me shiver slightly from how close it was to my ear. I just knew he was smiling even bigger, feeling the way he affected me so easily without any sort of effort at all.

"The rest of our lives is a pretty long time, don't you think you'll get tired after a year? How about five, ten?" I wondered as he turned his head to the side, his eye poking up to look lazily up at me.

"The rest of our lives isn't even long enough, but it'll have to do, I guess." I leaned down, my forehead pressed against his as I peered into the only eye I could see from how he was lying and he watched me curiously with a soft laugh spilling from his lips. "What are you doing, you weirdo?"

"You have gold in your eyes. Little gold flecks splattered over the green, like paint. It's pretty."

"You're pretty," He replied, making me crinkle my nose at him while he laughed. "This isn't a very good position to be laying in, I hope you know."

I grinned as I kissed a soft trail from his cheek to his jaw, down the side of his neck, before biting lightly against the skin on the back of his neck. "I don't see a problem with it," I whispered. He groaned as I laughed. I sat up and moved to sit on his back legs, smacking his butt through the blanket as he let out a startled gasp of surprise. "Come on, get up, we're going to be late," I said as I slid off of him.

"Parts of me are already up," he grumbled as he stood up and grabbed his boxers off of the ground, showing me just how true that statement was, before sleepily staggering into the bathroom. As fun as it was messing with him, the moment the bathroom door was closed I felt my smile tug, the frown pull at me, because there was no mention of last night, never.

We'd gone through it together, his nightmares, his episodes of sadness and self-doubt, the triggers that caused him to hyperventilate, but once the sun was up he never spoke of it. We never spoke of it, as if it was simply gone; buried away. I wondered how safe someone could truly feel, with so much chaos pushed deep down inside them.

I felt older than the almost eighteen that I was as I pulled on some clothes, grabbed my hoodie, and pulled it over my head. I walked down the stairs, leaving the door open so he knew I'd be right back. As expected, my house was not only silent, but it was pristine. All evidence of the fight was gone, the carpet was spotless from glass and stains, while my father was gone from the couch.

I could guess how it started based on their drunken fight. Mom's client came over to discuss a closing on a large house she'd been trying to get done. She was happy, my father was happy, and they invited the client into the kitchen for drinks. Kennedy was home, as rare as it was, because Wyatt's football team was in the next town over for a game, and it was one of the rare times everyone was home on a day that wasn't Sunday for the cursed dinners.

If the client touched Mom, I doubted she let him. The one thing about my parents that always seemed perfect was how much they loved each other and supported each other. I'm sure they fought like all couples did, but never like that. The alcohol was most likely the biggest part of the blame, and I wouldn't even be surprised if they didn't remember any of it. Not what I had said, not what they had done.

Honestly, they probably woke up in separate places and were confused, probably started to laugh with each other about it because they were oblivious in their ignorance. I grabbed some Pop-Tarts, a foil pack of brown sugar ones for me and a foil pack of chocolate chip ones for Luke, a few water bottles, and a foil pack of strawberry ones for Izzy. Luke said she wanted us to get her this morning, and while I didn't usually try to bribe her with food, I'd do anything to get her to stop being mad at me.

As I walked into the bedroom door, Luke was just finishing putting his shoes on. A smile was on his face as he leaned down and grabbed his jacket, slipping it onto his body. Without a pause, he grabbed my shoulder and pulled me against him, wrapping me into a tight hug. He pressed his nose against my neck, breathing me in as if he hadn't just seen me five minutes ago. "Good morning," his breath was warm against my throat, his lips slightly wet from shaving.

I could smell his aftershave mixed with his hair shampoo and took a minute to just breathe it in. I nuzzled my nose against his chest, feeling his heart pounding against my cheek. "Good morning," I replied, my lips pulled into a grin as he slowly pulled away from me. "Poptarts?" He nodded eagerly, like a little kid, and I laughed as he opened the foil packet and started to inhale one. I followed him out the door, both of us silently munching on our pop tarts.

Luke never cared to look out at the living room as we walked past it, but I wondered if he did anyway, not moving his head, but his eyes. His shoulders stiffened and I slid my fingers down the curve of his spine, feeling him melt against my touch. "It's okay, you don't have to be scared," I whispered as he paused, took a deep breath, and let it out slowly.

He turned to look at me, his eyes calm, despite the turmoil that was raging around inside them. "I'm not scared when I'm home," he said, his eyes studying mine as a small smile lifted his exhausted expression. After a second, he tapped my chest before turning around and continuing out the door. It took me a minute of silence to figure out what he meant, but when I did, it left me breathless.

Home. He called me his home. *I'm not scared when I'm with you.*

I bit my bottom lip, worrying it between my teeth as I followed him out the door and into the garage. I knew without needing to look that my cheeks were splattered with the brightest color of red, my heart racing as I replayed his words over and over in my mind. Luke slung our bags into the back as he sat down next to me. I backed out of the garage and started to drive. We were in a comfortable silence as I drove, Luke's fingers ghosted over my knee since he couldn't hold my hand while I ate and drove, and the soft sounds of whatever was playing on the radio spilled into the silence between us.

My mind was filled with so many thoughts I felt antsy, my fingers twitched as I wondered the best way to put them down. My secret, the thing I had never told anyone, not even Isabella, started to pull at me. Wanting me to say it out loud, as stupid as it might sound. I glanced at Luke and shoved it all down, his eyes glanced around and watched the buildings pass as he was lost in his thoughts and memories. For now, my thoughts would have to be placed on hold because, to me, his were the only important ones. I just needed to figure out how to untangle him from the bad ones, to entrap them and yank them away, so he was left with only the good, forever the good.

As we pulled up in front of Isabella's house, I beeped the horn and waved at Mami while she blew me kisses from her car window. Even Luke hesitantly waved because he barely knew her, but I had a feeling that wouldn't last much longer. Mami liked to have little get-togethers for Isabella and me, to pull me into the house and make dinner and catch up. She thought it was funny talking in a language I didn't understand and watching me squirm, or the many times I felt a shoe or a spoon smack against my butt while I tried and countlessly failed to help her cook anything.

She would love Luke, the way he could understand her, how he could cook. She backed away and left, and I felt a sadness flow through me as I wondered what she would think if she found out about us. Would she accept us as Luke's boss did? In a way, she was more my mother than my own, and the thought of her hating me made me want to cry.

Luke's fingers slid up my arm, soft touches through the fabric of my hoodie as I turned to look at him. His fingers slid over my cheek, and the rough pad of his thumb pressed a line under my eye. So unspoken, the words he didn't need to speak for me to hear. *It's okay, it's going to be okay. I'll always be here.*

I pressed my hand to his chest, and he sucked in a deep breath before wrapping his finger around my wrist, pressing down gently on the pulse. *I'll always be your home.*

"Even at four in the morning?" Luke whispered, his eyes lowered, a soft smile brushed against his lips as he watched me through his eyelashes.

I let out a soft laugh, my nose crinkled as his other hand slid down the groove of my dimple, up and down over the taut skin. "Especially at four in the morning."

Isabella surprised us as she opened the back door and slid in. Luke's and my hands fell to our laps as we both blushed a soft blush of embarrassment, having gotten lost in each other without thought of what was going on around us. "Oh, don't mind me, just keep on with your beautiful gay selves in the middle of a homophobic neighborhood. Don't worry, I'll kick everyone's asses for you," she said, fluttering her fingers at us with a bright smile on her face.

Luke and I stared at each other, and my lower lip trembled as I stared at her with wide eyes. "Love you, Pretty Boy," she said shyly. I unbuckled my seatbelt and climbed over the center console. Luke smacked my butt with a laugh as he shook his head at me.

I wrapped my arms around her, pulling her against me as she muttered things at me in Spanish that, judging by the way Luke was laughing, were probably pretty bad. Luke climbed into the driver's seat easily as the car started to move and I held Isabella and cried, feeling her finally calm down and hold me back. "Love you, Izzy," I muttered, sniffling against her shirt as she made a soft "ew" noise.

"You know I can't stay mad at you, Pretty Boy. I just needed a minute to breathe," she said as she lifted my face and squished my cheeks. I felt my lips enclosed in a fish-like shape as mirth danced in her eyes for a moment before they narrowed into a glare. "Don't you do it again, or I'll use my shoe next time," she threatened as I tried and failed to smile under the strain of her fingers on my face. I nodded and she narrowed her eyes at me before giving a sharp nod and pressing her lips against my forehead. "Good."

Luke was laughing at us as I buried my face in her neck again, and Izzy patted my back, trying to shush me while she awkwardly rocked me. "Love you too, Curly!" Izzy randomly called out as Luke laughed even harder. "Accept our crazy ways!"

I was laughing along with Luke for a moment before he replied. "I knew y'all were crazy the moment I met you and was dragged down the street from the police chasing us while you both just laughed without caring. But, it's okay. Your crazy is exactly the kind of crazy I want. Love you too, Izzy,"

"He's still my pretty boy though," Izzy threatened, her words clipped with her warning.

Luke not caring in the least grinned. "He's *MY* pretty boy,"

Then we were all laughing, as Isabella smacked Luke with her shoe, the car going side to side down the road, and I was glad everything was okay, that we were okay. I hoped it would always, always be okay.

Home. I really liked that
word. Maybe home could
be our always.

Chapter 31
Luke

I didn't have to work tonight, and Isabella had us rush her home, wanting to get an art stencil ready for tonight. Because she was fighting with Kinsley and didn't go out with him last night, she wanted all of us to go together tonight, to *'strengthen the bond again,'* as she called it.

Mostly, I was surprised when she invited Serina too. Serina had flushed the deepest shades of red she nodded her head eagerly, having pulled out her phone then and there to text her parents and tell them some lie about her and Kinsley going on a date.

It was strange, how all of this seemed to work out weirdly. Isabella ended up being my pretend girlfriend, Serina ended up being Kinsley's pretend girlfriend, while Kinsley and I dated secretly and Isabella and Serina did... whatever it was they were doing.

I wasn't quite sure what was going on with Isabella and Serina. I knew it wasn't my place to ask, especially since I felt guilty that all of us seemed to know Serina's feelings except for Isabella. But I would be here for her if ever she needed to talk, and I told myself that hopefully that made it okay.

It wasn't right, to tell Isabella Serina's feelings. They needed to work that out on their own. But I could tell from the way Kinsley stared at them with a frown on his face and a twitch of his fingers that he wasn't going to be content waiting for much longer. He wanted to see his friends happy, and I couldn't blame him for that.

"Where are we going?" I asked, my thumb brushed up and down against Kinsley's, our hands clasped together as he pulled into a parking lot. We had just dropped Isabella off and left Serina as she got into her car and drove home, so now Kinsley and I were shopping it seemed.

Kinsley looked at me with a smile on his face, and for a moment, I was blinded by it. The deep grooves from his dimples, how his cerulean blue eyes shined in the sunlight. His hoodie had been pulled off and thrown in the back seat when he first got into the car, his ash blond hair slightly tangled as his bangs fluttered around his eyes. I could even see a strip of skin from where his shirt lifted, the curve of his hip bone drew my eye again and again, wanting nothing more than to lean over and touch it.

I wondered if the whole world stopped when I admired Kinsley or if it was just me who was trapped in this feeling. Then again, he was my whole world, so for me, everything stopped, everything shut down, leaving just me and him. "You'll see," he said, giving me a soft wink that my heart responded with the flutter of wings lifting and falling in my chest, a flurry of movement that made me want to wrap him in my arms and never let him go.

Kinsley's cheeks took on a light red hue as he leaned forward and batted his nose against mine as if to snap me out of my thoughts. I cupped his cheeks, no thought of the cards around us, and I pressed my lips against his, swallowing every gasp of surprise that followed. As I slowly pulled away, he stared at me with wide eyes, not backing away, but surprised all the same. "Luke! Someone could see us!" he whispered, his fingers curling around my wrists as I gently lowered my hands from his cheeks.

I thought about his words as I got out of the car. Kinsley got out, a confused look on his face as he shivered and grabbed his hoodie to slip back on. We met at the front of the car, and he had a perplexed expression on his face as I held my hand out to him and wiggled my fingers. Confused, he handed me the keys, and I laughed, slipping them into my pocket and lacing my fingers with his.

Kinsley looked down at our fingers for a moment, his cheeks a lovely coral color as he looked around the group of parked cars, absently pulling his hood up to cover his face. "It shouldn't matter, you know?" I asked, pulling him next to me as we walked through the cars.

I knew what people would think if they saw us. Isabella was wearing one of Kinsley's hoodies for half of the school day, having spilled milk on her father's army jacket, and I knew that if anyone from school saw us they'd think Kinsley was Isabella. It kind of frustrated me, the way they'd just assume, the way they'd think it was strange if he was a boy as if it bothered them when it wasn't even their life.

Kinsley looked confused and I smiled, squeezing his hand tighter. "I guess in the end, I see it like this. Whoever I'm attracted to and whoever I love shouldn't matter to anyone else. The world is still going to spin the same way, whether I'm in love with a man or a woman, you know?" I looked at him and tilted his head up, my thumbs sliding up and down his jaw as I slowly pressed my lips against his.

For a moment we just existed, our bodies melded together in the middle of the parking lot, hidden by the empty cars that waited for their owners to come to claim them. As we broke away I smiled softly at him and took a step back. Because no matter what I said, we just weren't strong enough, we just weren't ready to be us in the middle of the chaos that would come from revealing who we were and what we were to each other. "See?" I said, holding my hands up and chuckling. "The world is still spinning."

He gave me a lopsided smile and shook his head at me. "You're incorrigible, Luke Wilson," he mumbled as I laughed at him. "The world might still be spinning, but we're still underage, still living with our parents. Just a little longer, and we can be free. Just a little longer," he said, a sad look on his face as we started to walk side by side. "The world was nothing but chaos. We're just trying to survive it."

I pulled on a strand of his hair, making him look at me once more as I smiled. "In the middle of my chaos, there's you. Standing there, calming the storm."

I laughed as Kinsley wrapped his arms around my stomach and pressed my back against a truck that was near us. Before he could press his lips to mine, however, the alarm went off and we jumped apart, and looked at each other for a moment, before bursting out laughing and running toward the mall.

I wasn't surprised that in the end, we were there because Kinsley wanted to go to the art store. Honestly, I should have expected it, from how excited he was. Reading Kinsley was my favorite thing in the world, seeing how excited he got, and how he'd smile, was everything to me.

I followed along beside him, my arms already filled with art supplies for him, and all I could do was smile. I loved the way he looked at art supplies, the way his eyes would light up as he stared at them like they were the most beautiful things in the world. I recognized that look because that's how I looked at him.

"Are we buying the store, Kins?" I wondered as we placed our stacks of supplies on the counter. The cashier looked at it with a look of mild disinterest.

Kinsley looked at me with doe eyes as the cashier rang everything up. "Is that allowed?" he wondered as I laughed out loud. He looked like a little kid as he turned to the cashier, his hands gripping the counter. "Can I buy the store?"

The cashier raised his eyebrow at him. "I didn't get paid enough for this nonsense, kid,"

Before Kinsley could go off and explain to the man just how wealthy he was, I pressed my fingers to his lips and smiled apologetically to the man since it was my fault in the first place. We ended up having four bags each to carry. "Are we done?" I wondered, grunting slightly in pain as some drawing pencils poked through the bag and stabbed into my leg.

Kinsley looked at me, his eyes narrowed, before giving me a little shake of his head. "Not yet, let's go," he said, leading me to his car.

I was entirely confused now but I followed him anyway because this was Kinsley, and I'd follow him anywhere without question. We had a moment of stupidity when Kinsley was looking for his keys, but then I remembered I had them in my pocket. We put the supplies in the car and got in, Kinsley driving again.

I gave up trying to question him then, simply leaning against the seat and turning my body towards him to watch him grin and bounce up and down in excitement. I never was one for surprises before, but anything that had to do with Kinsley was okay, no matter what it was. Maybe that made me a simp, but I didn't care. I'd do anything to see him smile.

He drove us to the grocery store and made me stay in the car while he accumulated things, coming back out with a few bags and placing them in the backseat. "Groceries? Are you planning on cooking? I'm scared, what if we die?" I asked as he slapped my knee gently, crinkling his nose at me with a laugh. "I mean, I can eat later, I'm too young to die. I'm not hungry-" I started to say but was quickly cut off by the sound of my stomach growling loudly. The traitor.

Kinsley grinned, his hand sliding up my jacket and my shirt, to press firmly against my stomach as he started to drive. "Are you going to argue when your stomach is crying for help?"

I smirked as his fingers moved back and forth against my lower stomach and sat back, pressing my hand against the back of his, and slid it down slightly lower. "I mean if you're that hungry," I mumbled, quirking my eyebrow at him as he flushed and yanked his hand back.

"Luke!" He exclaimed as he pulled the car off of the sidewalk and back onto the road. "You're being dirty." His cheeks lit up a darker and darker shade as I laughed at him.

"I'm not apologizing," I said as I held my hand out for him to take it once more. He stuck his tongue out at me, but after a few seconds, he shook his head and laced his fingers with mine. "I love you," I said, watching his false anger fade away as he smiled, a slightly shy look slipping onto his face as he nearly melted into his seat.

"I love you too, Luke," he slid his thumb against mine as he glanced at me for a moment before looking away. I closed my eyes, lost in the sound of his voice, those words echoing through me on repeat. I never thought I'd ever feel like this, want like this, love like this. I never thought someone would ever love me.

I had grown up being told I was broken, thrown around like I was nothing, and made to believe I would never have the one thing I wanted all along, someone to love me the way I loved them. But he was there, and I was there, and we were together. I hoped nothing would ever change, nothing would ever come to break us apart. It was funny, how I never believed in marriage until I met Kinsley, and now all I wanted to do was be eighteen, to buy a ring, and propose to him.

I didn't want him to ever fade away, he was everything to me. I wanted our books to join together, to the point where if someone flipped through them, read them, they wouldn't see Kinsley, they wouldn't see Luke, they'd see us, together, as one. Just two heartbeats, one soul, blended as one.

I didn't realize the car had stopped moving until Kinsley pulled his hand out of mine, a worried expression on his face as he got out of the car. I looked up at the building and smiled, unsure why Kinsley looked worried when this was our place. The abandoned building, the rooftop that was ours. I helped Kinsley carry up the grocery bags as we walked up the stairs and set down on top of the roof as the sky started to take a golden hue. It wasn't nighttime yet, and I had a feeling we'd end up staying there until it was, since Kinsley had all the supplies we'd need in his trunk. I didn't mind though, despite the cold it was fine, because we were all alone up there.

This building was higher up than most others around this area and if we laid down flat in the middle of it no one would see us. We could do anything, be anything on this rooftop, and I loved the freedom that came with that. No parents screaming, no fathers walking in, no interruptions. Just me, just Kinsley, just us.

Kinsley started to pull things out of the grocery bags and I grinned at the premade sandwiches, the bags of chips, and the little containers of prechopped fruits. The cans of soda and even little containers of our favorite ice cream were scattered in front of us. I breathed out a sigh of relief. "I'm glad it's not something you were going to try and cook. I don't know if I was a good enough boyfriend to pretend it tasted good when I'm withering on the ground dying." I mumbled as he punched me in the arm.

I grinned as he shoved me backward, his hand cupping the back of my head to make sure I didn't smack it into the cement, and I burst out laughing as he tickled his fingers up and down my sides, an evil grin on his face as he straddled my legs. I could have pushed him off of me even as he held both my wrists in one hand and pressed them above my head, but I didn't, allowing him to torture me because he was smiling, he was laughing. God, that laugh. I would have allowed him to tickle me for hours on end just to hear that laugh and to see the way his eyes shined.

Kinsley climbed off of me, trying to give me a pout as if he was still offended, but as I pressed my lips against his, the pout faded away, left with a complacent smile. My stomach grumbled once more as Kinsley started to distribute the food, both of us eating our ice cream first before it melted, before eating the rest. I couldn't help but chuckle in my mind because this was just one of the many things about Kinsley that he did but didn't realize he was doing.

To go grocery shopping for a cheap simple picnic when he was rich. He could have called a restaurant and rented out the whole thing, got us privacy and proper rich people gourmet foods, but he didn't even consider it. This was why I wasn't worried about money with Kinsley. Even if we moved away somewhere, and lost all of his parents' money, we'd be fine. He didn't need the money, he didn't care about it. As long as he could draw, as long as I could work on cars, and as long as we were together, we'd be fine. No matter what, we'd always be fine.

"I need to talk to you," Kinsley said, an hour after we were finished eating.

Our trash had been gathered in one bag, resting at our feet as we lay on our backs staring up at the clouds lazily floating across the dramatic dark golden sky. It was getting darker by the second, soon it would be nighttime. Serina said she was getting Isabella, so we were just waiting now. My heart jumped in my chest at the seriousness of his tone, and I instantly sat up, my heart racing as I looked down at him. "Are you... is this a bad talk?" I whispered.

Kinsley sat up slowly, his silence choking me with every second that passed as he slowly wrapped his fingers around mine, our knees touching as he stared at our fingers. I tried to tell myself that he wasn't going to touch me if he was breaking up with me, right? So maybe it wasn't that, right? "I um... I did something behind your back, and I think you're going to be mad at me. But I just... I don't know what else to do, Luke. I just wanted to help you," he whispered, lifting his eyes to mine.

His eyes were filled with a pleading look that made me shiver, unsure of what the hell was going on. What could he have possibly done? My eyes burned, unsure what to think as I blinked them rapidly. He wasn't leaving me, right? He didn't cheat on me, right? Then what could it be that was making him look like that? My thoughts were racing, worry spilling through me, and I was having trouble breathing. "What did you do?" I whispered, my voice breaking.

His eyes filled with sadness as they swept over my face, taking in my expression. "Oh, Luke," he cupped my cheeks as I leaned against his hands. I absorbed his warmth, trying to take deep breaths, to calm myself. I was always so on edge, always waiting for everything to fade away. I never expected to have happiness, not like this. Every day I was waiting for it to get taken away. I didn't deserve this, I didn't deserve him. I didn't deserve anything.

"I found a therapist," he nearly choked out.

My eyes went wide, confusion flowed at his words because they weren't anything that I was expecting. But then the confusion faded away, and frustration slipped in because I never wanted a therapist. My mother had one because she was depressed. But I didn't need one, I didn't. I wasn't one of those people that needed one. I wasn't like them, I wasn't.

"I called up an office that was in the next town over. It's a two-hour drive, but it's worth it there and back, once a week. I made sure to ask about... how accepting they were before I even gave them your name. To make sure you were given the best one, one without prejudice, who won't care if you're dating a boy if you chose to talk about me. She's nice. I talked to her. I... you didn't have to, Luke, but I just wanted to help," he whispered. "I didn't know how else to help."

I pulled back from him and stood, pacing as he watched me. I was frustrated. He had done it behind my back, hadn't asked me if I wanted it, just went ahead and did it anyway. "I didn't need to talk to some stranger, Kins, I have you! Why would I need anyone else?" I nearly spat at him. I ran my fingers through my hair and tugged hard at the strands, trying to will myself to breathe.

"Because I'm not good enough to help you through the darkness. I can be your light, I can protect you, shine on you, but there's still darkness surrounding you, waiting. As long as that darkness is there, you'll never fully be okay, Luke. You'll always have me, I'm not going anywhere. But I'm not good enough to help you get rid of the darkness. I'm not a professional," he said, watching me carefully, calmly.

I sunk to my knees in front of him, my heart racing as tears spilled down my cheeks. "I never accepted help, I didn't need it, Kinsley. Even back when I tried to kill myself. Dad said it made us crazy, needing a therapist. Only crazy people needed one, he'd say, like my mom. He knew Shawn was forced to see one, but it was ordered by the school and he assumed Shawn was brushing it off. He'd call me crazy, Kins. He'd-" I stammered.

Kinsley scooted closer to me, pressed his hands on my cheeks, slightly harder than he needed to, and pulled me out of my shock. "Luke," he said slowly, his eyes searching mine. "There is nothing wrong with getting a therapist. It doesn't make you crazy to need someone to talk to. It doesn't matter what your father would say, because he's the problem, not you. He's the broken one, not you."

I took a deep breath, my tears sliding over his hands, my hands clutching his hoodie as I pulled him closer to me. "What if she told me I was just like him? What if she told me I was broken, I wasn't good enough? What if you... leave?" I whimpered as I fell from my knees to my butt and stared up at him.

Kinsley didn't reply to me at first. He took me into his arms and hugged me tightly, without words or complaints. He waited for me to calm down, enveloping me in the safety of his arms. As I calmed down slowly, I felt his tears wet my hair and the throb of his heart beating through his chest, against my shoulder as he held me tightly.

His body shook against me, and I realized that while I was the one who was broken and fighting the demons inside my mind, he was the one suffering. I had taken every punch, every hit, every curse. I had been the one who had taken the beatings, but he took all the pain. "I'll never leave, Luke. Never,"

I lifted my head as he looked down at me. "I'll go, Kinsley. I'll talk to her." *I'll do anything, for you. To stop the pain that resides inside both of us. Anything.*

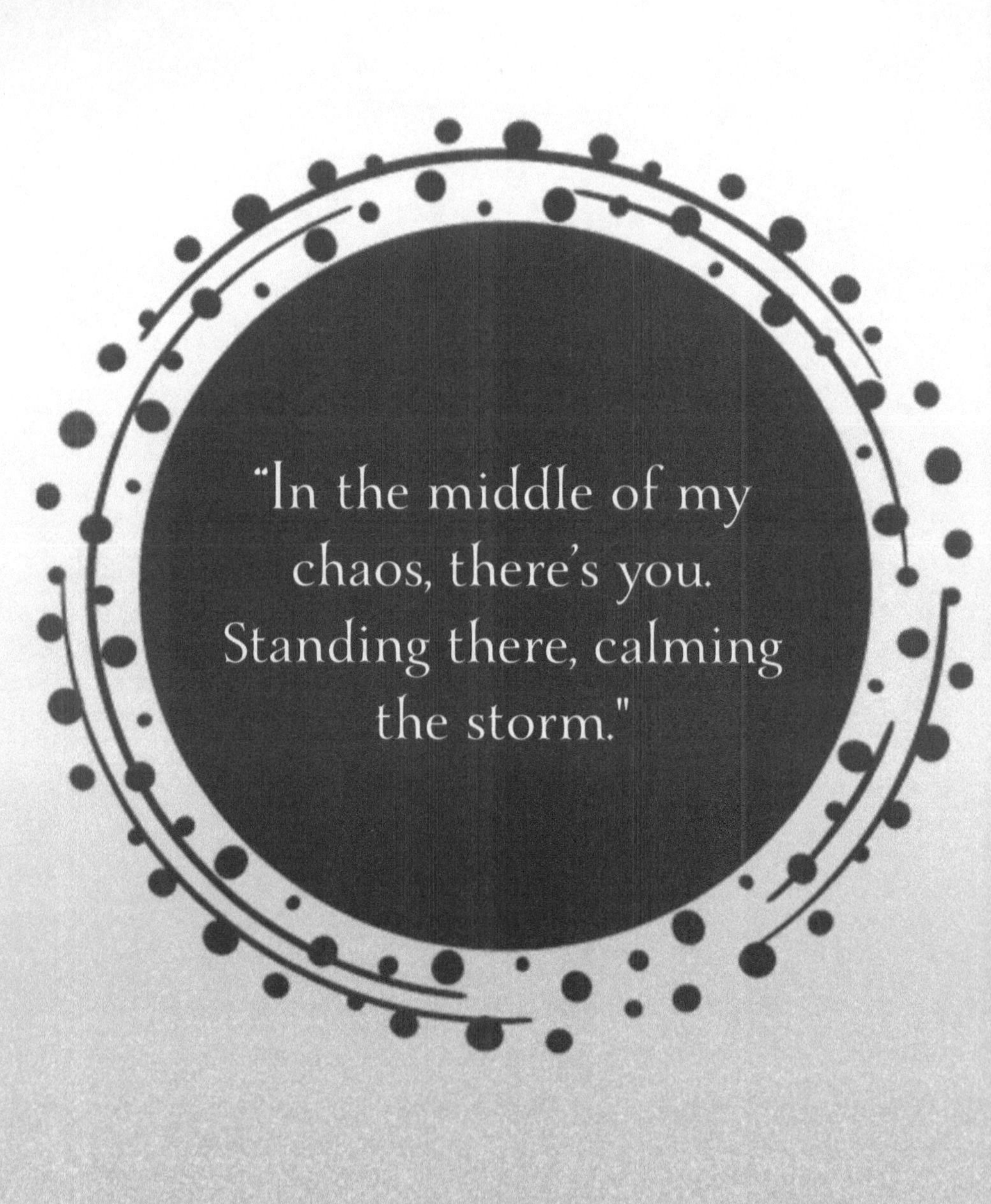
"In the middle of my chaos, there's you. Standing there, calming the storm."

Chapter 32
Kinsley

I had hoped everything would stay simple, or as simple as it could be with how secretive and complicated it all was. Luke was going to therapy twice a week now, and he barely had any nightmares. He was hesitant at first, but after a couple of weeks, it started to get easier for him.

He smiled more, his shoulders didn't hold as much weight on them, and I was glad to see he was finally starting to breathe the way I had always desperately wanted to see him breathe. He hadn't seen his mother yet, and while neither I nor the therapist was pushing for it, I knew he would go when he was ready. He was getting better, and we were still together strong, hidden under the disguise of both having girlfriends to appease everyone around us.

I didn't know much about Serina and Isabella, because they had been mostly secretive about their talks and their understanding of each other. I knew it was hard for Isabella because it was hard for her to let new people in. She loved Luke because she knew I loved him, and she never would have allowed him in if it wasn't for me. Serina was different because that was a love deeper than what she felt for me or Luke, and that scared her more than anything. The last time she loved someone that deeply, someone more than anyone else, was when she watched her father die in front of her eyes.

There was a moment when Isabella came to me crying, wanting to talk to me about what she should do, about everything that was going on, but all I could do was hold her close to me and help her through her sorrow. To remind her that not everyone she was going to love would die in front of her eyes.

We were getting closer to the end of school, and it was starting to put pressure on everyone. My parents fought me about college, they wanted me to go to an Ivy League for a business degree to take over for my father, but I didn't want any part of that. I didn't have the grades for it even if I did, but my parents ignored everything I said, as always. They started to arrange talks with headmasters they had done business with in the past. I was stressed over it, Luke was busy with therapy, and I had to admit we trapped ourselves in our little bubble more than we should have been.

I started going on dates with Luke under the pretense that I was dating Serina so she could get away from her overbearing parents too, and instead of the four of us staying together, we'd split into two, giving each other time to connect with our loved ones. It didn't mean that we were separating, Isabella and I were always going to be close and Luke had started to get close to Serina as well. We still had dreams of moving to New York and getting a big apartment together. Only now, those plans included Luke, and possibly even Serina, if they were together by then.

I guess we got... careless. Stupid, in a way. We were seventeen still, you know? Seventeen-year-old boys in love, and we did stupid things when we were in love. We should have known better, we should have tried harder to keep everything secret. We let it all get to our heads and didn't think we'd get caught. We had known each other for a year now and had been dating for half a year, and we got complacent with the fact that no one knew, that no one saw. Until someone did see.

I could still hear it, even now in my mind as I stared at my accuser in terror. I could still hear the sounds of Luke gasping in my ear, the feel of his lips against the back of my neck as he pushed me against the door in the janitor's closet. I could still feel the touch of his fingers on my skin, dancing against the sweat as he slid them up my shirt, and down my pants, touching everything and leaving behind trails of fire I never wanted him to extinguish.

We had been stupid, thinking no one would notice him grabbing my wrist, thinking that no one would see the darkened look in his eyes as he smirked at me and pulled me into the closet, locking the door behind us. It was locked, I knew it was locked, because I had been pressed up against it.

We were muffled, my mouth pressed against his arms that were pressed against the door for balance, his teeth biting into my neck to muffle his noises, but even muffled, we were noticed. The kids were all supposed to be in class, and Luke and I were supposed to be in separate classes, we didn't think we'd be noticed, except we were. Luke was beside me, both of us had just walked out of the janitor's closet with sweaty bodies and knowing grins, our mouths curved in silent happiness filled with secrets we thought only we knew. Until we were both shoved against the wall, barely a few steps away.

Roan stared at us with disgust in his eyes, fluttering them back and forth as his lips snarled, and a gag spilled from his lips just looking at us. Without a word, he took a step back and wiped his hands on his shirt as if just touching us was going to make him gay.

"So this is what you do?" he wondered, his eyes moving back and forth between us with his lips curled in a snarl. "They're fucking dykes, and you're both faggots, and you pretend you're all dating each other so people won't notice? Just one big gay group of friends?"

"I don't know what you're talking about, we weren't doing anything," Luke said, his voice low, threatening as he took a step forward, automatically shielding me from Roan's gaze.

Roan snorted at him. "Okay, tell me what you were doing in there then," he said, pointing at the janitor's closet.

I shrugged, even though my heart was racing, and peered around Luke. "We were playing Pokemon. You know, gotta catch 'em all."

Luke's shoulders shook in silent laughter as Roan looked at me like I was crazy, his lips lifting and falling as if he was trying his hardest not to allow what I said to make him laugh. "Really? Because whenever I screw a girl against that door, it rattles just like that. I'm not stupid, don't test my patience, you nasty faggot," he sneered.

I let out a sigh as I ran my fingers through my hair. I pressed my finger against the tender skin on the back of my neck from Luke's bites for a second then pulled my hood over my head, wanting to hide them just in case Roan noticed them.

Though he wasn't looking at me anymore, but at Luke. "So this is why you wanted to trade with me in psych class last year. You traded partners to sit next to him. Then after that, you were suddenly near him all the time, hanging out with him and Isabella. We all started to think you were dating Isabella, but no, you were just using her to be with Kinsley. How fucking nasty is that?"

"It's none of your business who we're with, Roan. We're just trying to get through the rest of the school year, and then we're all getting out of here. Don't worry yourself about us," Luke's hands clenched in tight fists as his muscles stiffened, ready to fight if need be.

Roan laughed, a low laugh as he glared at Luke. "We'll see whose business it is," he said with a low threatening tone. As the bell rang he gathered spit in his mouth, and spat on the ground near Luke's feet, giving us one last disgusted look before turning away. Almost the moment he turned away from us the doors opened and kids started to file out around us, some of them sparing a glance at us but moving past fast, not wanting to be late and not seeing anything strange to gossip about.

Luke looked at me, both of us confused and shaking in fear. I tilted my head up and he nodded, and we walked up the stairs to the art room. I locked the door as we moved through the room to the windows, opening them almost on impulse as we allowed the fresh air to slowly start moving the rancid smell of goo out of the room.

Together we slid down against the wall under the window, and for a moment I remembered a time when I had sat there, with Isabella beside me, holding me while I cried about how much I loved Luke. It was funny, in a way, that I was sitting there on the verge of tears in the same place, except instead of Isabella it was Luke beside me.

We didn't touch at first, almost scared of how the other would react, but it didn't take long for his fingers to seek out mine. They molded together without pause or care, as if they belonged together. We were silent in our sorrow, hands clasped together, and after a few minutes, Luke's head casually slid down the wall and into my lap. He looked up at me, and I stared down at him, our hands still clasped together as I draped them over his chest, right over his heart.

I pulled away from his fingers and pressed my hand against his chest, making sure it was still okay, because, in the end, that's all that mattered to me. If he was okay, if he was going to be alright, it was all that mattered. His fingers wrapped around my wrist, pressing against the pulse. His eyes fluttered closed for a moment as I stared at everything that I've always wanted, lying there in my lap, existing. Everything would be okay, as long as he kept existing.

"I'm scared," he whispered, his eyes opening to look up at me, fluttering back and forth as he read me.

"Me too," I whispered, but for probably a different reason. I was scared that we'd be outed, that the whole school would know, that my parents would find out, not to mention what this would do for Serina too, but I was mostly scared of his fear.

I trusted him, more than anyone, but a little part of me was always going to be scared that one day it would be too much for him, that it would all be too much, and he'd seek out the cold metal that he sought comfort in so long ago once more. I could live in a world that ridiculed me for loving the same gender as me, but I couldn't live in a world that didn't have him in it.

Luke hummed as I ran my fingers through his curls. Across from where we sat was a large canvas, a charcoal picture that I had started again. It wasn't the same. This time the black silhouette had curls, curls that framed light seafoam eyes. Isabella told me to draw another self-portrait, but to me, Luke was the reflection of my soul, and there was no way to explain myself without showing him. There was no me without him.

I was almost finished with it, and it was perfect. Despite what my parents wanted, I was going to submit it along with a few others in a portfolio to an art school in New York. I was going to name this one: *The reflection of my soul.*

"He called Serina and Isabella that... that word," Luke mumbled, pulling me out of my thoughts. "Did you hear him?"

I nodded, my teeth clenched in sudden anger, and my eyes narrowed on the door. My phone vibrated, and I knew it was probably Izzy, especially since Luke's vibrated as well, indicating a group chat. She was supposed to be in the next class with us, and we didn't show up.

"I don't know how he got to that conclusion. Maybe he saw them? Maybe he knows something? Why is he hiding their secret then? Wouldn't he have just assumed we were lying to our girlfriends and sneaking behind their backs? That would have been the normal conclusion," I tried to take a deep breath to calm myself.

Luke's long legs were straight as he crossed them at the ankles, and for a moment, I was reminded of a time long ago, on my seventeenth birthday, when we had laid like this on top of the roof. It was almost a year ago, and our positions were swapped since I was the one lying in his lap, and he was the one playing with my hair.

"Did you know what you were doing?" I blurted out, wanting to change the subject. Wanting to think of better things than what we were probably going to have to face later on today. Would Roan tell right now? Would we walk out there to lockers spray-painted again, and people pushing both of us, jeering at us, taunting us?

I couldn't help but think we wouldn't be, at least not yet, because Roan seemed to know about Izzy and Serina and he didn't tell on them either. But why? For what reason? I had no idea what was going on anymore. I wanted to ask them, but Izzy had been so quiet and pushing people away, and Serina had just been smiling such a big fake smile that neither of us knew what to say to any of them anymore. I kept hoping they'd fix it, and they'd be happy and smile, but as time passed, I was starting to wonder if I was keeping my distance because I was trying to let them fix it themselves, or because I was scared everything was going to crash apart and we'd split up, destroying all of us.

I realized Luke was looking at me like I was crazy, and I pulled myself out of my thoughts, remembering what it was I was trying to ask him. "Did you know that night on my birthday that you were holding my hand? That you were playing with my hair?"

Almost instantly, his cheeks started to glow a soft shade of pink as his eyes lowered, and his long eyelashes brushed against his cheeks. I counted time and time again each freckle, each little scar on his body, but no matter how many times I stared at them like it was the first time. Each time I pressed my finger against them, wanting to touch them, to memorize them again and again. To love every bit of him, again and again.

Worth it, I whispered in my mind as my eyes fluttered over the beauty that was Luke Wilson. *Whatever happens with Roan, it's worth it.* I wouldn't change anything if we went back in time. Not one single thing.

Maybe it was better this way, that someone knew. That everyone would know. Maybe it would be easier if it came out. Then we wouldn't have to hide and pretend anymore. I was fucking terrified, but I was relieved in a way too. A weight slowly lifted off my shoulders that I hadn't even realized was there this whole time.

Maybe it would have been okay if I showed my parents the real me. Maybe they would still love me. Luke was right, about what he had said before. The world would still spin, whether I loved a man or a woman. I wondered if they would see it that way, over time.

"I knew," he breathed, his eyes closed for a moment before staring up at me. "I did it anyway."

"If you could go back in time and change everything, would you? If we could go back to the letters, would you have thrown them away? Would you have left me in the art room and never tried to talk to me again? Would you have let everything never happen, if you could go back in time and start over?" I wondered, trying to hide the fear in my voice.

I wasn't even sure why I was scared because going back in time wasn't possible. But I was still scared all the same because now that something was going on with Roan, would he change his mind if he could? I knew he had already come out to his boss and his mom most likely knew too, but the school? My parents?

Would he go back in time and change knowing what could be coming for us? "Never, Kins. If I could go back in time when I met you in the art room, I would have grabbed you and kissed you right then and there. I already knew I was in love with Sparrow before I walked into that art room. I should have ignored your gender and just kissed you like I wanted to from the start."

He shrugged. "But I guess I went through denial first, and anger, then I just kind of tried to separate my feelings because I didn't think I was interested in guys. I guess that's kind of what they call gay panic, right?" he asked with a chuckle, scrunching his nose at me.

I pressed my finger against his nose, then slid it down his cheek, around his jaw, just enamored in the feel of him. "Even now that we don't know what's going to happen with Roan?"

"Baby," he whispered, making my heart flutter in response as he slid his fingers against my cheek and tangled them in my hair, shoving my hood down in the process. "I don't care if the whole world is against us. You have me. I have you. That's never change. Stop worrying about it. It's scary, but we'll get through it, one step at a time. Just don't let go of my hand, okay?"

I smiled at him, letting out a soft breath as his fingers slid from my wrist to my fingers on his chest, lacing them together. I leaned down, my lips a hair's breadth above his. "I'll never take my hand away from the gravity of your fingers. I promise," I whispered, pressing my lips against his.

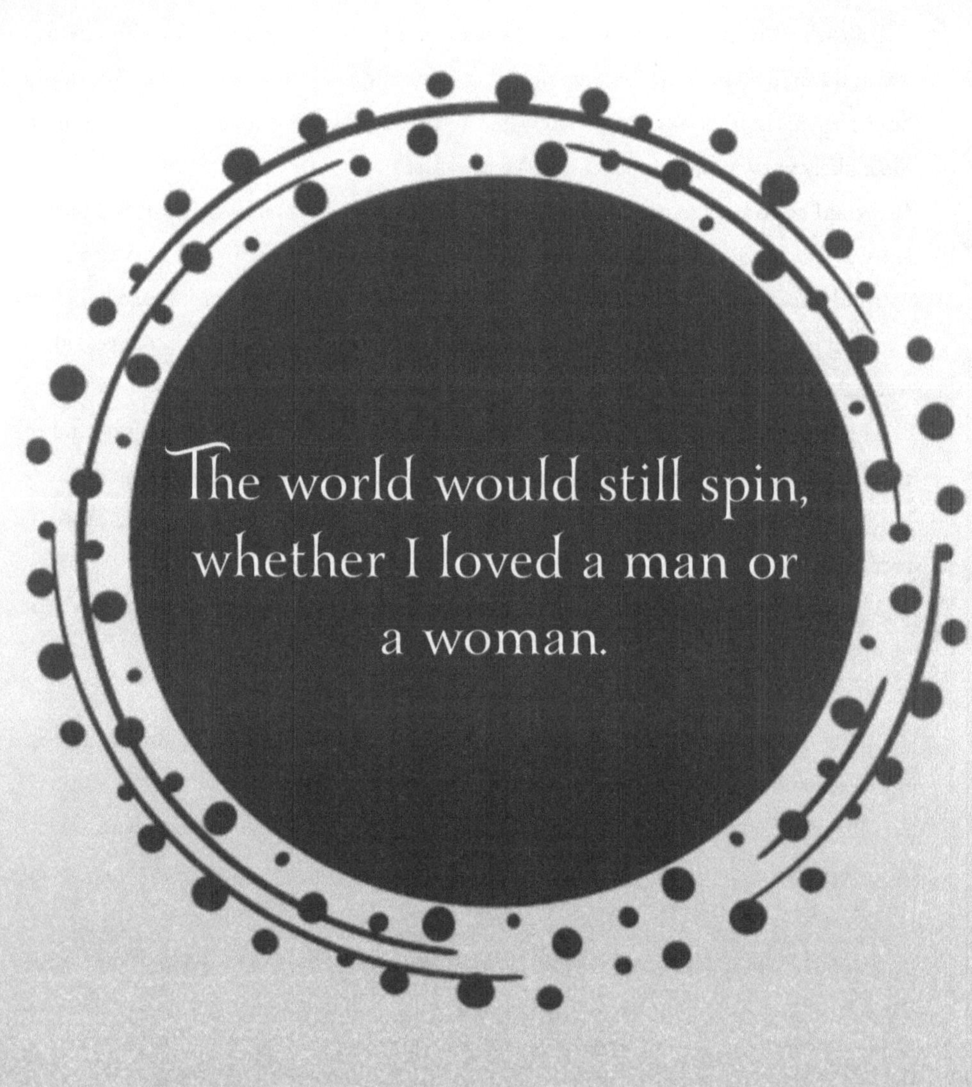

The world would still spin,
whether I loved a man or
a woman.

Chapter 33
Kinsley

We didn't know what to think as we went back to class. I was having trouble stopping myself from panicking over every little thing as we walked side by side but not touching. Every person that moved past us, everyone who stopped and looked at us, I wondered if they knew. But no one said anything, no one strayed a little longer, no one whispered under their fingers, not yet, anyway. We were only trying to miss that one class when we escaped into the janitor's closet, but we ended up skipping the next one as well just to sit there and think about all the ways our life was about to change in the art club room.

I would be worried about my parents if they were ever home to receive calls, but the office would just leave a voicemail about our absences on the machine, and I'd delete them as I've been doing all school year long. Not too many absences, not enough for the principal to feel the need to call me into the office. Every once in a while, we'd skip a class here or there, just to be together. Even before we realized we were both in love with each other, we'd skip class together. It was funny, the way we've always been together from the start, but we never even knew.

We had calculus now, the three of us. Isabella sat in between me and Luke. This teacher was a firm believer that if two girls sat together they'd do nothing but giggle all class long and gossip with each other, or if two guys sat together then they'd plan pranks and disrupt the class. The three of us sat in the back of this class, thankfully, and while our desks were inches apart from each other to allow room for a body to walk up and down the aisle, at least we were close.

I was positioned next to the window, while Isabella sat next to me, and Luke beside her. Roan was in this class too, unfortunately, and while we had all arrived at the same time, it didn't stop me from worrying he was looking too closely at us. Every time he flicked a piece of paper over the desk of the girl next to him to land on the desk of one of his basketball goons, I flinched, waiting for the guy to turn around and look at me with a nasty disgusted sneer.

I wasn't sure what to think, as nothing happened. Was Roan not going to tell anyone? Why? What was he trying to prove? I couldn't believe he was suddenly being nice, this was freaking Roan after all. I didn't think he even knew what redeeming qualities were to try and find his own.

I was startled out of my internal panic attack as a little folded triangle landed gently on my desk, landing perfectly in between my hands. I let out an agitated sigh, peering at Isabella from under my eyelashes as she stared back at me with an unamused glare.

She'd been being strange the past day or two, and I'd been trying to get her to tell me why, but she was closed up, reserved. Shaking, staring at everything, and making sure she was never alone. It made me worried, seeing her like that. I'd even seen her slide up against Tony once just so she wasn't standing by herself in the hallway and he looked down at her with a surprised blush on his face as Roan and his goons walked past them.

I hated the fact that we had secrets, and I wanted to ask her what was going on because I was scared she was mad at me again. It had always been Kinsley and Isabella, after all, the bestest friends for life. I never wanted that to change. I unfolded the intricately folded triangle carefully, the soft crinkle of the paper drowned out by the voices of the students as we mechanically replied to a question from the teacher, wanting to know what equation was needed to solve the problem on the board.

I could hear Luke's monotone answer blending in with the rest while Isabella and I remained quiet, our lips moving in a silent whisper as if we were pretending to be paying attention. Math sucked, I was horrible at it, and I knew later on I'd just end up grabbing Luke's notes and copying them. He loved math for some strange reason, but I guess that was a good thing. He probably needed to be good at math to be a mechanic.

'You and Curly ditched me last period and didn't answer any of my texts,' she had written. I nodded because I expected her to point it out, to be mad about it. I looked past her to Luke, noticing he was watching me, his eyes looking down at my note, then back at me before giving a soft nod of affirmation. I didn't need to ask him to know he was fine with me telling Izzy what happened.

I twirled my pencil around and around, staring down at the note for a second as I thought of how to word it. *'Luke pulled me into the janitor's closet and Roan discovered us. Not like walked in on us, we had the door locked, but I guess he noticed what we were doing cause of the door shaking. Then it probably didn't help that we came out of the closet together, not trying to make it look like one came out first or anything.'* I replied before folding the note into a square and throwing it back at her.

I still find it humorous that even after almost four years of high school, Isabella and I had never been caught or yelled at for throwing notes back and forth. Especially as the moment Isabella caught my note, the teacher's annoyed voice whipped through the air, yelling at Roan. "Roan, stand up and read the note for everyone to hear," he said, his eyes narrowed as he stared at Roan.

This was probably the only reason I loved Mr. McCormrick. I didn't like that he seemed to be the only math teacher in this school and taught all of the different math classes. Honestly, I hoped he got paid more for all of that. But I liked how he never seemed to give a shit about Roan.

Most of the other teachers babied Roan because of his parents' connections, scared they'd get in trouble with the principal if they didn't let him off the hook or leave him alone to his own devices. Not that I blamed them, since I had seen a teacher or two get fired for trying to discipline Roan, and Roan would make up some bullshit about the teacher being unjustified or flirting with him, and they'd get fired without having a chance to fight back against his wild and ludicrous claims.

I felt panic rising through me as Isabella slowly opened my note, not caring about what was going on with Roan as he stood, but as Isabella read over what I'd said, she lifted her head fast, her eyes wide as her mouth fell open, staring at me, then at Roan, horrified. I could see it, just as she did, the way Roan shifted from foot to foot, a grimace on his face. Luke's eyes met mine once more and I let out a soft shaky breath, panic wrapping around me tightly, settling deeply down inside me. Luke's eyes were so expressive I could tell exactly what he was thinking. *What if the note was about us? The whole class will find out now.*

I closed my eyes, and squeezed them shut tightly, as if thinking maybe if I couldn't see then no one would be able to hear. I wanted to open a hole in the middle of the room, to bury myself down into the foundation of the building, amidst the rocks and dirt below.

Suddenly, in the middle of my horror, Roan's deep voice filled the room with a mechanical uncaring tone to it, startling me even more. "I wrote: Coach just texted me, telling me to tell all of you that practice is canceled today. The basketball court has been getting holes in it, wear and tear, and he's finally got the okay from the principal to get it fixed. Then Charles said: Okay, got it, Captain. About time that jerk finally got around to getting that fixed. Our parents donate enough to the school for it to get done. Then I wrote: Don't you sass the coach. He had to get permission."

Roan lifted his eyes to look around the room and located another one of his goons, nodding his head at him. "Now you know too, no practice. But I still want y'all to be practicing at home. If you started slacking at all I'd make you run till you couldn't feel your legs anymore."

A shudder ran through both of the basketball players Roan was looking at, and Mr. McCormrick grumbled, grabbing the note from Roan to make sure he wasn't making this up. He ran his eyes over it with an annoyed sigh, before handing it back to Roan and walking back up to the class. "Tell your coach he needs to stop texting during class. This could have been announced on the PA system instead of making you tell everyone via notes and texts, which are both not allowed in my class. You know you're on your last warning, Roan. Even the principal is getting tired of it. Don't make me send you down to the office." He warned.

Roan narrowed his eyes at the teacher, and I frowned, wondering what that was about. Were they finally punishing Roan for his bullshit? I freaking hoped so. Maybe his parents were getting tired of bailing him out of everything constantly. "Now, back to the material on the board," he snapped.

It wasn't long after that when another note flew onto my desk. *'Now I'm getting pissed. Y'all were stupid to do that in the middle of school, but he had no right to care and call you out like that. What y'all do, what Serina and I do, is none of his business. He's on my last nerve, and I'm getting tired of the way he gets away with everything.'*

I widened my eyes at it, my head tilted to the side as I tried to read what she had written and what she hadn't written at the same time. She's always hated Roan just as much as I have, but how she wrote this reply made it sound like she was genuinely holding onto something even worse than I knew about. I kept thinking of the way Roan seemed to know about her, to have called her that word, and I wondered what it was that happened that I didn't know about.

*'When he saw us, he had said: 'So what, you and Luke are *insert rude gay slur here* and pretending to have girlfriends, while Isabella and Serina are *Insert rude lesbian slur here*.' I don't understand how he'd jump to the conclusion that something was going on with you and Serina. Wouldn't he have naturally assumed Luke and I were just secretly hooking up behind y'all's backs? Normal people would come to that conclusion.'*

My mouth was in a straight line as I waited for Isabella to flick a note towards Luke before looking towards me for my reply. I flicked my note at her once the teacher turned around and started to write on the board, oblivious to the three of us flinging notes back and forth.

It took a few minutes for Isabella to attempt to open the note since Mr. McCormrick had stopped to hand out test papers, making me realize I needed to open my textbook to the page he had written on the board and pretend I knew how to answer these freaking problems we were supposed to be working on.

Honestly, I had been getting better at math though, and I grinned as I was given a paper with a B on it, knowing that while I had trouble learning math from teachers, I was getting better since I made Luke start to tutor me. It worked out in a way. He sucked at English, I sucked at math, and to motivate each other, we were tasked to take a piece of clothing off every time we finished a whole paper without any problems on it. Seeing him take his clothes off was exactly the type of motivation I needed to study more.

As Mr. McCormrick went back up to the front, sitting down behind his computer while we were supposed to be working, Isabella threw her note back at me with a sad, hesitant look on her face. I opened it, noticing this time she hadn't done her perfect triangle, and frowned, wondering what was upsetting her to make her forget her triangle fold of frustration.

'Roan saw Serina and me. I don't want to get into details, not yet, Pretty Boy. It was yesterday, and I need a minute to breathe to get past it. I'm sorry Kins. Know that when I can force myself to talk about it, you'll be the first one to know.'

I could tell her hand had been shaking as she wrote it and I bit my lower lip hard enough to taste a little dot of blood. 'You don't have to tell me until you're ready, Izzy. I'm here for you, always.' I replied to her with a heavy angry hand.

I took deep breaths as she read it, giving me a soft nod, a sad smile on her face as she slipped the note in her pocket and started to work. I glanced at the back of Roan's head, wondering why he was such a hateful jerk. What the hell crawled up his ass and just died there? I mean yeah, okay. He hated me all through middle school because I broke his knee and he couldn't play. I understood his hatred for me over that. Basketball was his life, it was his everything, and even back then his dad put so much pressure on him.

Then it didn't help that I popped out of nowhere and I was better than him on the one position he liked the most, and his father would give him a disappointed look over that and send him to another position, making sure to praise me while Roan was forced to watch and get looks of disapproval. I even heard him once or twice tell Roan: *'Why can't you bend like that when you dribble the ball? Why can't you run that fast? You need to be more like Kinsley. He's a natural, he hasn't even played basketball before this year.'* Which was true, I hadn't, and maybe if I was one of those sporty kids I'd have been excited to hear my coach talk about me like that.

But I wasn't, and I didn't care. I was only doing it because my parents made me. Basketball was fun, but it wasn't that fun. It wasn't what I truly wanted to do. But then high school came and I assumed since he'd had surgery and recovered from it, that he was able to play again and only needed the brace, that he'd get over it. Then I was getting shoved into lockers, called names, and spat on, tortured for years, for something he'd already recovered from. I just didn't understand him. Now he was holding both of these large secrets inside him, something you'd expect a bully to use right away. I just wish I knew why.

My phone vibrated in my pocket and I slowly slipped it out, looking down at it with a soft smile sliding over my lips. *'I love you, babe. No matter what, we'll get through this. You know that, right?'*

I lifted my eyes to look at Luke. He had a soft blush on his cheeks as he pressed his eraser against his nose, ducking his head shyly as he glanced at me from under his eyelashes. So freaking cute, I swear. *'I love you too, Lukie. And I know, absolutely.'* I replied, before slipping my phone into my pocket.

Luke grinned, reading through my text as Mr. McCormrick's sharp voice flooded through the room. "Luke, texting in class isn't allowed. See me after class." Luke crinkled his nose in annoyance, and I could see him turning his phone off before slipping it into his pocket.

As the bell rang, the classroom emptied in waves, as it usually did. Isabella stood and I waved her on, knowing her next class wasn't with me anyway and I wanted to wait for Luke. I put my things away slowly, as did Luke, and followed him to the front as Roan and a few others finally left the classroom. "Go on, Kinsley. I won't bite him, you don't have to be his bodyguard." Mr. McCormrick said with a laugh.

I narrowed my eyes at him as Luke chuckled softly under his breath, and walked out the door, leaving the two alone. Even as I stepped out into the hall I could already hear Mr. McCormrick going off about how disappointed he was over one of his top students texting, and how he needed to set a good example. I smirked, knowing Luke was probably standing there staring at my ass and ignoring everything he was saying.

I took a few steps down the hallway, knowing I couldn't stay, but I lingered because I wanted to be near him for just a little longer. Maybe that was my mistake, wanting to stay, lingering, when I shouldn't have. A hand gripped my upper arm and I gasped in surprise as I was slammed against a locker hard enough to knock my breath out of me.

For a moment my vision went blank, and my head smacked sharply against the locker, as I was yanked away from it and slammed to the ground. "Fucking faggot," Roan growled in my ear as a knee pressed down against my stomach. There was a small circle forming, kids who were supposed to be filing into Mr. McCormrick's class but were standing outside waiting for him to stop lecturing Luke. They were chanting *'fight, fight'* over and over again as Roan grinned wickedly above me.

Then as quickly as he came, he was gone. Luke seemed to have known, as he jammed his way through the crowd. He flung himself on Roan to get him off of me, and as I forced myself to sit up I watched the two of them roll around, fighting. Roan was stronger than Luke this time, as even as they usually were. Luke was holding back, trying to rein in his punches even as they landed on Roan's jaw and his collarbone.

Roan was on top of Luke now as he punched Luke hard enough to leave a black eye. Fear raced through me as I ran and knocked him off of Luke by slamming my head into Roan's ribs. Before Roan could retaliate, however, he was being yanked backward. Luke and I were still on the ground, as Mr. McCormick glared at Roan.

"The principal's office, all of you, now," he said, glaring at the three of us. He glanced at those around us and locked eyes with a girl who was nearby, who had flinched at his attention. "Did you see everything? Who started this?"

"Um, Kinsley was walking down the hall and Roan shoved him in a locker. Luke knocked Roan off of Kinsley, and Roan started attacking Luke," she said, her eyes fluttering around everywhere.

Mr. McCormick looked around the crowd, at the kids that were nodding and saying she was telling the truth, before looking at her once more. "You're a witness, come with me as well."

I stood up slowly, my hand clutching my stomach where Roan had kneeled on it. I held out my hand for Luke as he slowly took it, and didn't let go. He was shaking, his other hand tugging at his curls, and I could see he was scared. It had been a while since he had been punched since his father had punched him. "It's going to be okay," I said, my voice strong despite how much I was in pain.

I could see the beginning of a black eye forming on his face, his eye swelling as he stared at me. The hallway was emptying fast, the students terrified of Mr. McCormrick's fury as he started to drag a cursing Roan down the hallway. "I know, because I have you," Luke whispered, squeezing my hand once more, before letting it go.

I smiled at him, batting my shoulder into his gently, as we followed them down the hall. "You'll always have me."

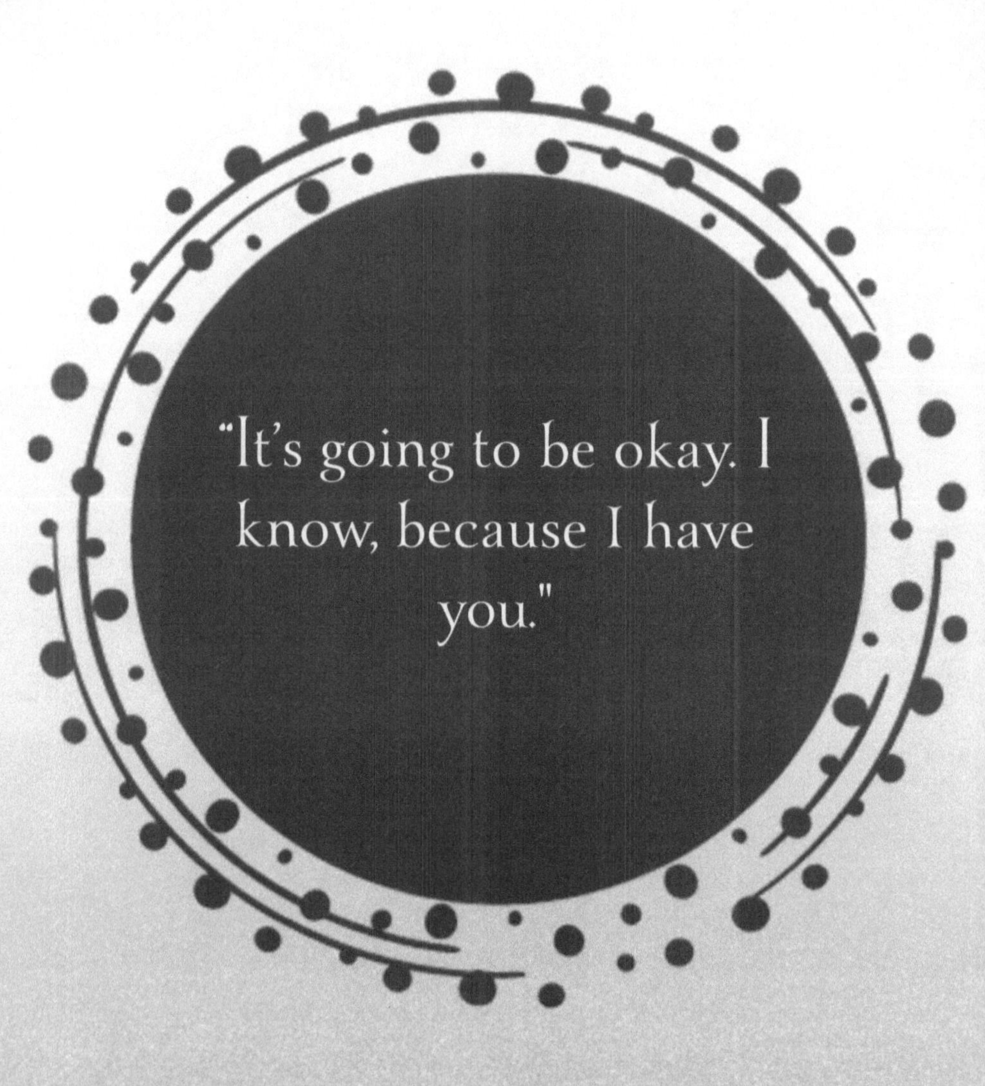
"It's going to be okay. I know, because I have you."

Chapter 34
Luke

I was shaking as I sat next to Kinsley in the chairs in front of the office. The girl was sitting beside Kinsley, Roan on the other side, and Mr. McCormick was glaring at Roan with his arms crossed over his chest. Roan's coach was standing in the doorway whisper yelling at Mr. McCormick and I was both disgusted and impressed that Mr. McCormick was just standing there ignoring the spit that was blasting out of Roan's coach's mouth as he screamed at him.

Roan was the captain of his basketball team, Roan was the best player on the team, and all of the teachers and coaches knew that Roan had one last strike. His coach wasn't happy Mr. McCormick didn't just let it all slide like the other teachers would have. My coach was there as well, glaring at Roan with his arms crossed over his chest. He wasn't happy that Roan had given me a black eye because for him it was one thing if Roan was beating up on a different kid, it was another thing entirely if he was beating up on one of his players. As sick and twisted as it was, the principal wasn't going to care about Kinsley as much as me.

Then again, Kinsley's parents donated a lot of money to this school, and I was fairly sure if Kinsley had ever complained to the principal once Roan probably would have gotten in more trouble sooner. Kinsley just never liked to stand out, he didn't like to cause problems, and he just wanted all of it to go away. Hopefully, this would be the end of it. Hopefully, they'd finally expel him.

"Luke? Oh my god, Luke!" I stood up fast, my heart racing as my mom stepped into the hallway. I hadn't seen her since the night Dad took Shawn away, but I had started to talk to her on the phone lately. Kinsley and my therapist had been encouraging me to visit her, but I wanted to start slow. We've had some decent conversations, she knew about

Kinsley and she never seemed to mind any of it. I was glad, I wasn't sure how I'd take it if she had.

Mom's wide-crazed eyes and her messy appearance were the last memories I had of her, but she looked like a completely different person now. She looked so much better. Her malnourished form was filling out nicely, and her pale skin and her broken nails were getting better. She looked pretty today, better than ever.

Her hair was pulled back into a bun, and she was wearing a soft blue dress, the skirt hanging to her knees as she walked in with a clatter from her heels on the tile ground. She had on a sprinkling of makeup and as I stood to greet her she wrapped her arms around me and held me tightly against her, making me let out a soft breath of surprise as I breathed in the memories of the past.

Her perfume, her hugs, her touches, her caring about me. I let out a soft shudder as she pulled away. "You're Kinsley, right?" My mother asked, turning to look at him as we all sat down. He blinked in surprise, his eyes fluttering to me, before looking at her again with a shy nod. "I remember you from the hospital. You're that boy who broke a few ribs and had a fractured wrist. Thank you for taking care of my son." She patted his hand as he smiled at her. "You're just as pretty as he said you are," She whispered, making Kinsley flush a bright red color as I bit back a grin.

Kinsley narrowed his eyes as I crinkled my nose at him, trying to ignore the pain in my left eye, but before he could reprimand me for gushing over him behind his back, another woman walked down the hall and moved straight past us, to Roan. She was wearing a sharp pantsuit, her long black hair pulled back into a ponytail as she glared at Roan with sharp dark brown eyes filled with anger. Without a word, she slapped her son across the face, causing a gasp to spill out of everyone's mouths as we all stared at her with mouths agape.

Even the coaches and Mr. McCormick shut up to watch her, but she said nothing as she sat down in the chair next to him and crossed her legs, waiting for us to be called. "Um..." Luke's mother said, clearly thrown. "Is your mother or father coming?" She asked me, looking around Kinsley.

"Hmm?" Kinsley asked, raising his eyebrow at her. "Nah, they don't care. They'd only come if I was in the hospital and then I'd just have to listen to them complain about wasting their time coming to release me again." He said with a shrug.

My mother frowned as Kinsley tapped his fingers against his knee, and I wished more than anything I could reach out and hold his hand, to quiet the sadness he always held inside him. I couldn't do anything about his parents, but I could promise him he'd never be alone again, not while I was with him.

It didn't take much longer than that until the principal's office opened and he beckoned us all inside. Roan's mother pulled the Principal out into the hallway since she was related to him, probably trying to find a way to save Roan, but I could tell by the way she thundered inside the room with a flustered principal following behind her that she didn't get her way.

"I need to know what happened. Susie, if you don't feel comfortable telling me without a parent present, I can wait until your parent comes," the principal said softly as the teacher and the coaches stood leaning against the door, watching us.

Kinsley, my mother, and I were sitting on one couch, while Roan stood to the side, leaning against the wall beside where his mother was sitting in her chair. Susie was sitting in a chair by herself, closer to me than Roan's mother, and I couldn't blame her. She was probably scared of the lady after watching her smack her son.

"Honestly, Roan had been bullying Kinsley for years. It has kind of stopped from what I could tell when Luke and Kinsley started being friends, but I guess it started up again. Um, I don't know if there was a reason for it, or if Roan just felt the need, but Kinsley was walking down the hallway and Roan slammed him against the locker. He called him a fa...a gay slur, and then just attacked him. Kinsley wasn't even bothering him, just walking to his next class.

"Then Luke ran at Roan to get him off of Kinsley. They were punching each other. Luke was on his back and Roan was hurting him. Kinsley slammed into Luke, shoving him off of Luke. That's when Mr. McCormick intervened," Susie said with a shaky voice. She kept looking over at Roan, as if she was scared speaking out against him would make him attack her next.

The principal looked at Mr. McCormick, who confirmed as much as he could that Susie was telling the truth. "You can go, Susie. Tell the secretary you need a late pass." She nodded, standing up slowly as she walked out of the room, Mr. McCormick patting her back as she left. "You can go as well, gentlemen. I don't think Mrs. Gee wants to keep watching your class, Bill," he said, looking at Mr. McCormick and the two coaches.

The two coaches argued with it for a while but accepted that he didn't want them to stay and left, leaving just us three kids and the two parents in the room. "Roan. Why have you been bullying Kinsley? What has he ever done to you? And don't start with your knee, that was in middle school and it has long since been healed. You've been attacking him for years? What the hell? Do you not know who his parents are? They do a lot for this school, I can't get on their bad side," The principal said, talking to him not as a principal, but as a family member.

Roan scoffed as he grabbed the chair Susie had been sitting in and moved it in the middle of everyone, sitting down and grumbling. "Because he has everything, and he's still a fucking faggot. Yeah, I said it. Both of them are faggots. I saw them," he sneered, glaring at Kinsley and me.

Kinsley's body stiffened beside me as my mom's body relaxed, but the way her arms crossed across her chest showed just how angry she was about his words. Deciding that there was no point caring anymore, I slipped my fingers against Kinsley's, lacing them together tightly and inconspicuously in between our legs as he shook against me.

Almost instantly, the principal's and Roan's mom's faces contorted in a disgusted grimace that I wished more than anything I could hide from, that I could hide Kinsley from. But I sat up straighter because this was something we'd have to get used to if we were going to stay together. I would get used to this, to see this every day if I needed to, if it meant I could live the rest of my life holding his hand.

"So you're telling me that you beat up someone for no reason, just because you think you saw something? Is there proof you saw it? And honestly, even if it was true, is it okay to hurt someone? He didn't have a weapon, and he didn't provoke you or say anything to you. You just attacked him for being what? Different from you? What's next, you're going to attack people who have long hair because yours is short? Or maybe you'll attack girls for having different body parts than you? Because that's all just as different from you as this is," my mother said, sitting up straight as she glared at Roan.

"Don't you talk to my son like that when yours is a fucking faggot," Roan's mother sneered, standing up and glaring at my mom. I felt my heart beating fast in my chest as my mom scoffed at her. "You should be ashamed, raising him like that. Have you not been taking him to church? He needs to get sent to a conversion camp at the earliest second, both of them. Where are Kinsley's parents? They would send him in a heartbeat, I know they would."

Kinsley's breath came out fast as he shuddered beside me, and I felt like an asshole for causing all of this. If only I hadn't pulled him into that freaking closet, everything would be okay. We were so close, just a few months away until we could graduate. Until we could get out of here. But we were still seventeen, and if his parents wanted to send him away, there wasn't anything we could do about it.

"As I said, where's your proof? All we have to go off of is a boy's word, a boy who has been bullying Kinsley for years. A boy who nearly killed Kinsley last year, and I know that for a fact because I was one of the nurses who took care of Kinsley. Is there documented proof that they were as he says?" She asked, glaring at Roan.

Everyone was quiet as Roan sputtered, frowning. "N-no, but I saw them!" he shouted.

"She's right, Roan. Without any proof of your accusation, it's just an accusation. And I know you have been bullying Kinsley because of that little Mexican girl. Just ask her out already," The principal said as he rolled his eyes.

I snorted as I pressed my fingers against my mouth. I looked at Kinsley, watching a sly smile spread over his lips as we realized exactly what he had said. I mean...it made sense. Here I had thought that he had been bullying Kinsley all that time because he secretly had a crush on him, but no, it was because he had a crush on Isabella. He picked on Kins because he thought he was with Izzy. Then seeing Kinsley and me together, after apparently seeing Izzy and Serina together, must have been too much for him to deal with.

"You have a crush on my girlfriend?" I asked as Kinsley laughed silently beside me.

My mom raised her eyebrow at me but remained silent because she knew I was dating Kinsley, but she didn't know anything about Isabella and me pretending to be dating to keep everyone off our backs. Roan sputtered, furious as he pointed at me. "He's fucking lying, he was in the janitor's closet with Kinsley, and I saw Serina and Isabella kissing the other day too, they're all gay and pretending to be together." He spat, frustrated things weren't going his way.

"Look, Roan crossed a line today and we all saw it coming, Marian," the principal said, looking at Roan's mom. "He had one strike left, and he attacked Kinsley for no reason.

Pretending he's gay isn't going to cut it, both of these boys have girlfriends, this is just outlandish. Roan is getting expelled today, there's no way around it."

She growled in frustration but didn't argue with him. "Roan, you have half an hour to gather your things from wherever they are, to clear out your lockers, and to get out of this school." He pressed his finger on a button on his desk, clearing his throat. "Escort Roan around the school to get his things and then make sure he leaves peacefully." He spoke, before looking at Roan again. "You cannot come back onto this property again. Not for games, not for visits, nothing. I can't stop you from going to away games, it's not my property, but if you come here you'll be escorted out by the police. You can go now."

Roan stood up fast and grabbed his chair, throwing it at the shelves on the wall beside the principal's desk. He was screaming curse words at the principal, at us, as his mother grabbed his ear and yanked him out of the office threatening to whip him for embarrassing her like this. The principal sighed as he shook his head at them, waiting until the door closed before turning to look at us. "Kinsley. You were the victim in this, so there's nothing for you. But Luke, you got in the middle and started to punch Roan, it wasn't even your fight and you didn't need to do that. You could have yanked Roan off of him, but you started to punch him. You're going to be suspended for two weeks for fighting him."

"If you suspend him, then I will sue you and this whole school system," my mom said, sitting up straight as she stared at the principal. My mouth fell open, and I wasn't surprised to see the principal's fall open as well as Kinsley gripped my hand tighter in surprise. "Did you know that it's considered a hate crime to attack someone simply for being gay? Whether he is or not is not your concern, or Roan's. The fact that Roan has been bullying Kinsley and nearly killed him once before with the only reason being because he thinks he's gay, is a hate crime and you've allowed it to happen. Don't pretend you've never seen or heard of Roan attacking Kinsley. And I remember you suspended my son once before because of what was it?

"Because Roan was once more beating up Kinsley, right after he had gotten out of the hospital, and Luke had defended him. If you had proper cameras placed inside your school as I'm sure you get enough money from Kinsley's parents to do so, then this wouldn't have happened from the beginning. I wonder if we gather up everyone's phones how many incidences of Roan beating on Kinsley can we find in the videos?"

Mom stood then, her arms crossed as she stared at the principal. "How many teachers would be in the background just standing there watching because Roan is related to you? Maybe his mother has this town in the back of her pocket, but if I take this to the school board, I wonder what they'd say? And I wondered if Kinsley's parents know that the school they've been donating all of this money to every year isn't even trying to ensure his safety after knowing he's been bullied all this time.

"The report from the school about Roan and the incident where Kinsley was almost killed was bullshit. All you did was place cameras outside, but not inside. This school claims to have a zero-tolerance policy for bullying but apparently, that doesn't apply to the students that are related to you. Maybe the school board would like to know how much you had been letting your school get out of control by allowing your family to run wild. Not only could you get in trouble, sir, but you could lose your job. So, are you sure you want to suspend my son?" She sat back down then, tapping her fingers on her knee as she stared him down.

The principal was speechless, and I felt giddy as Kinsley leaned closer to me, his breath against my cheek as he stared at my mother with a look of admiration in his eyes. I wanted more than anything to just run my fingers over the soft skin of his cheek, to slide my finger down the deep groove of his dimple, and to kiss him in the middle of the office, in the middle of the school, where everyone could see.

I took a deep breath, settling instead to slide my thumb up and down his knuckle, willing myself to wait until later when we were alone. Judging from my mom's argument I wouldn't be surprised if there were cameras placed all around the school now, which meant that Kinsley and I couldn't sneak into the janitor's closet anymore, and probably couldn't be alone in the art room either for a while until we weren't being watched anymore.

"He needs some sort of punishment for jumping into the brawl and throwing fists, Mrs. Wilson, be reasonable. Students were there, they saw him fighting Roan," the principal nearly begged, clearly feeling worried by her threat.

She sighed. "It's Ms. Stone. I had reverted to my maiden name," she spat at him as he paled, worried he had pissed her off even more. I loved seeing this side of my mom. She was a nurse, after all, and she was used to dealing with ridiculous patients' parents, or patients themselves that were just unreasonable. She was so strong until my father had torn her down, the only person that could. I was glad she was building herself back up, glad she was getting better. I was proud of her, proud that she was my mother. "After school detention? Surely that would be a better compromise."

I scrunched up my nose in annoyance as Kinsley chuckled softly beside me, and I knew without a doubt that every day I would be in the library for after-school detention he would probably be in there drawing so I did not have to be alone. "One week?" the principal asked, which I found funny that he was asking her, it showed how terrified he was right now.

She nodded, stood up, and looked down at me. "Starting today after school, one-week after-school detention. His coach will probably be annoyed but he'll get over it. Is that all then? The boys have a class to get to, I'm sure, and I have to get back home. I have a demanding dog that is probably waiting to be fed right now," I smirked knowing she was talking about my boss's dog.

"Yes ma'am, Ms. Stone. Thank you for coming in to see me. I take it you'll talk to Kinsley's parents, and make sure they know everything is okay?" He asked. She nodded, though I doubted she would. She hadn't tried to talk to Kinsley's parents, she knew I didn't want her to. They weren't the reason I was staying with Kinsley, and she knew that. "You're all dismissed, please get a late note from the secretary." He said as he stood up and shook my mother's hand.

We all walked into the hallway together, standing near the secretary's desk as we waited for her to write the notes. She had left to go get some more paper out of the back, leaving the three of us alone for a moment. I couldn't help but wrap my arms around my mom once more, pulling her tightly against me. "Thank you, Ma," I whispered, feeling her smile against me.

I pulled away from her as she grinned. "Anytime you need me, Luke, don't hesitate. You know I love you, no matter what. And you, come here, my bonus son." She said. I smiled as Kinsley's face flushed at her words.

I watched him hug her back slowly, almost uncertain as if he barely even knew what it felt like to hug a mother before finally hugging her back. It was heartbreaking to watch him melt against her, tears in his eyes as his body slightly shook in an overwhelmed shudder. "He's not my brother, so how is he your bonus son," I mumbled as she pulled away from Kinsley and smiled at me.

"Because obviously, you're going to marry him someday. I recognize the way you look at him, Luke. That's the look of someone who is staring at their future," she whispered into my ear, before winking at me. I was speechless as she walked away waving.

Kinsley looked at me, a twinkle in his eyes. I looked around the room, making sure we were alone before brushing my lips gently over his. He sputtered as I pulled away, his face the color of a cherry as he pressed his hands against his cheeks, pulling his hood over his face to try and cover it. "What was that for?" He stammered, clearly thrown.

"Just kissing my future," I replied as he stared at me like I was crazy.

"You're so strange sometimes, Luke," he mumbled as I grinned at him. "But it's okay, I still love you."

I tapped my shoulder into him gently. "I love you too, Kins."

"Just kissing my
future,"

Chapter 35
Kinsley

"What movie do you want to see?" I wondered as Serina and I stepped out of her car.

For a moment, she didn't answer me, her eyes trailing over the posters that were set up outside the movie theaters, looking at everything that had just come out and everything that was going to be coming out soon. As she stared at the pictures, she hummed along to a song, but I could tell by the way she hummed that she wasn't putting all of her efforts into it. A sadness was in her eyes and it pulled at me, making me wonder if it had to do with her and Isabella.

"I don't know, Kins. I guess we should just wait for Luke and Isabella. They'll be another hour though, right? Let's get hotdogs while we wait."

Serina nodded toward the hotdog stand that was right across from the movie theater. Her parents had gotten stricter than usual the past few weeks, making it harder for her to go out, but we started to find ways around that. As long as she was with me, it was okay for her to go anywhere. They were tracking her, but because I had a cab drop me off at her house, they knew she was with me, so they were fine with it.

It was pretty warm out that night, even though it had been raining a lot lately and you could still smell the tangy wet smell that hung heavily in the air. As we sat down against the side of the theater where it opened up to a small alley beside it, I couldn't help but wish it was raining once more.

Times like this when everything was quiet, when the air was thick with the smell of rain, all I could think about was Luke. Sitting in the gazebo behind my house, watching the rain with him, such an innocent time filled with two boys who loved each other desperately but were unable to figure out how.

We ate in a relaxed silence, sitting on the sidewalk without caring for our expensive clothes. It was funny how we were the ones who didn't particularly care about getting our fancy clothes dirty, but Isabella and Luke would be scolding both of us if they were here right now.

I went to pull my phone out of my pocket but decided against it because, as much as I craved to hear Luke's voice, to obsessively read his last few texts as I waited until I could see him again, I didn't. You'd think we'd be getting tired of each other with how much we saw each other, but we weren't. It didn't matter that we were only separated for a few classes every day in school, or his football practice, or even when he had to work at night.

Those small breaks from each other felt like torture to me. We spent every second of the day around that finding ways to touch and kiss and connect, to tangle ourselves together so seamlessly that we breathed together as one. The honeymoon phase, Izzy called it, but I wasn't so sure.

I couldn't imagine a day I would wake up wanting nothing more than to stare at him and marvel at how beautiful his skin looked with the sunlight glittering around him. I couldn't imagine a day I could look at him and my heart wouldn't call for his. That I wouldn't crave his touch more than breathing, that my heart wouldn't flutter like the wings of a hummingbird trying desperately to fly. No, I didn't think this was a honeymoon phase, not for me, not for us. It was just how we love.

Serina coughed, a soft smile on her face as she nodded her head towards my hand. "You're obsessed," she muttered as I flashed a grin. "Not that I can say otherwise myself, to be honest. But I just..." She sighed, looking off to the side as she took a small bite from her hotdog.

I frowned, remembering what Isabella had written in the note today, about Roan. "Are you okay? You and Izzy?"

She shrugged, brushing her head back against the stone of the theater with a sigh. As she pulled her head up again, her hood fell back, and her long black hair was pulled into two low ponytails, showing off some of the red that she had dyed underneath her hair. "I hope so," she choked out, her bottom lip quivering for a second as she blinked once, then once more, trying to get the sheen of tears to dry instead of falling.

I leaned over, lacing her fingers with mine, patting my free hand against the back of hers as she smiled a soft smile at me. "It's okay to break sometimes. That's why you have friends. To help you pick the pieces up when you're finished, and to make sure you look your absolute best afterward," I said, smiling as she breathed out a raspy breath.

"I've always wanted friends. I just didn't think I was allowed. Someone like me, someone so different from what my parents wanted me to be. But you know, I met you, and Izzy, and Luke, and now all I can think is: There was never anything wrong with me from the start. Even if I'm not good enough for them, it doesn't matter. I just have to be good enough for myself," I sucked in a deep breath, closing my eyes because for a moment all I could see was my parents' faces. How happy they were with me, now that I had been with Serina for a little while now.

But would they have been happy knowing it was all a lie? Would they have loved me knowing that I didn't want to go to Harvard, Princeton, or any of the schools they were sending applications to without caring if I even wanted them to? Would they have loved me knowing I didn't want to go to college for business, but for something else entirely?

All of that time Luke had been telling me I was brave, but how was I brave when I hid behind lies? They loved me because I let them fill out the applications and I didn't argue about it. They loved me because the person I held hands with in public was the gender they approved of. Would they have loved me if I had stopped trying to make them love me? If I had stopped worrying about what they thought about me, and more about what I thought about myself?

Serina was studying me, and while I felt like a jerk for making this about me while I was trying to help her feel better, she smiled, her head tilted to the side. "Are you good enough for yourself?"

I didn't say anything for a few minutes, lost in the thoughts of everything that had happened to me. How I had always pushed what I wanted to do to the side, thinking it was stupid and pointless. All my life, I had known the careers my parents deemed good, safe, and smart, and the ones they thought were stupid and a waste of time. Sure, a handful of people had succeeded at them, but why would I have thought I was good enough to be one of the handful?

So I had always pushed it down, a pipe dream, trying to focus on what they wanted me to focus on, to do whatever I could to make them happy. Pushing it down even more when Luke came, because for a while all I wanted to focus on was his happiness, and helping him get better. But I guess in a way, I was still shoving myself down, so far down that I forgot that I mattered too. *I matter too.*

I let out a shaky breath as I patted the back of her hand once more. "Not yet, but I will be," I promised.

She smiled brightly at me as she curled her knees up to her chest, her other hand resting on top of them, and pressed her cheek against them. "I know you will because you're Kinsley," she said with a nod. Then she stuck her tongue out at me, grinning. "My brother from another mother."

I laughed, shaking my head at her, knowing if Luke and Isabella were here they would be calling us dorks. "My sister from another mister," I added as we both started to laugh at each other over how cringy we were.

"So I wonder, do you guys know that you cheat on each other constantly, or is this like a weird four-person relationship?" I felt my heart drop into my stomach as Serina and I whipped our heads toward the road and stared at Roan.

Maybe if it had just been him, I wouldn't have been scared. I was so freaking tired of him constantly being there all the time, ruining every single thing for me over and over again. I would have fought back against him if he had been alone, but the fact that he was standing there with three other guys and two girls made me pause, a knot of fear settling in my stomach.

The first thought in my mind was: *Shit, Luke is going to be here in about ten or fifteen minutes.* I didn't want him to come and see this, to be here for this. Luke would have fought him, there in public, and he would have gone to jail. Roan's family would have put him in jail. While I was almost eighteen, Luke was still months away from it. Where would he have gone? Juvie? To his dad? The paperwork for him to be emancipated was just formalities, to be honest, because by the time it was one hundred percent done he would have been nearly eighteen. Maybe he would have still gone to jail after all.

My heart was racing as I stood, attempting to pull Serina behind me as she ignored my hand and scowled at Roan. "You're so jealous you can't get anyone that you just keep messing with us! Just leave us alone, Roan! People only like you because they're scared of your family! You don't even know what it's like to have friends!" Serina yelled, glaring at Roan as I stiffened in surprise.

Fear rushed through me as Roan took a step closer to us, pinning us against the theater wall even more. I was annoyed by the number of people who were just walking past us and ignoring us, or the parents who did indeed look worried until they saw Roan, and walked away, not wanting to be involved. Most everyone in town knew Roan and who his mother was, and how it was pretty much expected for him to take over her job one day as the chief. I wondered if that was still in the cards since he was expelled that day.

Roan surprised me, throwing his hands up in the air, laughing, and the small group behind him was only a half step behind as they laughed along with him, mindlessly copying him to stay in his good graces. "We don't want any trouble, Roan. We're just there to watch a movie, waiting for our friends to come. Please just go do whatever you were there for," I pleaded, eyes lowered in compliance.

I could see the clock from there, the large old-fashioned clock that rested at the end of the street, telling the time. *Luke is coming, go away, Roan.* I chanted in my mind. I could feel sweat breaking out on my forehead as I felt my phone vibrate, knowing it was probably Luke telling me he had gotten off work and was picking Izzy up from her job, and heading over towards us now. I wanted to cry, wishing I could just be done with all of this. Wishing we were eighteen already, graduated, packed, and loaded into cars, driving away from this fucked up town and these homophobic people.

Of course, Roan wasn't going to listen. He was Roan. He walked towards me, one hand grabbed the collar of my shirt as he grabbed Serina's arm, pulling us both into the alley while his friends followed behind. Serina screamed and he yanked her harder, and a handful of curses slipped from my mouth as I tried to kick him in the knee.

He must have seen it coming because he dodged the kick, let go of Serina, and shoved me into the side of the dumpster hard enough to knock the breath out of me. I had hoped that meant Serina was running away, but one of the girls caught her and grabbed the back of her hair, pulling out a whimper of pain as the girl held her tightly. Serina tried to yank the girl's hands out of her hair, but the other girl grabbed Serina's hands, a scowl on her face as they waited for Roan to say something.

Hands grabbed my arms as one guy grabbed each arm, hauling me to my feet and holding me against the dumpster. "Let her go! She has nothing to do with you getting expelled, Roan. You want to take it out on me, then take it out on me, but leave her out of this!"

Roan chuckled, his eyes flicking back and forth between me and Serina as I tried to catch my breath. He cracked his knuckles as he looked at the third guy, motioning with his head towards Serina. The guy grabbed her hands from the girl, and she took a step back, waiting. "My mom always said I couldn't hit girls, but I wonder if lesbians even count in that sense? Who's the man in the relationship? Or does it not work like that for girls? How about you, Kinsley? You're the girl in the relationship, right? So does that make you both the girls?"

I rolled my eyes because obviously, the fact that we were both guys meant there wasn't a girl in the relationship. The idea of labeling the *bottom* a girl was insulting. But I didn't expect much else from Roan, to be honest.

"You're just jealous I'm more of a man than you are," Serina sneered as she rotated her wrist to flip Roan off. "And no matter what you do to me, it'll never be your name she calls, it's always going to be mine."

The pride I felt for her was short-lived, as Roan screamed in anger. Without a word, the girl started to punch Serina, while the guy and the other girl held her tightly in their grasp. I screamed, fighting against the guys holding me, managing a kick or two as they grunted against me, but unfortunately held me tight.

"Get the fuck off of her! Roan, god dammit! What the fuck is your problem, huh? Did your mommy not hug you enough as a child? You can't bully your way to getting what you want. Eventually, you'll have to grow the fuck up!" I screamed as he turned to look at me.

I tried as hard as I could to block out Serina's breathless pleading as I struggled, refusing to stop trying to get out and help her even if I could barely move. As much as I didn't want Luke to come earlier, I didn't think Roan would stoop so low as to hurt Serina too, and now all I could do was scream for Luke repeatedly in my mind.

All I could see was Isabella's tear-stricken face in my mind. *Izzy, Serina, Luke,* I thought in my mind as Roan grabbed my hair, yanking my head back painfully. *I'm sorry, I tried.*

"You're wrong, Kinsley. Sometimes, the world hands people rainbows and gold, and people get the happiness they want, the happiness they fight for. But then some people just get fucking nothing. And I hate to break this to you, but the world is freaking corrupt. People like me, people with rich influential family members, people like you even, we get away with whatever the fuck we want to get away with. Why? Because my mom is in charge here, my family has connections you can't even dream of, and we have more money than anyone else in this town."

"What was that? What did you say?" He asked, moving closer to me as I whispered. I didn't even realize I was whispering.

"It's not fair?" He asked, before roaring out a laugh. "Let me tell you something, Kinsley. Life isn't fair. Life is money, politics, and the strong beating up the weak. I'm doing the world a favor! Getting rid of a few more sinners," he said with a grin, moments before punching me in the face.

The first punch was the worst. That's what they always said, right? The first punch always hurts the worst. Maybe it was because I had been anticipating it coming for so long that when it hit I was still surprised my body was in shock by it. As if I was holding on to a little bit of notion that maybe, just maybe he would change his mind. Maybe he would stop, see the silver lining, and take a step back instead of forward. Maybe he would see that his fist was moments away from being considered a deadly weapon.

But as that first punch landed my body was like a ripple in the ocean, the calm before the storm. I thought I was calm, as Luke told me I was, but I felt the furthest thing from calm as the fists landed, pulled away, and landed once more. Almost like I was in another body I felt numb. It was like I was watching the scene play out above me, but in my own body as well, at the same time. A punch to my stomach was second, and a third, and a fourth. Almost like he was a boxer, and my stomach was his bag.

I stopped counting when I stopped hearing Serina's cries, and I wasn't sure if it was because I blacked out or because she did. I couldn't hear... anything. Maybe going numb meant everything faded away, that I was distanced from it all. In a way, it was trippy, not being able to hear or feel but watching it all play out in front of me.

Then Roan was ripped off of me, and the hands holding me back let go fast. Luke, I breathed in my mind, falling to my knees as I looked up at the person holding Roan. But I was surprised to see it wasn't Luke, no. It was Roan's mother. She was angry, as she slammed her son against the alley wall without any ounce of sympathy.

I could see blood pouring down Roan's face as he tilted his head to the side in surprise, spitting a tooth out of his mouth and onto the ground with a stream of spit. She relentlessly shoved him against the wall again as she handcuffed him, ignoring his pleas for her to stop, that he was her son, and he was sorry. She looked at me as I fell onto my stomach, and I could tell just how little she cared about his sorry.

I was dizzy, everything was going in and out as I watched the cops pulling the girls off of Serina. Everything moved around me in slow motion as I watched the others caught and being dragged away. At the front of the alley, it was blinding, the lights of the police cars, and I glanced away and toward Serina. She was just lying there.

I didn't realize I was crying until I slid my face over the pool of tears I made, trying desperately to lift my body. I slid towards her slowly as an EMT screamed at people to move out of the way. He got to Serina before I did, and I lashed out, refusing to let anyone touch me until she was loaded onto the stretcher. For a brief terrifying moment, I wondered if I'd be able to let anyone touch me again.

Until I felt *him* touching me. *Oh, I'm safe. I'm home now.*

It was like everything was soundless until he touched me, and suddenly I could hear everything and feel every bit of the pain I was in. Like a switch, everything returned - the sirens, the screams, the cries, everything. But despite how loud it was, none of it was enough to wash him out. He looked down at me, horror in his eyes as he shoved the EMTs out of the way, falling to his knees in front of me.

I opened my mouth to talk to him, to tell him I loved him, to tell him how important he was to me. I couldn't find my voice, couldn't find the words, and it horrified me. "Kinsley," he choked out, his fingers gripping me tightly as he pulled me against his chest. Almost instantly, the pain was gone, and all I could feel was him as he stood, cradling me like a broken child in his arms.

"I got you, Baby." He pressed his lips against mine, in front of everyone, and I instantly melted against him, my fingers curled in his shirt, and I smiled.

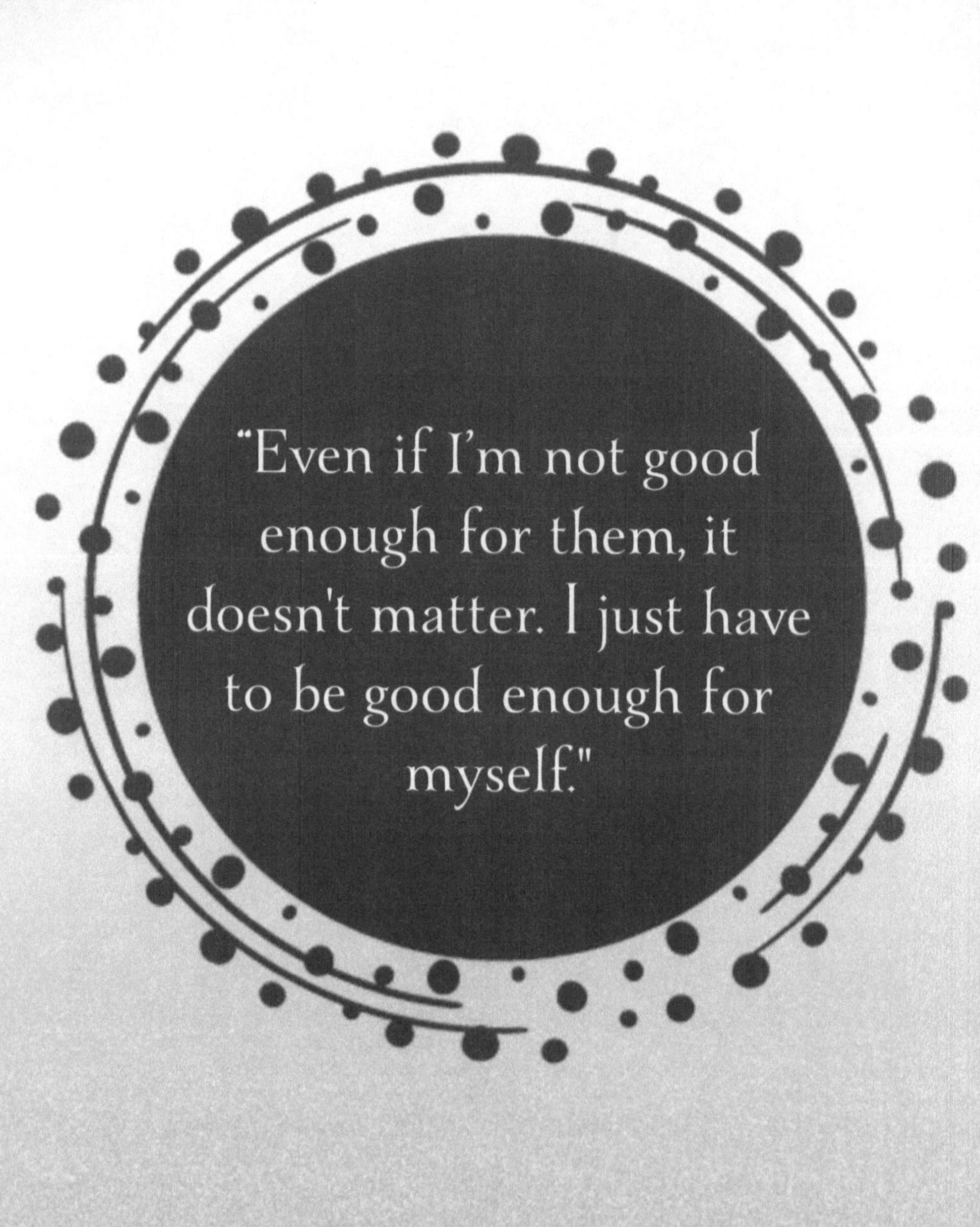

"Even if I'm not good enough for them, it doesn't matter. I just have to be good enough for myself."

Chapter 36
Luke

Some people might ask me if I regretted it. I refused to leave, even when his parents were glaring at us. But I didn't regret it, not one bit. Seeing him lying there bruised and battered once more, *once fucking more because of Roan*, it made me realize something. What was the point? What was the literal point? Sneaking around, hiding everything about us from everyone, and look where that got us? I wasn't going to waste another second without touching him, without kissing him, without showing the whole freaking world what he meant to me.

I had never been ashamed to show the world how much I loved him, I had been ashamed to live in a world that made me scared of losing him, *because* I loved him.

We rushed to the hospital in separate ambulances. Izzy was with Serina, and I was with Kinsley, both of us leaving behind Kinsley and Serina's cars without really caring about them right now. My mom was waiting for us when we got there. Serina was rushed to surgery since she had a large gash from one of the girls' rings, and Kinsley had to wait half an hour for an OR to open up.

It was the worst few hours of my life. It was worse than being in jail without being able to contact Kinsley. It was worse than watching him be with Serina without knowing it was all fake. I'd go back to pining away for him with my unrequited love if it meant he would be okay, he'd be healthy all over again. Those few hours were the darkest hours I've ever lived through. Sitting there watching the doors, watching people go in, watching them leave.

They didn't teach you in school how to wait for someone as their life hung in the balance. Kinsley was holding on, putting on a show, more adrenaline the doctors said because he was worried about Serina, but he had worse injuries than she did. Roan didn't even try to rein in his punches. They didn't teach you what to do when every little piece of the puzzle that was placed together started to unravel, and the only one who could ever put it back together might not make it.

I promise I'll be good, I chanted in my mind as I waited. I had Isabella's hand in one hand, and a little rubber ball in the other, squeezing it, over and over again as I ignored the feeling of being drained. *I won't ever say God's name in vain again.* Promises, so many promises. It was all I knew how to do, as the clock ticked and ticked, and the blood in my vein slowly filled up the bag.

"Luke, that's enough blood. Don't take any more blood from him, I don't care what he says." I could hear my mom, but she sounded so far away, while the clicking of the clock was so close, so loud. I was O negative, a universal donor. They didn't teach you in school what the hell you were supposed to do when the other half of your soul was dying. This was all I could think to do.

That, and pray. *I'll do anything you want, tell me, anything. Just please, please, please.* I had never prayed before and was unsure how to even go about it but I would do it, for him. I'd do anything for him. All I could see in my mind was his smile, his beautiful cerulean eyes, and how bright and shining they were. The deep lines on his cheeks, the large dimples that I loved more than anything else in the whole world. I could still feel his silky ash blond hair in between my fingers, I could still smell his skin on mine, embedded in my heart like a tattoo, forever.

Please don't take him from me.

I was relieved when Isabella's mother came because I wasn't sure how to help her. She was saying the word gone over and over again, her chant as it slipped from her lips, and without a word her mother fell to her knees in front of her and pulled her onto her lap, holding her as one would hold a baby.

My mother shoved a straw in between my lips and coaxed me to drink the tangy orange juice. She had tears in her voice, straining to hold them back, to be strong for me. I took a sip and nearly threw it up, too wound up to swallow, to move, to speak, to breathe. How could I breathe if he couldn't? Was he even breathing? I had never been so uncertain of anything in my life.

Then she pulled me onto her lap and I let her, her fingers in my hair, rocking me side by side. Isabella's mother patted my mother's knee, and my mother's hand patted hers, a silent plea of strength as they held each other together, so they could be strong for their babies. Across from us was a wall of judgment and cold stares.

Kinsley's parents were dressed in their finest, and I was unsure if they had stopped at home to get changed for the cameras or if they had worn that for work. Serina's parents arrived and my mother pulled the needle out of my arm. Both of them were stoic, with stern glares. There were no cameras back here for them to fake smiles. They didn't even care that we could all hear them whispering. "The kiss? Is it handled?" That was Serina's mother.

"I don't see why that has anything to do with you," Kinsley's father said angrily.

"He has been seen around town as her boyfriend for months, it makes her look like the girl who wasn't good enough for him. The girl that turned him gay," I wanted to scream at them, to tell them it didn't work like that, but I was still struggling to breathe, still unsure if I was allowed.

"The attack by the group of kids was seen and videotaped on at least five different phones, spread around all over by now. They can't deny Roan wasn't a part of it. He's been caught, his mother arrested him. She would lose her job if she didn't hold him as if any other criminal. The EMTs parked the ambulances in just the right places, no one saw the kiss except for the EMTs. I've paid them all already for their silence," Kinsley's mother informed her.

I was disgusted that their kids were dying and they were only concerned with their fucking image. I wanted nothing more than to stand up, to yell at them, but I couldn't move. Fortunately, I didn't need to.

"Could you?" Isabella's mother asked, sitting Isabella on the chair next to me and my mother. I wrapped my arms around a shaking non-verbal Isabella, pulling her against my chest and my mother's, the three of us rocked back and forth, a ball of fear and broken pieces trying our hardest to hold onto them as tightly as we could, trying to hold on to everything we had left; hope.

I wasn't sure what was going to happen until she started to curse at them. Her words were fast, angry, all in Spanish, and I wanted nothing more than to sink further and further into my chair to escape every bit of it. It was all so loud, and the clock was so loud. I heard a slap of her shoe and saw her smacking it against the palm of her hand as she screamed at them, pointing the toe of it at every one of them.

I already knew it wasn't going to do anything for them. You couldn't make them better people, as hard as you wished you could, you couldn't. The doors opened and we all held our breath as Serina was rolled out. I felt like an asshole for being disappointed it wasn't Kinsley. I shoved the disappointment down fast because Serina was my best friend, and I was so glad to see she was breathing. I wanted to go to her, to check on her, to make sure she was safe, but I was frozen, my heart was sputtering, and I couldn't move until Kinsley was safe.

Isabella nearly tore herself from my arms. I could tell that Serina's parents didn't want her to come, but one glare from Izzy's mother and the four of them were following the nurse and the doctor as they wheeled Serina away towards a room. "Oh, Luke," my mother whispered, curling me tighter against her. I didn't even realize I was crying until she said that, and then I realized I had been crying this whole time, without noticing it.

I found myself back to chanting or praying. I wasn't sure what it was called, to be honest, but I was doing it, anything, everything for him. *Please, please, please*, I was glad Serina was going to be okay. I could hear them, even as she was going down the hallway. She was okay, she was going to be okay. I wasn't sure about Kinsley. All I knew was, I wasn't breathing until I could see him breathe. *Please let him be okay.*

One hour later, the doors opened and everything inside me shifted. He came out with a tube down his throat, his eyes closed, and a large bandage pressed against the side of his forehead. The rest of him was covered, but I could see a large crack in the corner of his lower lip, his right cheekbone had a small bandage on it as well. I honestly didn't hear a single thing the doctor said as I stood, pulled out of my mom's arms, and moved to his side. The doctor was talking to Kinsley's parents and I ignored all of them as I walked beside the bed. I watched him, and I didn't breathe until I saw his chest rise. I didn't exhale until I saw it lower. Even if it was because of a machine, he was breathing, and so was I.

The rest of the day was horrible. Kinsley's parents were pretty much pulled away the whole time for press conferences, so much bad publicity for Roan and his mother. It seemed like all of the things Roan had been doing were starting to be aired, and how she was hiding all of it, every bit of it for him. They were losing everything, and Roan was getting charged with two counts of attempted murder. They were going to have a court hearing to see if he'd be tried as an adult or a child. For now, he was staying in jail.

The whole day I stayed by Kinsley's side, his hand in mine, and just stared. Isabella and I video-called each other from time to time, so she could see Kinsley, and I could see Serina, but mostly we just stared at the other halves of our souls, waiting for them to wake and make us complete all over again.

It was kind of funny how they both seemed to wake up at around the same time. My mom was in the room when he did, and she removed the tube from his throat fast, his eyes wide with panic as they scanned the room until they rested on me. Then he smiled, and I felt my heart beating again. He lifted his hand to my chest, pressed against it firmly, stared me in the eyes, and smiled. *I found you*, his heart whispered.

I burst out crying as I scooted closer to him, pressed my face against the side of his chest and Kinsley ran his fingers through my hair. I couldn't talk, couldn't move, all I could do was touch him and cry. *I'll always be right here, by your side.* My heart whispered to his. It seemed I didn't need words to reply anyway because as much as I knew him, he knew me.

"I know," Kinsley whispered, his voice raspy, filled with pain as I slowly lifted my head to look at him. He slid his hand to my cheek, the other hand had a cast on it but he pressed it gently against my other cheek, and he smiled at me. Even with the bruises, even with the cracked lip and the bandages, he's never looked so beautiful. "I know, baby."

I waited impatiently as Mom checked him over, asking him questions about the year, his name, my name, and so on. She checked his vitals, wrote down notes because she wasn't his nurse, but muttered how she'd be damned if someone came back in and interrupted us right now when she already did it all.

Once she was done and was writing on his chart, without a word I climbed onto the bed, making sure not to put any pressure on him. One knee on either side of his hips I hovered over him, my hands ghosting gently over his cheeks and I lowered my lips to his, as gently as I could. I kissed him softly, tracing my tongue against the top of his upper lip, keeping away from the cut on the bottom. He whined when I pulled away and I smiled at him even as he was pouting. "I'm not broken, Luke,"

"I was," I choked out, the tears sliding down my cheeks once more as I stared down at him. My mom made a quiet aww sound and ignored her. "Then I found you," I whispered. I was shaking as he lifted his hands to my shirt, tugged at me, and pulled my forehead against his. "Don't leave me all alone again, please,"

He yanked me against him, his lips crushed against mine almost painfully, and for a moment we were lost in each other as our tongues found each other over and over again. The door opened and shut as my mom quietly left us alone. "Never," Kinsley whispered against my lips, his nose sliding back and forth against mine. "Never again."

I pulled away from him and pressed a kiss against the skin in between his eyebrows, humming against his skin as I breathed him in. I moved to the side of him and slid under the covers, sliding his head on top of my shoulder, and holding him as tightly as I dared against me. "I'm sorry, Kins,"

He turned to look at me, watching me as I breathed him in. "Sorry for what?" His voice was light, slightly pained from the wounds on him. He was on pain meds, I was sure, but he had just had surgery not too many hours ago.

"I'm sorry I kissed you without your permission in front of people. I kind of outed both of us to your parents, the EMTs, and Isabella's mom. Your parents paid the EMTs to keep it quiet, but people know, and more will know. I doubt it will stay hidden for long."

He pressed his hand against my cheek, sliding his fingers up and down the side of my face absently. "Oops," Kinsley said with a soft laugh, crinkling his nose at me. "I guess, I kind of... did the same?"

I tilted my head, slightly confused. "What were you talking about?"

"Um, so last class, we had a substitute. She had us draw something. She said it's unfortunate that there's no art class in the school, and since she didn't exactly have the notes from the teacher to properly guide us through the day's topic, she just assigned us to draw something instead."

"Yeah, she did the same to us. I drew a butterfly. It was the only thing I could think of. You drew one for me before. Remember? In the art room when I wanted you to prove to me you were Sparrow?" I asked, chuckling slightly. "She told us to draw the most beautiful thing, and I remembered the butterfly because I had thought it was so pretty, even back then when I was freaking out."

For a second we both smiled, remembering the time so long ago as if it was yesterday. The time when two sixteen-year-old boys so excitedly would go back and forth pushing secret letters through little slots in lockers, caring about nothing else but what was going to be the next reply.

Finally, Kinsley spoke. "We had the same assignment. Draw the most beautiful thing you have ever seen."

"What did you draw? A butterfly? You tend to draw them a lot. Or maybe the rain? I know how much you love the rain. You said before it was your favorite thing." I said pushed a strand of his hair from his face, and gently ran my finger over the smaller bandage on top of his cheekbone.

His cheeks flushed in embarrassment as he let out a soft laugh as he mouthed the word *no*. His cerulean eyes twinkled in mirth, even now after being in so much pain. He was so strong, so much stronger than me. So beautiful. "I drew you, Luke. My most beautiful, favorite of all." My cheeks flushed at his words, a soft gasp spilling from my lips as I ran my nose up and down the middle of his. "So I guess I already outed us earlier today, and I didn't ask either so... surprise." His shoulders shook in silent laughter as he bit back a curse from the pain.

"You're a menace. We're so stupid," I mumbled, pressing my forehead against his.

"The stupidest," he agreed. "I don't regret it though. Do you?"

I shook my head, lowering my eyes to gaze into his. "Absolutely not."

We were quiet for a little while, holding each other amidst the soft chatter of the doctors and nurses who came in to check on him. I was scolded a few different times, but I never moved, and Kinsley point-blank refused to heal if they made me move, so they eventually stopped bugging us about it. His parents didn't come back that day. Never tried to visit him. While he smiled and shrugged at me, I could see it bothered him immensely.

The only time I moved off of the bed was when Isabella's mother came in, sending her shoe at the back of my head and telling me to get off of the patient. "You and Isabella are the same, in the same position, whispering the same promises. I swear, the four of you are connected," Mami muttered as I tried to smile around a wave of brain damage.

"Mami," Kinsley whined, his hands outstretched as he curled his fingers in a come here motion. Isabella's mother moved to the side of the bed and looked down at him. I could see tears in his eyes as he looked at her, and I took a step back, giving them room. After all, she was more a mother to him than his own, and while he didn't seem to care much that his parents knew he was with a boy, he did care what she thought. "Do you hate me now?"

"Oh *Dios mío, mi hijo*," she gasped, falling to her knees on the edge of the bed. My lips quivered as she leaned down and gently wrapped her arms around him, kissing the top of his head as she held him. "You'll always be *mi hijo*. I believe in a God that loves his children for who they are, not who they force themselves to be." She pulled away from him, cupping his cheek with one hand as she held out her other hand for me. I took it slowly, allowing her to pull me closer to her, so she could look at both of us.

"I don't care who you love, *mi hijos*, I care that you are loved, and that you're loved the way you deserve. That's all that matters to me." Her eyes sparkled with tears as Kinsley sat up and hugged her, cursing under his breath in her ear from the pain of his sudden movement.

Then she was smacking me with her shoe since she couldn't smack him as he was hugging her and cursing, and the three of us were laughing all over again. "Love you Mami!" We both screamed as we hugged her tightly, making her curse at us in Spanish even as she was squeezing us against her.

"Okay, okay, okay! Get off of me, I need to go make sure those people aren't being mean to my baby. You let him heal, or you know what will happen," she threatened, pointing her shoe at me.

I grinned at her, nodding as I laughed. "Yes, Mami." She left us alone as I slipped back into the bed with Kinsley, curling him against me as we both sighed in relief. "Everything is going to be okay, right Kins?" I whispered as he rubbed his nose against my collarbone.

"Always, no matter what," he muttered with a smile.

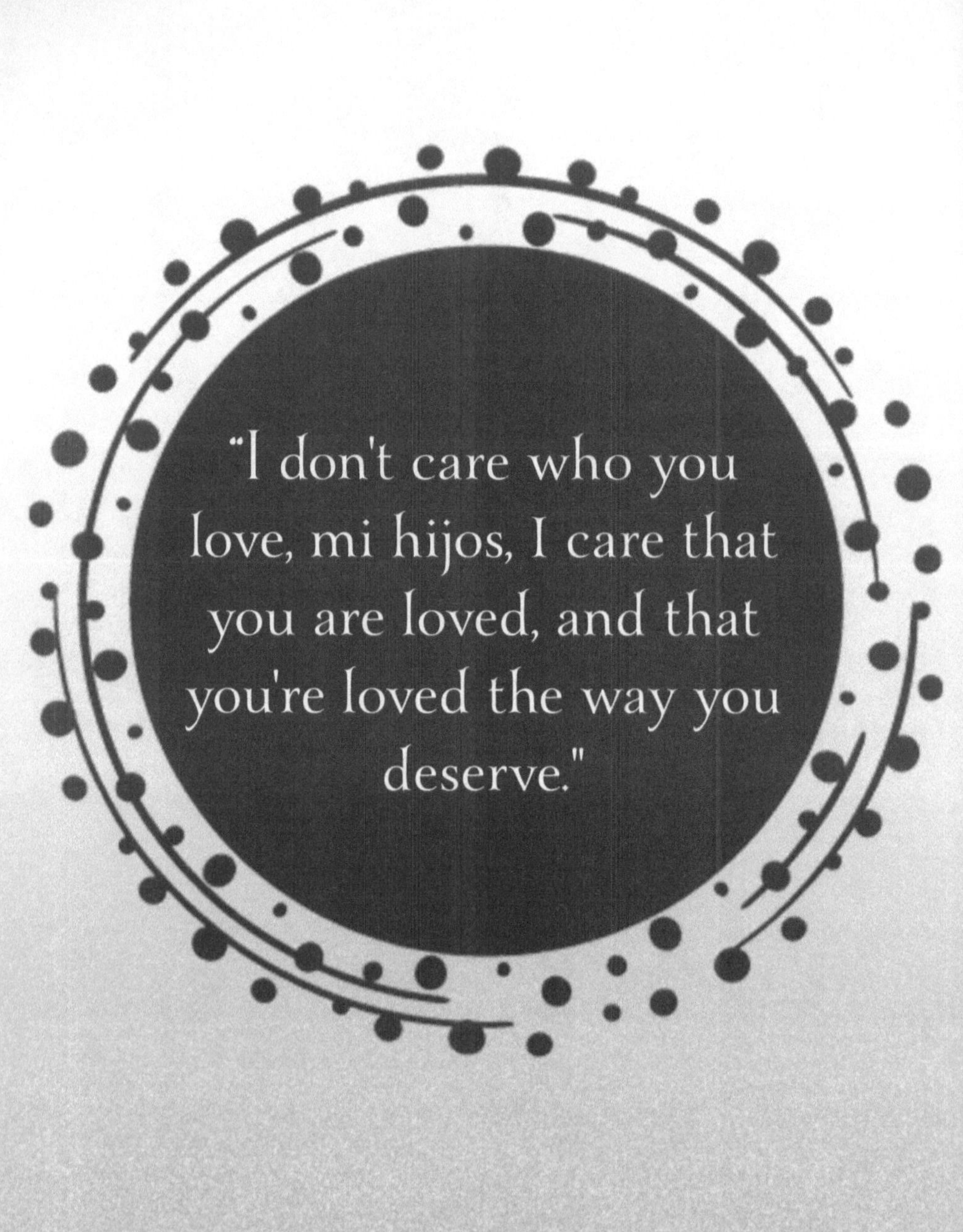

"I don't care who you love, mi hijos, I care that you are loved, and that you're loved the way you deserve."

Chapter 37
Kinsley

Love was like the rain. It came slowly in the form of sweet smells and dense air, a soft warning, for those who paid close enough attention to notice it. Then the sprinkling came, and even then, some people didn't see it. Some waited until the downpour when it hit them. I saw my love from the beginning. The soft smell of the air, the way everything felt heavy and thick, covering every part of me like a blanket I desperately never wanted to unravel.

Luke waited until it became so loud, so violent that he couldn't ignore it anymore, he waited until the downpour to notice, to know what it was he was feeling. It didn't matter now that our love was figured out slowly through the seasons, all that mattered was we were together now, whether it was sprinkling or a downpour, we were together, and we'd always be together. Because we were Kinsley and Luke, Sparrow and Green, two heartbeats side by side, inside one soul.

The day I left the hospital, everything changed for me. Luke had stayed by my side the whole time, so neither of us knew what it was we were going home to. We weren't surprised either, to be honest. Both of our stuff was boxed up and sat inside a U-Haul that was parked in the driveway, professionally packed because my parents couldn't be bothered to box up our things themselves. They had hired a moving company to pack up our room, emptying every part of it. They told so many lies; it was funny how everyone seemed to believe them.

Because Luke's mother was at the hospital, they told everyone Luke was going back home to his mother, that she had come back from out of town, and everyone believed it. As for me, they said I was coming back home happily after being beaten up by Roan, but in reality, my stuff was packed right along with Luke's, and both of us were kicked out. They didn't want someone like me in their house, corrupting their life and their daughter.

Luke's mother and Paul took us both in, without pause or question. To the eyes of the public, I was still with my parents. We went to court together, I went to galas with them, and as long as they didn't force me to date random girls anymore, I pretended to be their dutiful son. It was their compromise. They'd pay for my college, as long as I pretended to be happy with them in front of the public. Maybe it was stupid that I was letting them do that, but I was excited about college and I knew I couldn't afford it without them.

College was a hard topic for me for a while. They still wanted me to go to an Ivy League college, to get my business degree, and come back and run my father's shops when he decided to retire. He didn't think I was good enough to live in his home but he still wanted me to inherit his business, to keep up the pretenses.

If I was to agree to that, I wouldn't be able to marry Luke one day. He'd never be fine with me being so public with my relationship, to be part of the rich crowd but holding hands with a man instead of a woman. I wasn't even sure if Luke and I were going to last forever, but the idea that he was planning my future without Luke in it disturbed me, and I wanted no part of it.

I realized, finally, that it was time for me to put myself first, for the first time in a long time. So I sat down alone one night when Luke was at work with Paul, and his mother was at her job at the hospital, and I filled out college applications. My heart raced as I mailed them in, all of them in New York, and I waited. I waited until I heard back from them before I said anything to Luke, Isabella, or Serina. Maybe it was stupid waiting, but I'd kept this a secret for so long as it was, working on it here and there when no one knew. I wanted to be sure it was even possible for me to do it before I finally said anything. Maybe it was cowardly, but I'd never shown this part of myself to anyone before, and I wanted to make sure I had a chance before showing them.

The school year was strange after getting out of the hospital. Rumors of the kiss did start, and the four of us finally realized we didn't want to hide anything anymore. Serina and Isabella were handling everything themselves on their side, so Luke and I walked into school the next day holding hands, our heads high and our shoulders straight, ignoring everyone else around us.

To say we didn't get ridiculed would be an understatement. The kids were mostly disgusted, but there were a surprising few that were supportive, and even another surprising few that came to us for the rest of the year thanking us for being brave enough so they could be brave as well. Brave like Luke and Kinsley, they said. I'd just smile, look at Luke, and laugh. Because Luke knew how brave we both were and how brave we weren't.

We were brave because we had each other, something we didn't realize until recently. We had both leaned on each other, supported each other, and made each other the best we could be, together.

I sat on the rooftop overlooking the city that glittered with streetlights in the middle of the night. Most houses were dark, a few cast lights from nightlights or porch lights, but it was early in the morning now, as it usually was whenever we met up to tag walls, and I wasn't surprised to see the city as dark as it was.

I watched as Isabella and Serina spray-painted a picture together. From where I was sitting, I could just see them. They were giggling and smiling at each other, their gazes filled with a look I recognized because I looked at Luke the very same way. I was nervous because I didn't know what was going to happen. We were graduating tomorrow, and for the first time, I knew what it felt like to be scared and happy at the same time.

I knew what was going to happen. Luke had gotten his college acceptance letter in the mail this week and opened it with all four of us- Luke, me, his mother, and Paul- five if you counted his boss's dog. He had been so excited to get into college in New York, and Serina and Isabella did as well, leaving just me to wait for my results.

None of them were worried about it like I was, but then again, none of them realized I had applied to a different college, one still in New York but different than they were expecting. Both Isabella and Serina applied for the School of Visual Arts and got in, and I guess they were expecting me to do the same. Luke got into Lincoln Technical Institute, and his dream of being a mechanic already started since he had been working for a shop for the past four years at least with Paul. As for me, I applied to Columbia University. One of the top colleges in the world... for writers.

I held the thick envelope between my fingers, staring down at the park where we normally parked our cars, and waited a bit impatiently for Luke's car to arrive. He had finally gotten it finished and it drove perfectly, as I always knew he would. I ran my fingers through my hair, feeling anticipation and dread tugging at the pit of my stomach, the thick envelope feeling like a weight in my hand tugging me down deeper and deeper, burying me under the stress and the worry. It was the only college that I applied for, in the end, the only one that I desperately wanted to go to.

I didn't open it yet, didn't see if I was accepted, because I wanted to open it with Luke. He was the only one I wanted to be with when I saw it for the first time. I wasn't sure what I was going to do if I didn't get in, but I knew no matter what it would be okay because we'd be okay. Because we were Luke and Kinsley, and we'd always be.

I couldn't hear the girls giggling from up there, but I could see it in the way their shoulders dropped, the smile in their eyes as they looked at each other, even around the masks on their faces as they stared with red splatters of paint decorating their lovely complexions, lighting up brighter and brighter as they continued to catch each other staring. They had their rough spots, their own story, but I was glad to see them smiling then, looking forward to their future, the future all four of us were going to share, together.

I perked up as I saw Luke's car park next to mine, my heart already pounding as he turned it off and got out. I pulled my phone from my pocket, checking the time. It was later than he had said it would be. It was funny how it always seemed to be four in the morning when we were doing something important. Like me telling him about this paper, about my future, about the last little puzzle that was Kinsley Bryant.

From there, I could see he'd taken time to go home and shower first, to get the grease off his body and change his clothes. His hair looked damp, his soft brown curls hanging limply in his green eyes as he lifted his head and found me. While we were too far away from each other to make out the details, I had him so memorized that it didn't matter.

I didn't need to see him up close to know he had a light scattering of freckles that dotted against his cheeks, down his neck, and across his back. I didn't need to see him up close to know his seafoam-colored eyes were sparkling as he smiled a lazy smile up at me, his long eyelashes dancing against his cheekbones.

He had on dark clothes, a black hoodie, and black jeans, our usual attire for sneaking through town in the dark of the night and being illegal with our criminal activities. As he slowly made his way through the silent city, I watched him. He was taller than he was when we were sixteen, but so was I now. We seemed to get taller at the same time, in the same increments, and now that I was eighteen and he was almost eighteen, we were the same inch of difference from each other, except taller all the same.

I remembered how we had run down that road, Luke carrying a screaming Isabella over his shoulder, and my ribs feeling like death with every slap of my foot against the ground. But back then, it didn't matter that I could barely breathe, that I was in pain as we ran from the cops because my fingers were wrapped around Luke's wrist, and he was laughing. All that mattered to me was his smile. Even now, I could see the younger Luke in my mind, I could hear his laughter as he held me tightly against him in the stairwell, holding me in his arms as we joked around. It felt like it was yesterday, even though it was over a year ago.

I was never going to forget any part of it. Luke walked up the stairs, his feet slightly heavy with his steel-toe boots, the soft clink of his shoes on the metal stairs a sound that I forced myself to memorize. Little things, stupid things to others, were little treasures to me. We were graduating tomorrow, all four of us, and then after that, we were moving.

Serina's parents were doing just about the same as mine, paying us to stay away, and her parents along with mine gave us money for an apartment. They didn't know that we were all going to New York though, both of our parents hoping we'd change our minds, suddenly be straight, and suddenly agree to go to the schools they wanted us to go to. They were soon going to realize we were using it all for New York, as far away from them as we could, and none of us were ever going to look back.

"Hey, Baby," Luke said, his voice soft, filled with apprehension I didn't understand as I turned to look at him. His cheeks were flushed, his fingers running through his curls, and a soft smile on his face as his eyes twinkled in happiness. All at seeing me. I still wasn't used to hearing him call me that, and I loved every part of it. No matter how many months or years we'd been together, I'd never get tired of hearing him call me that.

"Hey babe," I said softly as he sat down across from me. We were right up against the edge of the roof, both of our legs dangling over the edge. His fingers were tugging at my pants, his knee touching mine, and I took a moment to drink in the beauty that was Luke Wilson. I never wanted to look away.

Luke tapped the envelope in my hands and I felt a shudder run through me, knowing it was finally time to tell my secret. "What's that?" His fingers slid down the length of the paper and curled against my fingers.

I let out a soft breath, and his eyebrows knitted together in confusion as I shoved the letter at him, my nerves already shot as he grabbed it. "Can you open it? I can't open it. Tell me what it says," I mumbled, tangling my fingers against his pants, holding him like an anchor as he watched me.

His gaze was filled with questions, but he didn't voice a single one of them, not yet anyway. His fingers were steady, unlike my shaking ones, and he opened the envelope with ease as he pulled his phone out to light up the words for him to read it. I watched him read it, his eyes moving back and forth, and I gripped his pants tighter, wanting to curl up in a ball in his lap and cry.

What if I didn't get in? What if I was the only one who didn't get accepted? What was going to happen now? I wondered, worried. *Oh, how stupid I was not to apply anywhere else!*

But before I could start hyperventilating, Luke lowered the paper, his eyes peering into mine, and he smiled. "You got accepted to Columbia University, Kinsley. I didn't know you applied for it though. I'm kind of confused," he admitted with a soft chuckle. "I guess I just assumed you'd go to the same school as Serina and Isabella."

I remembered the only time I'd ever said it before, back when I was little. I was in kindergarten, the first time I had lifted a children's book to show my mom, the widest smile on my lips as I waved it at her. *'It's so pretty, Mommy. I want to do it too. I want to write children's books too, I want to draw pictures too.'*

She had given me the most awful look and then, smacked the book out of my hands, telling me how ridiculous that was. A pipe dream, not possible. I'd be going to business school, she said, something more reliable, not a useless children's dream. I was crushed, and I had buried what I truly wanted to do deep down inside me, feeling stupid for even wanting it. Stupid for thinking I'd be good enough, that I'd be capable. But now, with Luke, everything felt possible. Serina asked me once if I was enough for myself, and now, it was time I started to try.

"I have always dreamed of being a writer, Luke. A children's book writer. To illustrate my books. Something I never said out loud before. I guess I was scared, you know? It's not a reliable job, but it's what I want to do." My body was shaking as I stared at him, worried he'd say the same thing my mom did so long ago. I knew the idea of becoming a writer was hard. So many people wanted to, but it was hard to be seen when so many others were out there. It was like throwing a needle in a haystack hoping someone would care enough to find it and love it enough to show it to the world.

Luke was quiet as he looked at the paper. He folded it carefully and slipped it back into the envelope. Gently, he slipped the envelope into my hoodie pocket, trying his best not to wrinkle it. His fingers moved up my sides, up my throat as he leaned even closer to me. Luke locked his hands behind my neck, and as his thumbs slid up and down my jaw, he smiled. "Then it's what you'll do if it's what you want to do. And I'll be right there supporting you, every step of the way."

I felt like I was going to cry as I tangled my fingers in his hoodie and yanked him against me. He smiled against my lips as he tugged gently on the little hairs that settled under my hairline. "I never want to live in a world without you in it, Luke," I whispered against his lips as he melted against me.

We were lost in each other for a little while. Finally, we pulled away, our foreheads pressed against each other. "I remember the first time we ran down this alley," Luke said as he pulled away and looked at the road below. A smile tugged on my lips as my heart slowly calmed down. We could see Serina and Isabella from here still, and I knew they were waiting for us to join them as they laughed and painted together.

"I thought you were the most beautiful boy I've ever seen, and I was already entranced with you from the beginning," he admitted. His hands moved down my legs and rested against his own. He looked nervous, his finger sliding back and forth over his upper thigh, his lip pulled in between his teeth before he let it go.

Since the beginning, the start of us, we'd been destined to be together. *'What's there to lose? Maybe we'll end up hating each other. It wouldn't matter anyway though, because no names, right?'*

"Um, I-" he stammered, his eyes lifted to mine, a soft blush on his cheeks as he watched me. I was speechless, enamored with everything that was Luke Wilson. "I wasted so much time Kins, so much time I could have been touching you, kissing you. So many tears that were unnecessary between the two of us, if I had just figured it out sooner. I don't want to waste any more time." He pulled a small box out and held it loosely in between his fingers. My eyes widened as I stared at the little black box.

'Or maybe...just maybe...we'll end up falling in love. Maybe we'll be the type of romance that's talked about, the type of romance that everyone envies and wishes they could have.'

I let out a breath, sucking it back in, holding the air steadily inside me. My heart pounded in my chest, the flutter of a thousand wings inside me.

"You asked me once before if I believed in marriage, and I told you no, do you remember? Because all I had ever seen were my parents, and how fucked up their marriage was. I was so worried I'd be like him. That I'd find someone I loved one day, and I'd end up hurting them. I'd start drinking, we'd have problems, and I'd cheat. I'd punch, and I'd shatter everything around me, burying everything that I claimed to love in a storm. I never wanted to see someone I love gazing up at me with pain and horror in their eyes as my mom looked at my dad.

"But then you came Kinsley, and everything changed. It took a while for me to find myself, but with your light, you helped me see that I was never broken all along. I was waiting for you, the other half of me, to find me. So no, I guess in a way whether I believe in marriage or not, it doesn't matter." He whispered. He looked at the little box, before looking up at me once more, a deep red blush sprinkled over his cheeks as his light green eyes sparkled, the little gold specks shining in the moonlight.

He opened the box, and I couldn't even look at it. I couldn't pull my eyes away from his. "It doesn't matter if I believe in marriage, because I believe in you. I believe that you will always be the light, to show me the way out of the darkness. You'll always be there, the other half of my soul, making me complete when I feel broken. I love you, Kinsley, with every piece of me, I love you. Will you marry me? I mean, not then, because I'm still seventeen, and we're still young. But one day, will you marry me?" His voice was a whisper filled with worry, hope, and fear.

I didn't even realize I was crying until I felt the soft plop of a tear against my fingers, my fingers wrapped tightly in the bottom of my hoodie as I stared at him with wide eyes. I looked at the two matching bands that sat side by side, before looking up at him once more, smiling. I breathed in a deep breath, and I wanted to laugh because all I could smell was the rain. *Oh, how I loved the rain.*

"Absolutely," I breathed. His body nearly folded as he let out a soft breath of relief. Then we both laughed, his lips pressed against mine as he fumbled with the rings, clumsily sliding them onto both of our fingers. "I love you, Luke," I whispered as I pressed my forehead against his.

I loved the feel of the ring on my finger as I pressed my fingers against his cheeks and the smile that lit up every part of his face as he felt it as well. "I love you too, Kinsley."

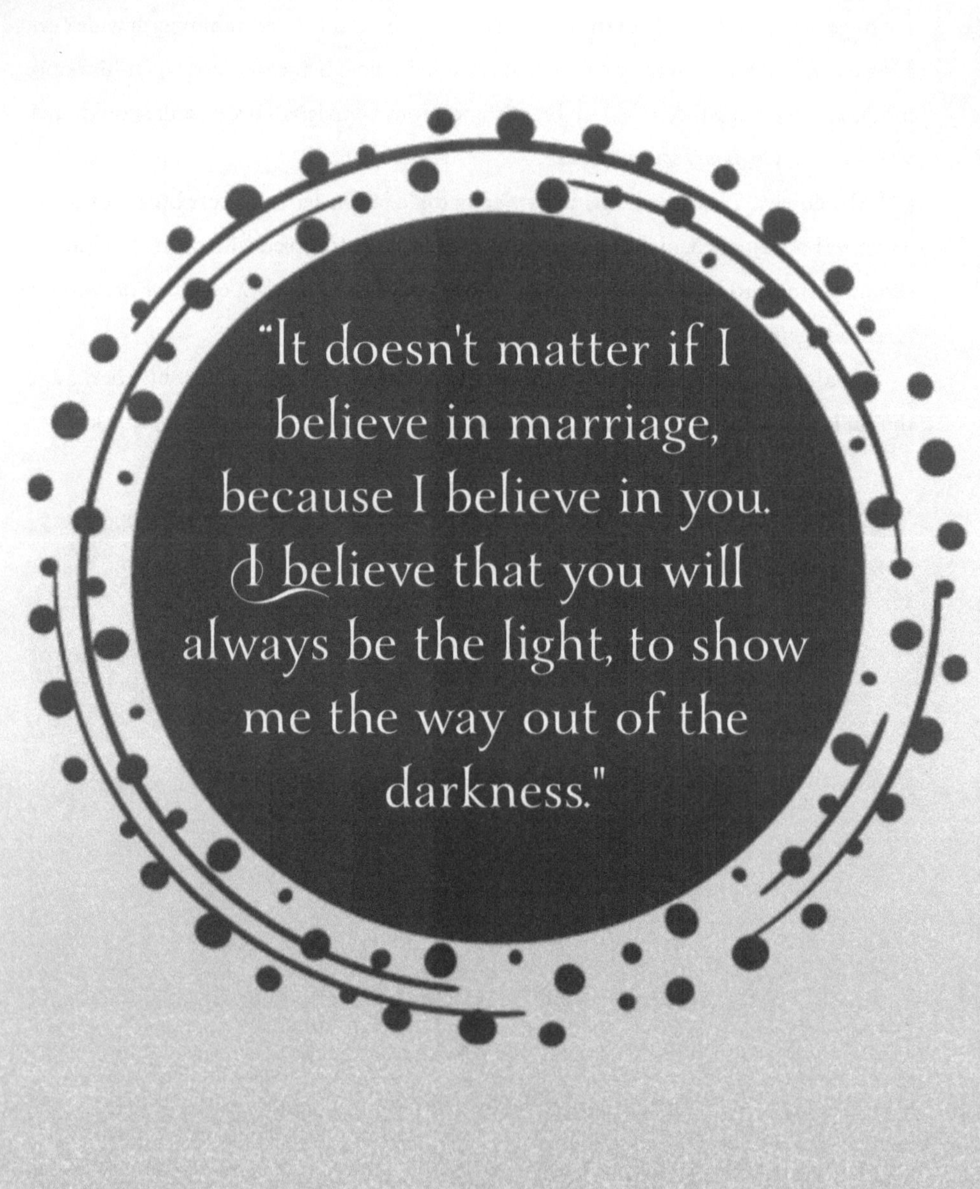

"It doesn't matter if I believe in marriage, because I believe in you. I believe that you will always be the light, to show me the way out of the darkness."

Chapter 38
Luke

They say life is measured in moments. We can't possibly remember everything that happened to us, every day, day after day. But the good things, we remember. The good things we'll always remember. I couldn't say Kinsley and I were perfect, we had our bad days along with the good. Small fights, or moments where we wanted nothing more than to go up to a rooftop and scream everything away.

Though the good outweighed the bad, standing out like lights in my mind, for me to recount every step of the way. I could still remember the way Kinsley looked when he turned around in the art room that day I found out he was Sparrow. How beautiful he looked, even when I didn't know who he was. How my soul called to him the moment I saw him, even if I didn't understand back then what it was I was feeling.

I can still remember calling him at four in the morning, simply because I couldn't stop crying, and all I needed was to hear him breathe on the other side of the phone. How it felt to slide my fingers down his back as I put ointment on his scars, scars that have long since flattened and nearly faded away by now. I remember sitting on the rooftop with Kinsley's head in my lap, his fingers cupped around my cigarette, helping me block the wind. My first birthday with Kinsley and Isabella, and how they had cut it before putting the candles on it and tried as hard as they could to rearrange it just so I could make a wish.

Ill never forget dancing with Kinsley. When he was drunk, and when he wasn't. The feel of our first kiss, even if it was filled with drunken silliness and misunderstandings. Even now I wondered if my shoes were still sitting there in the deep end of Kinsley's parents' pool, together, just like us, always. I'll always remember confessing my feelings for Kinsley at four in the morning, a morning filled with glow-in-the-dark paint and kisses that left our lips swollen for days.

When I was at my lowest, Kinsley was there, like an angel planted just to save me. I wasn't sure what happened when we died. If we were reincarnated, but if we were, somehow we found each other in this lifetime. I hoped we found each other in all of them. I had a feeling our souls were just too strong to stay apart, and I had a good feeling that we'd meet each other again and again, in every lifetime, in every dimension, in every way possible. There was never going to be anything stronger than Kinsley and Luke, never.

"Hey, baby, where are you?" My lips automatically lifted into a smile, just at the sound of his voice as he called for me.

Sometimes it was the little things in life that mean the most to us. To feel the breeze against our hair, to breathe in the air, and to have the ability to breathe again... and again.

"Babyyyy, oh, where is my babyyy," Kinsley sang, the smile on my lips tugging higher and higher as he opened doors and closed them, searching for me.

I moved to the side of Kinsley's office, standing near the boxes, waiting for him to find me. I had chosen this house specifically because of this room, for him. None of us had stayed in New York after we graduated. For some reason, Isabella and Kinsley had decided we needed to vacation after college in California, and the four of us had just fallen in love with it almost instantly. This house, we had purchased with our own money, together. Kinsley had cut off his parents when he published his first book when he was a senior in college, and it had shot off almost instantly.

Being a writer was hard, but he had been determined, and the look on his face as he watched his numbers rise every day had been worth every bit of me pushing him, telling him to keep going, that it was going to be okay. There had been so many days he had wanted to give up, to pick an easier career, but I had held him through the storm in his mind, and told him it would be fine, we'd be fine, because we had each other.

We had moved to California after the four of us had graduated, and Kinsley had written his second book, getting an award for it. I had chosen this office for him because I knew how much he had loved to sit there with a canvas and charcoal, his fingers sliding over the paper as he drew, and the view overlooking the sea had been spectacular there. It had four large windows, and bright curtains, to make the room sparkle, hoping that when he sat there in this room his eyes would shine brighter than the sea.

It didn't matter that we'd been together for years now, it still felt like yesterday, running through that alley getting chased by the cops with Isabella screaming curse words at me in Spanish, while Kinsley laughed and held my wrist, tugging me along. It would always feel like yesterday for me.

Every memory was like someone was annotating my life, marking my words, saving everything for me to flip through the pages and reread once more. Maybe it was rough at first, but so were diamonds that needed to be plucked out of the dirt and dusted off to show how they shined. I'd like to say our story was worth the effort, no matter how rough it was in the start, to see how in the end, we did indeed shine.

I had opened the windows, the sea breeze spilling in through the windows as Kinsley walked into the room slowly, hesitantly. He'd been away for a few days while I finalized the purchase of the house, got everything put up, and moved us in. He was getting popular in the world now, going on TV shows and off to book signings. Every chance he got he liked to tell everyone about his husband, rubbing me in his parents' faces knowing very well they were sitting there somewhere, watching.

Kennedy did end up marrying Wyatt, the two of them taking over Kinsley's parents' business as they had wanted. Recently, Kinsley had sent his books to Kennedy, for her baby shower present. I had held Kinsley the whole night as he cried, after she had called him and talked to him on the phone, and told him she was sorry.

He never did have the good relationship with his parents he always wanted, but it seemed to be enough for him to have Kennedy, to have my mom and Paul, and to have Isabella's mother as well. They might not be his parents by blood, but they were his family by choice, and over time he accepted it and moved on from his parents. There was nothing wrong with pushing your family out of your life if they were toxic to you.

Kinsley walked farther into the office, and I silently stared at him as he looked out at the view in awe. His ash blond hair was cut slightly shorter for a more adult professional look, resting more towards the middle of his ears. His bangs were set to the right, like a curtain bang, barely covering his eye anymore.

There was a sparkle in his cerulean eyes as he scanned the shelves I had put together painstakingly the night before, along with the shelf that had a light built-in to show off the trophies he had received. He leaned against the desk, and I took a minute to let my eyes trail down his frame, admiring him and wanting him just as much as I always had, from the beginning. His long graceful fingers were pressed against the top of the desk as I admired his wedding ring, how it sparkled in the light from the slowly setting sun.

Kinsley pulled out his phone, and as I expected, he was calling me. He jumped, hearing my phone ringing from the side of the room, and as he lifted his eyes to mine, they lit up with that sparkle I loved so much, his full lips curling into the widest smile, his dimples like deep caverns on either side of his lips.

"You jerk, you've been there the whole time!" His lips puffed out in a slight pout that remained only for a second or two until he started to laugh. I smiled, my head tilted to the side as I moved closer to him. Even after all this time, his cheeks lit up with a soft coral color just by seeing me, like a paintbrush across his cheeks. "What were you doing? Just watching me?"

I placed my hands on either side of the desk, trapping him in between them, and he let out a soft breath of surprise. "I was admiring the view," I muttered as I lowered my head and pressed my nose against the hollow of his throat. I slid my nose up and down his soft skin as he squirmed underneath my touch. "I missed you, Kins."

"I missed you," he replied, his fingers finding my cheeks and pulling my face to his. I stared down at him, a joke between us since we had always been an inch apart in high school, but somewhere along the way in college, I ended up gaining two more inches than him. Now we were three inches apart, and he would pout about it, feeling so small under my gaze. I didn't mind because it made him so much cuter, like I needed to hold him close and protect him. Even though he protected me more than I ever protected him.

My eyes closed as he brushed his fingers down them, his lips found purchase against mine as we took a moment to just breathe each other in. His tongue slid gently against mine, his taste flooding through every part of me, and I smiled as a soft moan spilled from his mouth into mine. Kinsley pulled me closer, for a moment, before I pulled away just enough to look at him.

"How was the book signing?" Kinsley's eyes fluttered open, a love-struck expression on his face as he slowly pulled himself away from what was building inside both of us. We'd only been apart for a few days, but even that was too long, and I had no doubt that tonight was going to end up being a long night filled with the swish of sheets, clasped hands, and lips finding purchase all night long.

"It was fine," Kinsley replied, his words simple even though his cheeks were flushed in an embarrassed hue.

I found it funny that most writers were introverts, people who liked to hide more than they liked to be seen, who spoke pretty words and drew beautiful pictures either on paper or in the reader's mind. Kinsley hated being so seen, sitting with a stranger talking about his books, the camera trained on his face as a small crowd cheered, or sitting there with a long line of parents and kids eagerly waiting for his autograph. After all the years he spent hiding under his hoods, he couldn't do it any longer, and while he was so very shy, I was proud. Proud he was trying his best, and succeeding. So proud he was mine.

"How's the garage doing? Is it all put together?" Kinsley asked, a wide smile on his face as he changed the subject away from him and to me.

I cocked my eyebrow at him, knowing just what he was doing, but let it pass all the same. My mom and Paul ended up moving to California too, not wanting to spend time away from any of us. I was surprised to find my stepdad had quite a bit of money, and Paul decided to put down on a new shop there, where he and I would run it together. "It's still closed while we're stocking it, but it's getting close to opening," I tried to hide how excited I was to get to mess with everything new and shiny and to start working on cars again.

He pressed his finger against my nose, and I shouldn't even be surprised by now because this was Kinsley, my Kinsley, and even without words, he would always know me. "Cute," he muttered, my cheeks flushed at his gaze. "You're the cutest." I ducked my head, backing a step away as he grinned at me. He always loved when I got shy since it was always only for him.

"So, is this how our story ends?" Kinsley asked lightly as he walked toward the middle of the room and stared at everything in earnest.

I grinned, watching the breeze swirl his hair around his face, his eyes trailing over every part of the office. "I don't know, you're the writer, Kins." Kinsley crinkled his nose at me, and a soft smile brushed across his lips. "How do you think it ends?"

He thought about my words for a moment, and shrugged, letting out a soft chuckle. "Here, with us. You and me, our ending," he said, turning to look at me once more.

I hummed as I slid my fingers against the picture frame on his desk, the picture frame I had been about to hang before he came home. "Possibly. I guess most stories end with periods, right? I think ours ends with a semicolon though. Because we'll never really end, not us. We'll always keep going, forever. There's no ending for us."

He sucked in a deep breath as he moved to stand beside me once more, his fingers trailing down my arm to settle beside my hand while he looked down at the picture frame. "You framed the letter?" His question came out sounding like an astonished whisper as his eyes skimmed over the letter, his first letter to me, rereading the words he had written so long ago.

"I had to, Kins. It was your first masterpiece, after all," I replied with a soft laugh as he looked up at me. "Back when I was trapped in the storm, and you were the calm that saved me."

You held out your hand, like a lifeline, and when I touched you, everything faded away, the calm.

Kinsley smiled as he pressed his hand against my chest, and I wrapped my fingers around his wrist, both of us feeling each other's heartbeat at the same time, as one.

"And to think, all of this started because of a single letter... and the wrong locker."

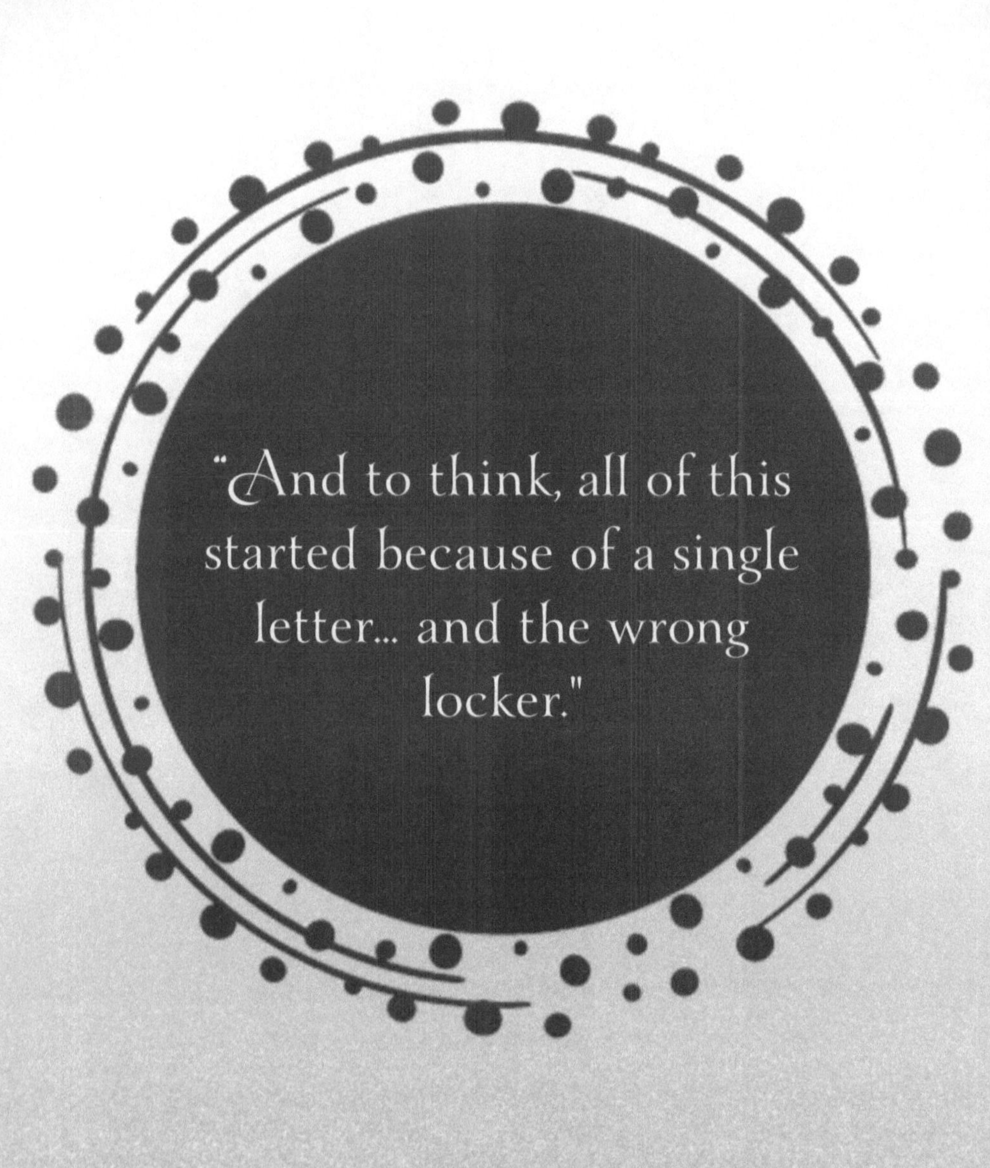
"And to think, all of this started because of a single letter... and the wrong locker."

Bonus Chapter 1
Age 18

"Hi, my gay babies!" The moment we opened the door, we were greeted with the scent of pine from the Christmas tree, and Kinsley chuckled at Isabella's remark. "Did you get the wrapping paper?"

Kinsley opened his mouth to tear into her, but I wrapped my arm around his shoulder, pulling him back against my chest as I held up the bag filled with various tubes of wrapping paper, some tape, ribbons, and bows. Kinsley cocked his eyebrow at me, and I didn't need him to speak to tell me what he was thinking. *I see what you did there.* His unspoken words were so strong that I couldn't help but laugh as I kissed his cheek and took an extra second to breathe in all that was Kinsley, my Kinsley, before pulling away.

Isabella was oblivious to Kinsley's fury, either that or she didn't care. She stood up and did a little shimmy in the middle of our living room, opening up the robe she was wearing to reveal a very revealing lingerie outfit, that was Christmas-themed. Almost instantly, Kinsley's fingers were pressed against my eyes, covering my view almost frantically. "Izzy! No, bad Izzy! Boundaries!"

I didn't need to see Izzy to know she was rolling her eyes. "Pretty Boy, all he sees is you, he's not attracted to me."

I nodded along with what she said, with a smile on my face, and Kinsley sputtered, his forehead leaning against my lips as I felt the familiar burn of him blushing. I puckered my lips against his hot skin, and he gasped in surprise, pulling away from me as I smiled. "Still, Izzy. You can't do indecent things in our common area. Here's the wrapping paper, I'm taking Luke to our room." Kinsley said. I could hear him throwing the roll at her as she let out a soft whine of protest.

"I just wanted to see if you'd wrap me up with it! So I could give myself as a present!" Isabella whined as I started to laugh.

"You already got her a present, if you give yourself to her like that we wouldn't see either of you for like a month." I reminded her.

It was kind of strange having a conversation when I couldn't even see who I was talking to, but I didn't fight Kinsley. I liked the feel of his fingers against my skin and the little possessive flair-ups that he showed every once in a while. "That's what I was hoping for," Isabella muttered.

"Whatever, don't be naughty. It's Christmas Eve," Kinsley said as he led me through the house. He let me go as he opened the door to our bedroom, tugging me inside and shutting the door behind us. Kinsley turned on the light and tugged his hoodie off.

Our room wasn't as big as Kinsley's had been back when we lived with his parents, but it was bigger than the room I shared with him at my mom's house. It didn't matter, we didn't need a lot of space anyway, because we were always ready to sit on each other, always ready to touch and hold each other, forever in our honeymoon phase even though we hadn't even been married yet. Kinsley sat down on the full-sized bed we had in the middle of the room, kicking his shoes off and watching them sail through the air to smack against the closet door.

There was one desk, but we mostly shared it. If he was working on it and I needed to I'd just take my laptop to the bed, or vice versa, but mostly it was Kinsley's. He had to write a lot of essays for his classes, and mine were mostly worksheets and textbooks. We'd only been in college for a few months now, but everything was perfect. It was harder, but being able to love Kinsley freely made it all the better. Meeting up for lunch every day, meeting after college, going on dates in the middle of New York where we could hold hands and no one ever freaking cared.

This city was refreshing and so different from the small town we grew up in. I wasn't sure if this city was going to end up being where we called our permanent home, but for now, we were happy to spend the next four years here. Kinsley laid down on his back as I took off my shoes, setting them down a little bit neater than he did his. He watched me with a soft look in his pretty cerulean eyes, the same look he'd always stared at me with, and I hoped he always would.

I dropped the bags on the ground at the foot of the bed, before climbing up the bed to straddle him, my fingers finding purchase against his chest as he slid up my thighs and curled in my belt loops. "Merry Christmas Eve," Kinsley said softly, his full lips curving into a sweet smile.

I slid my nose against his cheek, sliding it to tap against the underside of his ear lobe, before gently tugging on it with my teeth. "Merry Christmas Eve, baby," I replied, my voice an octave lower as a shudder rolled through his body underneath me. I was grinning as I pulled away, sitting back up to take my coat off.

I flung it against the desk chair as Kinsley's fingers slid over my wrist, down the length of the tattoo that was still healing. I had surprised him with it. One afternoon I picked him up after he finished his college classes for the day. I wanted to tattoo his key on top of my scar from the very first moment he drew it there, and when he had seen it he nearly cried.

I didn't hate my scar as much anymore, thanks to a lot of help with therapy, but I still wanted to cover it anyway. To start a new chapter in my life, where I wasn't looking at the results of the past over and over again. The key represented so much to me, so much more than Kinsley probably even realized. The key to his cage, the key to free him from everything that had been holding him back.

But I saw it as more than that. It wasn't just a key he drew for his cage, but the key he'd given me for my birthday, so I knew I always had a place to go. A key to him, who was in all sense my home. It didn't matter to me where we lived, or where we went. We could be homeless and staying on the street and it wouldn't matter to me as long as I had him; my home. He probably didn't realize, this was the same as getting his name tattooed on my skin. This was me telling the world I was his, and I was always going to be just his; forever.

He pressed his lips against my key gently to not agitate it, and I smiled. It was mostly healed, just a little tinge of pain, but I didn't mind. I was lost in the beauty that was Kinsley, my eyes drawing down his face, trailing down the vein on his throat, slipping against the bones of his collarbone that jutted out just barely under the collar of his shirt. I wanted to slide my tongue against his vein, to feel him shudder underneath me.

As if he were reading my mind, he opened his eyes and looked at me, a soft blush splashing across his cheeks. His lips turned up into a sly smile against my tattoo. "I can feel that," he muttered, his eyes lowering to where I was sitting on top of him.

I grinned sheepishly as I leaned down and pressed a kiss against his cheek. "Oops," I whispered. "It's your fault."

He laughed as he smacked my chest and I rolled off of him to sit down next to him as he sat up. His eyes were alight in mirth as he stared at me, his laugh like a song I never wanted to stop listening to. "You sat on me," he reminded me.

"Help me wrap Christmas presents," I whined, batting my eyelashes.

"You're hopeless, you know."

I grabbed the bag of presents from under the bed and placed them in between us. "I know, but I'm yours," I reminded him.

"You're always going to be mine," he replied with a smile, his dimples deeply engraved on his cheeks.

We both jumped as Isabella cursed under her breath and for a moment, we stared at each other before bursting out laughing. "Can y'all stop being mushy? I'm trying to listen in and see what you got me for Christmas!" She yelled from the other end of the door.

We were still laughing as I shoved against Kinsley's shoulder, trying to make him stop laughing so I could stop. It was almost impossible not to laugh when Kinsley was laughing; his laughter was contagious, and we could go for hours, even long after we had forgotten what it was we were laughing about.

"I got you a dildo!" Kinsley yelled out. I couldn't help but gasp as he grinned at me. "You too," he said with a wink as I buried my face against his shirt. "Kidding, maybe."

"You better be kidding," I mumbled.

"What!? I already have one of those!" Isabella yelled, making us both laugh even harder.

"Go away, Izzy! We won't tell you!" I hollered against Kinsley's chest. She grumbled, her footsteps heavy drama as she stomped away. I rolled my eyes, looking up at Kinsley with a laugh. "She was so dramatic sometimes,"

"Couldn't be helped, she was our Izzy," he said as I nodded, agreeing with him. "So what did you get me?"

We sat cross-legged, facing each other with the gifts and the wrapping paper in between us as I smiled shyly at him. "I'm not telling you yet. You have to wait until Christmas," I said as I looked at the clock beside the bed.

Kinsley pouted, though noticing the time, his lips curled in that mischievous smile I loved so much. "In five minutes?" He asked, pointing at the clock. "I'm the fiance, I should get the privilege of opening my present before everyone else."

"We'll see if you're good," I said with a wink.

For the next few hours, we wrapped presents. We had been putting it off since we had been so busy with exams, but it was okay. We had a box set up to put a few presents in, a few for my mom and Paul, along with a couple for Shawn. Kinsley had another box that he put one present for each parent into and one for Kennedy, his eyes pulling at it a few times as he tried not to let it bother him knowing that they probably would not open it, let alone return the gesture. I knew it hurt him, and I wished I knew what I could do to help. All I knew how to do was be there for him through his storm, as he had always been there with me through mine.

Finally, we were finished. We lay down side by side, not ready for bed yet but slightly exhausted nonetheless. I lifted my head to look at him, taking in the soft shape of his nose and the fullness of his lips, how his eyelashes brushed against his cheekbones when he closed them, before fluttering open again and revealing the beauty of his cerulean eyes underneath. I could endlessly stare at him and never get tired of it. I never wanted to live without it again. "Kins, it's four in the morning," I whispered.

Maybe if it had been someone else, they would have yawned, they would have complained about it being so late, but not us. Four in the morning had been our favorite time, our secret time, our time of us and only us. "Presents time?" He had asked, already opening his nightstand even as he was asking.

I couldn't help but grin in my excitement as I grabbed a small bag out of mine. We had laid side by side. I had pushed my bag over to him, a shy smile on my face as he gently took it, before pushing a rectangular-shaped present toward me. He had pulled a small velvet box out of the bag with a cute confused smile on his face.

"Are you proposing again?" The question had drawn my eyes to the soft white gold band that had been resting on his wedding finger, waiting for the day we would finally get married. We had plans to wait until after we both graduated, but who knew, with us? We had felt like we had been together all our lives and would be together forever, so the idea of waiting to share our name had been hard, especially surrounded in a city filled with so many gay and lesbian couples that showed just how okay it had been for us to just be us.

Well, maybe we would at least wait until we were nineteen. That way people couldn't say we hadn't at least stayed engaged for a little while first.

I had been silent as he had opened the box, his eyes lighting up widely in surprise. Slowly, he pulled out a key on a chain, the exact copy of my tattoo, as a necklace. He had reached back into the box and pulled out a cage with a little bird inside, just like his own tattoo, but as a necklace. "Couple necklaces?" he had asked.

"The kind of couple necklaces only we'd understand," I had said, flashing a smile at him. I liked the idea of having something different from the usual split heart couple necklaces, or lock and key that linked together. These had been custom-made to match our tattoos, to tell our own story that only we would know.

He placed the key around my neck, and I placed the cage around his. The brightest smile was on his face as he held the cage in the palm of his hand, constantly glancing at it with a loving look on his face. "Thank you," he whispered, pressing a kiss against my cheek. It wasn't cheap, but I had been worried it was going to be too small to be that good. However, the way he was looking at it wiped all of my doubts away, the pure awe on his expression as he kept lovingly tracing the design. Only after a few minutes of admiring it, did he remember I hadn't opened his yet. "Open mine."

I couldn't quite contain how excited I was as I started to tug at the wrapping paper. I pulled it off slowly, mostly to mess with him, but as the last piece came off, I was frozen in awe, my eyes wide as I looked at it. "It's an art book, The Adventures of Sparrow and Green," Kinsley announced with a grin.

The front cover was a picture of the two of us, but you couldn't see our faces. Our hands were clasped together in between us, Kinsley's hoodie on, and me wearing a white t-shirt. Throughout the art book were various pictures of the past, memories I'd never forget. A picture of us sitting on the rooftop, Kinsley cupping his fingers around my lighter, helping me light my cigarette, my fingers running through his hair.

A picture of my birthday, the cake that was melting underneath their strange cutting and candle style. Us dancing together in his room, and a picture of us covered in glow-in-the-dark paint, him hovering over me as he held my cheeks in his hands, telling me he was in love with me for the first time. So many pictures drawn from the memories of the past, our past, and so many more pages waiting for more, our future.

I didn't even realize I was crying until Kinsley took the book out of my hands and pulled me against him, burying my face into the hollow of his throat, his fingers tangled in my curls. "I love you," I whispered as he smiled against my hair. "I'll love you forever,"

"Good," he replied, his voice softer, a tint of a smile in it. "It would be so lonely loving you forever if you weren't doing the same."

I tickled his sides as he let out a sharp laugh, before pressing a kiss against his throat. "Merry Christmas, Kinsley," I said as I lifted my head to kiss him.

"Merry Christmas, Luke," he whispered, pressing his lips against mine.

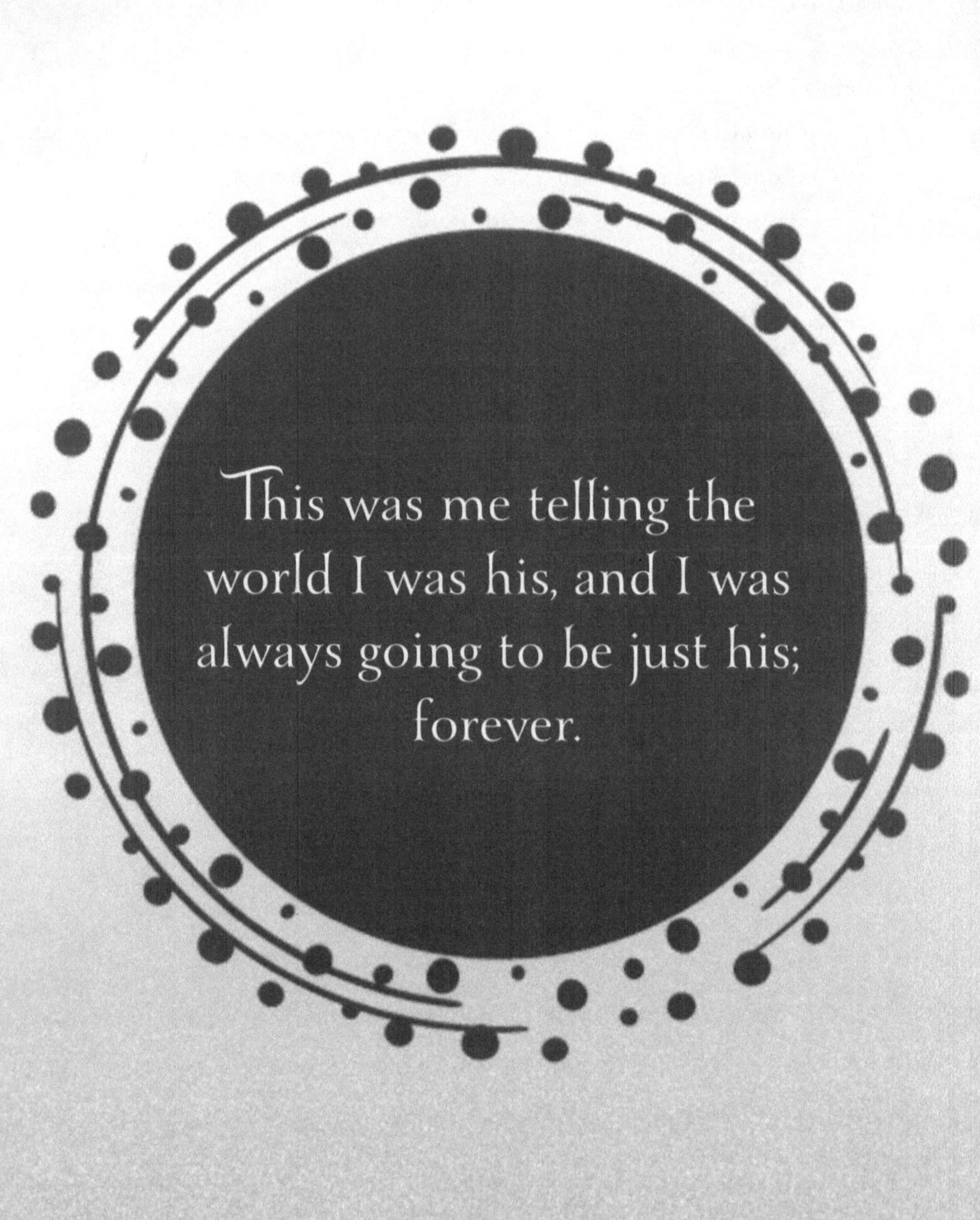
This was me telling the
world I was his, and I was
always going to be just his;
forever.

Bonus Chapter 2
Age 19

I couldn't breathe. No matter how hard I tried to suck in a deep breath, everything was trapped inside me. Contorted and closed, the air refused to go into my body to soothe the painful ache in my chest. I could see stars scattering across my vision as the dizzy feeling settled over me, mixing with the anxiety that was worming its way through every part of me. Only one thought raced through my mind. *I can't do this. I can't do this. I need Luke.*

As if he could read my thoughts, he was there, and I didn't even know how he could be. He grabbed my shoulders and pulled me into his lap, rocking me side to side. "Breathe, baby," he whispered into my ear. He picked up my hand and pressed it against his chest, the calm of his heart beating washing through me. "Feel me breathing? Breathe like me, baby, I got you. I'm not going to let you go."

Hot tears spilled down my cheeks as I buried my nose into his throat. I was filled with questions, but I couldn't speak, struggling to find the ability to breathe once more. *Why are you here? How did you get here? How do you always know?*

"Is he going to be okay? Because it's almost time for the show to start," a bored-sounding lady asked.

"You had three other people that are going to be interviewed first, so back the fuck up and give him some space," Luke's deep voice growled against my ear, making a shudder race through my spine. The lady muttered something I couldn't quite hear as I sucked in a deep breath, coughing at how painful it was. "That's it, baby, just like that. Breathe for me again, okay?" Luke whispered, his voice back to a soft mellow tone, my very own calm in the middle of my storm.

My tears soaked his shirt, and I smelled the grease of whatever it was he was working on. I was so angry with myself for dragging him out here when he was in the middle of a test. "I don't think I could do it, Luke." Luke shushed me.

"Just focus on me," he demanded softly. He pressed my hand tighter against his chest as he rocked me. I closed my eyes and breathed in his scent, his body wash mixed with the grease, not caring that it was probably getting on my suit. "I got you, Kins, always."

It didn't take long for me to calm down, once the other half of my soul was wrapped around me, taking all of the fear away. Slowly I pulled away from his throat as he cupped my cheeks. I could smell the orange soap he used to wash the grease off of his skin, a tangy smell against my face as he slid his thumbs underneath my eyes to wipe away the tears. "You're ruining your make-up, baby," he scolded. I couldn't help the weak laugh from slipping out.

"It's just eyeliner, it's fine." I crinkled my nose as he smiled. I loved the way he stared at me, even after a few years of being together, he still looked at me like I was the most important person in the world. Like I was the only person in the world, to him.

I wanted to slide my fingers over his eyes, to touch every little golden fleck that lit up in the bright luminescent lights back here in the dressing room. "Well, it looks sexy as fuck, just saying," he mumbled. His eyes darkened as he looked me up and down, and my cheeks flushed at his compliment. "I'm going to put you down in this chair, and you're going to keep breathing, okay?" I couldn't do anything else but nod in agreement.

I cleared my throat as Luke started to go through a bag that was left on the counter. "Luke, that's the make-up lady's bag, she's going to be mad at you."

"I don't care." He grabbed a headband and pulled my seat closer to him. "Come here, baby." He was talking to me softly, not like I was a child but like I was five seconds away from shattering. It made me feel calm. It was strange, normally I was the calm one out of both of us, but that day was a nightmare I had never foreseen when I chose this career. Luke put the headband on my head and pushed my bangs off of my face.

He took a second to scrub the mess off my face with a towel before he did anything else. "I never wore make-up before, it feels weird," I mumbled as he smirked at me.

"I'm going to have to say I accept this profession if it means I got to see you like this sometimes," Luke teased as I slapped his arm. "So, are you going to tell me why you had a panic attack?" He grabbed a vial of make-up and started to apply it to my skin.

I closed my eyes as he applied a slightly wet substance to my skin in almost the same skillful manner the woman did earlier. "You know how to put make-up on?"

I couldn't see him, but I could feel him smiling all the same. I didn't need to see him to know what he was doing, not anymore. "Mom, she had a lot of down days, you know? Before she started taking her meds properly. I helped her through it." he paused to clear his throat. I knew it was his way of trying to hide how memories of the past hurt him, to shove them down so I didn't see the pain, but I saw it all the same.

Every bit of pain he felt, I felt it too, as if it was my own. He started to pat my face with something powdery. The woman hadn't even done this much, but I didn't feel the need to stop him when he seemed to be having fun. "Don't change the subject, Kins. Tell me why you had a panic attack,"

I sighed as he tapped my chin to arch my head back so he could see my eyelids better. I guess I was getting eyeshadow that day. I kind of thought it was funny how he was sitting there wearing his mechanic clothes from class, a dirty rag in his back pocket, and that bandana pulling his curls out of his eyes while I was dressed up and sitting there for him to doll up. We must have looked quite the sight to anyone who came in there. "I've never been on TV before, Luke." I couldn't help it, even if it sounded silly. It was scary, knowing there were so many people watching. I felt so small and shy. It was like I was in high school all over again.

"Open your eyes, baby." His face was so close to mine that I could see all of the little light brown freckles scattered across his cheeks, a smudge of grease on the side of his face that he must have missed when he washed it. "You knew you'd have to go out there eventually, Kins. It's your first book, and it skyrocketed. Of course they want to interview you. You're still in college, that's such an impressive feat." He looked so proud, his lips tugged into a smile as he pulled down the skin on my left eye. I saw a black stick coming towards my eye and forced myself to stay still, my eyes lifting automatically to the ceiling as he applied a new layer of eyeliner.

"But I can't have my hood, and everyone can see me, and I... what if they don't like it?" I didn't think I had ever felt that self-conscious in my life. No one understood how hard it was, to be a writer. To put so much of yourself out there for others to enjoy. It was like we were holding our hearts out with extended palms, and wide eyes, begging someone to see them, to hold them close, and to love them exactly for what they were. When people threw them aside carelessly, when they called them stupid or disgusting, it felt like they took my heart and stabbed it through. I didn't think I had ever done anything that painful before in my life.

Luke sighed. He moved on to my other eye, before digging through the bag once more and pulling out a stick of mascara. He held it taunt in his hand as he pulled out his phone, clicking on something, before speaking. "How is this book so popular? It is boring as fuck," he read, making me furrow my eyebrows in confusion. "I hated this book. The whole thing was just unrelentingly dull from first to last," he barely paused before he clicked on something else. "I don't enjoy this book. Insanity, sadness, loss. What a joy!"

I realized finally he was reading reviews, and frowned, cringing over how harsh they were. "I know why you're having doubts, Kins. You were reading reviews on your book last night, and I saw you. I told you not to click on the one-star reviews."

"I don't remember those, are those new ones?" My breath caught in my throat once more.

"Nope, these were written like eight years ago," he muttered. "This was a complete disappointment." He clicked on something else and I frowned, watching him. "The characters were all boring, the writing style was one I couldn't get into, and the plot was vague and unexplained."

"Okay, Luke, I got it, those were horrible, why the Hell are you making me listen to this?" I whined, feeling uneasy all over again.

Luke put his phone down on the counter, pulling my face back to his once more as he opened the mascara bottle and started to slide it expertly on my eyelashes. "Because those are the one-star reviews on The Shining, by Stephen King, and look at him now. Do you think he cares? I mean, maybe. I'm sure even he sat there looking at these reviews and cried a little because people don't understand how hard it is for someone to pour their soul into a book and then have it torn down. But he's famous and has ten times as many five-star reviews. Stop focusing on the one-star reviews and look at your five-star ones. Not everyone is going to like everything, Baby, and there will be some assholes out there. But you have to ignore them and push past it, okay?"

I was speechless for a moment as I thought about his words. He threw the mascara back into the bag carelessly as he watched me. "You're right, I didn't even think about it like that." I felt slightly stupid for letting the small amount of bad criticism get to me when there were so many good ones I could have looked at instead.

He grinned as he grabbed a clear lip gloss and applied it as I opened my mouth for him. "You're going to go out there and blow them all away, babe. They probably won't even care what you say, they're just going to be looking at how pretty you are, my Pretty Boy. Don't tell them our address, I'll have to beat them all off with a stick."

I huffed out a laugh as I punched him gently in the stomach. "Did you walk out on your test because of me? I'm a really bad fiance."

"No, I finished it right before your editor called me. I got an A, it's okay. I passed the class. I just didn't have time to change or anything, so sorry about that."

I grabbed his shirt and yanked him close, the widest grin splitting my lips as excitement poured out of me. "You seriously think I care what you're wearing? I love this look, you should know that by now. We need to celebrate! We gotta call Izzy and Serina, and-" I started to say as he gently pressed his lips against mine, silencing me.

"Honestly right now, there's only one way I want to celebrate with you tonight, and I don't think the girls will want to be present for that," he whispered, his voice deeper as he stared down at me through his eyelashes.

I slid my finger against his lip, a blush creeping across my cheeks as I laughed softly at him. "You have lip gloss on you now."

"I want all of you on me, but I guess this will do for now," he replied with a wink, the menace.

The door opened and we moved apart slowly to see my editor standing there, sighing in visible relief. "Oh thank God, he's pretty and not crying again. You're a lifesaver, Luke. Can I please have your fiance now? It's his turn."

Luke and I stood, and he took a second to straighten my suit, his eyes only on me as he smiled. "You can borrow him for now, but afterward he's coming home with me," he demanded like the cocky shit he was, making my lips twitch at his tone.

"Of course, Luke. I expected nothing else," she said with a grin, laughing at us. "I need to get my husband to watch you two one of those days. You're the epitome of relationship goals. I can't even get him to pick up his dirty laundry from the ground, and you won't believe what he did yesterday–" She threw her hands in the air as she ranted, which was such a common occurrence that we were used to it by then. She was still ranting even as she walked off fast, leaving us behind to slowly follow. Luke laced his fingers with mine, pulling me gently after her out the door.

All of the things I was panicking over were gone, because all I could focus on was Luke's voice, his fingers clasped against mine, and his smile. "You're going to do fine, baby," Luke whispered into my ear as we came closer to the stage.

I sucked in a deep breath as the woman announced me, the crowd cheering as I turned to look at Luke once more. "I know because you're with me,"

He brushed his lips against my cheek, his eyes shining in mirth. "Always, babe. Always."

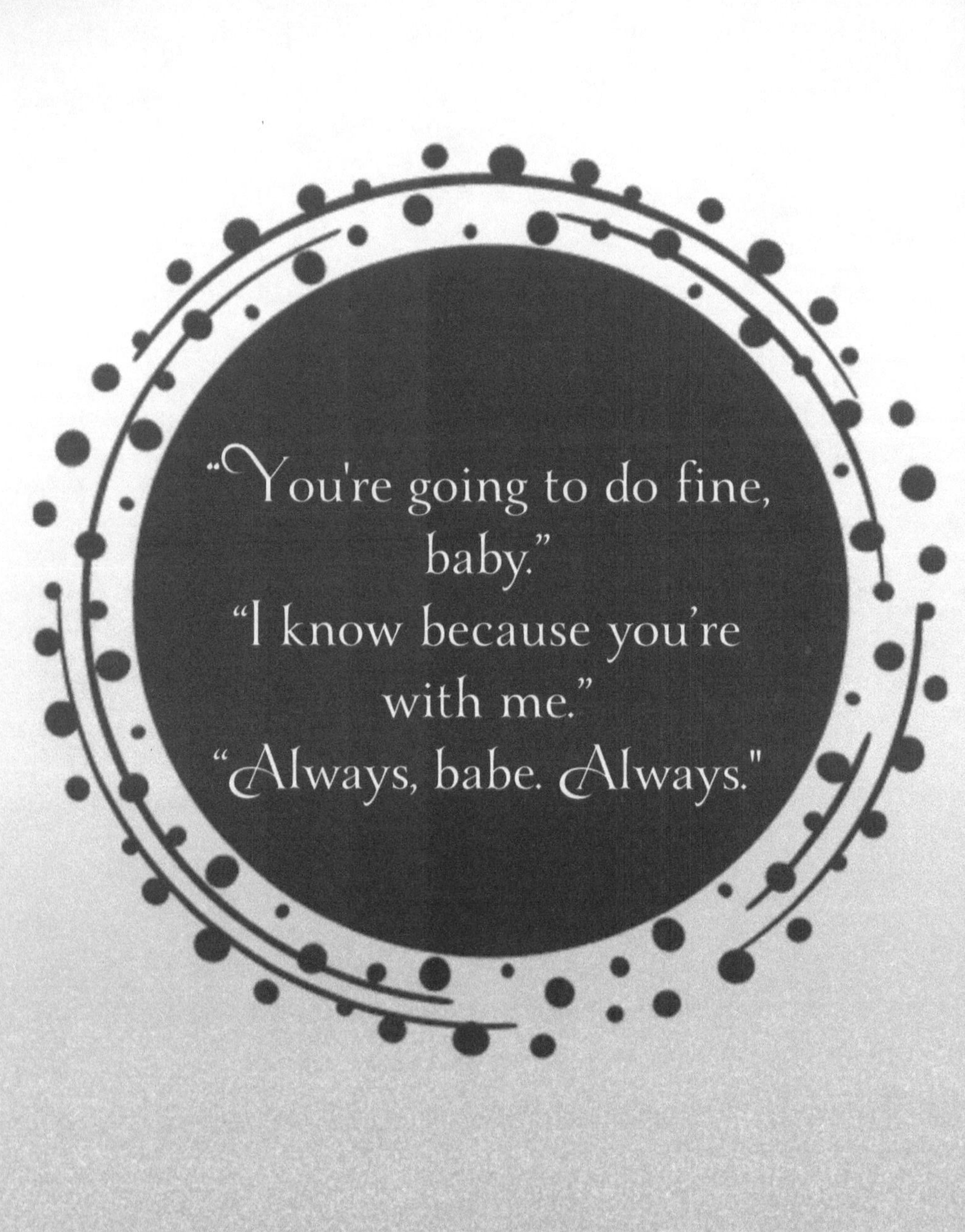

"You're going to do fine, baby."
"I know because you're with me."
"Always, babe. Always."

Bonus Chapter 3
Age 23

"So are we getting a puppy or a kitty?" Luke asked over the phone as I walked down the sidewalk.

I couldn't quite control my grin as I moved past people on the sidewalk. Because I was a writer, I didn't need to worry about my job or having certain hours. I didn't have a nine-to-five job, I could go out and grocery shop, or pet shop, whenever I wanted to as long as I got my manuscripts done in time for my editor to be happy. My third book was given to the editor just yesterday, and as a reward, Luke told me he'd be fine with us sharing our house with an animal.

It felt like it was just yesterday that we'd moved into that pretty house beside the sea, but it had been a few months now, and we'd both always wanted an animal, just never had the stable childhood lifestyle to get one. Luke had always been scared his father would use it against him, hurt it, or kill it when he was angry. My parents had thought all animals were disgusting and refused the few times I tried to bring it up.

"I don't know, I guess it depends on what jumps out at me unless you have a pref-erence," I could hear the sounds of machines clanking together behind me, and Luke's stepdad laughing over something in the background, making Luke laugh in return.

It didn't bother me that I didn't know what they were laughing about, knowing Luke he'd probably sit me down the moment he got home and tell me all about his day, as he always did, with his usual excited look in his eyes that always ended with me climbing onto his lap and kissing him. It didn't matter that we'd been together for years now, it still felt like yesterday when he looked at me like that. We might be getting older, but I still felt like the same sixteen-year-old boy who climbed out from behind a bench to watch the other sixteen-year-old boy who would eventually become my husband walking down the hallway. I hoped I felt like this forever, but I wasn't worried. Every day was warm, every day was special when every day had him in it.

Luke hummed a soft, sweet melody that made me lower my eyes with a smile, enjoying the way he was humming along to whatever song was playing in their garage. *"Whatever you want, baby. You'll be home more than me, I just want you to be happy. I'll love whatever you choose,"* he said with a smile in his voice. *"I'm just sorry I couldn't get out of work to come with you. I hope you're not mad at me."*

I was fairly annoyed to a degree, seeing as I had made this appointment with the pound ahead of time, but I understood why he had to miss it. "It's not your fault that there was a big car pile-up yesterday and like five cars were towed to your shop. I just feel so proud you're one of the first places they thought to go to. Such a new garage and you're getting so much business already. You're awesome, babe."

I hadn't been able to park right next to the pound, but I was close enough to it that I could walk to it. I stopped before crossing the street, waiting for the red hand to change so I could cross. All around me, the cars whooshed past, the sidewalk around me getting slightly crowded as others waited to cross. *"I have to go, baby, I love you. I need two hands to work on this."*

"It was okay, Luke, I understand. I love you too. I'll see you when you get home." As always, no matter where we went, there would always be someone who was homophobic, someone who was annoying and unnecessary. I wasn't surprised to feel the glare of an older gentleman who was crinkling his nose at me for saying the name Luke and I love you in the same sentence. The younger me would have burst into tears or wished Luke was here to hide behind. The younger me would have felt like shit for the rest of the day, but not now, not anymore. I had grown a lot since high school. Instead of trying to hide behind the hoods I no longer needed to wear, I gave him a wide smile and a nod of acknowledgment as he looked away with a disgusted huff, rolling his eyes.

A little hand tugged on the bottom of my shirt, and I looked down in surprise, looking into sweet little light green eyes that looked just like Luke's. "Can you hold my hand so I can cross the street?" The little girl asked. Her light brown hair was messy, and her clothes were falling apart and ripped in some places, making my heart ache to see her. Her feet looked like they hurt, shoved into such tiny shoes. She looked to be about five or six.

"Where's your mama or daddy?" I asked her, bending down to her level.

The little girl frowned as she tugged on the bottom of her shirt, clearly unhappy with how short it was. She splayed her fingers over the gap that showed off her little tummy. "I don't have a mommy or a daddy, I'm trying to find one."

Just then the light changed, and I lifted her into my arms automatically, feeling drawn to the sweet little girl as I crossed the street with her. "Do you know where you live?"

She wrapped her arms around my neck as she sat on my arm. "I lived with a mean lady who didn't want to share food with me. She returned me because I was crying a lot, but I was just hungry," she said with a sniffle, her eyes watering at the memory. "The orphanage was annoyed I was returned again, so I ran, wanting to find a new mommy or daddy. Can you be my daddy? You're pretty."

My heart ached as I listened to her story. Without hesitation, I started to walk down the street in the opposite direction of the pound. All thoughts of getting an animal were gone for now, and all I could think of was this little girl, and how uncomfortable she looked. I walked into a clothing store and the doorbell went off, a saleswoman stepped forward with a bright smile on her face. "Can you get her a whole new outfit? New shoes as well, these look awful," I said as the woman stepped away to get a tape measure. "Is that okay with you?" I asked the little girl. "Then you'll tell me the name of your orphanage, right?"

"But I don't want to go back there, they're mean," she said, tears in her eyes as she let out a soft sob.

"What's your name?" I asked her, trying to get her to stop looking so sad. "My name is Kinsley."

She stopped crying almost instantly, her eyes so wide and beautiful, so much like Luke's that I couldn't help but smile. "My name is Lakely, and I'm this many," She said, holding out six fingers on her hands. She smiled a wide smile, showing off a missing bottom tooth for a moment before the lady came back.

I was chewing on my bottom lip as the lady walked off with the little girl, before looking up orphanages near me on my phone. The idea of kids, I'd always thought of it before, but I wasn't sure how Luke felt about it. But the more I talked to this little girl the more I couldn't stop myself from wondering what our little family of two would feel like if there was a third. As the little girl giggled with the shop worker, I dialed an orphanage number, and then another, asking them over and over again if they were missing a little girl who was six named Lakely.

The third call ended up being the right one. "You found her? Oh my goodness, that little brat. She walked out the door. We were just about to call the police," the woman said, sounding frustrated.

I was annoyed that she called her a brat, and annoyed that she hadn't called the police yet. I had had her in this store for a good twenty minutes now, and the orphanage wasn't that close, she had to have been walking for a while. If I hadn't found her, who knows what could have happened to her? "I'd like to adopt her. Please explain to me the process and get the papers ready for when I get there with her," I said confidently over the phone.

For the next half hour, the woman on the phone explained everything I would need to do over the phone, what amount of money I'd need, and the family therapy sessions I'd have to attend with Lakely and Luke afterward to make sure we were situated properly. Lakely hadn't been adopted before, just in the foster system, but I wasn't planning on returning her like she was a used piece of clothing.

Finally, I hung up the phone with her as the saleswoman led Lakely to me with a shy smile on her face and an adorable little outfit. She had picked a soft yellow dress that had little black leggings underneath and a pair of comfortable-looking sneakers. Over the woman's arm were a couple of other outfits and shoes Lakely must have tried on, unsure which she liked the most. "Throw away her old clothes and ring up all of that," I said, making Lakely smile widely at me in surprise.

I wasn't as rich as I had been living with my parents, but with my books and Luke's garage, we were making enough not to worry about much. So while the price of adoption was high, I knew I could pay it. But first, I had to make sure she was okay with it. I held Lakely's hand as I led her down the sidewalk to an ice cream shop. She stared at everything with wide eyes as I ordered something and let her pick out her flavor as well, before leading her to a slightly isolated table in the back away from the other families that were there.

I stared at Lakely as she started to dig into her ice cream, the brightest smile on her face as she hummed excitedly. "I know you were looking for a mommy and a daddy, but what would you say if you got two daddies instead? You know, some families have no mommies, but two daddies. And some that have no daddies, but two mommies. Would that bother you, to have two daddies?"

She blinked, staring at me with wide eyes as she thought about it. I knew I needed to ask Luke too, but I didn't want to ask him until after I made sure she was okay with it.

I didn't want to get his hopes up, only for the little girl to not feel comfortable with us. "Those two girls are kissing, you mean like that?" Lakely asked, pointing fairly rudely at two women who were bent over a large cup of ice cream with two spoons, pressing their lips together with soft smiles on their faces.

I grabbed her hand gently, lowered it to the table, and patted it softly. "Yes, like that. I am married to a man, not a woman. So if I were to be your daddy, you'd get two daddies, not one. Would that bother you?" I asked her, watching her little six-year-old mind try to process this. I gave her time, knowing she was young and this was a hard decision. Maybe it would have been better to try and adopt an older child, one that could understand better.

It wasn't as easy as people thought it was for same-gender couples to adopt. We had to worry about everything. How the child would feel, and how the other kids in their school would react if they got bullied for it. How the parents would feel, and so on. "It doesn't matter, I just want people to be happy," she said with a wide smile. "It doesn't matter who they're happy with, as long as they're happy."

I wanted to cry, hearing the soft, non-judgmental words of the sweet little six-year-old girl. "I found the orphanage you stay at, and they're getting papers ready. I needed to get my husband to sign them as well, so they said for me to go by the orphanage and sign a release paper, where they would come and inspect my home, make sure it had enough room for you, and for a week you would stay with me while my husband and I get to know you and see if you'll be a good fit for us. After the week, my husband and I will go back to the orphanage and finalize the adoption. Is this something you're interested in?" I asked her, talking slowly, making sure she understood.

"I would get two daddies?" She asked, her eyes wide as she stared at me. Little tears started to form in her eyes as I felt my bottom lip tremble, hoping beyond all hope that Luke would agree. "I'll be so good, and I won't cry," She promised.

Later that evening, I was setting the table for three as Lakely explored the room that was going to be hers if Luke agreed. The orphanage was understanding; they knew I didn't have any furniture, but they also saw my bank account as per one of the conditions, and they had no worries that I wouldn't be able to afford her bedroom furniture. They gave me a cot for her for the night, and I hoped if all went well with Luke, we could go out and buy furniture together tomorrow since he was off on Thursdays.

I was humming under my breath as the front door opened, anxiety spilling through me at what he'd say as he closed the door and kicked off his shoes, letting out an exhausted breath of air as he trudged through the house toward me. Hearing the clatter of dishes and smelling the soft scent of dinner led him to me as he came up behind me.

Luke wrapped his arms around my waist, burying his mouth against my throat as he kissed my skin with light feather kisses. "Honey, I'm home," he whispered against my throat as I grinned, turning in his arms to kiss him.

The smell of the orange soap on him was strong, mostly masking the grease scent that was constantly clinging to him, the normal smells of Luke that I loved more than anything. His seafoam eyes were twinkling with happiness as he looked at me, and I traced over his cheeks as he pressed his forehead against mine. "So what animal did you get?" he asked, pressing a kiss against my nose as I let out a sheepish breath. *Damn, I completely forgot about the animal.*

"Um, about that-" I started to say the moment Lakely came bouncing into the kitchen and stared at us both with her wide eyes. Luke jolted in surprise, his eyes wide as he and Lakely appraised each other, and I let out an uncomfortable laugh. "Surprise?"

Luke took a step towards Lakely as she walked over to him, looking up at him with her wide matching eyes. "Kinsley, did you go and steal a whole kid from someone? I need to know. You do have a past of illegal tendencies. Dammit, I'm going to have to call Serina, Isabella probably stole a child too. The two of you do all of your illegal stuff together."

I chuckled, but before I could reply to him, Lakely tugged on the bottom of Luke's shirt, her eyes wide as she stared at him. "My name was Lakely, and I'm this many. Will you be my daddy number two?" She asked, her little voice loud as she stared at him with her tiny little fingers raised to show six fingers.

Luke looked at me with whiny pouting lips as I smirked, already sensing his resolve falling away at her adorableness. "She's here for a week, for us to get to know her, and see if the three of us can be a family together. I'll explain everything later, but after a week if we all like each other we have to go back and pay the adoption fee."

Luke stared at me for a few seconds, then at her, before falling to his knees in front of her and wrapping his arms around her. "She has my eyes, Kins," he whispered, rocking the giggling Lakely back and forth in his arms. "We can keep her?" He asked, looking back up at me with wide eyes. "I... I'm not sure how good of a father I'll be."

Lakely grabbed Luke's cheeks, patting them rather painfully as she smiled at him. "It's okay, we can figure it out together," she said in her soft voice, patting him on the head.

"Oh my God, absolutely yes," Luke said, crushing her giggling body against his once more. I fell to my knees behind Lakely and Luke pulled me against her as the two of us crushed her in a tight hug, making her giggle even louder. Luke's eyes were filled with happiness as he pressed a kiss against my forehead. *'I love you,'* He mouthed to me, grinning softly.

I love you too, babe,' I mouthed back at him with a laugh.

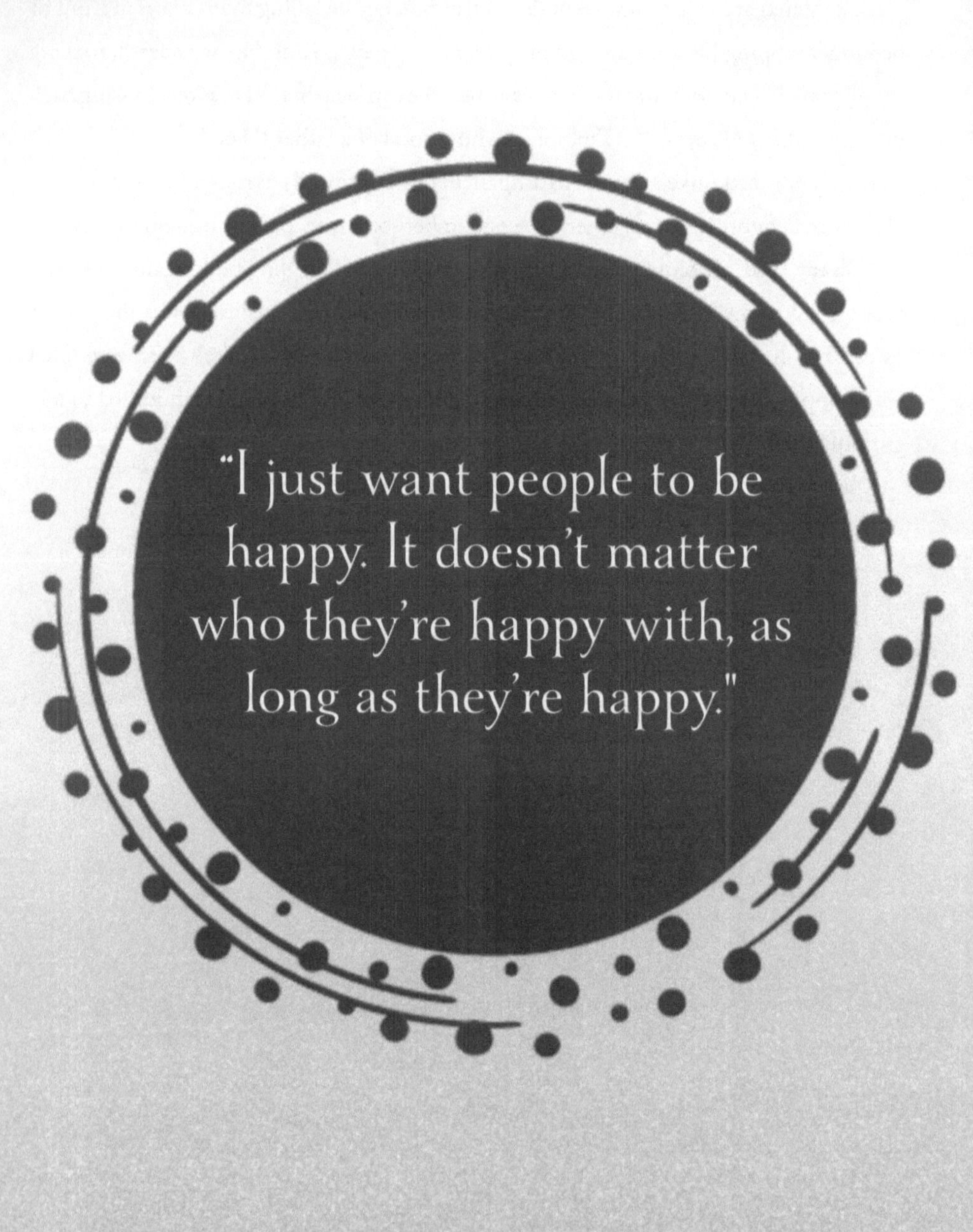

"I just want people to be happy. It doesn't matter who they're happy with, as long as they're happy."

Bonus Chapter 4
Age 19

Sometimes, your life comes to a point where everything just stops, and all you are left with is the overwhelming truth that everything led to this, to right now, to this moment in time. It's silly, really, when you think about it. You proposed to someone or got proposed to, and you stayed with them for usually at least a year before you even got married. Unless you were the adventurous type that married someone you just met five minutes ago and then Yolo, I guess, got it.

But I knew this was coming a year ago, a year before that, but no matter how long I had to prepare for what was about to happen it didn't matter, because it was happening right now, and I had no idea what the hell I was doing. My body was covered with sweat and I couldn't breathe properly. And dammit all, my hands wouldn't stop shaking.

"Izzy, I need help, I don't know what to do," I mumbled, my lips aching a little from how much I'd been biting them the last half hour.

Isabella giggled and I wanted nothing more than to punch her, but was trapped in the idea of whether it was ethical to punch a woman. Like they say it's not okay for a man to punch a woman but does that saying count for a woman that was with another woman? And what about the man, who was with the other man? Oh my god, I was about to get married.

"Would you put the phone down and help me please?" I asked Isabella desperately.

Isabella rolled her eyes at me. "You told me I had to take videos and pictures of everything. I only had two hands, I couldn't do both. And think about your future babies, wanting to watch how frantic you were right before marrying their other daddy."

I huffed as I clenched my hands tightly, only to uncoil them as they continued to shake. "You're not being funny right now, Izzy,"

"Well, you're being funny," she said, her lips curving up into a smirk. "What do you mean you need help? Help with what?"

"I was getting married in thirty minutes, and they won't stop shaking. I wasn't freaking out at the rehearsal dinner, I wasn't freaking out that morning in the car, or last night when you wanted to stay up late doing facials for some strange reason, I wasn't even freaking out five minutes ago when Serina popped her head in here, so why the hell was I freaking out now? It makes no sense!" I whined, waving my shaking hands around where she could see them.

Isabella chuckled, a fond look on her face mixed with exasperation. I started pacing back and forth across the small room. My clothes were fine, my tie was tied, but I wasn't ready yet because of my stupid fucking hands. How was he going to put the ring on my finger like this?

"You want to know the worst part of all of this? The worst part is I think about the fact that I'm stupidly freaking out, yes, I know it's stupid but I'm doing it anyway, and then I start freaking out over that too! Freaking out that I'm freaking out, and then I'm freaking out that I'm freaking out even more, and that just leads to a circle of freaking out that I have no idea how to get out of..." I continued miserably, a small bead of sweat sliding down between my shoulder blades that made me involuntarily shiver in frustration.

In a way, I knew one of the main things that was stressing me out the most was how I had sent a wedding invitation to my family, and they had replied with a simple no. Just the word no, written down on a little greeting card, time spent for a moment to slide the card into an envelope and send it in the mail. Kennedy sent her letter, which surprised me, but it didn't have anything more than an *I'm sorry* written on it. Maybe it would have been better if they hadn't replied at all.

"Oh my God, this is bad, isn't it?" I asked, inhaling and exhaling large amounts of air as I tensed again, looking at Isabella with shaking fucking hands. "Is this bad? Izzy, tell me, is this as bad as it looks-"

Isabella grabbed my shoulders and held me in place as I tried not to cry like a two-year-old. "You know what? Just forget about your hands, Kins. You're getting married, they aren't of use until tonight anyway. What are you supposed to hold anyway? Nothing, absolutely nothing, not until tonight, when he expects you to hold his di-" she started to say as I pressed my hands against her mouth with an annoyed groan.

She licked my hand, and I pulled it away with a disgusted look, dragging my hand against a random chair close by, hoping that didn't make God frown down at me. "I'm not kidding, Izzy, I don't know what to do."

She stood up straight, her head raised high as she straightened her shoulders. I was eyeballing her because this was Izzy, and either whatever she said was going to be profound or it was going to be horrible. There was never a middle ground with her. "Pretty boy, you could stand there across from him naked, wearing nothing but the little cushion for the ring over your junk, and Luke would still marry you without a moment's pause."

I stared at her with my mouth hanging open because, honestly, he'd probably get excited in a second if I even tried to be that bold and- oh my God, why was I even imagining it? I groaned, rolling my eyes at her as she stood there grinning, looking all proud of herself. "You groan, but your hands aren't shaking anymore."

I didn't reply to her; instead, I was too busy laughing a soft laugh, realizing that while I had been panicking at some point, Isabella had decided to take off her shoes and was standing there shoeless, the heel in her hand ready to impale me with the deadly spike. "Why are you shoeless? Please don't hit me with that; I won't survive that medieval death trap."

"You try wearing heels; they're so freaking painful," she replied. Isabella and Serina were wearing matching light blue dresses and black strappy high heels. We didn't tell them what to wear, just what color we wanted, both of us settling for a light blue and light green theme to match our eyes.

The night of the glow-in-the-dark paint was thick in our minds when we picked the color scheme for the wedding, and despite the way the wedding planner looked at us like we were crazy, she went along with it anyway when we flashed her my parents' unlimited credit card. For the most part, I wasn't using it much, only for emergencies, but I thought if they weren't going to show or even call, the least they could do was pay for their only son's wedding.

I wasn't sure when it started or why, but both of us ended up bursting into laughter for no reason, clutching onto each other as we tried desperately to suck in deep breaths, our arms wrapped around each other as we tried desperately to suck in deep breaths without fainting over lack of oxygen.

After a while, we fell silent again until Izzy let out a wistful sigh. "Why do you think you're freaking out?"

"I don't know, it just seemed to come out of nowhere."

"Are you thinking of running out on the wedding? Because I have my car out front, no judgment, I'll always have your back kins. We can go get donuts and eat a dozen and cry over why the world is so illogical if you want. I'm an art student, drama is what I do," she said, snapping her fingers back and forth between us.

I gave her a strange look, unsure why she'd even think I'd ever want to do that. "What? No, of course not. I've never been more excited about anything in my life, Izzy."

"Okay, then what is it?"

I blinked once, then twice, before shrugging. "Maybe I'm just scared, you know? What if he wakes up one day and looks at me and thinks: what the hell did I do? And ends up regretting everything?"

"Goodness Kinsley, push your fears aside and think. That was honestly the stupidest thing I've ever heard. This is Luke, we're talking about."

I sighed because she was right. This was Luke, my Luke, and I was so stupid to think he'd even have proposed to me in the first place if he wasn't sure about how he felt about me. It took him freaking forever to figure it out in the first place, so of course he wasn't going to wake up and regret it. I started laughing like a crazed lunatic as Isabella joined in for the hell of it, and for a moment I wondered how strange this must be to whoever could be walking down the hallway. "He loved you, *estupido*. Now go out there and make sure he cries first because I bet Serina he would."

We both jumped when the door opened, and Serina's head popped in. "You guys ready?"

"How's Luke doing?" I blurted out at her. Isabella chuckled as she and Serina shared a knowing look filled with their own language of glances and smiles only they knew.

"Honestly? He's freaking out about the flowers," Serina replied with an eye roll. "Whatever you do, don't mention the centerpieces. He's so annoyed with them. I find it hilarious because I guess when he's panicking he channels you. I never thought he'd ever care about flowers."

I couldn't help but laugh with her, feeling a wave of relief gush over my body. I thought it was funny he was freaking out over something so stupid, but I couldn't judge him since I was over there panicking over my stupid hands.

"Hurry up, I'll meet you guys out there," she said, winking at Isabella as she closed the door and left us alone.

Isabella grinned at me before holding up her finger and frowning. "Hold on, you're missing something." She started to dig through her purse for a few seconds before pulling out a blue handkerchief. "This was my father's. He had it in his drawer, and I took it a long time ago, back when Mami was trying to throw his stuff away. I kept this, and I kept Papa's jacket after he had died. You can't keep it, you know. I need it back," she said firmly, tucking it into my tux with a grin.

I smiled, my heart pounding as I tapped the handkerchief. "Something borrowed, something blue."

"Exactly, pretty boy. Now let's get you married."

"Rina," I whined, pacing back and forth as Serina stared at me with a mix of apprehension and laughter in her eyes. I was wearing my pants but that was about it, my tux in her hands as she watched me pacing back and forth, trying to hand me my shirt. I snapped my phone shut and shoved it into my pocket. I wasn't even sure why this bothered me so much, but they just weren't right! Kinsley was already upset over his parents, he deserved everything to be perfect. "I just want to kill them all for ruining everything."

"As your best man, I am compelled to remind you that killing people is illegal, though as your best friend, I guess I should add in the fact that Izzy parked out front and we have a very nice large trunk that'll fit a short person or two. Probably." I couldn't help but laugh as I remembered all of the many illegal things the four of us had done over the years. "Also, calm down. You're ruining your hair."

I scoffed, narrowing my eyes at her. "Why does it even matter? Everything is ruined already. I told them no red roses, but blue and green ones, and if they couldn't do blue and green, then do white. At least that would have matched more. But they still delivered red! It doesn't match anymore, it looks stupid."

Maybe this was a stupid thing to be upset about, and if someone had told me a few months ago I'd be having a tantrum about flowers right then I'd have probably laughed, but I couldn't help it, I was so fucking nervous. I was shaking, my heart was racing, and in a matter of minutes, I was about to be married to the most important person in my life. I felt like I was going to throw up. "I don't even have something new!"

Serina was being a complete dick, which wasn't helping. I started to rethink my best friend title. She laughed that laugh that made her snort a little every once in a while, and I was secretly glad her eyeliner was starting to smear. She deserved it, to be honest. "I'm sorry, I'm sorry, I'm being the worst best man ever," she said, coughing once more to clear her throat as she waved my shirt at me again. I grabbed the shirt and started to slip my hands into it, buttoning it up automatically with a frustrated sigh. "But is it at all possible that you were panicking about something other than the flowers?"

"What?" I asked her, cursing under my breath as I had to rebutton my shirt since I screwed it up the first time.

"Are you possibly rethink things?"

I looked at her with a dead look. "Are you serious right now? Of course not. There's no me without Kinsley, all I've wanted was to be with him forever."

Serina nodded, a bright smile on her face. "That is true, absolutely."

"Oh God, do you think he is? Having doubts?" I wondered, feeling faint all of a sudden.

"Kinsley has been in love with you since before he's ever even seen you. I remember when we first met, and how I had talked to him about how I felt for Isabella. He had told me he fell in love with you through letters, not knowing who you were, what your gender was, what you looked like, or even what your real name was. He said he knew you were the other half of his soul and he had told me once before that there would be no life without you in it. He said if there was life after death, then he was sure you and he had been reincarnated over and over again, led back to each other because something as strong as you and him isn't something that can ever be parted."

"Oh... wow," I said, my lips quivered as I looked down at my hands. "Fuck," I mumbled, feeling a hardness in my throat as I quickly wiped my hand underneath my eye.

Serina looked horrified. "No, you're not supposed to cry yet, Kinsley has to cry first."

"Rina," I whined. "What am I doing? Who fucking cares about flowers, they're going to be dead in a couple of hours anyway? I had to go, I have to marry my Pretty Boy, I have to get dressed, why the hell am I not dressed yet? Where is my tux, oh my God, what is going on with my hair?" I yelled, running around the room and finally stopping to stand in front of the mirror.

A hand on my shoulder caused me to momentarily pause as I turned to look at a smiling Serina, who handed me a small velvet box. I opened it, ignoring the fact that she had tried to scrape off the clearance sticker that was taped to the top of the box, and stared in confusion at a small sparkly hairpin that was light blue. "What's this?" I asked, sliding my finger down the hairpin with a frown on my face.

"I bought it for myself, but because of the sparkles, it doesn't match my dress so I never really used it before. And now I'm giving it to you, it's yours now. Something new," she said, looking proud of herself. "You didn't have your something new, right?" she asked.

"That's because you had left it at the house."

"And as your best man, I'm allowed to make up for it by giving you my sparkly hairpin," she said with a smile.

My lower lip jutted out as I pulled her into a hug, sighing. "Thank you, Serina," I whispered, my voice shaking as tears threatened to well up in my eyes once more. "I love you so much, I would die without you."

Serina chuckled, shaking her head against my shoulder. "What about your pretty fiancé?"

"Fuck him," I mumbled, squeezing her tighter as we laughed with each other.

"Ew, no thanks," she mumbled, making the two of us laugh for a good few minutes before we finally pulled away from each other. "I love you too, Luke. God, you're gonna get married! I can't believe it!" she exclaimed, clapping her hands as I took my tux from her and slipped it on.

I grinned, grabbed the tie, and held it up for her. "Fuck yeah, I'm getting married," I said, exhaling with a smile. "Now help me get dressed."

"Something as strong as you and him isn't something that can ever be parted."

Bonus Chapter 5
Age 19

I separated from Serina as I went out into the chapel. The murmur of voices from everyone we knew was slightly loud as they all waited for the procession to start. We had made a few friends over the last two years we'd been in New York and flown a few people out from our hometown, giving us a semi-full church filled with new and old faces. A little girl to the side was being coached on how to throw flowers since the priest had promised he knew a lovely couple that was willing to help. The little girl was wearing the same outfit as Serina and Isabella, her midnight-colored skin made the light blue of the dress sparkle as her lovely amber eyes floated around the room, only half listening to her mother as she waved at me with a bright smile on her face.

As if the others could sense I was there, most of the guests turned to look at me, watching me walk down the aisle alone toward the front of the church. Hoots and hollers from friends in my mechanics classes erupted through the group, pulling out quite a few chuckles from others that made a soft blush of embarrassment spread across my cheeks.

Everyone thought Kinsley and I were crazy for getting married so soon, but honestly, this was America, and the number of people who got married when they were eighteen was staggering, so the fact that Kinsley and I waited at least until we were nineteen was something we were slightly proud of since we'd been in love with each other since we were sixteen.

Maybe three years wasn't much to some people, but as I told Kinsley when I proposed to him, I was tired of wasting time. Time with him, a future with him, a life with him, everything with him. I didn't need to wait until we were both out of college to know he was the one I was going to spend the rest of my life with.

Serina had left me alone to go and rush Izzy and Kinsley. I met my mom and Paul at the front of the aisles, and she was already crying, her eyeliner running as she pressed kisses against both of my cheeks. "Mommm," I whined, wiping her lipstick off of my cheeks as Paul laughed and patted my back with a wide grin.

"Congratulations, Son."

"Thanks, Dad," I said as he patted my back once more before he dragged my mom away and forced her crying self to sit down in the front row. I smiled, remembering the first time I'd called him Dad, and seeing how shocked he was. It was the only time I'd ever seen him cry, but it was worth it. He had always been more of a father to me than my real dad was, and after my real father had left me and Kinsley alone in my mom's old house that day, I hadn't thought of him as my father since.

I wanted nothing to do with him, absolutely nothing because he was nothing to me. I had tried so hard for so long to get him to be proud of me, but I realized after a while it was pointless. I didn't need him to be proud of me, I just needed to be proud of myself, and I was, I finally was.

The music came on as Serina nearly ran down the aisle, her eyes wide as a soft chuckle spilled through the room. Everyone sat down as she stood beside me and smoothed down her dress, blinking at me a few times with a smile. "He looked fabulous."

The little flower girl walked slowly down the aisle, the brightest grin on her face as she walked and threw petals, stopping to wave at a few people she recognized as a soft chuckle filled the room over how cute she was. She twirled in a circle in the middle of the room, throwing petals and making the biggest scene, before finally taking a seat next to my mother who patted her head and whispered to her how much of a good job she did.

But I wasn't looking at her anymore, no. I was watching Isabella walk down the aisle, anticipation flooding through me, knowing that Kinsley was coming next. My Kinsley. My heart was racing as I saw him step into the room, the soft gasps spilling as everyone took in the beauty that was my Kinsley, my pretty boy, mine.

Kinsley walked down the aisle with Isabella's mother's hand resting in the crook of his elbow, and I kept thinking of the first time I saw him, in the art room. I didn't even see a gender at first, all I saw was him and his beautiful cerulean blue eyes, his soft ash-blond hair and how it framed his pristine face, and those dimples.

Back then, I thought he was the most beautiful boy I'd ever seen, and even now three years later nothing changed. Even now, he was still the most beautiful man, my most beautiful man, and I did not doubt that he always would be.

I imagined what it would look like to watch Kinsley walk down the aisle before. How many times? I wasn't entirely sure. A hundred? A thousand? It didn't matter, because none of them compared to this. I tried to control my breathing as Kinsley and Mami trudged the aisle, greeting guests as he passed by, but I couldn't. I told myself I wasn't going to cry until the end because Isabella bet it would be me who cried first, and Serina bet it would be Kinsley. I didn't want to make Serina lose her bet after all.

In the end, I lost, and I knew I lost because it was impossible not to cry when my future husband was looking at me like that. I fought the urge to press my hand against my chest as I watched him, unable to keep the tears to myself as they slowly slid down my cheeks because, *fucking hell, he's beautiful*.

They stood at the bottom of the stairs as Mami turned to Kinsley, tears running down her cheeks as she swatted him on the shoulder. "Look what you made me do, *Mijo*!" she said, making those in the first few pews laugh softly at her. I grinned as Kinsley winced with a laugh. She pulled Kinsley into a hug, patting his back lightly as she went to pull away. "I love you, *Mijo*."

"I love you too, Mami," Kinsley said softly, his voice enough to make me sigh after having gone over a day without hearing it. Serina and Isabella were so adamant we didn't see each other until now, and I had missed him so much last night.

I had no idea where the shoe came from, but Mami waved it at me, her eyes narrowed as she glared. "Don't you hurt my baby," she said, glaring at me, then at Kinsley, as if unsure which one of us she'd kill if we hurt each other.

I laughed as I held my hand out for Kinsley. "I won't," I promised, looking deeply into Kinsley's eyes.

She sat down next to Paul as I pulled Kinsley up to stand across from me, both of our hands clasped together. I was busy thinking of all the ways I didn't deserve to be standing there across from him, all the ways I didn't deserve him, when he interrupted my internal self-pity moment. "Hey you," he murmured, loud enough for only us to hear.

I had a lot of things to say to him, so many things I wanted to say after having gone a whole night and day without seeing him. But for some reason, standing there across from him, I couldn't think of a single one. All I could muster was the first thing that popped into my head. "You look sexy."

Serina must have been close enough to hear as she snorted behind me. I couldn't feel too upset about my random word vomit though when Kinsley started to blush in surprise, while the priest coughed to hide his laughter beside us. Kinsley's hands shook mine as we grinned at each other like a couple of idiots and I tightened my grip around them, smiling when I felt him relax a little.

"Everyone, we're here today..."

The priest started to say. I took a deep breath as I tried to settle the nerves and the excitement billowing inside me. "You nervous?" I whispered, watching him from under my eyelashes.

Kinsley was watching me as well, a soft smile on his lips. "I think we're both nervous."

I shrugged, not arguing with him since it was true. "How long are your vows?"

He grinned, winking at me. "I don't know, I'm winging it."

"Of course you were, Mr. Hot shot writer now that you have a book published," I muttered as he smirked at me, tapping the tip of his tongue against the top of his lip. "Damn it, mine's probably lame."

Finally, the priest went to the end of his speech, looking at both of us with a smile on his face. "Let's get started with the vows, shall we?"

I took a deep breath, closed my eyes, opened them again, and smiled. "Before you, I was nothing. Just a little boy stuck in the middle of a storm. I went through life contemplating what it would be like without me in it, wondering if I should... If I should try to kill myself again." A soft gasp spilled from the crowd, people who didn't know me very well or didn't know my past, pressed their hands against their mouths in surprise.

"But then I saw you."

"You came into my life in a flutter of exciting letters and someone who saw me, for me. Even after telling me you didn't know who I was, you still wanted to know me, you still liked me, and that was everything to me. I was already in love with you before I saw you in that room, I just didn't realize. I was so young, and the idea of liking another boy was something I had instilled in my mind was wrong, so I ran. But you never gave up on me. You were the constant, the calm in the middle of my storm.

"I learned over time that this was a different love from the kind most expected, but it was better, for me. You make me better, you've always made me better. You never gave up on me, and I'll never give up on you. You pushed me to go to therapy, to see that it was okay for me to be me, to be everything I wanted to be. And you never once left my side.

"I grew up being told I'd never be loved, that I was broken, that no one could ever love someone like me, but you proved them all wrong baby. Because you do, and you have, and you will, and I had the uttermost faith in you. Like a puzzle, you've always been the piece I'd been missing, ever since the beginning. You told me once that I wasn't broken, that you were a half, and I was a half, and together we were a whole. You were right, Kinsley, and I can't imagine going the rest of my life without you by my side, making me complete. It's always been you. It'll always be you. I'd never stop proving how much I love you, even if it takes the rest of our lives. I love you, Pretty Boy. My Sparrow, my Kinsley."

Kinsley's shoulders shook as he wiped his eyes with one hand, holding onto me tightly with the other. The crowd around us let out soft sighs and sniffles as some of them cried for us. It was so hard, finding a church that was willing to marry us, and maybe it would have been easier to take Isabella up on her offer of going to some beach and getting one of our friends to register to marry us, but Kinsley wanted to stand in church, to take pictures under the stained glass, with the sun setting in the background, to send to his parents and to show them that even if we were both guys, it was okay. That we were okay, even if we were different from them.

So I looked, and while this church ended up being a good hour and a half away from where we lived, it was worth it to see him standing there like that brushing his tears from his cheeks as he peered up at me through his eyelashes. The sun was setting, illuminating his cerulean eyes in a twinkling hue as the golden rays of the setting sun made everything just that much more dramatic.

"Damn," Kinsley finally muttered, letting out a soft laugh as he crinkled his nose at me. "And here I thought I could just wing it, but nothing I say is going to top that," he said, his dimples flashing in the way I wished I'd always see them for the rest of my life. I was determined to make that happen, a secret vow, just for me. To always, always make him happy.

He took a deep breath, and closed his eyes as he thought, before looking at me once more. "My life was nothing but hiding, waiting, and wishing. Hiding under hoodies, hiding from everyone. I wasn't what was expected from me, and no matter how hard I tried to be what they wanted. it was never good enough, so I hid. Waiting for the end of high school so we could all move away and never look back, to finally be me, and wishing that I was what my parents wanted. I wasted so much time trying to make them happy. Trying to be what they wanted me to be. I couldn't make them proud of me, even now I..." he trailed off, looking into the crowd, before looking at me once more.

"*I tried*," he whispered. He paused for a second, and it was my turn to squeeze his hands in encouragement.

"But I realized it didn't matter if they're not proud of me. Because all that matters is if I'm proud of myself. And if it wasn't for how hard I tried to get them to be proud of me, I wouldn't have ever written that letter, and I never would have slipped it into the wrong locker."

The soft laughter of those who knew of our story spilled through the crowd, but we only had eyes for each other as he stared at me, smiling. "It's funny, how I spent so many years hiding, but out of everyone, no matter how hard I tried to hide, you saw me. You saw the me that even I didn't see. You told me countless times that I was brave, that I made you brave, but it was the other way around, Luke. You were so brave, replying to my letter, and you were so brave when I confessed to you that I didn't know who you were, but you still wanted to talk to me.

"You went against everything you've ever believed in, befriended someone who wasn't straight, and stuck by me through everything. You stood up to Roan, you protected me, again and again. Without you, I wouldn't even be alive, do you realize that? He could have killed me that day in the hallway when I had just gotten out of the hospital, but you stopped him. You saved me, Luke, in more ways than one. You continue to save me, day after day. You chose me, when you could have had anyone."

"*Me*," he breathed, shaking his head as if it were the strangest thing, that I'd seen only him when there were so many others. But it wasn't strange, not to me. In a world full of gray silhouettes, his was the only one that was in color. The only one that would ever be in color.

"You love me, simply because I'm me," he said, inhaling deeply as he squeezed my hands tightly. The soft awes of the guests spilled around us, and I smiled, watching the beautiful hue of red slide over his lovely cheeks, embarrassed to be so exposed and so seen in front of so many. "I could be myself around you, even more so than with Isabella, who was the first person who ever accepted me for me," he took a second to turn around and smile at Isabella as she blew him a kiss.

"You made me see that while it sucks so much that my family hates me, that they don't accept me and probably won't ever accept me, that it doesn't matter. I don't need them to be happy because I have you, your mom, your stepdad, Izzy, her mom, and Serina. Even if none of them are related to me by blood, they're still our family, and I'm not alone. I'm not going to ever be alone because I'll always have you. You're the other half of my soul, my Green, my Luke. I'll love you and only you forever, I vow it."

As the church was filled with cries and awes in the wake of his silence, we stared at each other so deeply, peering into each other's souls, and heard all of the things that we didn't say out loud. The whispers of promises and vows that only we'd hear, only we'd understand.

'I vow to always love you. I vow to always be the calm in the midst of the storm. I vow to never leave you alone. I vow to always, always be proud of you.' Back and forth we vowed silently with our hearts, vows only we could hear, only we felt, embedded forever in our souls.

We were so incredibly immersed in each other's presence that Isabella and Serina needed to step towards us, tapping both of our shoulders as a peal of soft laughter spilled through the crowd. Both of us looked away from each other with a soft blush on our cheeks as the priest spoke. "I said, it's time for the rings, gentlemen," the priest said with a chuckle.

Isabella gave Kinsley my ring, and he slipped it on slowly, repeating the priest's words, my heart fluttering like a thousand wings as I watched him. *'I found you,'* Kinsley's heart whispered to mine, making mine beat even harder.

When it was my turn, Serina handed me Kinsley's ring, and I repeated the priest's words, slipping the ring onto his finger with a smile. *'Welcome home,'* my heart responded.

"You may kiss each other now," the priest said. The whole church broke out into loud cheers and whistles as Kinsley grabbed the front of my shirt and pulled me against him. A soft chuckle spilled from my lips as I lowered my head and pressed my lips against his.

"It's getting dark, baby. What if we're too tired to consummate our wedding?" I teased, whispering against his lips.

He laughed, pulling tighter against my tux as I hugged him tighter. "There's always time for that, silly."

I smirked, remembering once upon a time, in the time of letters and animosity. Letters filled with hope, with sweet words, letters between two boys who were desperate for something they didn't quite yet understand. "Even if it's four in the morning?"

Kinsley sucked in a deep breath, closing his eyes for a moment, lost in the past. Lost in the memories, just like I had been. He opened his eyes and smiled, his lips brushing against mine once more. "Even if it's four in the morning, Green."

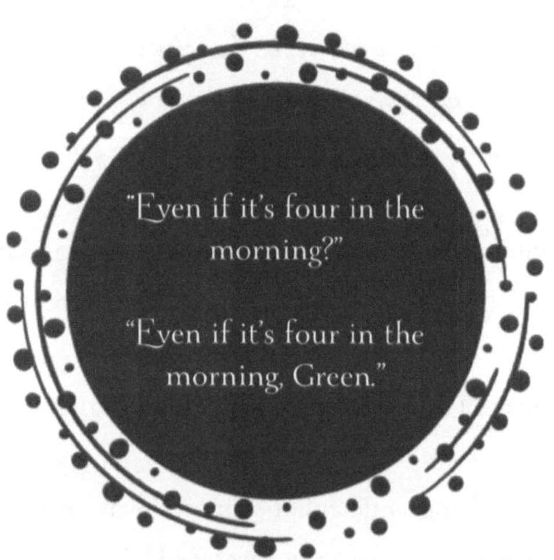

Acknowledgements

Wrong Timing is the continuation of Luke and Kinsley's story. To be honest, I had written Wrong Locker to end with all of the chapters, and the bonus chapters, but it was too long so I split it in half. The first book introduces the characters, and while it's a slow burn from the first book to the second, it's worth it in my opinion. Love isn't fast. Maybe it is for some, to instantly see someone and feel that trickle of rain and know, but most people grow towards others like a flower, slow and steady until they're ready to bloom. I wish more books were portrayed with the realism that showcases just how long it takes to fall in love with someone. While it's fast for some, but's slow for most, and those people are sitting there reading all of these books wondering what's wrong with them that it doesn't just come that easy for them.

I want to thank everyone who sat there and read all of my chapters one by one as I uploaded them, commenting on them, and telling me how much you enjoyed them because you have no idea how helpful that was for me. All of my readers have become such great friends and family to me, and for someone like me who doesn't have a family, it's nice to know that there are people out there who care.

I couldn't have done anything without the support of the readers who backed me every step of the way. To the ones who followed me on Patreon and Ream, I want to thank you all immensely for your continuing generosity and support. I'm able to write because of you, and I'm honored you chose to follow me. I want to thank all of my closest friends, the ones who took the time to help me go through the book and edit it, pointed out my mistakes, and helped me get where I am now. Desiree Lynn, Amanda Lilly, Nicole S., and Arielle Lavecchia.

I want to point out my sister who pushed me from day one, standing in my corner. My eldest sister Ashley Douglas, even when I was a little girl she'd religiously read all of my chapters and all of my ideas even when they probably weren't very good. She encouraged me to keep going, and even now ten plus years later she hasn't grown tired of me shoving more and more at her in search of her unwavering encouragement. I want to thank my kids, who get so excited and ooh and awe every new book I write because they love the covers and keep begging me to let them read them. Not yet, but one day haha.

Thank you again for all of my amazing readers, and I hope you stick around because this is just one of many.

About The Author

Mallory Grant is a mother, a wife, and a cat mom. Born in Ohio, she's lived in North Carolina most of her life until recently she moved to Oklahoma and has been living there for three years now. Mallory used to hide beside her nightlight after lights out with a book in between her hands and an imagination filled to the brim with stories. She grew up knowing from a young age that all she'd ever wanted to be is an author and to share her imagination with the rest of the world.

Other Books By Author

THE CHAINED SERIES
Chained To Fate

THE WRONG SERIES
Wrong Locker
Wrong Timing